SPORTS *Best*

SHORT STORIES

SPORTS *Best*
SHORT STORIES

Edited by Paul D. Staudohar

CHICAGO
REVIEW
PRESS

Library of Congress Cataloging-in-Publication Data
Is available from the Library of Congress.

Published by Chicago Review Press, Incorporated
814 North Franklin Street
Chicago, Illinois 60610
ISBN 1-55652-429-3

Printed in the United States of America
5 4 3 2 1

CONTENTS

ACKNOWLEDGMENTS

As always, the excellent staff of Chicago Review Press made important contributions. Publisher Linda Matthews and executive editor Cynthia Sherry got the ball rolling and provided creative insights. Editor Drew Hamrick was on the project from start to finish, and his fine work is much appreciated. Useful suggestions came from Mark Duran at *Playboy*, Michael Callahan at Harcourt, Inc., Edith Golub at Simon and Schuster, Barry Malzberg at Scott Meredith Literary Agency, Laurel Maury at the *New Yorker*, Lucie Prinz at the *Atlantic Monthly*, and Bob Scheffler at *Esquire*. Thanks also to Sharon Melnyk and Carol Vendrillo at the University of California, Berkeley; writer W. C. Heinz; and reader Gene Holloway. At California State University, Hayward, Florence Bongard and Linda Wickwire were helpful associates. Also at Cal State, librarians Lynne LeFleur, Kristin Ramsdell, and Ilene Rockman gave capable assistance, as did Karen Hansen-Smith from the Contra Costa County Central Library.

—Paul D. Staudohar

INTRODUCTION

This is the first volume of two new books devoted to short stories on a variety of sports. It is part of the Best Short Stories series, which began with baseball in 1995 and includes golf (1997), football (1998), boxing (1999), fishing (2000), and hunting (2000). Our objective in these books is to present the very best short fiction on sports.

What constitutes sport is in the eye of the beholder. Some observers think that only robust physical games qualify. However, for this collection we have adopted a more expansive definition. We include traditional games of baseball, football, golf, and hockey, but also sedentary contests like card playing and chess.

Every sport has riches that can be mined by a good author. Sports stories can provide a realism and intensity that are nearly as good as the real thing, and in some cases better. Stories inform, too, so readers can learn about sports with which they are not conversant. But the stories in this book are not just about particular sports. They give us character studies, often revealing people stuck in difficult situations who have to overcome obstacles. Some typical motifs are believing in oneself, coping with adversity, self-destruction, fear of failure (or success), and redemption through a second chance.

Americans have a long-standing love affair with their favorite sports. Contests in skill, strength, and speed occupy an important place in modern society, as they have throughout the ages. Some people associate sports with the games they see on television. College students may be caught up in the welter of intercollegiate and intramural sports on campus. Parents with young children may think more of sports as developing the bodies and character of their offspring. To many, sports are simply playful recreation that they engage in for health and happiness. Whatever the case, people usually find more than one sport attractive.

The authors of the stories in this book understand how sport is a microcosm of life, and they draw on a full range of human expression to afford the reader an enjoyable respite from the pressures of the everyday world. This is especially the case with stories that contain pleasant touches of humor, love, satire, mystery, and spoof.

While not all of the authors are equally well known, most of them are familiar to lovers of fine literature. A. Conan Doyle, one of the very best, has the inimitable Sherlock Holmes investigating the disappearance of a racehorse. Other British writers are Leslie Charteris, whose poker story involves his famous detective, the Saint; P. G. Wodehouse, who is up to whimsical tricks on the golf course; Jeffrey Archer on the mystery of "Dougie Mortimer's Right Arm"; and W. Somerset Maugham, with a curiously enticing piece woven around both bridge and swimming.

Many of these selections come from prominent American literary magazines like the *New Yorker, Esquire, Collier's, Playboy, Atlantic Monthly,* and *Cosmopolitan.* Of the twenty-four stories, four are on baseball, three each on horse racing and hunting, and two each on golf and boxing. Other stories concern auto racing, fishing, hockey, football, chess, swimming, poker, bullfighting, rowing, and dog shows. This last is the classic story of a bulldog who becomes a show champion, by Richard Harding Davis.

Davis is one of the great American writers in the volume. Others include Jack London, E. Annie Proulx, Irwin Shaw, Joyce Carol Oates, John Cheever, Paul Horgan, Ellery Queen, John D. MacDonald, Howard Nemerov, André Dubus, and Ring Lardner.

The stories bring sports to life, capturing the essence of athletic skill and the sights, sounds, and thrills of competition. So let's turn the page to our first adventure, Lardner's quintessential baseball yarn, "Hurry Kane."

Hurry Kane is a pitching phenom with a blazing fastball. A sentimental goof with a weakness for the ladies, he's hard to keep on the straight and narrow. The story is told in the colloquial prose and humorous dialogue for which its author is renowned. Ringgold Wilmer Lardner (1885–1933) was a sportswriter for the Chicago Tribune *who achieved recognition for his revealing coverage of the infamous Black Sox World Series in 1919. But it was as a writer of short fiction that he became an icon of American literature. "Hurry Kane," first published in* Cosmopolitan, *is vintage Lardner. His best-known stories are found in* Round Up *(1929) and the* Collected Stories of Ring Lardner *(1941).*

Ring Lardner

HURRY KANE
(1927)

IT SAYS HERE: "Another great race may be expected in the American League, for Philadelphia and New York have evidently added enough strength to give them a fighting chance with the White Sox and Yankees. But if the fans are looking for as 'nervous' a finish as last year's, with a climax such as the Chicago and New York clubs staged on the memorable first day of October, they are doubtless in for a disappointment. That was a regular Webster 'thrill that comes once in a lifetime,' and no oftener."

"Thrill" is right, but they don't know the half of it. Nobody knows the whole of it only myself, not even the fella that told me. I mean the big sap, Kane, who you might call him, I suppose, the hero of the story, but he's too dumb to have realized all that went on, and besides, I got some of the angles from other sources and seen a few things with my own eyes.

If you wasn't the closest-mouthed bird I ever run acrost, I wouldn't spill this to you. But I know it won't go no further and I think it may give you a kick.

Well, the year before last, it didn't take no witch to figure out what was going to happen to our club if Dave couldn't land a pitcher or two to help out Carney and Olds. Jake Lewis hurt his arm and was never no good after that and the rest of the staff belonged in the Soldiers' Home. Their aim was perfect, but they were always shooting at the pressbox or somebody's bat. On hot days I often felt like leaving my mask and protector in the clubhouse; what those fellas were throwing up there was either eighty feet over my head or else the outfielders had to chase it. I could have caught naked except on the days when Olds and Carney worked.

In the fall–that's a year and a half ago–Dave pulled the trade with Boston and St. Louis that brought us Frank Miller and Lefty Glaze in exchange for Robinson, Bullard and Roy Smith. The three he gave away weren't worth a dime to us or to the clubs that got them, and that made it just an even thing, as Miller showed up in the spring with a waistline that was eight laps to the mile and kept getting bigger and bigger till it took half the Atlantic cable to hold up his baseball pants, while Glaze wanted more money than Landis and didn't report till the middle of June, and then tried to condition himself on wood alcohol. When the deal was made, it looked like Dave had all the best of it, but as it turned out, him and the other two clubs might as well have exchanged photographs of their kids in Girl Scout uniforms.

But Dave never lost no sleep over Glaze or Miller. We hadn't been in Florida three days before him and everybody on the ball club was absolutely nuts about big Kane. Here was a twenty-year-old boy that had only pitched half a season in Waco and we had put in a draft for him on the recommendation of an old friend of Dave's, Billy Moore. Billy was just a fan and didn't know much baseball, but he had made some money for Dave in Texas oil leases and Dave took this tip on Kane more because he didn't want to hurt Billy's feelings than out of respect for his judgment. So when the big sapper showed up at Fort Gregg, he didn't get much of a welcome. What he did get was a laugh. You couldn't look at him and not laugh; anyway, not till you got kind of used to him.

You've probably seen lots of pictures of him in a uniform, but they can't give you no idear of the sight he was the first day he blew in the hotel, after that clean, restful little train ride all the way from Yuma. Standing six foot three in what was left of his stockings, he was wearing a suit of Arizona store clothes that would have been a fair fit for Singer's youngest Midget and looked like he had pressed it with a tractor that had been parked on a river bottom.

He had used up both the collars that he figured would see him through his first year in the big league. This left you a clear view of his Adam's apple, which would make half a dozen pies. You'd have thought from his shoes that he had just managed to grab hold of the rail on the back platform of his train and been dragged from Yuma to Jacksonville. But when you seen his shirt, you wondered if he hadn't rode in the cab and loaned it to the fireman for a wash-cloth. He had a brown paper suitcase held together by bandages. Some of them had slipped and the raw wounds was exposed. But if the whole thing had fell to pieces, he could have packed the contents in two of his vest pockets without bulging them much.

One of the funniest things about him was his walk and I'll never forget the first time we seen him go out to take his turn pitching to the batters. He acted like he was barefooted and afraid of stepping on burrs. He'd lift one dog and hold it in the air a minute till he could locate a safe place to put it down. Then he'd do the same thing with the other, and it would seem about a half-hour from the time he left the bench till he got to his position. Of course Dave soon had him pretty well cured of that, or that is, Dave didn't, but Kid Farrell did. For a whole week, the Kid followed him every step he took and if he wasn't going fast enough, he either got spiked in the heel or kicked in the calf of his hind leg. People think he walks slow yet, but he's a shooting star now compared with when he broke in.

Well, everybody was in hysterics watching him make that first trip and he looked so silly that we didn't expect him to be any good to us except as a kind of a show. But we were in for a big surprise.

Before he threw a ball, Dave said to him: "Now, go easy. Don't cut loose and take a chance till you're in shape."

"All right," says Kane.

And all of a sudden, without no warning, he whammed a fast ball acrost that old plate that blew Tierney's cap off and pretty near knocked me down. Tierney hollered murder and ran for the bench. All of us were pop-eyed and it was quite a while before Dave could speak. Then he said:

"Boy, your fast one *is* a fast one! But I just got through telling you not to cut loose. The other fellas ain't ready for it and neither are you. I don't want nobody killed this time of year."

So Kane said: "I didn't cut loose. I can send them through there twice as fast as that. I'm scared to yet, because I ain't sure of my control. I'll show you something in a couple more days."

Well, when he said "twice as fast," he was making it a little strong. But his real fast one was faster than that first one he threw, and before the week was over we looked at speed that made it seem like Johnson had never pitched nothing but toy balloons. What had us all puzzled was why none of the other clubs had tried to grab him. I found out by asking him one night at supper. I asked him if he'd been just as good the year before as he was now.

"I had the same stuff," he said, "but I never showed it, except once."

I asked him why he hadn't showed it. He said:

"Because I was always scared they would be a big league scout in the stand and I didn't want to go 'up.'"

Then I said why not, and he told me he was stuck on a gal in Waco and wanted to be near her.

"Yes," I said, "but your home town, Yuma, is a long ways from Waco and you couldn't see much of her winters even if you stayed in the Texas League."

"I got a gal in Yuma for winters," he says. "This other gal was just for during the season."

"How about that one time you showed your stuff?" I asked him. "How did you happen to do it?"

"Well," he said, "the Dallas club was playing a series in Waco and I went to a picture show and seen the gal with Fred Kruger. He's Dallas's manager. So the next day I made a monkey out of his ball club. I struck out of fifteen of them and give them one hit—a fly ball that Smitty could have caught in a hollow tooth if he hadn't drunk his lunch."

Of course that was the game Dave's friend seen him pitch and we were lucky he happened to be in Waco just then. And it was Kane's last game in that league. Him and his "during the season" gal had a brawl and he played sick and got himself sent home.

Well, everybody knows now what a whale of a pitcher he turned out to be. He had a good, fast-breaking curve and Carney learned him how to throw a slow ball. Old Kid Farrell worked like a horse with him and got him so he could move around and field his position. At first he seemed to think he was moored out there. And another cute habit that had to be cured was his full wind-up with men on bases. The Kid starved him out of this.

Maybe I didn't tell you what an eater he was. Before Dave caught on to it, he was ordering one breakfast in his room and having another downstairs, and besides pretty near choking himself to death at lunch and supper, he'd sneak out to some lunchroom before bedtime, put away a Hamburger steak and eggs and bring back three or four sandwiches to snap at during the night.

He was rooming at the start with Joe Bonham and Joe finally told on him, thinking it was funny. But it wasn't funny to Dave and he named the Kid and Johnny Abbott a committee of two to see that Kane didn't explode. The Kid watched over him at table and Johnny succeeded Bonham as his roommate. And the way the Kid got him to cut out his wind-up was by telling him, "Now if you forget yourself and use it with a man on, your supper's going to be two olives and a finger-bowl, but if you hold up those runners, you can eat the chef."

As I say, the whole world knows what he is now. But they don't know how hard we worked with him, they don't know how close we came to losing him altogether, and they don't know the real story of that final game last year, which I'll tell you in a little while.

First, about pretty near losing him: As soon as Dave seen his possibilities and his value to us, he warned the boys not to ride him or play too many jokes on him because he was simple enough to take everything in dead earnest, and if he ever found out we were laughing at him, he might either lay down and quit trying or blow us entirely. Dave's dope was good, but you can't no more prevent a bunch of ball players from kidding a goofer like Kane than you can stop the Century at Herkimer by hollering "Whoa!" He was always saying things and doing things that left him wide open and the gang took full advantage, especially Bull Wade.

I remember one night everybody was sitting on the porch and Bull was on the railing, right in front of Kane's chair.

"What's your first name, Steve?" Bull asked him.

"Well," says Kane, "it ain't Steve at all. It's Elmer."

"It would be!" says Bull. "It fits you like your suit. And that reminds me, I was going to inquire where you got that suit."

"In Yuma," said Kane. "In a store."

"A store!" says Bull.

"A clothing store," says Kane. "They sell all kinds of clothes."

"I see they do," said Bull.

"If you want a suit like it, I'll write and find out if they've got another one," says Kane.

"They couldn't be two of them," says Bull, "and if they was, I'll bet Ed Wynn's bought the other. But anyway, I've already got a suit, and what I wanted to ask you was what the boys out West call you. I mean, what's your nickname?"

"'Hurry,'" says the sap. "'Hurry' Kane. Lefty Condon named me that."

"He seen you on your way to the dining-room," said Bull.

Kane didn't get it.

"No," he said. "It ain't nothing to do with a dining-room. A hurricane is a kind of a storm. My last name is Kane, so Lefty called me 'Hurry' Kane. It's a kind of a storm."

"A brainstorm," says Bull.

"No," said Kane. "A hurricane is a big wind-storm."

"Does it blow up all of a sudden?" asked Bull.

"Yeah, that's it," says Kane.

"We had three or four of them on this club last year," said Bull. "All pitchers, too. Dave got rid of them and he must be figuring on you to take their place."

"Do you mean you had four pitchers named Kane?" says the big busher.

"No," said Bull. "I mean we had four pitchers that could blow up all of a sudden. It was their hobby. Dave used to work them in turn, the same afternoon; on days when Olds and Carney needed a rest. Each one of the four would pitch an innings and a half."

Kane thought quite a while and then said: "But if they was four of them, and they pitched an innings and a half apiece, that's only six innings. Who pitched the other three?"

"Nobody," says Bull. "It was always too dark. By the way, what innings is your favorite? I mean, to blow in?"

"I don't blow," says the sap.

"Then," said Bull, "why was it that fella called you 'Hurry' Kane?"

"It was Lefty Condon called me 'Hurry,'" says the sap. "My last name is Kane, and a hurricane is a big wind."

"Don't a wind blow?" says Bull.

And so on. I swear they kept it up for two hours, Kane trying to explain his nickname and Bull leading him on, and Joe Bonham said that Kane asked him up in the room who that was he had been talking to, and when Joe told him it was Wade, one of the smartest ball players in the league, Hurry said: "Well, then, he must be either stewed or else this is a damn sight dumber league than the one I came from."

Bull and some of the rest of the boys pulled all the old gags on him that's been in baseball since the days when you couldn't get on a club unless you had a walrus mustache. And Kane never disappointed them.

They made him go to the club-house after the key to the batter's box; they wrote him mash notes with fake names signed to them and had him spending half his evenings on some corner, waiting to meet gals that never lived; when he held Florida University to two hits in five innings, they sent him telegrams of congratulation from Coolidge and Al Smith, and he showed the telegrams to everybody in the hotel; they had him report at the ball park at six-thirty one morning for a secret "pitchers' conference"; they told him the Ritz was where all the unmarried ball players on the club lived while we were home, and they got him to write and ask for a parlor, bedroom and bath for the whole season. They was nothing he wouldn't fall for till Dave finally tipped him off that he was being kidded, and even then he didn't half believe it.

Now I never could figure how a man can fool themself about their own looks, but this bird was certain that he and Tommy Meighan were practically twins. Of course the boys soon found this out and strung him along. They advised him to quit baseball and go into pictures. They sat around his room and had him strike different poses and fix his hair different ways to see how he could show off his beauty to the best advantage. Johnny Abbott told me, after he began rooming with him, that for an hour before he went to bed and when he got up, Kane would stand in front of the mirror staring at himself and practising smiles and scowls and all kinds of silly faces, while Johnny pretended he was asleep.

Well, it wasn't hard to kid a fella like that into believing the dames were mad about him and when Bull Wade said that Evelyn Corey had asked who he was, his chest broke right through his shirt.

I know more about Evelyn now, but I didn't know nothing than except that she was a beautiful gal who had been in Broadway shows a couple of seasons and didn't have to be in them no more. Her room was two doors down the hall from Johnny's and Kane's. She was in Florida all alone, probably because her man friend, whoever he was at that time, had had to go abroad or somewheres with the family. All the ball players were willing to meet her, but she wasn't thrilled over the idear of getting acquainted with a bunch of guys who hadn't had a pay day in four or five months. Bull got Kane to write her a note; then Bull stole the note and wrote an answer, asking him to call. Hurry went and knocked at her door. She opened it and slammed it in his face.

"It was kind of dark," he said to Johnny, "and I guess she failed to recognize me." But he didn't have the nerve to call again.

He showed Johnny a picture of his gal in Yuma, a gal named Minnie

Olson, who looked like she patronized the same store where Kane had bought his suit. He said she was wild about him and would marry him the minute he said the word and probably she was crying her eyes out right now, wishing he was home. He asked if Johnny had a gal and Johnny loosened up and showed him the picture of the gal he was engaged to. (Johnny married her last November.) She's a peach, but all Kane would say was, "Kind of skinny, ain't she?" Johnny laughed and said most gals liked to be that way.

"Not if they want me," says Kane.

"Well," said Johnny, "I don't think this one does. But how about your friend, that Miss Corey? You certainly can't call her plump, yet you're anxious to meet her."

"She's got class!" said Kane.

Johnny laughed that off, too. This gal of his, that he's married to now, she's so far ahead of Corey as far as class is concerned—well, they ain't no comparison. Johnny, you know, went to Cornell a couple of years and his wife is a college gal he met at a big houseparty. If you put her and Evelyn beside of each other you wouldn't have no trouble telling which of them belonged on Park Avenue and which Broadway.

Kane kept on moaning more and more about his gal out West and acting glummer and glummer. Johnny did his best to cheer him up, as he seen what was liable to happen. But they wasn't no use. The big rube "lost" his fast ball and told Dave he had strained his arm and probably wouldn't be no good all season. Dave bawled him out and accused him of stalling. Kane stalled just the same. Then Dave soft-soaped him, told him how he'd burn up the league and how we were all depending on him to put us in the race and keep us there. But he might as well have been talking to a mounted policeman.

Finally, one day during the last week at Fort Gregg, Johnny Abbott got homesick himself and put in a long-distance call for his gal in New York. It was a rainy day and him and Kane had been just laying around the room. Before the call went through Johnny hinted that he would like to be alone while he talked. Kane paid no attention and began undressing to take a nap. So Johnny had to speak before an audience and not only that, but as soon as Kane heard him say "Darling" or "Sweetheart," or whatever he called her, he moved right over close to the phone where he wouldn't miss nothing. Johnny was kind of embarrassed and hung up before he was ready to; then he gave Kane a dirty look and went to the window and stared out at the rain, dreaming about the gal he'd just talked with.

Kane laid down on his bed, but he didn't go to sleep. In four or five minutes he was at the phone asking the operator to get Minnie Olson in Yuma. Then he laid down again and tossed a while, and then he sat up on the edge of the bed.

"Johnny," he says, "how far is it from here to New York?"

"About a thousand miles," said Johnny.

"And how far to Yuma?" said Kane.

"Oh," says Johnny, "that must be three thousand miles at least."

"How much did that New York call cost you?" asked Kane.

"I don't know yet," said Johnny. "I suppose it was around seven bucks."

Kane went to the writing table and done a little arithmetic. From there he went back to the phone.

"Listen, girlie," he said to the operator, "you can cancel that Yuma call. I just happened to remember that the party I wanted won't be home. She's taking her mandolin lesson, way the other side of town."

Johnny told me afterwards that he didn't know whether to laugh or cry. Before he had a chance to do either, Kane says to him:

"This is my last day on this ball club."

"What do you mean?" said Johnny.

"I mean I'm through; I'm going home," says Kane.

"Don't be a fool!" says Johnny. "Don't throw away the chance of a life-time just because you're a little lonesome. If you stay in this league and pitch like you can pitch, you'll be getting the big money next year and you can marry that gal and bring her East with you. You may not have to wait till next year. You may pitch us into the world's series and grab a chunk of dough this fall."

"We won't be in no world's series," says Kane.

"What makes you think so?" said Johnny.

"I can't work every day," says Kane.

"You'll have help," says Johnny. "With you and Carney and Olds taking turns, we can be right up in that old fight. Without you, we can't even finish in the league. If you won't do it for yourself or for Dave, do it for me, your roomy. You just seen me spend seven or eight bucks on a phone call, but that's no sign I'm reeking with jack. I spent that money because I'd have died if I hadn't. I've got none to throw away and if we don't win the pennant, I can't marry this year and maybe not next year or the year after."

"I've got to look out for myself," says Kane. "I tell you I'm through and that's all there is to it. I'm going home where my gal is, where they ain't no smart Alecks kidding me all the while, and where I can eat without no assistant manager holding me down to a sprig of parsley, and a thimbleful of soup. For your sake, Johnny," he says, "I'd like to see this club finish on top, but I can't stick it out and I'm afraid your only hope is for the other seven clubs to all be riding on the same train and hit an open bridge."

Well, of course Johnny didn't lose no time getting to Dave with the bad news, and Dave and Kid Farrell rushed to the sapper's room. They threatened him and they coaxed him. They promised him he could eat all he wanted. They swore that anybody who tried to play jokes on him would either be fined or fired off the club. They reminded him that it cost a lot of money to go from Florida to Yuma, and he would have to pay his own way. They offered him a new contract with a five-hundred-dollar raise if he would stay. They argued and pleaded with him from four in the afternoon till midnight. When they finally quit, they were just where they'd been when they started. He was through.

"All right!" Dave hollered. "Be through and go to her! If you ain't out of here by tomorrow noon, I'll have you chased out! And don't forget that you'll never pitch in organized baseball again!"

"That suits me," says Kane, and went to bed.

When Johnny Abbott woke up about seven the next morning, Hurry was putting his extra collar and comb in the leaky suitcase. He said:

"I'm going to grab the eleven-something train for Jacksonville. I got money enough to take me from here to New Orleans and I know a fella there that will see me the rest of the way—if I can find him and he ain't broke."

Well, Johnny couldn't stand for that and he got up and dressed and was starting out to borrow two hundred dollars from me to lend to Kane, when the phone rang loud and long. Kane took off the receiver, listened a second, and then said "Uh-huh" and hung up.

"Who was it?" asked Johnny.

"Nobody," says Kane. "Just one of Bull Wade's gags."

"What did he say?" Johnny asked him.

"It was a gal, probably the telephone operator," said Kane. "She said the hotel was on fire and not to get excited, but that we better move out."

"You fool!" yelled Johnny and run to the phone.

They was no gag about it. The hotel had really caught fire in the basement and everybody was being warned to take the air. Johnny tossed some of his stuff in a bag and started out, telling Kane to follow him quick. Hurry got out in the hall and then remembered that he had left his gal's picture on the dresser and went back after it. Just as he turned towards the door again, in dashed a dame with a kimono throwed over her nightgown. It was Evelyn Corey herself, almost in the flesh.

"Oh, please!" she said, or screamed. "Come and help me carry my things!"

Well, here was once that the name "Hurry" was on the square. He dropped his own suitcase and was in her room in nothing and no-fifths. He grabbed her four pieces of hand baggage and was staggering to the hall with them when a bellhop bounced in and told them the danger was over, the fire was out.

This seemed to be more of a disappointment than Evelyn could stand. Anyway, she fainted—onto a couch—and for a few minutes she was too unconscious to do anything but ask Kane to pour her a drink. He also poured himself one and settled down in the easy chair like he was there for the day. But by now she had come to and got a good look at him.

"I thank you very much," she said, "and I'm so exhausted with all this excitement that I think I'll go back to bed."

Kane took his hint and got up.

"But ain't I going to see you again?" he asked her.

"I'm afraid not," says Evelyn. "I'm leaving here this evening and I'll be getting ready from now till then."

"Where are you headed for?" Kane asked her.

"For home, New York," she said.

"Can't I have your address?" said Kane.

"Why, yes," said Evelyn without batting an eye. "I live at the Ritz."

"The Ritz!" says Kane. "That's where I'm going to live, if they ain't filled up."

"How wonderful!" said Evelyn. "Then we'll probably see each other every day."

Kane beat it down to the dining-room and straight to Dave's table.

"Boss," he said, "I've changed my mind."

"Your what!" says Dave.

"My mind," says Kane. "I've decided to stick."

It was all Dave could do not to kiss him. But he thought it was best to act calm.

"That's fine, Hurry!" he said. "And I'll see that you get that extra five hundred bucks."

"What five hundred bucks?" says Kane.

"That five hundred I promised you if you'd stay," says Dave.

"I hadn't heard about it," said Kane. "But as long as I ain't going home, I'm in no rush for money. Though I'm liable to need it," he says, "as soon as we hit New York."

And he smiled the silliest smile you ever seen.

I don't have to tell you that he didn't live at the Ritz. Or that Evelyn Corey didn't live there neither. He found out she hadn't never lived there, but he figured she'd intended to and had to give it up because they didn't have a suite good enough for her.

I got him a room in my boarding house in the Bronx and for the first few days he spent all his spare time looking through city directories and different telephone directories and bothering the life out of Information, trying to locate his lost lady. It was when he had practically give up hope that he told me his secret and asked for help.

"She's all I came here for," he said, "and if I can't find her, I ain't going to stay."

Well, of course if you went at it the right way, you wouldn't have much trouble tracing her. Pretty near anybody in the theatrical business, or the people that run the big night clubs, or the head waiters at the hotels and restaurants—they could have put you on the right track. The thing was that it would be worse to get a hold of her than not to, because she'd have give him the air so strong that he would have caught his death of cold.

So I just said that they was no question but what she had gone away somewheres, maybe to Europe, and he would hear from her as soon as she got back. I had to repeat this over and over and make it strong or he'd have left us flatter than his own feet before he pitched two games. As it was, we held him till the end of May without being obliged to try any tricks, but you could see he was getting more impatient and restless all the while and the situation got desperate just as we were starting on our first trip West. He asked me when would we hit St. Louis and I told him the date and said:

"What do you want to know for?"

"Because," he says, "I'm going home from there."

I repeated this sweet news to Dave and Kid Farrell. We finally called in Bull Wade and it was him that saved the day. You remember Bull had faked up a note from Evelyn to Kane down at Fort Gregg; now he suggested that he write some more notes, say one every two or three weeks, sign her name to them, send them to Bull's brother in Montreal and have the brother mail them from there. It was a kind of a dirty, mean thing to do, but it worked. The notes all read about the same——

"Dear Mr. Kane:—I am keeping track of your wonderful pitching and looking forward to seeing you when I return to New York, which will be early in the fall. I hope you haven't forgotten me."

And so on, signed "Your friend and admirer, Evelyn Corey."

Hurry didn't answer only about half of them as it was a real chore for him to write. He addressed his answers in care of Mr. Harry Wade, such and such a street number, Montreal, and when Bull's brother got them, he forwarded them to Bull, so he'd know if they was anything special he ought to reply to.

The boys took turns entertaining Kane evenings, playing cards with him and staking him to picture shows. Johnny Abbott done more than his share. You see the pennant meant more to Johnny than to anybody else; it meant the world's series money and a fall wedding, instead of a couple of years' wait. And Johnny's gal, Helen Kerslake, worked, too. She had him to her house to supper—when her folks were out—and made him feel like he was even handsomer and more important than he thought. She went so far as to try and get some of her gal friends to play with him, but he always wanted to pet and that was a little too much.

Well, if Kane hadn't stuck with us and turned out to be the marvel he is, the White Sox would have been so far ahead by the Fourth of July that they could have sat in the stand the rest of the season and let the Bloomer Girls play in their place. But Hurry had their number from the first time he faced them till the finish. Out of eleven games he worked against them all last year, he won ten and the other was a nothing to nothing tie. And look at the rest of his record! As I recall it, he took part in fifty-eight games. He pitched forty-three full games, winning thirty-six, losing five and tying two. And God knows how many games he saved! He had that free, easy side-arm motion that didn't take much out of him and he could pitch every third day and be at his best.

But don't let me forget to credit myself with an assist. Late in August, Kane told me he couldn't stand it no longer to just get short notes from the Corey gal and never see her, and when we started on our September trip West, he was going to steal a week off and run up to Montreal; he would join us later, but he must see Evelyn. Well, for once in my life I had an idear hit me right between the eyes.

The Yuma gal, Minnie Olson, had been writing to him once a week and though he hardly ever wrote to her and seemed to only be thinking of Corey, still I noticed that he could hardly help from crying when Minnie's letters came. So I suggested to Dave that he telegraph Minnie to come East and visit with all her expenses paid, wire her money for her transportation, tell her it would be doing Kane a big favor as well as the rest of us, and ask her to send Kane a telegram, saying when she would reach New York, but to be sure and never mention that she wasn't doing it on her own hook.

Two days after Dave's message was sent, Kane got a wire from El Paso. She was on her way and would he meet her at the Pennsylvania Station on such and such a date. I never seen a man as happy as Hurry was when he read that telegram.

"I knew she was stuck on me," he said, "but I didn't know it was that strong. She must have worked in a store or something since spring to save up money for this trip."

You would have thought he'd never heard of or seen a gal by the name of Evelyn Corey.

Minnie arrived and was just what we expected: a plain, honest, good-hearted, small-town gal, dressed for a masquerade. We had supper with her and Kane her first night in town–I and Johnny and Helen. She was trembling like a leaf, partly from excitement over being in New York and amongst strangers, but mostly on account of seeing the big sap again. He wasn't no sap to her and I wished they was some dame would look at me the way she kept looking at Hurry.

The next morning Helen took her on a shopping tour and got her fixed up so cute that you couldn't hardly recognize her. In the afternoon she went to the ball game and seen Kane shut the Detroit club out with two hits.

When Hurry got a glimpse of her in her Fifth Avenue clothes, he was as proud as if he had bought them himself and it didn't seem to occur to him that they must have cost more than she could have paid.

Well, with Kane happy and no danger of him walking out on us, all we had to worry about was that the White Sox still led us by three games, with less than twenty left to play. And the schedule was different than usual—we had to wind up with a Western trip and play our last thirteen games on the road. I and Johnny and Dave was talking it over one day and the three of us agreed that we would be suckers not to insist on Miss Olson going along. But Dave wondered if she wouldn't feel funny, being the only girl.

"I'll make my gal go, too," said Johnny.

And that's the way it was fixed.

We opened in St. Louis and beat them two out of three. Olds was trimmed, but Carney and Kane both won. We didn't gain no ground, because the White Sox grabbed two out of three from Washington. We made a sweep of our four games in Detroit, while the Sox was winning three from Philadelphia. That moved us up to two and a half games from first place. We beat Cleveland three straight, Kane licking them 6 to 1 and holding Carney's one run lead through the eighth and ninth innings of another game. At the same time, Chicago took three from Boston.

So we finally struck old Chi, where the fans was already counting the pennant won, two and a half games behind and three to go—meaning we had to win all three or be sunk.

I told you how Kane had the Chicago club's number. But I didn't tell you how Eddie Brainard had been making a monkey of us. He had only worked against us six times and had beat us five. His other game was the nothing to nothing tie with Hurry. Eddie is one sweet pitcher and if he had been the horse for work that Kane was, that last series wouldn't have got us nowheres. But Eddie needs his full rest and it was a cinch he wouldn't be in there for more than one game and maybe part of another.

In Brainard's six games against us, he had give us a total of four runs, shutting us out three times and trimming us 3 to 2, 4 to 1 and 2 to 1. As the White Sox only needed one game, it was a cinch that they wouldn't start Eddie against Kane, who was so tough for them, but would save him for Carney or Olds, whichever one worked first. Carney hadn't been able to finish a game with Chicago and Olds' record wasn't much better.

Well, we was having breakfast in our hotel the morning we got in from Cleveland, and Kane sent for Dave to come to the table where him and Johnny Abbott and the two gals was eating.

"Boss," he says, "I'm thinking of getting married and so is Johnny here, but they ain't neither of us can do it, not now anyway, unless we grab some of that world's series jack. And we can't get into the series without we win these three games. So if I was managing this ball club, I'd figure on that and know just how to work my pitchers."

"Maybe I've thought about it a little myself," says Dave. "But I'd like to listen to your idears."

"All right," says Kane. "I'd start Kane today, and I'd start Kane tomorrow, and I'd start Kane the day after that."

"My plan is a little different," said Dave. "Of course you start today, and if you win, why, I want to play a joke on them tomorrow. I intend to start

Olds so they'll start Brainard. And if the game is anywheres near close at the end of the third or fourth innings, you're going in. It will be too late for them to take Brainard out and expect him to be as good the third day. And if we win that second game, why, you won't have to beg me to pitch the last one."

You'll think I'm getting long-winded, but they ain't much more to tell. You probably heard the details of those first two games even if you was on the Other Side. Hurry beat them the first one, 7 to 1, and their one run was my fault. Claymore was on second base with two men out in the sixth innings. King hit a foul ball right straight up and I dropped it. And then he pulled a base-hit inside of Bull, and Claymore scored. Olds and Brainard started the second game and at the end of our half of the fourth innings, the score was one and one. Hurry had been warming up easy right along, but it certainly was a big surprise to the Chicago club and pretty near everybody else when Dave motioned him in to relieve Olds. The White Sox never came close to another run and we got to Brainard for one in the eighth, just enough to beat him.

Eddie had pitched his head off and it was a tough one for him to lose. But the best part of it was, he was through and out of the way.

Well, Johnny and Kane had their usual date with the two gals for supper. Johnny was in his bathroom, washing up, when the phone rang. Kane answered it, but he talked kind of low and Johnny didn't hear what he was saying. But when Hurry had hung up, he acted kind of nervous and Johnny asked him what was the matter.

"It's hard luck," said Kane. "They's a friend of mine from Yuma here, and he's in trouble and I've got to go over on the North Side and see him. Will you take both the gals to supper yourself? Because I may not be back till late. And don't tell Min who I'm going to see."

"How could I tell her when you ain't told me?" said Johnny.

"Well," said Kane, "just tell her I'm wore out from working so hard two days in a row and I went right to bed so I'd be all right for tomorrow."

Johnny was kind of worried and tried to coax him not to go. But Kane ducked out and didn't come in till midnight. Johnny tried to find out where he'd been and what had happened, but he said he was too sleepy to talk. Just the same, Johnny says, he tossed around and moaned all night like he was having a nightmare, and he usually slept like a corpse.

Kane got up early and went down to breakfast before Johnny was dressed. But Johnny was still worried, and hustled up and caught him before he was out of the dining-room. He was hoping Hurry would explain his getting in late and not sleeping. Kane wouldn't talk, though, and still acted nervous. So Johnny finally said:

"Hurry, you know what this game today means to me and you ought to know what it means to you. If we get trimmed, a lot of people besides ourselves will be disappointed, but they won't nobody be as disappointed as me. I wished you'd have had a good sleep last night and if you'll take my advice, you'll go up in the room and rest till it's time to go to the ball yard. If you're anywheres near yourself, this Chicago club is licked. And for heaven's sakes, be yourself, or your roomy is liable to walk out into Lake Michigan tonight so far that I can't get back!"

"I'm myself," says Kane and got up and left the table, but not quick enough so that Johnny didn't see tears in his eyes.

That afternoon's crowd beat all records and I was tickled to death to see it, because Hurry had always done his best work in front of crowds that was pulling against him. He warmed up fine and they wasn't nobody on our club, nobody but Kane himself and two others, who didn't feel perfectly confident that we were "in."

The White Sox were starting Sam Bonner and while he had beat us three or four times, we'd always got runs off him, and they'd always been lucky to score at all against Kane.

Bonner went through the first innings without no trouble. And then we got the shock of our lives. The first ball Hurry pitched was high and outside and it felt funny when I caught it. I was used to that old "zip" and I could have caught this one in my bare hand. Claymore took a cut at the next one and hit it a mile to left center for three bases. King hit for two bases, Welsh was safe when Digman threw a ground ball into the seats, and Kramer slapped one out of the park for a homer. Four runs. The crowd was wild and we were wilder.

You ought to have heard us on that bench. "Yellow so-and-so" was the mildest name Hurry got called. Dave couldn't do nothing but just mumble and shake his fists at Kane. We was all raving and asking each other what in hell was going on. Hurry stood in front facing us, but he was looking up in the stand and he acted like he didn't hear one word of the sweet remarks meant for his ears.

Johnny Abbott pulled me aside.

"Listen," he says. "This kid ain't yellow and he ain't wore out. They's something wrong here."

By this time Dave had found his voice and he yelled at Kane: "You so-and-so so-and-so! You're going to stay right in there and pitch till this game is over! And if you don't pitch like you can pitch, I'll shoot you dead tonight just as sure as you're a yellow, quitting—!"

We'd forgot it was our turn to bat and Hildebrand was threatening to forfeit the game before he could get Bull Wade to go up there. Kane still stood in front of us, staring. But pretty soon Dave told young Topping to run out to the bull pen and warn Carney and Olds to both be ready. I seen Topping stop a minute alongside of Kane and look up in the stand where Kane was looking. I seen Topping say something to Kane and I heard Kane call him a liar. Then Topping said something more and Hurry turned white as a sheet and pretty near fell into the dugout. I noticed his hand shake as he took a drink of water. And then he went over to Dave and I heard him say:

"I'm sorry, Boss. I had a bad inning. But I'll be all right from now on."

"You'd better!" says Dave.

"Get me some runs is all I ask," says Kane.

And the words wasn't no sooner out of his mouth when Bull smacked one a mile over Claymore's head and came into the plate standing up. They was another tune on the bench now. We were yelling for blood, and we got it. Before they relieved Bonner, we'd got to him for three singles and a double—mine, if you must know—and the score was tied.

Say, if you think you ever seen pitching, you ought to have watched Kane cut them through there the rest of that day. Fourteen strike-outs in the last eight innings! And the only man to reach first base was Kramer, when Stout dropped an easy fly ball in the fifth.

Well, to shorten it up, Bull and Johnny Abbott and myself had some luck against Pierce in the seventh innings. Bull and Johnny scored and we licked them, 6 to 4.

In the club-house, Dave went to Hurry and said:

"Have you got anything to tell me, any explanation of the way you looked at the start of that game?"

"Boss," said Kane, "I didn't sleep good last night. Johnny will be a witness to that. I felt terrible in that first innings. I seemed to have lost my 'fast.' In the second innings it came back and I was all right."

And that's all he would say.

You know how we went ahead and took the big series, four games out of five, and how Hurry gave them one run in the three games he pitched. And now you're going to know what I promised to tell you when we first sat down, and I hope I ain't keeping you from a date with that gal from St. Joe.

The world's series ended in St. Louis and naturally I didn't come back East when it was over. Neither did Kane, because he was going home to Yuma, along with his Minnie. Well, they were leaving the next night, though most of the other boys had ducked out right after the final game. Hurry called me up at my house three or four hours before his train was due to leave and asked me would I come and see him and give him some advice. So I went to the hotel and he got me in his room and locked the door.

Here is what he had to say:

On the night before that last game in Chi, a gal called him up and it was nobody but our old friend Evelyn Corey. She asked him to come out to a certain hotel on the North Side and have supper with her. He went because he felt kind of sorry for her. But when he seen her, he lost his head and was just as nuts about her as he'd been at Fort Gregg. She encouraged him and strung him along till he forgot all about poor Minnie. Evelyn told him she knew he could have his pick of a hundred gals and she was broken-hearted because they was no chance for her. He asked her what made her think that, and she put her handkerchief to her eyes and pretended she was crying and that drove him wild and he said he wouldn't marry nobody but her.

Then she told him they had better forget it, that she was broke now, but had been used to luxury, and he promised he would work hard and save up till he had three or four thousand dollars and that would be enough for a start.

"Four thousand dollars!" she says. "Why, that wouldn't buy the runs in my stockings! I wouldn't think of marrying a man who had less than twenty thousand. I would want a honeymoon in Europe and we'd buy a car over there and tour the whole continent and then come home and settle down in some nice suburb of New York. And so," she says, "I'm going to get up and leave you right now because I see that my dream won't never come true."

She left him sitting in the restaurant and he was the only person there outside of the waiters. But after he'd sat a little while—he was waiting till the first shock of his disappointment had wore off—a black-haired bird with a waxed mustache came up to him and asked if he wasn't Hurry Kane, the great pitcher. Then he said: "I suppose you'll pitch again tomorrow," and Kane said yes.

"I haven't nothing against you," says the stranger, "but I hope you lose. It will cost me a lot of money if you win."

"How much?" said Kane.

'So much," says the stranger, "that I will give you twenty thousand dollars if you get beat."

"I can't throw my pals," said Kane.

"Well," said the stranger, "two of your pals has already agreed to throw you."

Kane asked him who he referred to, but he wouldn't tell. Kane don't know yet, but I do. It was Digman and Stout, our shortstopper and first baseman, and you'll notice they ain't with our club no more.

Hurry held out as long as he could, but he thought of Evelyn and that honeymoon in Europe broke him down. He took five thousand dollars' advance and was to come to the same place and get the balance right after the game.

He said that after Johnny Abbott had give him that talk at the breakfast table, he went out and rode around in a taxi so he could cry without being seen.

Well, I've told you about that terrible first innings. And I've told you about young Topping talking to him before he went down to the bull pen to deliver Dave's message to Carney and Olds. Topping asked him what he was staring at and Hurry pointed Evelyn out to him and said she was his gal.

"You gal's grandmother!" said Topping. "That's Evelyn Corey and she belongs to Sam Morris, the bookie. If I was you, I'd lay off. You needn't tell Dave, but I was in Ike Bloom's at one o'clock this morning, and Sam and she were there, too. And one of the waiters told me that Sam had bet twenty thousand dollars on the White Sox way last spring and had got six to one for his money."

Hurry quit talking and I started to bawl him out. But I couldn't stay mad at him, especially when I realized that they was a fifty-three-hundred-dollar check in my pocket which I'd never have had only for him. Besides, they ain't nothing crooked about him. He's just a bone-headed sap.

"I won't tell Dave on you," I said, and I got up to go.

"Wait a minute," says Kane. "I confessed so I could ask you a question. I've still got that five thousand which Morris paid me in advance. With that dough and the fifty-three hundred from the series, I and Min could buy ourself a nice little home in Yuma. But do you think I should ought to give it back to that crook?"

"No," said I. "What you ought to do is split it with young Topping. He was your good luck!"

I run acrost Topping right here in town not long ago. And the first thing he said was, "What do you think of that goofey Kane? I had a letter from him and a check. He said the check was what he owed me."

"Twenty-five hundred dollars?" I says.

"Two hundred," said Topping, "and if I ever lent him two hundred or two cents, I'll roll a hoop from here to Yuma."

E. Annie Proulx is one of the very best writers anywhere. Her first novel, Post-cards, *won the 1993 PEN/Faulkner Award, and she won the 1994 Pulitzer Prize for* The Shipping News. *Accomplished also as a short-story stylist, Proulx's collection* Close Range: Wyoming Stories *won the inaugural fiction award from* New Yorker *magazine in 2000. The story that follows is ostensibly about deer hunting, but deals more with a deadly game of one-upmanship between two grumpy old men. "On the Antler" was originally published in* Harrowsmith *magazine.*

E. Annie Proulx

ON THE ANTLER (1983)

HAWKHEEL'S FACE WAS as finely wrinkled as grass-dried linen, his thin back bent like a branch weighted with snow. He still spent most of his time in the field and on the streams, sweeter days than when he was that half-wild boy who ran panting up the muddy logging road, smashing branches to mute the receding roar of the school bus. Then he had hated books, had despised everything except the woods.

But in the insomnia of old age he read half the night, the patinated words gliding under his eyes like a river coursing over polished stones: books on wild geese, nymph patterns for brook trout, wolves fanning across the snow. He went through his catalogues, putting red stars against the few books he could buy and black crosses like tiny grave markers against the rarities he would never be able to afford—Halford's *Floating Flies and How to Dress Them,* Lanman's *Haw-Ho-Noo,* Phillips' *A Natural History of the Ducks* with color plates as fine as if the wild waterfowl had been pressed like flowers between the pages.

His trailer was on the north bank of the Feather River in the shadow of Antler Mountain. These few narrow acres were all that was left of the home place. He'd sold it off little by little since Josepha had left him, until he was down to the trailer, ten spongy acres of river bottom and his social security checks.

Yet he thought this was the best part of his life. It was as if he'd come into flat water after half a century and more of running the rapids. He was glad to put the paddle down and float the rest of the way.

He had his secret places hidden all through Chopping County and he visited them like stations of the cross; in order, in reverence and in expectation of results. In late May he followed the trout up the narrow, sun-warmed streams, his rod thrusting skillfully through the alders, crushing underfoot ferns whose broken stems released an elusive bitter scent. In October, mists came down on him as he waded through drenched gold-enrod meadows, alert for grouse. And in the numb silence of November Hawkheel was a deer hunter up on the shoulder of Antler Mountain, his back against a beech while frozen threads of ice formed on the rifle's blue metal.

The deer hunt was the end and summit of his year: the irrevocable shot, the thin, ringing silence that followed, the buck down and still, the sky like clouded marble from which sifted snow finer than dust, and the sense of a completed cycle as the cooling blood ran into the dead leaves.

Bill Stong couldn't leave things alone. All through their lives there had been sparks and brushfires of hatred between Hawkheel and him, never quite quenched, but smoldering until some wind fanned up the flames.

In school Hawkheel had been The Lone Woodsman, a moody, insubordinate figure prowling the backcountry. Stong was a wiseacre with a streak of meanness. He hunted with his father and brothers and shot his first buck when he was eleven. How could he miss, thought woman-raised Hawkheel bitterly, how, when he sat in a big pine right over a deer trail and his old man whispered, "Now! Shoot now!" at the moment?

Stong's father farmed a little, ran a feed store and got a small salary to play town constable. He broke up Saturday-night dance fights, shot dogs that ran sheep and sometimes acted as the truant officer. His big, pebbled face was waiting for Hawkheel one school morning when he slid down the rocks to a trout pool.

"Plannin' to cut school again? Well, since your old man's not in a position to do it for you, I'm going to give you a lesson you'll remember." He flailed Hawkheel with a trimmed ash sapling and then drove him to school.

"You don't skip no more school, buddy, or I'll come get you again."

In the classroom Bill Stong's sliding eyes told Hawkheel he had been set up. "I'll fix him," Hawkheel told his sister, Urna, at noon. "I'll think up something. He won't know what hit him when I'm done." The game began, and the thread of rage endured like a footnote to their lives.

In late October, on the Sunday before Stong's fifteenth birthday, an event that exposed his mother's slovenly housekeeping ways took his family away.

Chopping County farmers soaked their seed corn in strychnine to kill the swaggering crows that gorged on the germinating kernels. One of the Stongs, no one knew which one, had mixed the deadly solution in a big roasting pan. The seed was sown and the unwashed pan shoved beneath the blackened iron griddles on the pantry floor where it stayed until autumn hog butchering.

The day was cold and windy, the last of summer thrown up into the sky by turbulent air. Stong's mother pulled out the pan and loaded it with a pork roast big enough to feed the Sunday gathering of family. The pork killed them all except Bill Stong, who was rolling around in Willard Iron's hayloft on a first shameful adventure. The equation of sex and death tainted his adolescent years.

As Stong grew older, he let the farm go down. He sat in the feed store year after year listening in on the party line. His sharp-tongued gossip rasped at the shells of others' lives until the quick was exposed. At the weekend dances Stong showed up alone, never dancing himself, but watching the women gallop past, their print blouses damp with sweat under the arms, their skirts sticking to their hot legs. At night he walked through town seeing which ones left the window shades up. He went uninvited to church suppers and card parties, winked out juicy tales and stained the absent with mean innuendo. Often his razor tongue stropped itself on the faults and flaws of his dead parents as though he had come fresh from a rancorous argument with them, and at other times he called them saints in a tearful voice.

Stong caught Hawkheel with petty tricks again and again. After Hawkheel started farming, once or twice a year he found the mailbox knocked over, water in the tractor's gas tank or the gate opened so the cows got onto the highway. He knew who'd done it.

Still, he kept on buying grain at the feed store until Stong told him about Josepha. Stong's eyes shone like those of a greedy barn cat who has learned to fry mice in butter.

"Hell, everybody in town knows she's doin' it but you," he whispered. He ate Hawkheel up with his eyes, sucked all the juice out of his sad condition.

It was cold in the store and the windows were coated with grain dust. Hawkheel felt the fine powder between his fingers and in his dry mouth. They stared at each other, then Stong scurried out through the chilly passageway that led to the house.

"He's got something coming now," said Hawkheel to Urna. "I could wire him up out in the woods and leave him for the dogs. I could do something real bad to him any time, but I want to see how far he goes."

Stong had sour tricks for everybody. Trade dropped away at the feed store, and there were some, like Hawkheel, who spat when they saw the black pickup heading out of town, Stong's big head turning from side to side to get his fill of the sights before the woods closed in.

For a long time Urna made excuses for Stong, saying that his parents' death had "turned" him, as though he were a bowl of milk gone sour in thundery weather. But when Stong told the game warden there was a summer doe in her cellar she got on the phone and burned Hawkheel's ear.

"Leverd, what kind of a man turns in his neighbor over some deer meat he likes to eat just as good as anybody?"

Hawkheel had an answer, but he didn't give it.

A few years after Josepha left, Hawkheel began to slide deep into the books. He was at Mosely's auction hoping the shotguns would come up early so he could get out of the crowd and take off. But it dragged on, hundreds of the old lady's doilies and quilts going one by one to the summer people. Hawkheel poked through the boxes on the back porch, away from the noise. A book called *Further Adventures of the One-Eyed Poacher* sounded good and he dipped into it like a swallow picking mosquitoes off the water, keeping one ear on the auctioneer's patter. He sat on the broken porch glider and read until the auctioneer, pulling the crowd behind him like a train, came around to the back and shouted "Who'll give me five dollars for them boxes a books!"

Surrounded in his trailer by those books and the hundreds he'd added to them over the decades, Hawkheel enjoyed his solitude.

Stong, too, was more and more alone up at the store. As he got older, his trade dwindled to a few hard-pressed farmers who still bought feed from him because they always had and because Stong carried them until their milk checks came in. Listening in on the phone wasn't enough now; he interrupted conversations, shouting "Get off the line! I got a emergency."

"You ask me," said Urna to Hawkheel, "he's funny in the head. The only emergency he's got is himself. You watch, they'll find him laying on the kitchen floor some day as stiff as a January barn nail."

"When I get through with him," said Hawkheel, "he'll be stiff, all right."

Stong might have fallen to the cold kitchen linoleum with an iron ringing sound, but in his sixties his hair turned a fine platinum white and his face thinned to show good bones. It was a time when people were coming into the country, buying up the old farmhouses and fields and making the sugarhouses into guest cottages.

"Bill, you look like a character out of a Rupert Frost poem," said the woman who'd bought Potter's farm and planted a thousand weedy birches on prime pasture. The new people said Stong was a character.

They liked his stories, they read morals into his rambling lies and encouraged him by standing around the feed store playing farmer—buying salt blocks for the deer, sunflower seeds for the bluejays and laying mash for the pet chickens they had to give away each fall.

Stong set his tattered sails to catch this changing wind. In late life he found himself admired and popular for the first time, and he was grateful. He saw what the summer people liked, and to please them he carried armloads of canning jars, books, tools and other family goods down from the house to the store. He arranged generations of his family's possessions on the shelves beside the work gloves and udder balm. He filled the dusty window with pieces of old harness, wooden canes and chipped china.

In autumn he laid in ammunition for the summer men who came back for their week of deer hunting. The sign in his window read GUNS BLUE SEAL FEED WINE ANTIQUES, a small part of what he offered, for all his family's interests and enterprises were tangled together on the shelves as if he had drawn a rake through their lives and piled the debris in the store.

"They say," said Urna, "that he's cleaned out everything from kettles to cobwebs and put a price tag on it. You know, don't you, that he's selling all them old books his grandfather used to have. He's got them out there in the barn, higgledy-piggledy where the mice can gnaw on them."

"Has he," said Hawkheel.

"I suppose you're going up there to look at them."

"Well," said Hawkheel, "I might."

The Stong place was high on a bluff, a mile upstream from Hawkheel's trailer as the crow flew. To Hawkheel, every turn of the road was like the bite of an auger into the past. He did not remember his adult journeys up Stong's driveway, but recalled with vivid clarity sitting in the dust-colored passenger seat of their old Ford while his father drove over a sodden mat of leaves. The car window had been cranked down, and far below, the hissing river, heavy with rain, cracked boulders along its bottom. His father drove jerkily, lips moving in whispered conversation with invisible imps. Hawkheel had kept his hand on the door handle in case the old man steered for the edge and he had to jump. It was one of the last memories he had of his father.

The Stong place, he saw now, had run down. The real-estate agents would get it pretty soon. The sagging clapboard house tapered away into a long ell and the barn. The store was still in the ell, but Hawkheel took the old shortcut around back, driving through the stinging nettles and just catching a glimpse through the store window of Stong's white head bobbing over a handful of papers.

The barn was filled with dim, brown light shot through like Indian silk with brilliant threads of sunlight. There was a faint smell of apples. On the other side of the wall a rooster beat his wings. Hawkheel looked around and saw, behind the grain sacks, hundreds of books, some in boxes, some stacked on shelves and windowsills. The first one he took up was a perfect copy of Thad Norris's 1865 *The American Angler's Book*. He'd seen it listed in his catalogue at home at $85. Stong wanted one dollar.

Hawkheel went at the boxes. He turned out Judge Nutting's nice little book on grouse, *The History of One Day Out of Seventeen Thousand*. A box of stained magazines was hiding a rare 1886 copy of Halford's *Floating Flies,* the slipcase deeply marked with Stong's penciled price of $1.50.

"Oh god," said Hawkheel, "I got him now."

He disguised the valuable books by mixing them with dull-jacketed works on potatoes and surveying, and carried the stack into the feed store. Stong sat at the counter, working his adding machine. Hawkheel noticed he had taken to wearing overalls, and a bandana knotted around his big neck. He looked to see if there was a straw hat on a nail.

"Good to see you, Leverd," said Stong in a creamy voice. He gossiped and joked as if Hawkheel were one of the summer people, winked and said, "Don't spend your whole social security check on books, Leverd. Save a little out for a good time. You seen the new Ruger shotguns?" A mellowed and ripened Stong, improved by admiration, thought Hawkheel.

The books had belonged to Stong's grandfather, a hero of the waters whose name had once been in the Boston papers for his record trout. The stuffed and mounted trout still hung on the store wall beside the old man's enlarged photograph showing his tilted face and milky eyes behind the oval curve of glass.

"Bill, what will you take for your grandpa today?" cried the summer people who jammed the store on Saturdays, and Stong always answered, "Take what I can get," making a country virtue out of avarice.

Stong was ready to jump into his grandfather stories with a turn of the listener's eye. "The old fool was so slacked-brained he got hisself killed with crow bait."

Hawkheel, coming in from the barn with book dust on him, saw that Stong still lied as easily as he breathed. The summer people stood around him like grinning dogs waiting for the warm hearts and livers of slain hares.

Stong's best customers were the autumn hunters. They re-opened their summer camps, free now from wives and children, burned the wood they had bought in August from Bucky Pincoke and let the bottle of bourbon stand out on the kitchen table with the deck of cards.

"Roughin' it, are you?" Stong would cry jovially to Mr. Rose, splendid in his new red L. L. Bean suspenders. The hunters bought Stong's knives and ammunition and went away with rusted traps, worn horseshoes, and bent pokers pulled from the bins labeled "Collector's Items." In their game pockets were bottles of Stong's cheap Spanish wine, faded orange from standing in the sun. Stong filled their ears to overflowing with his inventions.

"Yes," he would say, "that's what Antler Mountain is named for, not because there's any big bucks up there, which there is *not*"–with a half wink for Hawkheel who stood in the doorway holding rare books like hot bricks–"but because this couple named Antler, Jane and Anton Antler, lived up there years ago. Kind of simple, like some old families hereabouts get."

A sly look. Did he mean Hawkheel's father, who was carted away with wet chin and shaking hands to the state asylum believing pitchford handles were adders?

"Yes, they had a little cabin up there. Lived off raccoons and weeds. Then old Jane had this baby, only one they ever had. Thought a lot of it, couldn't do enough for it, but it didn't survive their care and when it was only a few months old it died."

Stong, like a petulant tenor, turned away then and arranged the dimes in the cash register. The hunters rubbed their soft hands along the counter and begged for the rest of the story. Hawkheel himself wondered how it would come out.

"Well, sir, they couldn't bear to lay that baby away in the ground, so they put it in a five-gallon jar of pure alcohol. My own grandfather—used to stand right here behind the counter where I'm standing now—sold 'em the jar. We used to carry them big jars. Can't get 'em any more. They set that jar with the baby on a stump in front of their cabin the way we might set out a plaster duck on the lawn." He would pause a moment for good effect, then say, "*The stump's still there.*"

They asked him to draw maps on the back of paper bags and went up onto the Antler to stare at the stump as if the impression of the jar had been burned into it by holy fire. Stong, with a laugh like a broken cream separator, told Hawkheel that every stick from that cut maple was in his woodshed. For each lie he heard, Hawkheel took three extra books.

All winter long Hawkheel kept digging away at the book mine in the barn, putting good ones at the bottom of the deepest pile as no one else would find them, cautiously buying only a few each week.

"Why, you're getting to be my best customer, Leverd," said Stong, looking through the narrow, handmade Dutch pages of John Beever's *Practical Fly-fishing,* which Hawkheel guessed was worth $200 on the collector's market, but for which Stong wanted only fifty cents. Hawkheel was afraid Stong would feel the quality of paper, notice that it was a numbered copy, somehow sense its rarity and value. He tried a diversion.

"Bill! You'll be interested that last week I seen the heaviest buck I seen in many years. He was pawing through the leaves about thirty yards from My Place."

In Chopping County "My Place" meant the speaker's private deer stand. It was a county of still hunting, and good stands were passed from father to son. Hawkheel's Place on the Antler regularly gave him big deer, usually the biggest deer in Feather River. Stong's old Place in the comfortable pine was useless, discovered by weekend hunters from out of state who shot his bucks and left beer cans under the tree while he tended the store. They brought the deer to be weighed on Stong's reporting scales, bragging, not knowing they'd usurped his stand, while he smiled and nodded. Stong had not even had a small doe in five years.

"Your Place up on the Antler, Leverd?" said Stong, letting the cover of the Beever fall closed. "Wasn't that over on the south slope?"

"No, it's in that beech stand on the shoulder. Too steep for flatlanders to climb so I do pretty good there. A big buck. I'd say he'd run close to one-eighty, dressed."

Stong raked the two quarters toward him and commenced a long lie about a herd of white deer that used to live in the swamp in the old days, but his eyes went back to the book in Hawkheel's hands.

The long fine fishing days began a few weeks later, and Hawkheel decided to walk the high northeast corner of the county looking for new water. In late summer he found it.

At the head of a rough mountain pass a waterfall poured into a large trout pool like champagne into a wine glass. Images of clouds and leaves lay on the slowly revolving surface. Dew, like crystal insect eggs, shone in the untrodden moss along the stream. The kingfisher screamed and clattered his wings as Hawkheel played a heavy rainbow into the shallows. In a few weeks he came to think that since the time of the St. Francis Indians, only he had ever found the way there.

As August waned Hawkheel grew possessive of the pool and arranged stones and twigs when he could not come for several days, searching later for signs of their disarray from trespassing feet. Nothing was ever changed, except when a cloudburst washed his twigs into a huddle.

One afternoon the wind came up too strong to cast from below the pool, and Hawkheel took off his shoes and stockings and crept cautiously onto the steep rock slab above the waterfall. He gripped his bare white toes into the granite fissures, climbing the rough face. The wind blew his hair up the wrong way and he felt he must look like the kingfisher.

From above the pool he could see the trout swimming smoothly in the direction of the current. The whole perspective of the place was new; it was as if he were seeing it for the first time. There was the back of the dead spruce and the kingfisher's hidden entrance revealed. There, too, swinging from an invisible length of line wound around a branch stub, was a faded red and white plastic bobber that the Indians had not left.

"Isn't anything safe any more?" shouted Hawkheel, coming across the rock too fast. He went down hard and heard his knee crack. He cursed the trout, the spruce, the rock, the invader of his private peace, and made a bad trip home leaning on a forked stick.

Urna brought over hot suppers until he could get around and do for himself again. The inside of the trailer was packed with books and furniture and the cramped space made him listless. He got in the habit of cooking only every three or four days, making up big pots of venison stew or pea soup and picking at it until it was used up or went bad.

He saw in the mirror that he looked old. He glared at his reflection and asked, "Where's your medicine bottle and sweater?" He thought of his mother who sat for years in the rocker, her thick, ginger-shellacked cane hooked over the arm, and fled into his books, reading until his eyes stung and his favorites were too familiar to open. The heavy autumnal rain hammered on the trailer and stripped the leaves from the trees. Not until the day before deer season was he well enough to drive up to Stong's feed store for more books.

He went though the familiar stacks gloomily, keeping his weight off the bad leg and hoping to find something he'd overlooked among the stacks of fine-printed agricultural reports and ink-stained geographies.

He picked up a big dark album that he'd passed over a dozen times. The old-fashioned leather cover was stamped with a design of flowing feathers in gold, and tortured gothic letters spelled "Family Album." Inside he saw photographs, snapshots, ocher newspaper clippings whose paste had disintegrated, postcards, prize ribbons. The snapshots showed scores of curd-faced Stongs squinting into the sun, Stong children with fat knees holding wooden pull-along ducks, and a black and white dog Hawkheel dimly remembered.

He looked closer at one snapshot, drawn by something familiar. A heavy boy stood on a slab of rock, grinning up into the sky. In his hand a fishing rod pointed at the upper branches of a spruce where a bobber was hopelessly entangled in the dark needles. A blur of moving water rushed past the boy into a black pool.

"You bastard," said Hawkheel, closing the album on the picture of Stong, Bill Stong of years ago, trespassing at Hawkheel's secret pool.

He pushed the album up under the back of his shirt so it lay against his skin. It felt the size of a Sears' catalogue and made him throw out his shoulders stiffly. He took a musty book at random—*The Boy's Companion*—and went out to the treacherous Stong.

"Haven't seen you for quite a while, Leverd. Hear you been laid up," said Stong.

"Bruised my knee." Hawkheel put the book on the counter.

"Got to expect to be laid up now and then at our age," said Stong. "I had trouble with my hip off and on since April. I got something here that'll fix you up." He took a squat, foreign bottle out from under the counter.

"Mr. Rose give me this for checking his place last winter. Apple brandy, and about as strong as anything you ever tasted. Too strong for me, Leverd. I get dizzy just smelling the cork." He poured a little into a paper cup and pushed it at Hawkheel.

The fragrance of apple wood and autumn spread out as Hawkheel tasted the Calvados. A column of fire rose in the chimney of his throat with a bitter aftertaste like old cigar smoke.

"I suppose you're all ready for opening day, Leverd. Where you going for deer this year?"

"Same place I always go—My Place up on the Antler."

"You been up there lately?"

"No, not since spring." Hawkheel felt the album's feathered design transferring to his back.

"Well, Leverd," said Stong in a mournful voice, "there's no deer up there now. Got some people bought land up there this summer, think the end of the world is coming so they built a cement cabin, got in a ton of dried apricots and pinto beans. They got some terrible weapons to keep the crowds away. Shot up half the trees on the Antler testing their machine guns. Surprised you didn't hear it. No deer within ten miles of the Antler now. You might want to try someplace else. They say it's good over to Slab City."

Hawkheel knew one of Stong's lies when he heard it and wondered what it meant. He wanted to get home with the album and examine the proof of Stong's trespass at the secret pool, but Stong poured from the bottle again and Hawkheel knocked it back.

"Where does your fancy friend get this stuff?" he asked, feeling electrical impulses sweep through his fingers as though they itched to play the piano.

"Frawnce," said Stong in an elegant tone. "he goes there every year to talk about books at some college." His hard eyes glittered with malice. "He's a liberian." Stong's thick forefinger opened the cover of *The Boy's Companion*, exposing a red-bordered label Hawkheel had missed; it was marked $55.

"He says I been getting skinned over my books, Leverd."

"Must of been quite a shock to you," said Hawkheel, thinking he didn't like the taste of apple brandy, didn't like librarian Rose. He left the inflated *Boy's Companion* on the counter and hobbled out to the truck, the photograph album between his shoulder blades giving him a ramrod dignity. In the rearview mirror he saw Stong at the door staring after him.

Clouds like grey waterweed under the ice choked the sky and a gusting wind banged the door against the trailer. Inside, Hawkheel worked the album out from under his shirt and laid it on the table while he built up the fire and put on some leftover pea soup to heat. "'Liberian!'" he said once and snorted. After supper he felt queasy and went to bed early thinking the pea soup might have stood too long.

In the morning Hawkheel's bowels beat with urgent tides of distress and there was a foul taste in his mouth. When he came back from the bathroom he gripped the edge of the table which bent and surged in his hands, then gave up and took to his bed. He could hear sounds like distant popcorn and thought it was knotty wood in the stove until he remembered it was the first day of deer season. "Goddammit," he cried, "I already been stuck here six weeks and now I'm doing it again."

A sound woke him in late afternoon. He was thirsty enough to drink tepid water from the spout of the teakettle. There was another shot on the Antler and he peered out the window at the shoulder of the mountain. He thought he could see specks of brightness in the dull grey smear of hardwood and brush, and he shuffled over to the gun rack to get his .30–.30, clinging to the backs of the chairs for balance. He rested the barrel on the breadbox and looked through the scope, scanning the slope for his deer stand, and at once caught the flash of orange.

He could see two of them kneeling beside the bark-colored curve of a dead deer at his Place. He could make out the bandana at the big one's neck, see a knife gleam briefly like falling water. He watched them drag the buck down toward the logging road until the light faded and their orange vests turned black under the trees.

"Made sure I couldn't go out with your goddamned poison brandy, didn't you?" said Hawkheel.

He sat by the stove with the old red Indian blanket pulled around him, feeling like he'd stared at a light bulb too long. Urna called after supper. Her metallic voice rang in his ear.

"I suppose you heard all about it."

"Only thing I heard was the shots, but I seen him through the scope from the window. What'd it weight out at?"

"I heard two-thirty, dressed out, so live weight must of been towards three hundred. Warden said it's probably the biggest buck ever took in the county, a sixteen-pointer, too, and probably a state record. I didn't know you could see onto the Antler from your window."

"Oh, I can see good, but not good enough to see who was with him."

"He's the one bought Willard Iron's place and put a tennis court onto the garden," said Urna scornfully. "Rose. They say he was worse than Bill, jumping around and screaming for them to take pictures."

"Did they?"

"Course they did. Then they all went up to Mr. Tennis Court's to have a party. Stick your head out the door and you'll hear them on the wind."

Hawkheel did not stick his head out the door, but opened the album to look at the Stongs, their big, rocklike faces bent over wedding cakes and infants. Many of the photographs were captioned in a spiky, antique hand: "Cousin Mattie with her new skates," "Pa on the porch swing," simple statements of what was already clear as though the writer feared the images would someday dissolve into blankness, leaving the happiness of the Stongs unknown.

He glared, seeing Stong at the secret pool, the familiar sly eyes, the fatuous gaping mouth unchanged. He turned the pages to a stiff portrait of Stong's parents, the grandfather standing behind them holding what Hawkheel thought was a cat until he recognized the stuffed trout. On the funeral page the same portraits were reduced in size and joined by a flowing black ribbon that bent and curled in ornate flourishes. The obituary from the *Rutland Herald* was headlined "A Farm Tragedy."

"Too bad Bill missed that dinner," said Hawkheel.

He saw that on many pages there were empty places where photographs had been wrenched away. He found them, mutilated and torn, at the end of the album. Stong was in every photograph. In the high school graduation picture, surrounded by clouds of organdy and stiff new suits, Stong's face was inked out and black blood ran from the bottoms of his trousers. Here was another, Stong on a fat-tired white bicycle with a dozen arrows drawn piercing his body. A self-composed obituary, written in a hand like infernal corrosive lace that scorched the page, told how this miserable boy, "too bad to live" and "hated by everybody" had met his various ends. Over and over Stong had killed his photographic images. He listed every member of his family as a survivor.

Hawkheel was up and about the next morning, a little unsteady but with a clear head. At first light the shots had begun on the Antler, hunters trying for a buck to match the giant that Stong had brought down. The Antler, thought Hawkheel, was as good as bulldozed.

By afternoon he felt well enough for a few chores, stacking hay bales around the trailer foundation and covering the windows over with plastic. He took two trout out of the freezer and fried them for supper. He was washing the frying pan when Urna called.

"They was on T.V. with the deer," she said. "They showed the game commissioner looking up the record in some book and saying this one beat it. I been half expecting to hear from you all day, wondering what you're going to do."

"Don't you worry," said Hawkheel. "Bill's got it comin' from me. There's a hundred things I could do."

"Well," said Urna, "he's got it coming."

It took Hawkheel forty minutes to pack the boxes and load them into the pickup. The truck started hard after sitting in the cold blowing rain for two days, but by the time he got it onto the main road it ran smooth and steady, the headlights opening a sharp yellow path through the night.

At the top of Stong's drive he switched the lights off and coasted along in neutral. A half-full moon, ragged with rushing clouds, floated in the sky. Another storm breeder, thought Hawkheel.

The buck hung from a gambrel in the big maple, swaying slowly in the gusting wind. The body cavity gaped black in the moonlight. "Big," said Hawkheel, seeing the glint of light on the hooves scraping an arc in the leaves, "damn big." He got out of the truck and leaned his forehead against the cold metal for a minute.

From a box in the back of the truck he took one of his books and opened it. It was *Haw-Ho-Noo*. He leaned over a page as if he could read the faint print in the moonlight, then gripped it and tore it out. One after another he seized the books, ripped the pages and cracked their spines. He hurled them at the black, swaying deer and they fell to the bloodied ground beneath it.

"Fool with me, will you?" shouted Hawkheel, tearing soft paper with both hands, tossing books up at the moon, and his blaring sob rose over the sound of the boulders cracking in the river below.

With his deerstalker cap, pipe, overcoat, and detective genius, Sherlock Holmes is widely recognized as the world's most famous sleuth. In this story, mystery blends with sport as Holmes and his companion, Dr. Watson, seek to unravel the kidnapping of a champion racehorse and the murder of its trainer. Sir Arthur Conan Doyle (1859–1930) was a medical doctor by training who created Holmes as a central character in a series of short stories. This was a unique idea in Victorian England, and the success of the stories launched Doyle into prominence. "Silver Blaze" first appeared in Strand Magazine, *along with other masterpieces such as "The Red-Headed League," "The Adventure of the Speckled Band," and "A Scandal in Bohemia."*

A. Conan Doyle

THE ADVENTURE OF SILVER BLAZE (1892)

I AM AFRAID, WATSON, that I shall have to go," said Holmes, as we sat down together to our breakfast one morning.

"Go! Where to?"

"To Dartmoor—to King's Pyland."

I was not surprised. Indeed, my only wonder was that he had not already been mixed up in this extraordinary case, which was the one topic of conversation through the length and breadth of England. For a whole day my companion had rambled about the room with his chin upon his chest and his brows knitted, charging and re-charging his pipe with the strongest black tobacco, and absolutely deaf to any of my questions or remarks. Fresh editions of every paper had been sent up by our newsagent only to be glanced over and tossed down into a corner. Yet, silent as he was, I knew perfectly well what it was, over which he was brooding. There was but one problem before the public which could challenge his powers of analysis, and that was the singular disappearance of the favourite for the Wessex Cup and the tragic murder of its trainer. When, therefore, he suddenly announced his intention of setting out for the scene of the drama, it was only what I had both expected and hoped for.

"I should be most happy to go down with you if I should not be in the way," said I.

"My dear Watson, you would confer a great favour upon me by coming. And I think that your time will not be mis-spent, for there are points about this case which promise to make it an absolutely unique one. We have, I think, just time to catch our train at Paddington, and I will go further into the matter upon our journey. You would oblige me by bringing with you your very excellent field-glass."

And so it happened that an hour or so later I found myself in the corner of a first-class carriage, flying along, on route for Exeter, while Sherlock Holmes, with his sharp, eager face framed in his earflapped travelling cap, dipped rapidly into the bundle of fresh papers which he had procured at Paddington. We had left Reading far behind us before he thrust the last of them under the seat, and offered me his cigar case.

"We are going well," said he, looking out of the window, and glancing at his watch. "Our rate at present is fifty-three and a half miles an hour."

"I have not observed the quarter-mile posts," said I.

"Nor have I. But the telegraph posts upon this line are sixty yards apart, and the calculation is a simple one. I presume that you have already looked into this matter of the murder of John Straker and the disappearance of Silver Blaze?"

"I have seen what the *Telegraph* and the *Chronicle* have to say."

"It is one of those cases where the art of the reasoner should be used rather for the sifting of details than for the acquiring of fresh evidence. The tragedy has been so uncommon, so complete, and of such personal importance to so many people that we are suffering from a plethora of surmise, conjecture, and hypothesis. The difficulty is to detach the framework of fact—of absolute, undeniable fact—from the embellishments of theorists and reporters. Then, having established ourselves upon this sound basis, it is our duty to see what inferences may be drawn, and which are the special points upon which the whole mystery turns. On Tuesday evening I received telegrams, both from Colonel Ross, the owner of the horse, and from Inspector Gregory, who is looking after the case, inviting my co-operation."

"Tuesday evening!" I exclaimed. "And this is Thursday morning. Why did you not go down yesterday?"

"Because I made a blunder, my dear Watson—which is, I am afraid, a more common occurrence than anyone would think who only knew me through your memoirs. The fact is that I could not believe it possible that the most remarkable horse in England could long remain concealed, especially in so sparsely inhabited a place as the north of Dartmoor. From hour to hour yesterday I expected to hear that he had been found, and that his abductor was the murderer of John Straker. When, however, another morning had come and I found that, beyond the arrest of young Fitzroy Simpson, nothing had been done, I felt that it was time for me to take action. Yet in some ways I feel that yesterday has not been wasted."

"You have formed a theory then?"

"At least I have got a grip of the essential facts of the case. I shall enumerate them to you, for nothing clears up a case so much as stating it to another person, and I can hardly expect your co-operation if I do not show you the position from which we start."

I lay back against the cushions, puffing at my cigar, while Holmes, leaning forward, with his long thin forefinger checking off the points upon the palm of his left hand, gave me a sketch of the events which had led to our journey.

"Silver Blaze," said he, "is from the Isonomy stock, and holds as brilliant a record as his famous ancestor. He is now in his fifth year, and has brought in turn each of the prizes of the turf to Colonel Ross, his fortunate owner. Up to the time of the catastrophe he was first favourite for the Wessex Cup, the betting being three to one on. He has always, however, been a prime favourite with the racing public, and has never yet disappointed them, so that even at those odds enormous sums of money have been laid upon him. It is obvious, therefore, that there were many people who had the strongest interest in preventing Silver Blaze from being there at the fall of the flag, next Tuesday.

"This fact was, of course, appreciated at King's Pyland, where the Colonel's training stable is situated. Every precaution was taken to guard the favourite. The trainer, John Straker, is a retired jockey, who rode in Colonel Ross's colours before he became too heavy for the weighing chair. He has served the Colonel for five years as jockey, and for seven as trainer, and has always shown himself to be a zealous and honest servant. Under him were three lads, for the establishment was a small one, containing only four horses in all. One of these lads sat up each night in the stable, while the others slept in the loft. All three bore excellent characters. John Straker, who is a married man, lived in a small villa about two hundred yards from the stables. He has no children, keeps one maid-servant, and is comfortably off. The country round is very lonely, but about half a mile to the north there is a small cluster of villas which have been built by a Tavistock contractor for the use of invalids and others who may wish to enjoy the pure Dartmoor air. Tavistock itself lies two miles to the west, while across the moor, also about two miles distant, is the larger training establishment of Mapleton, which belongs to Lord Backwater, and is managed by Silas Brown. In every other direction the moor is a complete wilderness, inhabited only by a few roaming gipsies. Such was the general situation last Monday night when the catastrophe occurred.

"On that evening the horses had been exercised and watered as usual, and the stables were locked up at nine o'clock. Two of the lads walked up to the trainer's house, where they had supper in the kitchen, while the third, Ned Hunter, remained on guard. At a few minutes after nine the maid, Edith Baxter, carried down to the stables his supper, which consisted of a dish of curried mutton. She took no liquid, as there was a water-tap in the stables, and it was the rule that the lad on duty should drink nothing else. The maid carried a lantern with her, as it was very dark, and the path ran across the open moor.

"Edith Baxter was within thirty yards of the stables when a man appeared out of the darkness and called to her to stop. As he stepped into the circle of yellow light thrown by the lantern she saw that he was a person of gentlemanly bearing, dressed in a grey suit of tweed with a cloth cap. He wore gaiters, and carried a heavy stick with a knob to it. She was most impressed, however, by the extreme pallor of his face and by the nervousness of his manner. His age, she thought, would be rather over thirty than under it.

"'Can you tell me where I am?' he asked. 'I had almost made up my mind to sleep on the moor when I saw the light of your lantern.'

"'You are close to the King's Pyland training stables,' she said.

"'Oh, indeed! What a stroke of luck!' he cried. 'I understand that a stable boy sleeps there alone every night. Perhaps that is his supper which you are carrying to him. Now I am sure that you would not be too proud to earn the price of a new dress, would you?' He took a piece of white paper folded up out of his waistcoat pocket. 'See that the boy has this tonight, and you shall have the prettiest frock that money can buy.'

"She was frightened by the earnestness of his manner, and ran past him to the window through which she was accustomed to hand the meals. It was already open, and Hunter was seated at the small table inside. She had begun to tell him of what had happened, when the stranger came up again.

"'Good evening,' said he, looking through the window, 'I wanted to have a word with you.' The girl has sworn that as he spoke she noticed the corner of the little paper packet protruding from his closed hand.

"'What business have you here?' asked the lad.

"'It's business that may put something into your pocket,' said the other. 'You've two horses in for the Wessex Cup—Silver Blaze and Bayard. Let me have the straight tip, and you won't be a loser. Is it a fact that at the weights Bayard could give the other a hundred yards in five furlongs, and that the stable have put their money on him?'

"'So you're one of those damned touts,' cried the lad. 'I'll show you how we serve them in King's Pyland.' He sprang up rushed across the stable to unloose the dog. The girl fled away to the house, but as she ran she looked back, and saw that the stranger was leaning through the window. A minute later, however, when Hunter rushed out with the hound he was gone, and though the lad ran all round the buildings he failed to find any trace of him."

"One moment!" I asked. "Did the stableboy, when he ran out with the dog, leave the door unlocked behind him?"

"Excellent, Watson; excellent!" murmured my companion. "The importance of the point struck me so forcibly, that I sent a special wire to Dartmoor yesterday to clear the matter up. The boy locked the door before he left it. The window, I may add, was not large enough for a man to get through.

"Hunter waited until his fellow grooms had returned, when he sent a message up to the trainer and told him what had occurred. Straker was excited at hearing the account, although he does not seem to have quite realized its true significance. It left him, however, vaguely uneasy, and Mrs. Straker, waking at one in the morning, found that he was dressing. In reply to her inquiries, he said that he could not sleep on account of his anxiety about the horses, and that he intended to walk down to the stables to see that all was well. She begged him to remain at home, as she could hear the rain pattering against the windows, but in spite of her entreaties he pulled on his large mackintosh and left the house.

"Mrs. Straker awoke at seven in the morning, to find that her husband had not yet returned. She dressed herself hastily, called the maid, and set off for the stables. The door was open; inside, huddled together upon a chair, Hunter was sunk in a state of absolute stupor, the favourite's stall was empty, and there were no signs of his trainer.

"The two lads who slept in the chaff-cutting loft above the harness-room were quickly aroused. They had heard nothing during the night, for they are both sound sleepers. Hunter was obviously under the influence of some powerful drug; and, as no sense could be got out of him, he was left to sleep it off while the two lads and the two women ran out in search of the absentees. They still had hopes that the trainer had for some reason taken out the horse for early exercise, but on ascending the knoll near the house, from which all the neighbouring moors were visible, they not only could see no signs of the favourite, but they perceived something which warned them that they were in the presence of a tragedy.

"About a quarter of a mile from the stables, John Straker's overcoat was flapping from a furze bush. Immediately beyond there was a bowl-shaped depression in the moor, and at the bottom of this was found the dead body of the unfortunate trainer. His head had been shattered by a savage blow from some heavy weapon, and he was wounded in the thigh, where there was a long, clean cut, inflicted evidently by some very sharp instrument. It was clear, however, that Straker had defended himself vigorously against his assailants, for in his right hand he held a small knife, which was clotted with blood up to the handle, while in his left he grasped a red and black silk cravat, which was recognised by the maid as having been worn on the preceding evening by the stranger who had visited the stables.

"Hunter, on recovering from his stupor, was also quite positive as to the ownership of the cravat. He was equally certain that the same stranger had, while standing at the window, drugged his curried mutton, and so deprived the stables of their watchman.

"As to the missing horse, there were abundant proofs in the mud which lay at the bottom of the fatal hollow, that he had been there at the time of the struggle. But from that morning he has disappeared; and although a large reward has been offered, and all the gipsies of Dartmoor are on the alert, no news has come of him. Finally an analysis has shown that the remains of his supper, left by the stable lad, contain an appreciable quantity of powdered opium, while the people at the house partook of the same dish on the same night without any ill effect.

"Those are the main facts of the case, stripped of all surmise and stated as baldly as possible. I shall now recapitulate what the police have done in the matter.

"Inspector Gregory, to whom the case has been committed, is an extremely competent officer. Were he but gifted with imagination he might rise to great heights in his profession. On his arrival he promptly found and arrested the man upon whom suspicion naturally rested. There was little difficulty in finding him, for he inhabited one of those villas which I have mentioned. His name, it appears, was Fitzroy Simpson. He was a man of the excellent birth and education, who had squandered a fortune upon the turf, and who lived now by doing a little quiet and genteel book-making in the sporting clubs of London. An examination of his betting-book shows that bets to the amount of five thousand pounds had been registered by him against the favourite.

"On being arrested he volunteered the statement that he had come down to Dartmoor in the hope of getting some information about the King's Pyland horses, and also about Desborough, the second favourite, which was in charge of Silas Brown, at the Mapleton stables. He did not attempt to deny that he had acted as described upon the evening before, but declared that he had no sinister designs, and had simply wished to ob-tain first-hand information. When confronted with his cravat he turned very pale, and was utterly unable to account for its presence in the hand of the murdered man. His wet clothing showed that he had been out in the storm of the night before, and his stick, which was a Penang lawyer, weighted with lead, was just such a weapon as might, by repeated blows, have inflicted the terrible injuries to which the trainer had succumbed.

"On the other hand, there was no wound upon his person, while the state of Straker's knife would show that one, at least, of his assailants must bear his mark upon him. There you have it all in a nutshell, Wat-son, and if you can give me any light I shall be infinitely obliged to you."

I had listened with the greatest interest to the statement which Holmes, with characteristic clearness, had laid before me. Though most of the facts were familiar to me, I had not sufficiently appreciated their relative importance, nor their connection to each other.

"Is it not possible," I suggested, "that the incised wound upon Straker may have been caused by his own knife in the convulsive struggles which follow any brain injury?"

"It is more than possible; it is probable," said Holmes. "In that case, one of the main points in favour of the accused disappears."

"And yet," said I, "even now I fail to understand what the theory of the police can be."

"I am afraid that whatever theory we state has very grave objections to it," returned my companion. "The police imagine, I take it, that this

Fitzroy Simpson, having drugged the lad, and having in some way obtained a duplicate key, opened the stable door, and took out the horse, with the intention, apparently, of kidnapping him altogether. His bridle is missing, so that Simpson must have put this on. Then, having left the door open behind him, he was leading the horse away over the moor, when he was either met or overtaken by the trainer. A row naturally ensued, Simpson beat out the trainer's brains with his heavy stick without receiving any injury from the small knife which Straker used in self-defence, and then the thief either led the horse on to some secret hiding-place, or else it may have bolted during the struggle, and be now wandering out on the moors. That is the case as it appears to the police, and improbable as it is, all other explanations are more improbable still. However, I shall very quickly test the matter when I am once upon the spot, and until then I really cannot see how we can get much further than our present position."

It was evening before we reached the little town of Tavistock, which lies, like the boss of a shield, in the middle of the huge circle of Dartmoor. Two gentlemen were awaiting us at the station; the one a tall fair man with lion-like hair and beard, and curiously penetrating light blue eyes, the other a small alert person, very neat and dapper, in a frockcoat and gaiters, with trim little side-whiskers and an eye-glass. The latter was Colonel Ross, the well-known sportsman, the other Inspector Gregory, a man who was rapidly making his name in the English detective service.

"I am delighted that you have come down, Mr. Holmes," said the Colonel. "The Inspector here has done all that could possibly be suggested; but I wish to leave no stone unturned in trying to avenge poor Straker, and in recovering my horse."

"Have there been any fresh developments?" asked Holmes.

"I am sorry to say that we have made very little progress," said the Inspector. "We have an open carriage outside, and as you would no doubt like to see the place before the light fails, we might talk it over as we drive."

A minute later we were all seated in a comfortable landau and were rattling through the quaint old Devonshire town. Inspector Gregory was full of his case, and poured out a stream of remarks, while Holmes threw in an occasional question or interjection. Colonel Ross leaned back with his arms folded and his hat tilted over his eyes, while I listened with interest to the dialogue of the two detectives. Gregory was formulating his theory, which was almost exactly what Holmes had foretold in the train.

"The net is drawn pretty close round Fitzroy Simpson," he remarked, "and I believe myself that he is our man. At the same time, I recognise that the evidence is purely circumstantial, and that some new development may upset it."

"How about Straker's knife?"

"We have quite come to the conclusion that he wounded himself in his fall."

"My friend Dr. Watson made that suggestion to me as we came down. If so, it would tell against this man Simpson."

"Undoubtedly. He had neither a knife nor any sign of a wound. The evidence against him is certainly very strong. He had a great interest in the disappearance of the favourite, he lies under the suspicion of having poisoned the stable boy, he was undoubtedly out in the storm, he was armed with a heavy stick, and his cravat was found in the dead man's hand. I really think we have enough to go before a jury."

Holmes shook his head. "A clever counsel would tear it all to rags," said he. "Why should he take the horse out of the stable? If he wished to injure it, why could he not do it there? Has a duplicate key been found in his possession? What chemist sold him the powdered opium? Above all, where could he, a stranger to the district, hide a horse, and such a horse as this? What is his own explanation as to the paper which he wished the maid to give to the stable-boy?'

"He says that it was a ten-pound note. One was found in his purse. But your other difficulties are not so formidable as they seem. He is not a stranger to the district. He was twice lodged at Tavistock in the summer. The opium was probably brought from London. The key, having served its purpose, would be hurled away. The horse may lie at the bottom of one of the pits or old mines upon the moor."

"What does he say about the cravat?"

"He acknowledges that it is his, and declares that he had lost it. But a new element has been introduced into the case which may account for his leading the horse from the stable."

Holmes pricked up his ears.

"We have found traces which show that a party of gipsies encamped on Monday night within a mile of the spot where the murder took place. On Tuesday they were gone. Now, presuming that there was some understanding between Simpson and these gipsies, might he not have been leading the horse to them when he was overtaken, and may they not have him now?"

"It is certainly possible."

"The moor is being scoured for these gipsies. I have also examined every stable and outhouse in Tavistock, and for a radius of ten miles."

"There is another training stable quite close, I understand?"

"Yes, and that is a factor which we must certainly not neglect. As Desborough, their horse, was second in the betting, they had an interest in the disappearance of the favourite. Silas Brown, the trainer, is known to have had large bets upon the event, and he was no friend to poor Straker. We have, however, examined the stables, and there is nothing to connect him with the affair."

"And nothing to connect this man Simpson with the interests of the Mapleton stables?"

"Nothing at all."

Holmes leaned back in the carriage and the conversation ceased. A few minutes later our driver pulled up at a neat little red-brick villa with overhanging eaves, which stood by the road. Some distance off, across a paddock, lay a long grey-tiled out-building. In every other direction the low curves of the moor, bronze-coloured from the fading ferns, stretched away to the sky-line, broken only by the steeples of Tavistock, and by a cluster of houses away to the westward, which marked the Mapleton stables. We all sprang out with the exception of Holmes, who continued to lean back with his eyes fixed upon the sky in front of him, entirely absorbed in his own thoughts. It was only when I touched his arm that he roused himself with a violent start and stepped out of the carriage.

"Excuse me," said he, turning to Colonel Ross, who had looked at him in some surprise. "I was day-dreaming." There was a gleam in his eyes and a suppressed excitement in his manner which convinced me, used as I was to his ways, that his hand was upon a clue, though I could not imagine where he had found it.

"Perhaps you would prefer at once to go on to the scene of the crime, Mr. Holmes?" said Gregory.

"I think that I should prefer to stay here a little and go into one or two questions of detail. Straker was brought back here, I presume?"

"Yes, he lies upstairs. The inquest is to-morrow."

"He has been in your service some years, Colonel Ross?"

"I have always found him an excellent servant."

"I presume that you made an inventory of what he had in his pockets at the time of his death, Inspector?"

"I have the things themselves in the sitting-room if you would care to see them."

"I should be very glad."

We all filed into the front room and sat round the central table, while the Inspector unlocked a square tin box and laid a small heap of things before us. There was a box of vestas, two inches of tallow candle, an A.D.P. briar-root pipe, a pouch of sealskin with half an ounce of long-cut Cavendish, a silver watch with a gold chain, five sovereigns in gold, an aluminium pencil-case, a few papers, and an ivory-handled knife with a very delicate inflexible blade marked Weiss and Co., London.

"This is a very singular knife," said Holmes, lifting it up and examining it minutely. "I presume, as I see bloodstains upon it, that it is the one which was found in the dead man's grasp. Watson, this knife is surely in your line."

"It is what we call a cataract knife," said I.

"I thought so. A very delicate blade devised for very delicate work. A strange thing for a man to carry with him upon a rough expedition, especially as it would not shut in his pocket."

"The tip was guarded by a disc of cork which we found beside his body," said the Inspector. "His wife tells us that the knife had lain for some days upon the dressing-table, and that he had picked it up as he left the room.

It was a poor weapon, but perhaps the best that he could lay his hand on at the moment."

"Very possibly. How about these papers?"

"Three of them are receipted hay-dealers' accounts. One of them is a letter of instructions from Colonel Ross. This other is a milliner's account for thirty-seven pounds fifteen, made out by Madame Lesurier, of Bond Street, to William Darbyshire. Mrs. Straker tells us that Darbyshire was a friend of her husband's, and that occasionally his letters were addressed here."

"Madame Darbyshire had somewhat expensive tastes," remarked Holmes, glancing down the account. "Twenty-two guineas is rather heavy for a single costume. However, there appears to be nothing more to learn, and we may now go down to the scene of the crime."

As we emerged from the sitting-room a woman who had been waiting in the passage took a step forward and laid her hand upon the Inspector's sleeve. Her face was haggard, and thin, and eager; stamped with the print of a recent horror.

"Have you got them? Have you found them?" she panted.

"No, Mrs. Straker; but Mr. Holmes, here, has come from London to help us, and we shall do all that is possible."

"Surely I met you in Plymouth, at a garden party, some little time ago, Mrs. Straker," said Holmes.

"No, sir; you are mistaken."

"Dear me; why, I could have sworn to it. You wore a costume of dove-coloured silk, with ostrich feather trimming."

"I never had such a dress, sir," answered the lady.

"Ah; that quite settles it," said Holmes; and, with an apology, he followed the Inspector outside. A short walk across the moor took us to the hollow in which the body had been found. At the brink of it was the furze bush upon which the coat had been hung.

"There was no wind that night, I understand," said Holmes.

"None; but very heavy rain."

"In that case the overcoat was not blown against the furze bushes, but placed there."

"Yes, it was laid across the bush."

"You fill me with interest. I perceive that the ground has been trampled up a good deal. No doubt many feet have been there since Monday night."

"A piece of matting has been laid here at the side, and we have all stood upon that."

"Excellent."

"In this bag I have one of the boots which Straker wore, one of Fitzroy Simpson's shoes, and a cast horseshoe of Silver Blaze."

"My dear Inspector, you surpass yourself!" Holmes took the bag, and descending into the hollow he pushed the matting into a more central position. Then stretching himself upon his face and leaning his chin upon his hands he made a careful study of the trampled mud in front of him.

"Halloa!" said he, suddenly, "what's this?"

It was a wax vesta, half burned, which was so coated with mud that it looked at first like a little chip of wood.

"I cannot think how I came to overlook it," said the Inspector, with an expression of annoyance.

"It was invisible, buried in the mud. I only saw it because I was looking for it."

"What! You expected to find it?"

"I thought it not unlikely." He took the boots from the bag and compared the impressions of each of them with marks upon the ground. Then he clambered up to the rim of the hollow and crawled about among the ferns and bushes.

"I am afraid that there are no more tracks," said the Inspector. "I have examined the ground very carefully for a hundred yards in each direction."

"Indeed!" said Holmes, rising, "I should not have the impertinence to do it again after what you say. But I should like to take a little walk over the moor before it grows dark, that I may know my ground to-morrow, and I think that I shall put this horseshoe into my pocket for luck."

Colonel Ross, who had shown some signs of impatience at my companion's quiet and systematic method of work, glanced at his watch.

"I wish you would come back with me, Inspector," said he. "There are several points on which I should like your advice, and especially as to whether we do not owe it to the public to remove our horse's name from the entries for the Cup."

"Certainly not," cried Holmes, with decision: "I should let the name stand."

The Colonel bowed. "I am very glad to have had your opinion, sir," said he. "You will find us at poor Straker's house when you have finished your walk, and we can drive together into Tavistock."

He turned back with the Inspector, while Holmes and I walked slowly across the moor. The sun was beginning to sink behind the stables of Mapleton, and the long sloping plain in front of us was tinged with gold, deepening into rich, ruddy brown where the faded ferns and brambles caught the evening light. But the glories of the landscape were all wasted upon my companion, who was sunk in the deepest thought.

"It's this way, Watson," he said at last. "We may leave the question of who killed John Straker for the instant, and confine ourselves to finding out what has become of the horse. Now, supposing that he broke away during or after the tragedy, where could he have gone to? The horse is a very gregarious creature. If left to himself his instincts would have been either to return to King's Pyland, or go over to Mapleton. Why should he run wild upon the moor? He would surely have been seen by now. And why should gipsies kidnap him? These people always clear out when they hear of trouble, for they do not wish to be pestered by the police. They could not hope to sell such a horse. They would run a great risk and gain nothing by taking him. Surely that is clear."

"Where is he, then?"

"I have already said that he must have gone to King's Pyland or to Mapleton. He is not at King's Pyland, therefore he is at Mapleton. Let us take that as a working hypothesis and see what it leads us to. This part of the moor, as the Inspector remarked, is very hard and dry. But it falls away towards Mapleton, and you can see from here that there is a long hollow over yonder, which must have been very wet on Monday night. If our supposition is correct, then the horse must have crossed that, and there is the point where we should look for his tracks."

We had been walking briskly during this conversation, and a few more minutes brought us to the hollow in question. At Holmes' request I walked down the bank to the right and he to the left, but I had not taken fifty paces before I heard him give a shout, and saw him waving his hand to me. The track of a horse was plainly outlined in the soft earth in front of him, and the shoe which he took from his pocket exactly fitted the impression.

"See the value of imagination," said Holmes. "It is the one quality which Gregory lacks. We imagined what might have happened, acted upon the supposition, and find ourselves justified. Let us proceed."

We crossed the marshy bottom and passed over a quarter of a mile of dry, hard turf. Again the ground sloped and again we came on the tracks. Then we lost them for half a mile, but only to pick them up once more quite close to Mapleton. It was Holmes who saw them first, and he stood pointing with a look of triumph upon his face. A man's track was visible beside the horse's.

"The horse was alone before," I cried.

"Quite so. It was alone before. Halloa, what is this?"

The double track turned sharp off and took the direction of King's Pyland. Holmes whistled, and we both followed along after it. His eyes were on the trail, but I happened to look a little to one side, and saw to my surprise the same tracks coming back again in the opposite direction.

"One for you, Watson," said Holmes, when I pointed it out; "you have saved us a long walk which would have brought us back on our own traces. Let us follow the return track."

We had not to go far. It ended at the paving of asphalt which led up to the gates of the Mapleton stables. As we approached a groom ran out from them.

"We don't want any loiterers about here," said he.

"I only wished to ask a question," said Holmes, with his finger and thumb in his waistcoat pocket. "Should I be too early to see your master, Mr. Silas Brown, if I were to call at five o'clock to-morrow morning?"

"Bless you, sir, if anyone is about he will be, for he is always the first stirring. But here he is, sir, to answer your questions for himself. No sir, no; it's as much as my place is worth to let him see me touch your money. Afterwards, if you like."

As Sherlock Holmes replaced the half-crown which he had drawn from his pocket, a fierce-looking, elderly man strode out from the gate with a hunting-crop swinging in his hand.

"What's this, Dawson?" he cried. "No gossiping! Go about your business! And you—what the devil do you want here?"

"Ten minutes' talk with you, my good sir," said Holmes, in the sweetest of voices.

"I've no time to talk to every gadabout. We want no strangers here. Be off, or you may find a dog at your heels."

Holmes leaned forward and whispered something in the trainer's ear. He started violently and flushed to the temples.

"It's a lie!" he shouted. "An infernal lie!"

"Very good! Shall we argue about it here in public, or talk it over in your parlour?"

"Oh, come in if you wish to."

Holmes smiled. "I shall not keep you more than a few minutes, Watson," he said. "Now, Mr. Brown, I am quite at your disposal."

It was quite twenty minutes, and the reds had all faded into greys before Holmes and the trainer reappeared. Never have I seen such a change as had been brought about in Silas Brown in that short time. His face was ashy pale, beads of perspiration shone upon his brow, and his hands shook until the hunting-crop wagged like a branch in the wind. His bullying, overbearing manner was all gone too, and he cringed along at my companion's side like a dog with its master.

"Your instructions will be done. It shall be done," said he.

"There must be no mistake," said Holmes, looking round at him. The other winced as he read the menace in his eyes.

"Oh, no, there shall be no mistake. It shall be there. Should I change it first or not?"

Holmes thought a little and then burst out laughing. "No, don't," said he. "I shall write to you about it. No tricks now or—"

"Oh, you can trust me, you can trust me!"

"Yes, I think I can. Well, you shall hear from me to-morrow." He turned upon his heel, disregarding the trembling hand which the other held out to him, and we set off for King's Pyland.

"A more perfect compound of the bully, coward and sneak than Master Silas Brown I have seldom met with," remarked Holmes, as we trudged along together.

"He has the horse, then?"

"He tried to bluster out of it, but I described to him so exactly what his actions had been upon that morning, that he is convinced that I was watching him. Of course, you observed the peculiarly square toes in the impressions, and that his own boots exactly corresponded to them. Again, of course, no subordinate would have dared to have done such a thing. I described to him how when, according to his custom, he was the first down, he perceived a strange horse wandering over the moor; how he went out to it, and his astonishment at recognising from the white forehead which has given the favourite its name that chance had put in his power the only horse which could beat the one upon which he had put his money. Then I described how his first impulse had been to lead him back to King's Pyland, and how the devil had shown him how he could hide the horse until the race was over, and how he had led it back and concealed it at Mapleton. When I told him every detail he gave it up, and thought only of saving his own skin."

"But his stables had been searched."

"Oh, an old horse-faker like him has many a dodge."

"But are you not afraid to leave the horse in his power now, since he has every interest in injuring it?"

"My dear fellow, he will guard it as the apple of his eye. He knows that his only hope of mercy is to produce it safe."

"Colonel Ross did not impress me as a man who would be likely to show much mercy in any case."

"The matter does not rest with Colonel Ross. I follow my own methods, and tell as much or as little as I choose. That is the advantage of being unofficial. I don't know whether you observed it, Watson, but the Colonel's manner has been just a trifle cavalier to me. I am inclined now to have a little amusement at his expense. Say nothing to him about the horse."

"Certainly not, without your permission."

"And, of course, this is all quite a minor point compared to the question of who killed John Straker."

"And you will devote yourself to that?"

"On the contrary, we both go back to London by the night train."

I was thunderstruck by my friend's words. We had only been a few hours in Devonshire, and that he should give up an investigation which he had begun so brilliantly was quite incomprehensible to me. Not a word more could I draw from him until we were back at the trainer's house. The Colonel and the Inspector were awaiting us in the parlour.

"My friend and I return to town by the midnight express," said Holmes. "We have had a charming little breath of your beautiful Dartmoor air."

The Inspector opened his eyes, and the Colonel's lip curled in a sneer.

"So you despair of arresting the murderer of poor Straker," said he.

Holmes shrugged his shoulders. "There are certainly grave difficulties in the way," said he. "I have every hope, however, that your horse will start upon Tuesday, and I beg that you will have your jockey in readiness. Might I ask for a photograph of Mr. John Straker?"

The Inspector took one from an envelope in his pocket and handed it to him.

"My dear Gregory, you anticipate all my wants. If I might ask you to wait here for an instant, I have a question which I should like to put to the maid."

"I must say that I am rather disappointed in our London consultant," said Colonel Ross, bluntly, as my friend left the room. "I do not see that we are any further than when he came."

"At least, you have his assurance that your horse will run," said I.

"Yes, I have his assurance," said the Colonel, with a shrug of his shoulders. "I should prefer to have the horse."

I was about to make some reply in defence of my friend, when he entered the room again.

"Now, gentlemen," said he, "I am quite ready for Tavistock."

As we stepped into the carriage one of the stable-lads held the door open for us. A sudden idea seemed to occur to Holmes, for he leaned forward and touched the lad upon the sleeve.

"You have a few sheep in the paddock," he said. "Who attends to them?"

"I do, sir."

"Have you noticed anything amiss with them of late?"

"Well, sir, not of much account; but three of them have gone lame, sir."

I could see that Holmes was extremely pleased, for he chuckled and rubbed his hands together.

"A long shot, Watson; a very long shot!" said he, pinching my arm. "Gregory, let me recommend to your attention this singular epidemic among the sheep. Drive on, coachman!"

Colonel Ross still wore an expression which showed the poor opinion which he had formed of my companion's ability, but I saw by the Inspector's face that his attention had been keenly aroused.

"You consider that to be important?" he asked.

"Exceedingly so."

"Is there any other point to which you would wish to draw my attention?"

"To the curious incident of the dog in the night-time."

"The dog did nothing in the night-time."

"That was the curious incident," remarked Sherlock Holmes.

Four days later Holmes and I were again in the train bound for Winchester, to see the race for the Wessex Cup. Colonel Ross met us, by appointment, outside the station, and we drove in his drag to the course beyond the town. His face was grave and his manner was cold in the extreme.

"I have seen nothing of my horse," said he.

"I suppose that you would know him when you saw him?" asked Holmes.

The Colonel was very angry. "I have been on the turf for twenty years, and never was asked such a question as that before," said he. "A child would know Silver Blaze with his white forehead and his mottled off fore leg."

"How is the betting?"

"Well, that is the curious part of it. You could have got fifteen to one yesterday, but the price has become shorter and shorter, until you can hardly get three to one now."

"Hum!" said Holmes. "Somebody knows something, that is clear!"

As the drag drew up in the inclosure near the grand stand, I glanced at the card to see the entries. It ran:—

Wessex Plate. 50 sovs. each, h ft, with 1,000 sovs. added, for four and five-year olds. Second £300. Third £200. New course (one mile and five furlongs).

1. Mr. Heath Newton's The Negro (red cap, cinnamon jacket).
2. Colonel Wardlaw's Pugilist (pink cap, blue and black jacket).
3. Lord Backwater's Desborough (yellow cap and sleeves).
4. Colonel Ross's Silver Blaze (black cap, red jacket).
5. Duke of Balmoral's Iris (yellow and black stripes).
6. Lord Singleford's Rasper (purple cap, black sleeves).

"We scratched our other one and put all hopes on your word," said the Colonel. "Why, what is that? Silver Blaze favourite?"

"Five to four against Silver Blaze!" roared the ring. "Five to four against Silver Blaze! Fifteen to five against Desborough! Five to four on the field!"

"There are the numbers up," I cried. "They are all six there."

"All six there! Then my horse is running," cried the Colonel, in great agitation. "But I don't see him. My colours have not passed."

"Only five have passed. This must be he."

As I spoke a powerful bay horse swept out from the weighing inclosure and cantered past us, bearing on its back the well-known black and red of the Colonel.

"That's not my horse," cried the owner. "That beast has not a white hair upon its body. What is this that you have done, Mr. Holmes?"

"Well, well, let us see how he gets on," said my friend, imperturbably. For a few minutes he gazed through my field-glass. "Capital! An excellent start!" he cried suddenly. "There they are, coming round the curve!"

From our drag we had a superb view as they came up the straight. The six horses were so close together that a carpet could have covered them, but half way up the yellow of the Mapleton stable showed to the front. Before they reached us, however, Desborough's bolt was shot, and the Colonel's horse, coming away with a rush, passed the post a good six lengths before its rival, the Duke of Balmoral's Iris making a bad third.

"It's my race anyhow," gasped the Colonel, passing his hand over his eyes. "I confess that I can make neither head nor tail of it. Don't you think that you have kept up your mystery long enough, Mr. Holmes?"

"Certainly, Colonel. You shall know everything. Let us all go round and have a look at the horse together. Here he is," he continued, as we made our way into the weighing inclosure where only owners and their friends find admittance. "You have only to wash his face and his leg in spirits of wine and you will find that he is the same old Silver Blaze as ever."

"You take my breath away!"

"I found him in the hands of a faker, and took the liberty of running him just as he was sent over."

"My dear sir, you have done wonders. The horse looks very fit and well. It never went better in its life. I owe you a thousand apologies for having doubted your ability. You have done me a great service by recovering my horse. You would do me a greater still if you could lay your hands on the murderer of John Straker."

"I have done so," said Holmes, quietly.

The Colonel and I stared at him in amazement. "You have got him! Where is he, then?"

"He is here."

"Here! Where?"

"In my company at the present moment."

The Colonel flushed angrily. "I quite recognise that I am under obligations to you, Mr. Holmes," said he, "but I must regard what you have just said as either a very bad joke or an insult."

Sherlock Holmes laughed. "I assure you that I have not associated you with the crime, Colonel," said he; "the real murderer is standing immediately behind you!"

He stepped past and laid his hand upon the glossy neck of the thoroughbred.

"The horse!" cried both the Colonel and myself.

"Yes, the horse. And it may lessen his guilt if I say that it was done in self-defence, and that John Straker was a man who was entirely unworthy of your confidence. But there goes the bell; and as I stand to win a little on this next race, I shall defer a more lengthy explanation until a more fitting time."

We had the corner of a Pullman car to ourselves that evening as we whirled back to London, and I fancy that the journey was a short one to Colonel Ross as well as to myself, as we listened to our companion's narrative of the events which had occurred at the Dartmoor training stables upon that Monday night, and the means by which he had unravelled them.

"I confess," said he, "that any theories which I had formed from the newspaper reports were entirely erroneous. And yet there were indications there, had they not been overlaid by other details which concealed their true import. I went to Devonshire with the conviction that Fitzroy Simpson was the true culprit, although, of course, I saw that the evidence against him was by no means complete.

"It was while I was in the carriage, just as we reached the trainer's house, that the immense significance of the curried mutton occurred to me. You may remember that I was distrait, and remained sitting after you had all alighted. I was marvelling in my own mind how I could possibly have overlooked so obvious a clue."

"I confess," said the Colonel, "that even now I cannot see how it helps us."

"It was the first link in my chain of reasoning. Powdered opium is by no means tasteless. The flavour is not disagreeable, but it is perceptible. Were it mixed with any ordinary dish, the eater would undoubtedly detect it, and would probably eat no more. A curry was exactly the medium which would disguise this taste. By no possible supposition could this stranger, Fitzroy Simpson, have caused curry to be served in the trainer's family that night, and it is surely too monstrous a coincidence to suppose that he happened to come along with powdered opium upon the very night when a dish happened to be served which would disguise the flavour. That is unthinkable. Therefore Simpson becomes eliminated from the case and our attention centres upon Straker and his wife, the only two people who could have chosen curried mutton for supper that night. The opium was added after the dish was set aside for the stable-boy, for the others had the same for supper with no ill effects. Which of them, then, had access to that dish without the maid seeing them?

"Before deciding that question I had grasped the significance of the silence of the dog, for one true inference invariably suggests others. The Simpson incident had shown me that a dog was kept in the stables, and yet, though someone had been in and had fetched out a horse, he had not barked enough to arouse the two lads in the loft. Obviously the midnight visitor was someone whom the dog knew well.

"I was already convinced, or almost convinced, that John Straker went down to the stables in the dead of the night and took out Silver Blaze. For what purpose? For a dishonest one, obviously, or why should he drug his own stable-boy? And yet I was at a loss to know why. There have been cases before now where trainers have made sure of great sums of money by laying against their own horses, through agents, and then preventing them from winning by fraud. Sometimes it is a pulling jockey. Sometimes it is some surer and subtler means. What was it here? I hoped that the contents of his pockets might help me to form a conclusion.

"And they did so. You cannot have forgotten the singular knife which was found in the dead man's hand, a knife which certainly no sane man would choose for a weapon. It was, as Dr. Watson told us, a form of knife which is used for the most delicate operations known in surgery. And it was to be used for a delicate operation that night. You must know, with your wide experience of turf matters, Colonel Ross, that it is possible to make a slight nick upon the tendons of a horse's ham, and to do it subcutaneously so as to leave absolutely no trace. A horse so treated would develop a slight lameness which would be put down to a strain in exercise or a touch of rheumatism, but never to foul play."

"Villain! Scoundrel!" cried the Colonel.

"We have here the explanation of why John Straker wished to take the horse out on to the moor. So spirited a creature would have certainly roused the soundest of sleepers when it felt the prick of the knife. It was absolutely necessary to do it in the open air."

"I have been blind!" cried the Colonel. "Of course, that was why he needed the candle, and struck the match."

"Undoubtedly. But in examining his belongings, I was fortunate enough to discover, not only the method of the crime, but even its motives. As a man of the world, Colonel, you know that men do not carry other people's bills about in their pockets. We have most of us quite enough to do to settle our own. I at once concluded that Straker was leading a double life, and keeping a second establishment. The nature of the bill showed that there was a lady in the case, and one who had expensive tastes. Liberal as you are with your servants, one hardly expects that they can buy twenty-guinea walking dresses for their women. I questioned Mrs. Straker as to the dress without her knowing it, and having satisfied myself that it had never reached her, I made a note of the milliner's address, and felt that by calling there with Straker's photograph, I could easily dispose of the mythical Darbyshire.

"From that time on all was plain. Straker had led out the horse to a hollow where his light would be invisible. Simpson, in his flight, had dropped his cravat, and Straker had picked it up with some idea, perhaps, that he might use it in securing the horse's leg. Once in the hollow he had got behind the horse, and had struck a light, but the creature, frightened at the sudden glare, and with the strange instinct of animals feeling that some mischief was intended, had lashed out, and the steel shoe had struck Straker full on the forehead. He had already, in spite of the rain, taken off his overcoat in order to do his delicate task, and so, as he fell, his knife, gashed his thigh. Do I make it clear?"

"Wonderful!" cried the Colonel. "Wonderful! You might have been there."

"My final shot was, I confess, a very long one. It struck me that so astute a man as Straker would not undertake this delicate tendon-nicking without a little practice. What could he practice on? My eyes fell upon the sheep, and I asked a question which, rather to my surprise, showed that my surmise was correct."

"You have made it perfectly clear, Mr. Holmes."

"When I returned to London I called upon the milliner, who at once recognised Straker as an excellent customer, of the name of Darbyshire, who had a very dashing wife with a strong partiality for expensive dresses. I have no doubt that this woman had plunged him over head and ears in debt, and so led him into this miserable plot."

"You have explained all but one thing," cried the Colonel. "Where was the horse?"

"Ah, it bolted and was cared for by one of your neighbours. We must have an amnesty in that direction, I think. This is Clapham Junction, if I am not mistaken, and we shall be in Victoria in less than ten minutes. If you care to smoke a cigar in our rooms, Colonel, I shall be happy to give you any other details which might interest you."

This is a story about a talented but down-on-his-luck boxer who is tempted into "taking a dive," or purposely losing a fight. His opponent is a fighter with limited skills, supported by mobsters who are betting that their man will win. These hard-edged themes plus a tough-guy narrative provide a compelling realism. Harry Sylvester (1908–1974) was a popular short story writer who also authored several novels, including Dearly Beloved *(1942),* All Your Idols *(1948), and* A Golden Girl *(1950). The story was originally published in* Esquire.

Harry Sylvester

I WON'T DO NO DIVE (1937)

AL LAY FLAT ON THE BED, waiting for the phone to ring. It didn't ring and he tried to remember the last time it had rung and why. He didn't do this very long; he began to think of what might come in the mail. He called the desk clerk and was told that the afternoon mail wasn't in yet. When Al called again ten minutes later the clerk said there was no mail for him.

Al sat on the bed, his face in his hands. After all, he thought, who the hell would write to me? He hadn't answered his father's last letter, saying in a roundabout way that it might be a good idea if Al came back to the farm. He didn't want to go back there, Al thought again. It was an all right place but he didn't want to go back there like this, broke and kind of a has-been. He wanted to go back there a successful prizefighter, with a string of wins, a light grey suit and plenty of money to buy new farm equipment and to scatter around, careless-like. That was the way he wanted to go back.

He felt dull, sitting in the warm, poorly ventilated room, and his thoughts were like a weight in his head and he let himself fall back onto the pillow again.

Pete Krevitz came into the room. He was a little man who, like most managers of prizefighters, was always hoping that somewhere he would stumble over a young fighter who would be the next heavyweight champion. Coming into the room, Pete cursed and said that he'd expected Al would be out doing some road work.

"Why should I be doing any?" Al said. "You ain't got me no fights lately. Anyhow, I'm in shape, all right. I can take a day off."

"The least you could of done would be out taking a walk or something."

"Why should I take a walk? I ain't got no place to go and if I walk I'll get hungry. I only got thirty-five cents and I'm saving that for supper."

"Here's a buck," Pete Krevitz said. "I got a fight for you. How do you like that?"

"That's fine," Al said, sitting up. "That's great. Who with?"

"This big, new guy, what's his name—Waller. Eddie Waller."

"He's a bum," Al said. "You certainly got me a snap."

"We're getting nine hundred for it," Pete said. He kept looking at Al's face, without taking his hat off or the cigar out of his mouth or his finger tips from the foot of the bed.

Al whistled. "Nine C's. Say, for nine C's I'd fight the Marines."

"They don't want you to fight the Marines."

"What do you mean?"

"Just that that ain't what they want you to do."

"What do they want, then?"

Pete looked at Al for a few seconds. There was almost a glint in his small eyes. "You gotta take a dive," he said.

Al got up and stood, straddle-legged, one hand and a finger pointing at Pete. "I ain't taking no dive," he said. "Not for no one and leastways not for a bum like Waller."

"Don't be a damn fool," Pete said. He wasn't angry. That was what Al noticed and it made him uneasy.

"I got a rep," Al said.

"Ever try eating a rep?"

"I'll get by without doing no dives."

"You ain't been getting by."

"I'd of been all right the night I fought the boog if I wasn't sick. I'd of beat him and I'd be up there."

"Maybe you would," Pete said. "But Antrim beat you down in Indianapolis. Anyway, the idea is you ain't up there and we gotta eat."

"All right, we gotta eat, but I won't do no dive. You can always get dough."

"I can't get it now or we'd be eating more regular. Nine C's is nine C's. You never got no more than a grand before for anything."

"I won't do no dive," Al said. He turned and looked out the window, leaning on the sill.

"Tomorrow," Pete said, still without anger, "you'll feel different when that buck is gone." He took off his hat, sat down and read a tabloid.

After a while, Al said, without turning from the window: "What the hell does anyone want to build Waller up for? He's a bum and he'll always be a bum."

"It wouldn't be healthy to talk about it too much, so keep what I tell you under your bonnet. The Magrid bunch has got him. They're a bunch of mobsters that made so much dough shaking down laundries that they thought they'd buy themselves a boxfighter and now they're building him up."

"They sure bought themselves a daisy," Al said. "I should fool around with bastards like that bunch."

"When you ain't eating you'll do a lot of funny things," Pete said. "I don't like to play around with mobsters myself. But if we get this dough we can get to New York or out to the Coast or maybe pick up some change in Florida. It'll be nice down there for the winter."

"I won't take no dive," Al said.

"All right. All right. You're one holy son of a bitch, that's all I gotta say. I gotta tell these guys tomorrow so they'll give me an advance for us to eat. So you better make up your mind about it by then. And if you do, don't renege, or they'll fill you so full of slugs you could stand on your head without trying."

"I won't take no dive," Al said.

"All right, you bastard, you'll think different tomorrow," Pete slammed the door as he went out.

Al looked out the window a long time. Lights were coming on all over the city. Between him and the lake, a mile away, two lines of young poplars were blowing. Fingering in his pocket the quarter, the dime and the crumpled dollar bill, Al knew without much anger that he would take the dive.

When he was dressing the night of the bout, Al didn't feel nervous as he usually did before a fight. The fact that the ending was arranged and known, holding no mystery, was quieting. Al was alone in one of two small dressing rooms reserved for main-bout fighters. Pete was there and a handler they usually had, named Joe Moody. But it was as though these other two were not there.

Al sat on a bench, the bathrobe on and a towel over his throat and chest. Absently but carefully he wrapped gauze about his hand and thumb and knuckles. He looked up and was surprised to see Pete nearby and watching him.

"How are you?"

"I'm all right. When do I go on?"

"Pretty quick," Pete said. "You don't have to fix those bandages so good."

"I don't want to hurt my hands."

"You ain't gonna hit him hard enough to hurt them."

"No, but I might hit him accidental in the back of the head or the top."

"You know what to do, now?" Pete said in a lower voice. "The boog got you in the seventh and tonight they want you to dive any time before the seventh so's Waller'll look better than the boog."

"That boog would never of got me if I hadn't been sick."

"I know all about that." Pete was nervous. "The idea is you're supposed to go before the seventh tonight."

"All right, I know. I don't know how he'll ever hit me, though, he's such a bum. I'll just have to stand there and let him hit me."

"I don't care what you do," Pete said in a low, savage voice; "so long as you go down and stay down before the seventh."

"Okay. Did I say anything?" Al asked. His calmness surprised him. He felt very quiet. "You got all the dough?"

"I just got most of it."

Joe Moody answered a knock at the door and a fat man looked in and said it was time to go on. A minute later the three of them went through the doorway into a corridor. It was colder there and a wind blew. They went along the corridor and turned right up a runway into a place of warmth, dull yellow light and tobacco smoke. The sound of voices rose in intensity as they came along the aisle and with his handlers near him, his big shoulders swinging loose and easy, and the feel of the eyes looking at him, Al was keen and fine for a minute. Then they were in the ring and Waller was already there, across it, bigger than Al but square in the shoulders and no hitter.

"Go over and shake hands with him," Pete said.

"He should come over to me," Al said.

Pete cursed and Al went over. "Luck," he said. Waller smiled the forced, false grin of the unsure fighter. Al saw that Waller was a little scared even knowing he was going to win.

"Thanks, kid," Waller said, taking Al's hand in both his own. Waller's handlers looked at Al. They were smiling two ways, with the mouth and with the eyes.

Back in the corner Pete whispered to Al: "There's the Magrid bunch near the ring."

Al saw some flashily-dressed men talking and smoking together. They didn't look much different from the other people near the ring, only a little better dressed. It wasn't a very big fight club they were all in that night.

Joe Moody held the six-ounce gloves and Al slipped his hands into them. These gloves always felt small after the big training gloves. Joe Moody was pale and quiet. Al had had him for a handler before and he was usually gabby. After all, Al thought, what the hell is there to talk about tonight.

When Al and then Waller were introduced, neither of them got a very big hand although Al got the bigger one and when Waller was introduced someone in the rear yelled: "Throw him out. He's a bum. He stinks."

Al glanced at the Magrid bunch near the ring. They didn't seem bothered much. Their heavy-lidded eyes blinked slowly and they seemed very satisfied with their cigars.

The first round was easy for Al. Waller was as bad as he had thought. Waller swung clumsily and didn't land a solid punch. Al shook him with short rights under the heart and made him look silly with straight lefts. The crowd gave Al a big hand when the round ended.

"What the hell's the matter with you?" Pete said.

"Why, isn't it all right for me to look pretty good for a while? I got to dive soon enough."

In the third and fourth rounds Al let Waller hit him, although he cushioned the punches pretty well with gloves and arms. When Waller swung his left hook it was wide and long, not quick and short and snapped as a hook should be. A couple of times Al just caught himself as he was going to let go with a straight right, which is always the answer to a wide left hook, since the right goes straight and inside the hook and you not only hit your opponent but the deltoid of your right arm cushions his blow. It was Al's best punch and he caught himself as he started to throw it a couple of times and just blocked Waller's hook, instead.

After the fourth round, Pete said he thought it was time Al took the dive. "You're making me nervous the way you got that right cocked. Every time he swings that round house left I think you're going to let go."

"I won't let it go," Al said. He felt tired. Not from fighting. It was a new kind of tiredness. "I'll dive now. I don't know how the hell you do it, but—"

"Just drop if he swings anywhere near you," Pete said.

"That's swell," Al said. "That'll look swell."

He'd do it early, Al thought. They were sparring near the center of the ring. Al purposely dropped his guard more than usual and Waller swung his long left. It hit Al with surprising force before he could even partly block it. Al shook his head to clear it. Eagerly, for the first time almost savagely, Waller came in for the kill. He swung his left again and Al's right moved inside it in a straight line, although Al didn't know it. All Al felt and knew at first was the shock of Waller's punch where it struck his deltoid. Then he saw Waller's face growing blank and dropping and twisting away in the same movement, the mouth falling into a startled roundness and the eyes growing empty, the face twisting down and to the left. It was a beautiful punch, perfectly timed and well delivered.

Al was standing over Waller who was out cold on the canvas. The referee was pushing and tugging at Al to get him into a neutral corner. The crowd was on its feet yelling as they hadn't yelled for Al in a long time and Al was stupidly looking at Waller, limp and on the floor and quite small.

Al was in a corner and the crowd was still yelling. Waller was counted out and Al turned to his own corner. He felt pretty good. Then he saw Pete Krevitz's face and it was different from any way it had ever been before. Al began to feel uneasy.

"I didn't mean it," Al said. "I don't know how it happened. Honest to Christ I didn't mean it. I didn't think. I—"

Pete stared at him as though Al had suddenly died. "Christ," Pete said, "Christ," and turned and went up the aisle alone. He almost ran. Joe Moody had disappeared.

Al threw the robe over his shoulders and raised his glove to the crowd which was yelling a little. Then he started up the aisle alone. The yelling rose some and men and boys and one woman reached out to pat his back or to touch and finger his robe. They liked a good, clean knockout. Al felt pretty good, hearing them. But in the dimness of the corridor and the wind blowing along it he felt no way at all, good or bad. No one was there. The crowd was going out another way. Cops would not let them down the runways leading into that corridor. Al opened the door of his dressing room and it was empty. He had thought Pete would be there.

He wondered why Pete wasn't there. It seemed funny to be undressing alone after a fight. He had always had someone near him to help if he was too tired to undress; to treat cuts and give him a rub after the shower. Al moved slowly. He didn't feel tired or hurt as after most fights. He really felt pretty good although the sweat was cold on him before he went into the shower. He stayed under the water longer than usual. His thought was slow and heavy and he figured it must have been a pretty good crack Waller had hit him. He must have stood wide open and waiting for it, because a square-shouldered guy like Waller had no right to be hitting that hard.

Al came out of the shower and again the loneliness of the room under a single light bulb impressed him. He wondered if Pete could be getting drunk; he often did after a fight. The least he could of done was leave a dollar or two for a steak before going. It couldn't really be that Pete was afraid of the Magrid bunch. They wouldn't really get tough. They might hold out the rest of the dough that was coming, but they wouldn't really get tough.

Al stood up after drying himself, naked in the dim, granular light. He had a beautiful, loosely-muscled build. His muscles were not hard but pliant and firm and his skin was smooth and silky. Women liked to touch it. He paused, standing erect, naked and beautiful and alone, and gravely considered whether the Magrid bunch would really do anything. Gravely he decided that they wouldn't and began to dress.

There was the noise of feet in the corridor and Al paused and looked at the door. The feet went swiftly by. Al felt himself relax. He wondered what was the matter with him, anyway. Everything would be all right tomorrow. He'd have Pete explain that it had all been a mistake, that he really hadn't intended it. And he hadn't. There had been the opening and without thinking he had put the right into it. Tomorrow Pete would explain for him and everything would be all right. Everything would be fine.

When he was dressed, he packed his bag. He really needed a new bag. He would ask Pete about that tomorrow. When he was ready to go, Al put his hand on the light cord, then took it away without pulling it. When he approached the door to open it he had begun to sweat a little. What the hell's the matter with me, he thought. He decided he hadn't stayed under the cold shower long enough to stop sweating.

Al put his hand on the door. His hand hesitated on the knob and, angry with the hand, Al flung the door open. The corridor was empty. He stepped into it. Fifty yards long, it lay under a faint light from small bulbs. No one was in it. As Al walked slowly, carrying his bag, he thought of how he hadn't seen anyone since he had left the arena and the crowd yelling for him. The wind blowing along the corridor made him feel the wetness on his forehead.

He walked along. In the arena to his right, through the occasional runways, Al heard the noises of chairs being folded and benches moved. These came slowly and far apart as though only a few men were working. Noise came at him sharply as he passed the last runway and his whole body jumped. For Christ sake, he thought, what's the matter with me? It was only a chair being folded nearby.

At the end of the corridor were two doors, one going straight into the lobby, the other, on the left, opening directly into the street. Al tried the lobby door but it was locked. He turned to the street door and felt the sweat come out on him again. In the name of Christ, he thought, what the hell's the matter with me? Nothing's going to happen, he told himself, what the hell are you so jittery about?

He took a long breath and opened the street door. There was no one outside and it was colder than in the corridor. He had truly expected or hoped that Pete or Joe Moody might be waiting for him. There was no one on the street, not even a cop. A single light in the middle of the block cast shadows but did little else. The concrete wall of the fight club ran unbrokenly along the side Al was on. Across the street there was a big garage, dark now, and a big, empty lot. Nothing else. There was no one on the street. Al felt the breath go out of him and he felt better. Then he noticed a car parked down the street, forty or fifty yards away. It was on the same side he was and the lights were out. He looked at it a while, feeling himself tense again. The car didn't move and he turned and began to walk away from it. A couple of punks necking, he thought. He didn't know why he was so nervous. "Everything's all right," he said aloud. "Everything's okay."

Behind him the car began to move, gathering speed slowly. He noticed it come closer but didn't turn to look. Why the hell don't they turn their lights on? he thought. That's a hell of a way to drive! Why don't they turn their lights on? The car was almost abreast of him. Its lights were off and it was just drifting along in second.

Al felt a sudden, sharp, light push on his shoulder, then another lower down, then a third. Quick, like jabs. Then he was lying on the sidewalk and he heard the noise, quickly repeated like the push. No pain. Only more noise and the quick, sharp, small pushes all along his body and it being hard to breathe on account of stuff coming up in your throat. He opened his mouth to yell but it wasn't sound that came out. The noise died slowly in his ears. Sleep was a much better thing, some part of him quietly thought. He lay there in the silent street.

For the freshwater angler it doesn't get any better than trout fishing in Alaska. And no trout fights harder than the rainbow. These are among the delights of this story, which also features a crafty guide and a lunker of a fish. It was first presented in Field and Stream *and reissued in the* Field and Stream Treasury *(1955). Author Frank Dufresne has written extensively about the outdoors. Among his books are* Alaska's Animals and Fishes *(1946),* No Room for Bears *(1965), and* My Way Was North *(1966).*

Frank Dufresne

THE KELLY RAINBOW (1933)

THE NORTHBOUND TRAIN ON the Government-owned Alaska Railroad hesitated briefly at the whistling station of Willow before puffing and groaning into the dusk on its way up through the white peaks of the Alaska Range toward its terminus at Fairbanks, 470 miles from the seaport of Seward. Momentary as was its stop at Willow, however, the train carried one passenger less when it creaked slowly across the high wooden trestle, one lone fisherman seeking the truth concerning one of the most highly touted trout streams in all of Alaska.

For years this particular fisherman had journeyed up and down the far, wild lengths of the Territory, wetting a line wherever and whenever opportunity allowed. In its time and place many a stream and lake had been labeled superlative, only to be checked off somewhat regretfully in favor of newer conquests. Was this to be the case again? Could Big Willow River, not far from the thriving, bustling city of Anchorage, compare with the remote silvery reaches of the Upper Kobuk, many miles north of the Arctic Circle; with Pilgrim River on the "pupmobile" line from Nome; with certain icy-cold tributaries of the great Yukon, or with the scores of trout-filled creeks in the southeastern Alaska archipelgo? Well, I had my doubts—in fact, plenty of them.

Up the steep, sandy siding strode a tallish individual of indeterminate age, cheery of eye, all whalebone and sinew. "The name's Kelly," said he briskly.

I introduced myself, supposing I was meeting one of the many transients, better known in Alaska as *cheechakos*, who visit this place. "When did you get here?" I asked.

Kelly laid two capable paws on my duffle and swung the heavy bag to his shoulder in a manner which betokened plenty of pack-board experience. "Nine years ago," he answered.

Nine years on one trout stream! My indifference did a right-about-face and raced quickly to respect, a reversal of opinion destined to be much heightened in the twenty-four hours which were to follow.

"Come on down to the shack, an' look at what I got sliced up for supper," invited Kelly. "Tomorrow we'll go out after 'em."

He led the way down to where a couple of abandoned railroad cars had been jacked up and fitted out as overnight camps for the accommodation of visiting fishermen.

I started slightly at the size of the rainbow trout slabs waiting to fulfill their fate in the skillet. Nothing less than a five-pound fish could have produced the like of them. However, one big fish does not make a trout stream by any means. I felt an urge to voice doubts on the matter. Things were looking entirely too good to be true. Numerous wild-goose chases have taught me the pessimistic lesson that rare are the occasions when a local guide cannot hide himself behind one or the other of these time-honored alibis.

"What about the water?" I asked. "Isn't it too low or too high, too cloudy, too clear, too—something?"

Instead of equivocating, Kelly leaped at the question. "Big Willow ain't too nothin'," he stated flatly. "She's just right. Mighty few times when she ain't. Now if you'll drag a box up to the table, we'll tear into this fish while it's still smokin' hot. Plenty of time tomorrow to settle that other question."

Afterward, when the dishes had been washed and stacked away, we sat outside in the cool night air and watched Big Willow put on its regular evening show. "Watched" is not the correct word, for the performance appealed mostly to the sense of hearing—the intermittent purr of the current and the chatter of fast water over the gravel, broken now and then by the splash and glistening flash of feeding trout in the big pool in front of our door, and the heavy spatterings of salmon fighting their way up-river over the shallows. It was restful, soul-satisfying.

While we smoked in silence a big old boss beaver came swimming out of the gloom of the far cottonwoods, furrowed a gleaming trail across the river and slid itself half out of water on the sand within five paces of us. Its small eyes glowed with an odd appearance of hostility, bright as the cigar ends in our hands, while it sized us up briefly before plunging into the water. Shortly afterward it popped to the surface well out on the bosom of the river and sounded an alarm to all night-roving wild folk by slapping its "nightstick" smartly on the water.

"'Tis the traffic cop," said Kelly softly, digging his cigar butt into the damp earth. "He comes on shift about this hour every night. Now that he's on the job, we'll turn in and leave him run the river till sunup."

In the morning a slick o' frost covered the ground where the sun of late August had not already searched it out.

"She's a dinger for rainbows," mused Kelly as he leaned his spare frame in the door of the car and looked out upon the river over which a bower of golden and crimson leaves rattled faintly on their drying stems, while now and then a single leaf fluttered downward into the rushing water. "Yes, sir; a dinger! A mite late for flies mebbe, but spinners'll take 'em."

We struck out along a newly brushed-out tractor trail which led at right angles from the railroad, penetrating for many miles up Big Willow watershed to a recently developed gold mine. The weather was clear, the slightest bit tingly, and the air filled with the tiny twitterings of migrating songsters. Nearer at hand, magpies and gray jays flirted furtively about in the underbrush as though fearful of being caught in some mischief. Kelly appeared to know every foot of the country, pointing out spots here and there where he had set out his traps for fur-bearers during the winter. Here he had come off second best in a scuffle with a cub bear; there a wily wolverine had finally made the fatal step after weeks of trap robbing.

Where a punky, fallen birch had been ground to snuff-colored powder by the tread of passing caterpillars we surprised a brood of spruce grouse dusting themselves. Like exploding smoke bombs they took to the air, somewhat spoiling the effect of their picturesque getaway by crashing pellmell into the first trees, clucking like a bunch of idiots as we passed under them close enough to knock off their silly heads with our rods.

After an hour or more of brisk walking, Kelly led the way through a thicket of dead-ripe high-bush cranberries to the bank of the Big Willow just above where it poured its racing flood against a log jam and came swirling back in a deep, scud-flecked eddy.

"Go after 'em," said Kelly. "'Tis an old story with me."

I dropped a line into the current. Scarcely had it straightened when I was fast to a fish. A living, iridescent rainbow leaped high out of the gray waters and danced halfway across the river on its tail, as though charged with lightning. In a few minutes I landed the trout, a beautifully colored specimen about eighteen inches long and looked to Kelly for approval. There was none.

"'Tis no fish fit for a man to creel unless he's hungry, or wants to make a show of numbers. Turn it loose and try again. Cast well out and let your lure go with the current. The big ones lay deep."

Following Kelly's advice, I soon learned that it was easy to catch fish in Big Willow, but to take one worthy of his stamp of approval was quite another matter. Rapidly I hooked and landed five good-sized trout, all of which he shamed me into releasing, although one of them exceeded twenty inches in length. I began to wonder just how big a rainbow would have to be to suit him.

Suddenly I got a savage strike with plenty of weight behind it, and for a moment believed I had established connections with such a fish. Deep in the water an unseen force ripped yard after yard of line from the reel in sullen fury. Settling myself for a long fight, I was astonished to see the waters split, followed by a huge bolt of bright scarlet shooting into the air and scattering jeweled spray in all directions. Above the dull roar of the water I heard Kelly's shout, "Leaping Lena!"

This was his pet name for the coho salmon in its bright-red spawning colors, its "wedding dress," as it has been aptly termed.

Although it was not a fish I desired to keep, the "Leaping Lena" put on a glorious, reckless battle. Like all of the salmon family I have encountered in Alaska, it fought with senseless ferocity, succumbing to the fly rod only after it had worn itself completely out by twenty minutes of maniacal leaping and gyrating. Its weight was about fifteen pounds.

Occasionally I have hooked this particular variety of salmon in other Territorial streams, but never with such regularity as on Big Willow that day. As they take no nourishment after leaving their home in the sea to spawn and die in the headwaters of the rivers and creeks, the strike appears to be delivered in pure anger. At least twenty of them hit my lure that day. Before night my rod tip was a sorry-looking affair.

Failing to secure a rainbow worthy of the Kelly trademark, we moved on downstream. Where a small, glass-clear side stream had its confluence with the main river I took a half dozen fine grayling with a Black Gnat—slim, graceful beauties which found their way into my basket without protest from my companion. It was at this same place that we came near to argument. An extraordinarily brilliant specimen of rainbow trout took the fly, and after a cautious, long-drawn-out struggle was led into the shallow water, where Kelly stretched a tape over it. I saw his thumb-nail slide up the tape to the figure 24, hesitate, then move along another half inch. My heart leaped.

"Is it a fit fish?" I asked.

Kelly shook his head. "'Tis a fair trout, but if you're a fisherman you'll do better," he said, and batted not an eye when, half peeved, I twitched the hook from the trout's lip and allowed it to fan itself wearily back into the current.

This grand gesture gave me some cause for regret later on, for it seemed that I was not to take a better fish. More than once I thought the moment had come, but each time it turned out to be one of the vivid, hook-nosed "Leaping Lenas" or a rainbow not quite up to the mark. Not that I could find any fault with the fishing. It was comparable to the best I had ever experienced; of such caliber that I can honestly proclaim Big Willow to be one of the very finest trout streams in Alaska. Its accessibility is a decided point in its favor. One has but to step off the railroad car and commence fishing, whereas a great many of my favorite places are buried in the wilderness. During the course of my day astream with Kelly I hooked upward of a hundred fish varying from one foot to two feet in length. That's fishing!

Determined to stay with it until Lady Luck showered down, I trudged behind my long-legged host as he led me along game trails beside Big Willow, portaging a hundred yards or more at a stretch to reach his favorite pools, although as far as I was concerned one spot was as good as another. On this trend of thought I asked Kelly how much of Big Willow offered such wonderful fishing, as we were enjoying.

Said he, "From the headwaters of this river to the Susitna below the railroad it's above twenty-five miles, and I've taken fish in every mile of it. It ain't all so good, though, for in the upper six or seven miles they run pretty small. I figure it's about eighteen miles of first-class fishing.

"Another thing that'll surprise you," he added. "Big Willow is purely a migratory stream. During the winter months there ain't a fish in it. They've all gone down into the Susitna, and mebbe into the salt water of Cook's Inlet, for all I know. But in the spring they come back thicker'n hair on a dog's back. If I was to name the best month of the year for you to come back here and try Big Willow, I'd say May; that's when the king salmon run. Rainbows is good fishin', sure enough; but if you never had a forty- or fifty-pound king on a trout rod, you just ain't had fun—that's all. Takes me from two to four hours to land one under the best of conditions. Mostly, though, I don't land 'em."

I looked sorrowfully at the tip of my rod, twisted like a corkscrew by mere 12- and 15-pounders of the "Leaping Lena" variety, and I made a mental resolve to bring along several extra tips if fortunate enough to pass this way during the May run of the giants.

By midafternoon it became evident that Kelly had given me too much river to work in one day at the rate we were going; so again and again we took to portaging the bends, racing against the lowering sun, even now casting long shadows through the cottonwoods and birches. On the last of these cut-offs we traversed a series of beaver dams and sunken brush piles in the center of which stood an enormous beaver house which showed several years' work in the making.

Kelly noticed my interest. "The traffic cop's home," he commented briefly, and pushed on a few yards farther to reach an open gravel bar not far above and across the river from the railroad cars we had left in the morning. The shadows of the trestlework actually darkened the waters as I made my last and most eventful cast of the day.

So swift was the water at this point that my spinner, though weighted, danced and strained at the surface like a thing alive while I stripped off sixty or seventy feet of line. When the strike came, there was nothing about it to indicate a large fish; the spinner simply disappeared. When I set the hook, the line cut slowly and diagonally across stream with but little strain on it. Thinking to test the size of the fish, I began pumping. Then I felt the first smashing, unleashed force telegraphed along the line and rod, and knew I was fast to a real fish. It was not another scarlet coho. Indirect testimony of this came to me through Kelly's low admonition: "Steady, man! Watch your slack!"

Suddenly, far downstream, a rainbow trout of magnificent dimensions rolled to the surface and began such a vicious, breath-taking battle that I was almost sure it would end in a limp line. More and more line was yielded from the reel as the great fish catapulted itself into the air, one leap following another in rapid succession, while the red jaws wrenched angrily at the stinging bit of steel which held it captive. Combined with the rushing force of the water, the fish was straining my tackle to the limit; and now, at the end of the day, I felt none too secure about any part of it. For a while I played the game safe by giving out line, until all at once I found myself staring at a very nearly emptied reel.

Already it had been demonstrated quite to my satisfaction that my equipment was far too frail to lead that whopper back against the current. This left but one procedure open. I floundered downstream in the wake of the fish, wet to the waist, until it swung back under the influence of a wide, strong eddy. Now the battle became more localized, although it was fully twenty minutes before I got a close-up view of the trout.

Thrilled by its great size and gorgeous coloration, and believing the fight won, something akin to horror struck me when I noticed the tiny hook dangling loosely in the torn lip, ready to fall out at the first slack in the line. The battle was not over. The trout had plenty of strength, for like a bolt it dove back into the deep water, boring, boring, boring until I just about decided it would never stop.

Luckily it indulged in no more acrobatics. Some time later—I have no recollection of minutes involved—the big fellow showed up again and allowed himself to be led, unresisting, over Kelly's booted feet as he stood knee-deep in the water. It was without question the largest rainbow I had ever seen—close to thirty inches in length, perfect in proportions.

This time Kelly produced no tape measure, but slid a practiced hand under the gleaming gill plates. The game was won, I knew, but vanity demanded verbal acknowledgment.

"Don't pull that fish out of the water until you answer me one question. Is it a Kelly rainbow?"

Kelly gained a secure grip with both hands and heaved himself upright. "Aye," he answered gravely, "'tis a fit fish."

Irwin Shaw (1913–1984) was a celebrated American author whose Selected
Short Stories *were published in 1961 by the prestigious Modern Library. He is
also well known for his novels, plays, and screenplays.* The Young Lions *(1948)
became an outstanding movie starring Marlon Brando, Montgomery Clift, and
Dean Martin.* Rich Man, Poor Man *(1970) and* Evening in Byzantium *(1973)
were made into blockbuster miniseries on television. Shaw played football at
Brooklyn College before serving in World War II. In the following story, a jour-
neyman National Football League linebacker develops extrasensory perceptions
that affect his life in surprising ways.*

Irwin Shaw

WHISPERS IN
BEDLAM (1969)

HE WAS A TYPICAL 235-pound married American boy, rosy-
cheeked, broken-nosed with an excellent five-tooth bridge across the
front of his mouth and a 63-stitch scar on his right knee, where the doctors had done some remarkable things with floating cartilage. His father-
in-law had a thriving insurance agency and there was a place open in it
for him, the sooner, his father-in-law said, the better. He was growing progressively deafer in the left ear, due to something that had happened to
him during the course of his work the year before on a cold Sunday afternoon out in Green Bay, Wisconsin. He was a professional football

player. He played middle linebacker on defense and a certain amount of physical wear and tear was to be expected, especially in Green Bay.

His name was Hugo Pleiss. He was not famous. He had played on three teams, the sort of teams that are always around the bottom of their division. When coaches said that they were going to rebuild their clubs for next year, the first thing they did was to trade Hugo or declare him a free agent. But with all the new teams coming into the league, and the consequent demand for experienced players, Hugo always managed to be on somebody's roster when a new season started. He was large and eager to learn and he liked to play football and he had what coaches called "desire" when talking to sportswriters. While intelligent enough in real life (he had been a B student in college), on the field he was all too easily fooled. Perhaps, fundamentally, he was too honest and trusting of his fellow man. Fake hand-offs sent him crashing to the left when the play went to the right. He covered decoys with religious devotion while receivers whistled past him into the clear. He had an unenviable record of tackling blockers while allowing ball carriers to run over him. He hadn't intercepted a single pass in his entire career. He was doing well enough, though, until the incident of his ear at Green Bay. The man who played left corner back with him, Johnny Smathers, had a quick instinct for reading plays and, as the offense shaped up, would shout to Hugo and warn him where the play was going. Smathers was small, distrustful and crafty, with a strong instinct for self-preservation and more often than not turned out to be right. So Hugo was having a pretty fair season until he began to go deaf in the ear on Smathers' side and no longer could hear the corner back's instructions.

After two games in which Smathers had correctly diagnosed and called dozens of plays, only to see Hugo go hurtling off in the opposite direction, Smathers had stopped talking to Hugo at all, on or off the field. This hurt Hugo, who was a friendly soul. He liked Smathers and was grateful for his help and he wished he could explain about his left ear; but once the word got around that he was deaf, he was sure he'd be dropped from the squad. He wasn't yet ready to sell insurance for his father-in-law.

Luckily, the injury to Hugo's ear came near the end of the season and his ordinary level of play was not so high that the drop in his efficiency had any spectacular effect on the coaches or the public. But Hugo, locked in his auditory half-world, fearful of silent enemies on his left and oblivious to the cheers and jeers of half the stadium, brooded.

Off the field, despite occasional little mishaps, he could do well enough. He learned to sit on the left of the coach at all meetings and convinced his wife that he slept better on the opposite side of the bed than on the one he had always occupied in the three years of their marriage. His wife, Sibyl, was a girl who liked to talk, anyway, mostly in protracted monologs, and an occasional nod of the head satisfied most of her demands for conversational responses. And a slight and almost unnoticeable twist of the head at most gatherings put Hugo's right ear into receiving position and enabled him to get a serviceable fix on the speaker.

With the approach of summer and the imminence of the pre-season training sessions, Hugo brooded more than ever. He was not given to introspection or fanciful similes about himself, but he began to think about the left side of his head as a tightly corked carbonated cider bottle. He poked at his eardrum with pencil points, toothpicks and a nail clipper, to let the fizz out; but aside from starting a slight infection that suppurated for a week, there was no result.

Finally, he made hesitant inquiries, like a man trying to find the address of an abortionist, and found the name of an ear specialist on the other side of town. He waited for Sibyl to go on her annual two-week visit to her parents in Oregon and made an appointment for the next day.

Dr. G. W. Sebastian was a small oval Hungarian who was enthusiastic about his work. He had clean, plump little busy hands and keen, merry eyes. Affliction, especially in his chosen field, pleased him and the prospect of long, complicated and possibly dangerous operations filled him with joy. "Lovely," he kept saying, as he stood on a leather stool to examine Hugo's ear, "Oh, absolutely lovely." He didn't seem to have many patients. "Nobody takes ears seriously enough," he explained, as he poked with lights and curiously shaped instruments into Hugo's ear. "People always think they hear well enough or that other people have suddenly all begun to mumble. Or, if they do realize they're not getting everything, that there's nothing to be done about it. You're a wise young man, very wise, to have come to me in time. What is it you told Miss Cattavi your profession was?"

Miss Cattavi was the nurse. She was a six-foot, 165-pounder who looked as though she shaved twice a day. She had immigrated from northern Italy and was convinced that Hugo played soccer for a living. "That Pele," she had said. "The money he makes!"

Dr. Sebastian had never seen a football game in his life, either, and an impatient look came over his face as Hugo tried to explain what he did on Sundays and about Johnny Smathers and not being able to hear cleats pounding perilously on his left side when he went in to stop a draw over center. Dr. Sebastian also looked a little puzzled when Hugo tried to explain just exactly what had happened at Green Bay. "People do things like that?" he had said incredulously. "Just for money? In America?"

He probed away industriously, clucking to himself and smelling of peppermint and newly invented antiseptics, orating in little bursts that Hugo couldn't quite hear. "We are far behind the animals," was one thing Hugo *did* hear. "A dog responds to a whistle on a wave length that is silence for a human being. He hears a footfall on grass fifty yards away and growls in the darkness of the night. A fish hears the splash of a sardine in the water a mile away from him, and we have not yet begun to understand the aural genius of owls and bats."

Hugo had no desire to hear whistles on dogs' wave lengths or footfalls on grass. He was uninterested in the splash of distant sardines and he was not an admirer of the genius of owls and bats. All he wanted to be able to hear was Johnny Smathers ten yards to his left in a football stadium. But he listened patiently. After what doctors had done for his knee, he had a childlike faith in them; and if Dr. Sebastian, in the course of restoring his hearing, wanted to praise the beasts of the field and the birds of the air, Hugo was prepared to be polite and nod agreement from time to time, just as he did when Sibyl spoke about politics or miniskirts or why she was sure Johnny Smathers' wife was no better than she should be when the team was on the road.

"We have allowed our senses to atrophy," Hugo winced as Dr. Sebastian rose on his toes for leverage and went rather deep with a blunt instrument. "We have lost our animal magic. We are only one third in communication, even the best of us. Whole new fields of understanding are waiting to be explored. When Beethoven's last quartets are played in a concert hall, a thousand people should fall out of their seats and writhe in unbearable ecstasy on the floor. Instead, what do they do? They look at their programs and wonder if there will be time for a beer before catching the last train home."

Hugo nodded. He had never heard any of Beethoven's last quartets and the floor of a concert hall didn't seem like the place a nice, well-brought-up married American boy should choose to writhe in ecstasy; but now that he had taken the step of going to a doctor, he was going to see it through. Still, with talk like that, about dogs and owls and sardines, he could see why there were no patients waiting in Dr. Sebastian's outer office.

"A crusade," Dr. Sebastian was saying, his eye glued to a lighted chromium funnel whose narrow end seemed to be embedded deep in Hugo's brain. Dr. Sebastian's breath pepperminted warmly on Hugo's bare neck. "A crusade is called for. You have a most unusually arranged collection of bones, Mr. Pleiss. A crusade to lift the curtain of sound, to unmuffle, to recapture our animal heritage, to distinguish whispers in bedlam, to hear the rustle of roses opening in the morning sun, to catch threats before they are really spoken, to recognize promises that are hardly formulated. I never did see a bone structure like this, Mr. Pleiss."

"Well, that feller in Green Bay weighed nearly three hundred pounds and his elbow—"

"Never mind, never mind." Dr. Sebastian finally pulled various bits of machinery out of his ear. "We will operate tomorrow morning, Miss Cattavi."

"OK," Miss Cattavi said. She had been sitting on a bench, looking as though she were ready to go in as soon as her team got the ball. "I'll make the arrangements."

"But—" Hugo began.

"I'll have everything ready," Dr. Sebastian said. "You've got nothing to worry about. Merely present yourself at the Lubenhorn Eye, Ear and Nose Clinic at three P.M. this afternoon."

"But there're one or two things I'd like to—"

"I'm afraid I'm terribly busy, Mr. Pleiss," Dr. Sebastian said. He whisked out of the office, peppermint receding on the aseptic air.

"He'll fix you," Miss Cattavi said, as she showed him to the door.

"I'm sure he will," said Hugo, "but—"

"I wouldn't be surprised," Miss Cattavi said, "if you came back to have the other ear done."

When Hugo woke up after the operation, Dr. Sebastian was standing next to his bed, smiling merrily. "Naturally," Dr. Sebastian said, "there is a certain slight discomfort."

The left side of Hugo's head felt as though it were inside the turret of a tank that was firing 60 rounds a minute. It also still felt like a corked cider bottle.

"You have an extraordinary bone structure, Mr. Pleiss." The doctor raised himself on tiptoe, so as to be able to smile approvingly down into Hugo's face. He spent a lot of time on his toes, Dr. Sebastian. In one way, it would have been more sensible if he had specialized in things like knees and ankles, instead of ears. "So extraordinary that I hated to finish the operation. It was like discovering a new continent. What a morning you have given me, Mr. Pleiss! I am even tempted not to charge you a penny."

It turned out later that Dr. Sebastian resisted this temptation. He sent a bill for $500. By the time Hugo received the bill, on the same day that Sibyl came back from Oregon, he was happy to pay it. The hearing in his left ear was restored. Now, if only Johnny Smathers wasn't traded away and if their relationship could be patched up, Hugo was sure he'd be in there at middle linebacker for the whole season.

There was a red scar behind his ear, but Sibyl didn't notice it for four days. She wasn't a very observant girl, Sibyl, except when she was looking at other girls' clothes and hair. When Sibyl finally did notice the scar, Hugo told her he'd cut himself shaving. He'd have had to use a saw-toothed bread knife to shave with to give himself a scar like that, but Sibyl accepted his explanation. He was rock-bottom honest, Hugo, and this was the first time he'd ever lied to his wife. The first lie is easy to get away with.

When he reported in to training camp, Hugo immediately patched up his friendship with Johnny Smathers. Johnny was a little cool at first, remembering how many times at the end of last season he had been made to look bad, all alone out there with two and three blockers trampling over him as Hugo was dashing away to the other side of the field, where nothing was happening. But when Hugo went as far as to confide in him that he'd had a little ringing in his left ear after the Green Bay game, a condition that had subsided since, Smathers had been understanding, and they even wound up as roommates.

Pre-season practice was satisfactory. The coach understood about the special relationship between Hugo and Smathers and always played them together and Hugo's performance was respectable, even though nobody was confusing him with Sam Huff or Dick Butkus or people like that.

The exhibition games didn't go badly and while Hugo didn't distinguish himself particularly, he made his fair share of tackles and batted down a few passes, listening carefully to Johnny Smathers' instructions and not being caught out of position too many times. It was a more-or-less normal September for Hugo, like so many Septembers of his life—sweaty, full of aches and bruises and abuse from coaches, not making love on Friday and Saturday, so as not to lose his edge for Sunday, feeling frightened for his life on Sunday morning and delighted to be able to walk out of the stadium on his own two feet in the dusk on Sunday afternoon. For want of a better word, what Hugo felt was happiness.

Then, just a minute before the end of the first regular league game of the season, something peculiar happened. Hugo's team was ahead, 21 to 18, and the other team had the ball on his team's eight-yard line. It was third down and four to go and the crowd was yelling so much, the opposing quarterback, Brabbledoff, kept holding up his arms to get them to quiet down enough so that he could be heard in the huddle. The crowd hushed a bit; but, even so, Hugo was afraid he wouldn't be able to hear Smathers when the play started. He shook his head to clear the sweat from the inside of his helmet and, for a moment, his left ear was parallel to the opposing huddle. Then the peculiar thing happened. He heard what Brabbledoff was saying, just as if he were right there next to him in the huddle. And the huddle was a good 15 yards away from Hugo, at least, and the crowd was roaring. "I'm going to bootleg it to the weak side," Brabbledoff was saying. "And, for Christ's sake, make it look real!"

The opposing team lined up and just before the snap, Hugo heard Smathers yell, "Around end to the strong side, around end to the strong side, Hugo!"

The two lines leaped into action; the guards pulled out to lead the run to the strong side. Hugo could have sworn he saw Brabbledoff hand off to Frenzdich, the halfback, who churned after the screen of interference, while Brabbledoff sauntered back, as though out of the play. Everybody on Hugo's team scrambled to stop the strong-side thrust. Everybody but Hugo. It was as though a button had been pushed somewhere in his back, making his moves mechanical. Struggling against the tide of traffic, he trailed Brabbledoff, who suddenly, in the clear, with no one near him, began to run like a frightened deer toward the weak-side corner, the ball now pulled out from behind the hip that had been hiding it. Hugo was there on the line of scrimmage, all alone, and he hurled himself at Brabbledoff. Brabbledoff said something unsportsmanlike, as he went down with Hugo on top of him, then fumbled the ball. Hugo kneeled on Brabbledoff's face and recovered the ball.

Hugo's teammates pummeled him in congratulation and they ran out the clock with two line bucks and the game was over, with the score 21 to 18.

The team voted Hugo the game ball in the locker room and the coach said, "It's about time you read a play correctly, Pleiss," which was high praise, indeed, from that particular coach.

In the shower, Johnny Smathers came over to him. "Man," Johnny said, "I could have killed you when I saw you drifting over to the weak side after I yelled at you. What tipped you off?"

"Nothing," Hugo said, after a moment's hesitation.

"It was a hell of a play," said Smathers.

"It was just a hunch," Hugo said modestly.

He was quieter than usual that Sunday night, especially after a win. He kept thinking about Dr. Sebastian and the sound of roses opening.

The next Sunday, Hugo went out onto the field just like every Sunday. He hadn't heard anything all week that a man wouldn't ordinarily hear and he was sure that it had been an acoustical freak that had carried Brabbledoff's voice to him from the huddle. Nothing unusual happened in the first half of the game. Smathers guessed right about half of the time and while there was no danger that Hugo was going to be elected defensive player of the week by the newspapers, he served creditably for the first 30 minutes.

It was a rough game and in the third quarter, he was shaken breaking into a screen and got up a little groggy. Moving around to clear his head while the other team was in the huddle, he happened to turn his left side toward the line of scrimmage. Then it happened again. Just as though he were right there, in the middle of the opposing huddle, he heard the quarterback say, in a hoarse whisper, "Red right! Flood left! Wing square in! R down and out . . . on five!"

Hugo looked around to see if any of his teammates had heard, too. But they looked just the way they always looked—muddy, desperate, edgy, overweight, underpaid and uninformed. As the opposing team came out of the huddle, up to the line of scrimmage, Hugo moved automatically into the defensive formation that had been called by Krkanius, who played in the front four and ran the defense positions. "Red right! Flood left! Wing square in! R down and out . . . on five!" he repeated silently to himself. Since he didn't know the other team's signals, that didn't help him much, except that "on five" almost certainly meant that the ball was going to be snapped on the fifth count.

Smathers yelled, "Pass. On the flank!" and, again, Hugo felt as though a button had been pushed in his back. He was moving on the four count and was across the line of scrimmage, untouched, a fraction of a second after the ball was snapped, and laid the quarterback low before he could take a half step back into the pocket.

"Have you got a brother on this team, you son of a bitch?" the quarterback asked Hugo as Hugo lay on the quarterback's chest.

After that, for most of the rest of the afternoon, by turning to his right, Hugo heard everything that was said in the opposing huddle. Aside from an occasional commonplace remark like "Where were you on that play, fat ass, waving to your girl?" or "If that Hunsworth puts his fingers into my eye once more, I'm going to kick him in the balls," the only operational intelligence that came across to Hugo was in the quarterback's coded signals, so there wasn't much advantage to be gained from Hugo's keenness of hearing. He knew *when* the ball was going to be snapped and could move a step sooner than otherwise, but he didn't know where it was going and still had to depend upon Smathers in that department.

Going into the last two minutes of the game, they were ahead, 14 to 10. The Studs were one of the strongest teams in the league and Hugo's team was a 20-point underdog on the Las Vegas line and a win would be a major upset. But the Studs were on his team's 38-yard line, first down and ten to go, and moving. Hugo's teammates were getting up more and more slowly from the pile-ups, like losers, and they all avoided looking over toward the bench, where the coach was giving an imitation of General George S. Patton on a bad day along the Rhine.

The Studs went briskly into their huddle, keyed up and confident. Hugo had been blocked out of the last three plays ("wiped out like my three-year-old daughter" had been the phrase the coach had used) and he was preparing his excuses if he was pulled out of the game. The Studs were talking it up in the huddle, a confused babel of sound, when suddenly Hugo heard one voice, very clearly. It was Dusering, the leading pass catcher in the league. Hugo knew his voice well. Dusering had expressed himself to Hugo with some eloquence after Hugo had pushed him out of bounds in what Dusering considered an ungentlemanly manner after a 30-yard gain on a pass to the side line.

"Listen." Dusering was saying in the huddle 15 yards away. "I got Smathers all set up. I can beat him on a buttonhook on the inside."

"OK," Hugo heard the quarterback say, and then the signal.

The Studs trotted up to the line of scrimmage. Hugo glanced around at Smathers. Smathers was pulling back deep, worried about Dusering's getting behind him, too busy protecting his area to bother about calling anything to Hugo. Hugo looked at Dusering. He was wide, on the left, looking innocent, giving nothing away.

The ball was snapped and Dusering went straight down the side line, as though for the bomb. A halfback came charging out in front of Hugo, yelling, his arms up, but Hugo ignored him. He cut back to his left, waited for a step, saw Dusering stop, then buttonhook back inside, leaving Smathers hopelessly fooled. The ball came floating out. Just as Dusering set himself to get it at waist height, Hugo flung himself across the trajectory of the pass and gathered it in. He didn't get far with it, as Dusering had him on the first step, but it didn't matter. The game was, to all intents and purposes, over, a stunning victory. It was the first pass Hugo had ever intercepted.

He was voted the game ball that Sunday, too.

In the locker room, the coach came over to Hugo while he was taking off his jockstrap. The coach looked at him curiously. "I really ought to fine you," the coach said. "You left the middle as open as a whore's legs on Saturday night."

"Yes, Coach," Hugo said, modestly wrapping a towel around him. He didn't like rough language.

"What made you cover the buttonhook?" the coach asked.

"I . . ." Hugo looked guiltily down at his bare toes. They were bleeding profusely and one nail looked as though he was going to lose it. "Dusering tipped it off. He does something funny with his head before the buttonhook."

The coach nodded, a new light of respect in his eyes.

It was Hugo's second lie. He didn't like to lie, but if he told the coach he could hear what people were whispering in a huddle 15 yards away, with 60,000 people screaming in the stands like wild Indians, the coach would send him right over to the doctor to be treated for concussion of the brain.

During the week, for the first time, he was interviewed by a sportswriter. The article came out on Friday and there was a picture of him crouching with his hands spread out, looking ferocious. The headline over the article said, "MR. BIG PLAY MAN."

Sibyl cut the article out and sent it to her father, who always kept saying that Hugo would never amount to anything as a football player and ought to quit and start selling insurance before he got his brains knocked out, after which it would be too late to sell anything, even insurance.

Practice that week was no different from any other week, except that Hugo was limping because of his crushed toes. He tested himself, to see if he could hear what people were saying outside of normal range, but even in the comparative silence of the practice field, he didn't hear any better or any worse than he had before his ear was hurt. He didn't sleep as well as he usually did, as he kept thinking about the next Sunday, and Sibyl complained, saying he was making an insomniac out of her, thrashing around like a beached whale. On Thursday and Friday nights, he slept on the couch in the living room. The clock in the living room sounded like Big Ben to him, but he attributed it to his nerves. On Saturday, the whole team went to a hotel for the night, so Sibyl had nothing to complain about. Hugo shared a room with Smathers. Smathers smoked, drank and chased girls. At two in the morning, still awake, Hugo looked over at Johnny sleeping beatifically, and wondered if perhaps he was making a mistake somewhere in the way he led his life.

Even limping from his crushed toes, Sunday was a remarkable day for Hugo. In the middle of the first quarter, after the opposing tackle had given him the knee to the head on a block, Hugo discovered that he not only could hear the signals in the other team's huddle but *knew what they meant*, just as though he had been studying their playbook for months. "Brown right! Draw fifty-five . . . on two!" came through in the quarterback's voice to his left ear, as though on a clear telephone connection, and was somehow instantly translated in Hugo's brain to "Flanker to the right, fake to the fullback over right guard, hand-off to right halfback and cutback inside left end."

Hugo still lined up obediently in the defensive formations called by Krkanius; but once the plays got under way, he disregarded his regular assignments and went where he knew the plays were going. He intercepted two passes, knocked down three more and made more tackles than the rest of the team put together. It was with somber satisfaction mixed with a curious sense of guilt that he heard Gates, the opposing quarterback, snarl in the huddle, "Who let that fish face Pleiss in there again?" It was the first time that he had heard any quarterback in the league mention him by name.

It was only as he was leaving the field that Hugo realized that Smathers hadn't called a play to him once during the whole game. He tried to catch Smathers' eye in the locker room, but Smathers always seemed to be looking the other way.

On Monday morning, when they ran the game films, the coach kept stopping the film on plays in which Hugo figured and rerunning those bits in slow motion over and over again. Hugo began to feel even more uncomfortable than he usually felt at these Monday-morning entertainments. The coach didn't say anything, except, "Let's look at that once more"; but seeing himself over and over again, in the center of plays so many times, embarrassed Hugo, as though he were showboating in front of his teammates. It was also embarrassing to see how often, even though he was right there, he allowed himself to be knocked down by blockers who were primarily going for another man, and how many tackles he had made that should have been clean but that developed into dogged, drag-me-along-with-you-Nellie yard-eating affairs. It was a stern rule with the coach that no comments were allowed by the players at the showings, so Hugo had no notion of what his teammates' estimate of his performance might be.

When the film was finally over, Hugo tried to be the first man out the door, but the coach signaled to him and pointed with his thumb to the office. Leaning heavily on his cane, Hugo hobbled into the office, prepared for the worst. The cane was not merely window dressing. The toes on Hugo's right foot looked like a plate of hamburger and, while he waited for the coach, Hugo thought of ways to introduce his infirmity as an excuse for some of the less glorious moments of his performance as revealed by the movies of the game.

The coach came in, opening the collar of his size-19 shirt so that he could express himself freely. He shut the door firmly, sat down and grunted. The grunt meant that Hugo could sit down, too. Hugo seated himself on a straight wooden chair, placing his cane prominently in front of him.

Behind the coach, on the wall, there was a blown-up photograph of a player in a 1940ish uniform. The player's name was Jojo Baines and he had once been voted the dirtiest lineman ever to play in the National Football League. The only time Hugo had ever heard a note of tenderness creep into the coach's voice was when he mentioned Jojo Baines.

"Ever since you joined this club, Pleiss," said the coach, "I have been appalled when I looked down at the starting line-up and seen your name on it—in my own handwriting."

Hugo smiled weakly, hoping to recognize a pleasantry.

"I won't keep it a secret from you, Pleiss," the coach went on. "For two years, I've been trying to get rid of you. I have made the circuit of every city in this league with my hat in hand, eating the bread of humiliation, trying to beg, borrow or steal another middle linebacker. To no avail." The coach had an ear for rhetoric, when he was so inclined. "No avail," he repeated. "They all knew that as long as I had to start you every Sunday, we were never a threat to anybody. I am going to give you an impersonal estimate of your abilities, Pleiss. You're slow, you have a miserable pair of hands, you don't hit hard enough to drive my grandmother out of a rocking chair, you close your eyes on contact, you run like a duck with gout, you wouldn't get angry if a man hit you over the head with an automobile jack and raped your wife in front of your eyes, and you get fooled on plays that would have made a high school cheerleader roar with laughter in 1910. Have I left out anything?"

"Not that I can think of sir," Hugo said.

"With all that," the coach went on, "you have saved three games in a row for us. You make a mockery out of the holy sport of football, but you have saved three games in a row for us and I am hereby increasing your salary by one thousand dollars for the season. If you tell this to anyone else on the team, I will personally nail you by the hands to the locker-room wall."

"Yes, sir," said Hugo.

"Now, get out of here," the coach said.

"Yes, sir," Hugo said. He stood up.

"Give me that cane," the coach said.

Hugo gave him the cane. The coach broke it in two, without rising from his chair. "I can't stand the sight of cripples," he said.

"Yes, sir," Hugo said. He tried not to limp as he walked out of the office.

The next Sunday was unsettling.

It started on an audible.

When the opposing team lined up after the huddle. Hugo knew that the play that had been called in the huddle was a short pass to the right flank. But when the quarterbook took his position behind the center, Hugo saw him scanning the defensive setup and frowning. The quarterback's lips didn't move, but Hugo heard, just as though the man were talking directly to him, the word "No." There was a little pause and then, "It won't work, they're overshifting on us."

Hugo didn't have time to wonder at this new extension of his powers, as the quarterback began to call a set of signals aloud, changing the play he'd picked in the huddle. Everybody could hear the signals, of course, but Hugo was the only one on his team who knew that the quarterback was calling for an end around, from left to right. Just before the snap, when it was too late for the quarterback to call any changes, Hugo broke for the left side. He knew, without thinking about why he knew it, that the end would take two steps to his left, hesitate for one beat, then whirl around and streak for the quarterback and the ball on the way around the opposite end. As the ball was snapped, Hugo was knifing in between the end and the tackle, and when the end, after his two steps, came around, Hugo flattened him with a block. The quarterback was left all alone, holding the ball, like a postman delivering a package to the wrong door, and was downed for a five-yard loss.

But it was an expensive exploit for Hugo. The end's knee caught him in the head as they went down together and he was stretched out unconscious when the whistle blew.

When he woke up some minutes later, he was lying behind the bench, with the doctor kneeling over him, prodding the back of his neck for broken vertebrae, and the trainer jamming spirits of ammonia under his nostrils. The jolt had been so severe that when the coach asked him at half time how he had been able to nip the end-around play in the bud, Hugo had to confess that he didn't remember anything about the play. In fact, he didn't remember leaving the hotel that morning, and it took him a good ten minutes after the coach had spoken to him to remember the coach's name.

The doctor wouldn't let him go back into the game and his value to the team was neatly demonstrated to the coach by the fact that they lost by three touchdowns and a field goal.

The plane was quiet on the flight home. The coach did not appreciate a show of youthful high spirits or resilience in adversity by teams of his when they had lost by three touchdowns and a field goal. And, as usual on such occasions, he had forbidden any drinks to be served, since he didn't believe the fine, full flavor of defeat should be adulterated by alcohol. So the plane sped through the night sky in a long funereal hush.

Hugo himself was feeling better, although he still didn't remember anything about the game that afternoon. He had a nagging sensation that something peculiar and fundamentally unwholesome had occurred *before* his injury, but he couldn't bring it up to the level of consciousness. There was a small poker game going on up front in low whispers and Hugo decided to sit in, to stop himself from profitless probing into the afternoon's events. He usually lost in these games, since one glance at his open face by any normally acquisitive poker player showed whether Hugo had a pair, two pairs or was buying to a straight.

Either because it was too dark in the plane for the other players to get a clear look at Hugo's face or because the head injury had hurt some nerve and rendered him expressionless, Hugo kept winning a fair proportion of the pots. He was a careless player and didn't keep track of his winnings and merely felt that it was about time that luck was turning his way.

After about an hour of play, he had a sizable stack of chips in front of him. He was sitting with three aces in his hand, having gotten two of them on a four-card draw, and he was about to raise the man on his left, Krkanius, who had drawn three cards, when somehow, just as though

Krkanius had nudged him and whispered the news into his ear, he knew that Krkanius had a full house, jacks and fours. He didn't raise Krkanius but threw his cards in. Someone else saw Krkanius and Krkanius put his cards down. Full house. Jacks and fours.

"I'm not feeling so well," Hugo said. "I'm cashing in." He stood up and went back to his seat.

It was a miserable night and the plane was bucking through thick cloud and Hugo sat at the window, looking out and feeling horrible. He was a cheat. He could make all sorts of excuses to himself, he could say he had acted out of surprise, without thinking, that it was the first time anything like that had ever happened to him, but he knew that if that weird message hadn't come through to him from Krkanius, on his left, he'd have raised Krkanius $10 and Krkanius would have raised him and Krkanius would be at least $20 or $30 richer right now. No matter how he tried to wriggle out of it, his conscience told him he was just as guilty as if he had taken $30 out of Krkanius' wallet.

Then, in a flash, he remembered the afternoon—the moment on the field when he was sure that he knew what the quarterback was thinking on the end-around play and his automatic reaction to it and his blotting out the end. It was another form of cheating, but he didn't know what to do about it. He could keep from playing poker, but he made his living out of playing football.

He groaned. He came from a deeply religious family, with a stern sense of morality. He didn't smoke or drink and he believed in hell.

After the plane landed, Hugo didn't go right home. Sibyl was away in Chicago, attending the wedding of one of her sisters, and he didn't feel like rattling around in an empty house. Krkanius, who had emerged from the poker game the big winner, invited him and a couple of the other boys to join him for a drink and, while Hugo didn't drink, he went along for the company.

The bar Krkanius took them to was crowded and noisy. There was a group of men with some girls at the bar, and as Hugo followed Krkanius to the back room, he heard a woman's voice say, "Uh-huh. That's for me. That big innocent-looking one."

Hugo looked around. A round blonde at the bar was staring directly at him, a sweet small smile on her full lips. If you didn't know what went on in her head, she looked like somebody's pure young daughter. "I'm going to teach you a few things tonight, baby," Hugo heard, staring, frozen, at the girl. The girl's mouth had never shown the slightest tremor of movement.

Hugo wheeled and hurried into the back room. When the waiter asked him what he wanted to drink, he ordered bourbon.

"Man," Krkanius said, surprised, "you really must've got shaken up today." Nobody had ever seen Hugo drink anything stronger than ginger ale before.

Hugo drank his bourbon quickly. He didn't like the taste, but it seemed to help his nerves. The blonde girl came into the back room and leaned over a table nearby to talk to somebody she knew. Remembering what she had been thinking as he passed her on the way in, Hugo ordered another bourbon. She glanced, as though by accident, at the table of football players. The way her sweater fit around her bosom made a peculiar ache come up in Hugo's throat.

"What're you waiting for, sweets?" he heard her think as her glance swept over him. "The night's not getting any younger."

He drank the second bourbon even more quickly than the first. "Oh, God," he thought, "I'm becoming a drunkard." The bourbon didn't seem to do anything for his nerves this time.

"It's time to go home," he said, standing up. His voice didn't sound like his. "I'm not feeling so well."

"Get a good night's sleep," Krkanius said.

"Yeah." If Krkanius knew that he'd had $30 stolen from him that evening, he wouldn't have been so solicitous.

Hugo walked quickly past the bar, making sure not to look at the girl. It was raining outside now and all the taxis were taken. He was just about to start walking when he heard the door open behind him. He couldn't help but turn. The girl was standing there, alone, with her coat on. She was scanning the street for a taxi, too. Then she looked at him. "Your move, baby," he heard, in a voice that was surprisingly harsh for a girl so young.

Hugo felt himself blush. Just then, a taxi drove up. Both he and the girl started for it.

"Can I give you a lift?" Hugo heard himself saying.

"How kind of you," the girl said, demurely.

On the way home, in the dawn, many hours later, Hugo wished for the first time in his life that he had been born a Catholic. Then he could have gone directly to a priest, confessed, accepted penance and been absolved of sin.

Sibyl called in the morning to tell him that her parents, who had come East for the wedding, were taking a trip to New York and wanted her to go along with them. Ordinarily, he wouldn't have been able to keep the disappointment at news like that out of his voice. He loved Sibyl dearly and usually felt lost without her. But now a wave of relief swept over him. The moment of confrontation, the moment when he would have to tell his innocent and trusting young wife about his appalling lapse from grace or, even worse, lie to her, was postponed.

"That's all right, honey," he said, "you just go along with your mother and dad and have a good time. You deserve a holiday. Stay as long as you like."

"Hugo," Sibyl said, "I just could break down and cry, you're so good to me."

There was the sound of a kiss over the telephone and Hugo kissed back. When he hung up, he leaned his head against the wall and closed his eyes in pain. One thing he was sure of, he wasn't going to see that girl, that Sylvia, again. Sylvia. Almost the same name as Sibyl. How rotten could a man be?

Passion spent for the moment, he lay in the largest double bed he had ever seen, next to the dazzling body that had opened undreamed-of utopias of pleasure for him. Ashamed of himself even for thinking about it, he was sure that if Sibyl lived to the age of 90, she wouldn't know one tenth as much as Sylvia must have known the day she was born.

In the soft glow of a distant lamp, he looked at the bedside clock. It was past four o'clock. He had to report for practice, dressed, at ten o'clock. After a losing game, the coach gave them wind sprints for 45 minutes every day for a week. He groaned inwardly as he thought of what he was going to feel like at 10:45 that morning. Still, for some reason, he was loath to go.

An hour later, he was finally dressed. He leaned over Sylvia to kiss her goodbye. She lay there, fresh as the morning, smiling, breathing placidly. He wished he were in as good condition as she was. "G'night, sweets," she said, an arm around his neck. "Don't let those rough boys hurt you today. And bring Baby a little giftie tonight. Try Myer's, on Sanford Street. They're full of goodies."

Walking home along the dark streets, Hugo thought, "Of course. Girls like little tokens of affection. Flowers, candy. Sentimental creatures." He didn't remember any store called Myer's on Sanford Street, but he supposed it was a confectionery shop that had some specialties that Sylvia had a taste for. He resolved to get her the best five-pound box of candy money could buy.

That afternoon, feeling a little light-headed from lack of sleep and the wind sprints, he walked along Sanford Street, searching for a shop called Myer's. He stopped short. MYER, the thin lettering read on the window. But instead of boxes of candy displayed behind the glass there was a blaze of gold and diamonds. Myer's sold jewelry. Expensive jewelry.

Hugo did not go in. Thrift was another of the virtues his excellent family had instilled in him as a boy. He walked along Sanford Street until he found a candyshop and bought a five-pound box of chocolates. It cost $15 and Hugo felt a twinge at his extravagance as the clerk wrapped the box in festive paper.

That night, he didn't stay more than ten minutes in Sylvia's apartment. She had a headache, she said. She didn't bother to unwrap the candy.

The next night, he stayed longer. He had visited Myer's during the afternoon and bought a gold bracelet for $300. "I do like a generous man," Sylvia said.

The pain Hugo had felt in handing over the $300 to the clerk in Myer's was considerably mitigated by the fact that the night before, when he had left Sylvia with her headache, he had remembered that every Tuesday there was a poker game at Krkanius' apartment. Hugo had sat in for three hours and had won $416, the record for a single night's winnings since the inception of the game. During the course of the evening, by twisting his head a little now and then to get a fix with his left ear, he had been warned of lurking straights, one flush and several full houses. He had discarded a nine-high full house himself because Croker, of the taxi squad, was sitting in the hole with a jack-high full house; and Hugo had won with a pair of sevens after Krkanius had bluffed wildly through a hand with a pair of fives. Somehow, he told himself piously, as he stuffed bills and checks into his wallet when the game broke up, he would make it up to his teammates. But not just now. Just now, he couldn't bear the thought of Sylvia having any more headaches.

Luckily, Sibyl didn't return until Friday. On Friday nights during the season, Hugo slept on the living-room couch, so as not to be tempted to impair his energies for Sundays' games, so *that* problem was postponed. He was afraid that Sibyl's woman's intuition would lead her to discover a fateful change in her husband, but Sibyl was so grateful for her holiday that her intuition lay dormant. She merely tucked him in and kissed him chastely on the forehead and said, "Get a good night's sleep, honey."

When she appeared with his breakfast on a tray the next morning, his conscience stirred uneasily; and after the light Saturday-morning practice, he went into Myer's and bought Sibyl a string of cultured pearls for $85.

Sunday was triumphal. Before the game, suiting up, Hugo decided that the best way he could make up to his teammates for taking $416 away from them was by doing everything he could to win the game for them. His conscience clear, obeying the voices within his head, he was in on half the tackles. When he intercepted a pass in the last quarter and ran for a touchdown, the first of his life, to put the game on ice, the entire stadium stood and cheered him. The coach even shook his hand when he came off the field. He felt dainty footed and powerful and as though he could play forever without fatigue. The blood coursing through his veins felt like a new and exhilarating liquid, full of dancing bubbles.

After the game, he was dragged off to a television interview in a little makeshift studio under the stands. He had never been on television before, but he got through it all right and later that night, somebody told him he was photogenic.

His life entered a new phase. It was as definite as opening and going through a door and closing it behind him, like leaving a small, shabby corridor and with one step emerging into a brilliantly lit ballroom.

His photograph was in the papers every week, with laudatory articles. Newspapermen sought him out and quoted him faithfully when he said, "The trick is to study your opponents. The National Football League is no place for guesswork."

He posed for advertising stills, his hair combed with greaseless products. He modeled sweaters and flowered bathing trunks and was amazed at how simple it was to earn large sums of money in America merely by smiling.

His picture was on the cover of *Sports Illustrated* and small boys waited for him at the players' entrance after practice. He autographed footballs, and taxi drivers recognized him and sometimes refused to take payment for their fares. He took to eating out in restaurants with Sibyl, because the managers more often than not tore up the check when he asked for it. He learned to eat caviar and developed a taste for champagne.

He was invited to parties at the home of Bruce Fallon, the quarterback, who had been paid $200,000 to sign and who was called a superstar by the sportswriters. Until then, Fallon, who only went around with the famous old-timers and the upper-bracket players on the club, had never even said hello to him when they passed on the street. "Do you play bridge, Hugo?" Fallon asked.

They played bridge, Fallon and Fallon's wife, Nora, and Hugo and Sibyl, in the huge living room of the Fallons' apartment, which had been decorated by an imported Norwegian. "Isn't this cozy?" Nora Fallon said, as the four of them sat around the pale wood table before the fire, playing for ten cents a point. Hugo's left ear worked for bridge as well as poker and Hugo wound up the first evening with an $800 profit, and Fallon said, "I've heard about your poker from the boys, Hugo. I've never met anybody with a card sense like yours."

Fallon discussed the coach with him. "If Bert would really let me call my own game," Fallon said, pouring whiskeys for himself and Hugo, "we'd be twenty points better a Sunday."

"He's a little primitive, Bert, that's true," Hugo said, "but he's not a bad guy at heart." He had never heard anybody criticize the coach before and had never even thought of him by his first name. Even now, with the coach a good seven miles away across town and safely in bed, Hugo felt a curious little tickling in the small of his back as he realized that he had actually said, "Bert."

When they left that night, with Fallon's check for $800 in his pocket, Nora Fallon put up her cheek to be kissed. She had gone to school in Lausanne. She said, "We have to make this a weekly affair," as Hugo kissed her, and he knew she was thinking, "Wouldn't it be nice if we could have a little quiet tête-à-tête, you and I, sometime soon?"

That night, when Hugo got home, he wrote the Fallon telephone number in his little pocket address book. He wondered what it could be like, making love to a woman who thought in French.

The trainer took a fussy interest in him now and, when he came up with a small bruise on his knee, insisted on giving him whirlpool baths for six days. The coach let him off a half hour early one day to make a speech at a local high school. Brenatskis, the publicity man, rewrote his biography for the programs and said that he had made Phi Beta Kappa in college. When Hugo protested, mildly, Brenatskis said, "Who'll know?" and, "It's good for your image." He also arranged for a national magazine to have Hugo photographed at home for a feature article. Sibyl insisted on buying a pair of gold-lamé pajamas if she was going to be photographed for a national magazine, and on having new curtains in the living room and new slipcovers made. When the article came out, there was only one picture accompanying it—Hugo in an apron, cooking in the kitchen. He was supposed to be making a complicated French dish. He never actually even made coffee for himself.

He bought three loud checked sports jackets for himself and a $400 brooch for Sylvia, who was still subject to headaches. He couldn't tear himself away from Sylvia, although he was beginning to find her rather common, especially compared with Nora Fallon. He bought a $100 pair of earrings for Sibyl.

On Sundays, he raged over all the fields in the league, and at the end of home games, he had to get to the locker room fast to keep from being mobbed by fans. He began to receive love letters from girls, who sometimes included photographs taken in surprising positions. He knew that these letters disturbed Sibyl, but the mails were free, after all. By now, everybody agreed that he was photogenic.

Sibyl one day announced that she was pregnant. Until then, although Hugo had wanted children from the beginning of their marriage, she had insisted that she was too young. Now, for some reason, she had decided that she was no longer too young. Hugo was very happy, but he was so occupied with other things that he didn't have quite the time to show it completely. Still, he bought her a turquoise necklace.

Fallon, who was born gambler, said that it was a shame to waste Hugo's card sense on penny-ante poker games and ten-cent-a-point family bridge. There was a big poker game in town that Fallon played in once a week. In the game, there were a stockbroker, a newspaper publisher, the president of an agricultural-machinery firm, an automobile distributor and a man who owned, among other things, a string of race horses. When Fallon brought Hugo into the hotel suite where the game was held, there was a haze of money in the room as palpable as the cigar smoke that eddied over the green table and against the drawn curtains. Hugo and Fallon had made a private deal that they would split their winnings and their losses. Hugo wasn't sure about the morality of this, since they weren't letting the others know that they were up against a partnership, but Fallon said, "What the hell, Huge, they're only civilians." Anybody who wasn't in some way involved in professional football was a civilian in Fallon's eyes. "Huge" was Fallon's friendly corruption of Hugo's name and it had caught on with the other men on the team and with the newspapermen who followed the club. When the offensive team trotted off the field, passing the defensive team coming in, Fallon had taken to calling out, "Get the ball back for me, Huge." A sportswriter had picked it up and had written a piece on Hugo using that as the title; and now, whenever the defensive team went in, the home crowd chanted, "Get the ball back for me, Huge." Sometimes, listening to all that love and faith come roaring through the autumn air at him, Hugo felt like crying for joy out there.

The men around the green table all stood up when Fallon and Hugo came into the room. The game hadn't started yet and they were still making up the piles of chips. They were all big men, with hearty, authoritative faces. They shook hands with the two football players as Fallon introduced Hugo. One of them said, "It's an honor," and another man said, "Get the ball back for me, Huge," as he shook Hugo's hand and they all roared with kindly laughter. Hugo smiled boyishly. Because of the five-tooth bridge in the front of his mouth, Hugo for years had smiled as little as possible; but in the past few weeks, since he had become photogenic, he smiled readily. He practiced grinning boyishly from time to time in front of the mirror at home. People, he knew, were pleased to be able to say about him, "Huge? He looks rough, but when he smiles, he's just a nice big kid." Civilians.

They played until two o'clock in the morning. Hugo had won $6020 and Fallon had won $1175. "You two fellers are just as tough off the field as on," said the automobile distributor admiringly as he signed a check, and the other men laughed jovially. Losing money seemed to please them.

"Beginner's luck," Hugo said. Later on, the automobile distributor would tell his wife that Huge didn't look it, but he was witty.

They hailed a taxi outside the hotel. Fallon hadn't brought his Lincoln Continental, because there was no sense in taking a chance that somebody would spot it parked outside the hotel and tell the coach his quarterback stayed out till two o'clock in the morning. In the taxi, Fallon asked, "You got a safe-deposit box, Huge?"

"No," Hugo said.

"Get one tomorrow."

"Why?"

"Income tax," Fallon said. In the light of a street lamp, he saw that Hugo looked puzzled. "What Uncle Sam doesn't know," Fallon said lightly, "won't hurt him. We'll cash these checks tomorrow, divvy up and stash the loot away in nice dark little boxes. Don't use your regular bank, either."

"I see," Hugo said. There was no doubt about it; Fallon was a brainy man. For a moment, he felt a pang of regret that he had taken Nora Fallon to a motel the week before. He hadn't regretted it at the time, though. Quite the contrary. He had just thought that if the child Sibyl was carrying turned out to be a girl, he wouldn't send her to school in Lausanne.

Sibyl awoke when he came into the bedroom. "You win, honey?" she asked sleepily.

"A couple of bucks," Hugo said.

"That's nice," she said.

By now, Hugo was free of doubt. If God gave you a special gift, He obviously meant you to use it. A man who could run the hundred in nine flat would be a fool to allow himself to be beaten by a man who could do only nine, five. If it was God's will that Hugo should have the good things of life—fame, success, wealth, beautiful women—well, that was God's will. Hugo was a devout man, even though, in the season, he was busy on Sunday and couldn't go to church.

During next week's poker game, Hugo saw to it that he didn't win too much. He let himself get caught bluffing several times and deliberately bet into hands that he knew were stronger than his. There was no sense in being greedy and killing the goose that laid the golden eggs. Even so, he came out almost $2000 ahead. Fallon lost nearly $500, so nobody had reason for complaint.

When the game broke up, Connors, the automobile distributor, told Hugo he'd like to talk to him for a minute. They went downstairs and sat in a deserted corner of the lobby. Connors was opening a sports-car agency and he wanted Hugo to lend his name to it. "There's nothing to it," Connors said. "Hang around the showroom a couple of afternoons a week and have your picture taken sitting in a Porsche once in a while. I'll give you ten thousand a year for it."

Hugo scratched his head boyishly, turning his left ear slightly toward Connors. The figure $25,000 came through loud and clear. "I'll take twenty-five thousand dollars and ten percent of the profits," Hugo said.

Connors laughed, delighted with his new employee's astuteness. "You must have read my mind," he said. They shook on the deal. Hugo was to go on the payroll the next day.

"He's got a head on his shoulders, old Huge," Connors told his wife. "He'll sell cars."

Another of the poker players, Hartwright, the race-horse owner, called Hugo and, after swearing him to secrecy, told him that he and what he called "a few of the boys" were buying up land for a supermarket in a suburb of the city. There was inside information that a superhighway was being built out that way by the city. "It'll be a gold mine," Hartwright said. "I've talked it over with the boys and they think it'd be a nice idea to let you in on it. If you don't have the cash, we can swing a loan. . . ."

Hugo got a loan for $50,000. He was learning that nothing pleases people more than helping a success. Even his father-in-law, who had until then never been guilty of wild feats of generosity, was moved enough by the combination of Hugo's new-found fame and the announcement that he was soon to be a grandfather to buy Hugo and Sibyl an eight-room house with a swimming pool in a good suburb of the city.

So the season went on, weeks during which Hugo heard nothing, spoken or unspoken, that was not for his pleasure or profit, the golden autumn coming to a rhythmic climax once every seven days in two hours of Sunday violence and huzzas.

The newspapers were even beginning to talk about the possibility of "The Cinderella Boys," as Fallon and Hugo and their teammates were called, going all the way to the showdown with Green Bay for the championship. But on the same day, both Fallon and Hugo were hurt—Fallon with a cleverly dislocated elbow and Hugo with a head injury that gave him a severe attack of vertigo that made it seem to him that the whole world was built on a slant. They lost that game and they were out of the running for the championship of their division and the dream was over.

Before being injured, Hugo had had a good day; and in the plane flying home, even though it seemed to Hugo that it was flying standing on its right wing, he did not feel too bad. All that money in the bank had made him philosophic about communal misfortunes. The team doctor, a hearty fellow who would have been full of cheer at the fall of the Alamo, had assured him that he would be fine in a couple of days and had regaled him with stories of men who had been in a coma for days and had gained more than 100 yards on the ground the following Sunday.

An arctic hush of defeat filled the plane, broken only by the soft complaints of the wounded, of which there were many. Amidships sat the coach, with the owner, forming glaciers of pessimism that flowed inexorably down the aisle. The weather was bad and the plane bumped uncomfortably through soupy black cloud and Hugo, seated next to Johnny Smathers, who was groaning like a dying stag from what the doctor had diagnosed as a superficial contusion of the ribs, was impatient for the trip to end, so that he could be freed from this atmosphere of Waterloo and return to his abundant private world. He remembered that next Sunday was an open date and he was grateful for it. The season had been rewarding, but the tensions had been building up. He could stand a week off.

Then something happened that made him forget about football.

There was a crackling in his left ear, like static. Then he heard a man's voice saying, "VHF one is out." Immediately afterward he heard another man's voice saying, "VHF two is out, too. We've lost radio contact." Hugo looked around, sure that everybody else must have heard it, too, that it had come over the public-address system. But everybody was doing just what he had been doing before, talking in low voices, reading, napping.

"That's a hell of a note." Hugo recognized the captain's voice. "There's forty thousand feet of soup from here to Newfoundland."

Hugo looked out the window. It was black and thick out there. The red light on the tip of the wing was a minute blood-colored blur that seemed to wink out for seconds at a time in the darkness. Hugo closed the curtain and put on his seat belt.

"Well, kiddies," the captain's voice said in Hugo's ear, "happy news. We're lost. If anybody sees the United States down below, tap me on the shoulder."

Nothing unusual happened in the passenger section.

The door to the cockpit opened and the stewardess came out. She had a funny smile on her face that looked as though it had been painted on sideways. She walked down the aisle, not changing her expression, and went to the tail of the plane and sat down there. When she was sure nobody was looking, she hooked the seat belt around her.

The plane bucked a bit and people began to look at their watches. They were due to land in about ten minutes and they weren't losing any altitude. There was a warning squawk from the public-address system and the captain said, "This is your captain speaking. I'm afraid we're going to be a little late. We're running into head winds. I suggest you attach your seat belts."

There was the click of metal all over the plane. It was the last sound Hugo heard for a long time, because he fainted.

He was awakened by a sharp pain in one ear. The right one. The plane was coming down for a landing. Hugo pulled the curtain back and looked out. They were under the cloud now, perhaps 400 feet off the ground and there were lights below. He looked at his watch. They were nearly three hours late.

"You better make it a good one," he heard a man's voice say, and he knew the voice came from the cockpit. "We don't have enough gas for another thousand yards."

Hugo tried to clear his throat. Something dry and furry seemed to be lodged there. Everybody else had already gathered up his belongings, placidly waiting to disembark. They don't know how lucky they are, Hugo thought bitterly as he peered out the window, hungry for the ground.

The plane came in nicely and as it taxied to a halt, the captain said cheerily, "I hope you enjoyed your trip, folks. Sorry about the little delay. See you soon."

The ground hit his feet at a peculiar angle when he debarked from the plane, but he had told Sylvia he would look in at her place when he got back to town. Sibyl was away in Florida with her parents for the week, visiting relatives.

Going over in the taxi, fleeing the harsh world of bruised and defeated men and the memory of his brush with death in the fogbound plane, he thought yearningly of the warm bed awaiting him and the expert, expensive girl.

Sylvia took a long time answering the bell and when she appeared, she was in a bathrobe and had her headache face on. She didn't let Hugo in, but opened the door only enough to speak to him. "I'm in bed, I took two pills," she said, "I have a splitting–"

"Aw, honey," Hugo pleaded. There was a delicious odor coming from her nightgown and robe. He leaned gently against the door.

"It's late," she said sharply. "You look awful. Go home and get some sleep." She clicked the door shut decisively. He heard her putting the chain in place.

On the way back down the dimly lit staircase from Sylvia's apartment, Hugo resolved always to have a small emergency piece of jewelry in his pocket for moments like this. Outside in the street, he looked up longingly at Sylvia's window. It was on the fourth floor and a crack of light, cozy and tantalizing, came through the curtains. Then, on the cold night air, he heard a laugh. It was warm and sensual in his left ear and he remembered, with a pang that took his breath away, the other occasions when he had heard that laugh. He staggered down the street under the pale lampposts, carrying his valise, feeling like Willy Loman coming toward the end of his career in *Death of a Salesman*. He had the impression that he was being followed slowly by a black car, but he was too distracted to pay it much attention.

When he got home, he took out a pencil and paper and noted down every piece of jewelry he had bought Sylvia that fall, with its price. The total came to $3468.30, tax included. He tore up the piece of paper and went to bed. He slept badly, hearing in his sleep the sound of faltering airplane engines mingled with a woman's laughter four stories above his head.

It rained during practice the next day and as he slid miserably around in the icy, tilted mud, Hugo wondered why he had ever chosen football as a profession. In the showers later, wearily scraping mud off his beard, Hugo became conscious that he was being stared at. Croker, the taxi-squad fullback, was in the next shower, soaping his hair and looking at

Hugo with a peculiar small smile on his face. Then, coming from Croker's direction, Hugo heard the long, low, disturbing laugh he had heard the night before. It was as though Croker had it on tape inside his head and was playing it over and over again, like a favorite piece of music. Croker, Hugo thought murderously, Croker! A taxi-squadder! Didn't even get to make the trips with the team. Off every Sunday, treacherously making every minute count while his teammates were fighting for their lives.

Hugo heard the laugh again over the sound of splashing water. The next time there was an intrasquad scrimmage, he was going to maim the son of a bitch.

He wanted to get away from the locker room fast, but when he was dressed and almost out the door, the trainer called to him.

"The coach wants to see you, Pleiss," the trainer said, "Pronto."

Hugo didn't like the "pronto." The trainer had a disagreeable habit of editorializing.

The coach was sitting with his back to the door, looking longingly up at the photograph of Jojo Baines. "Close the door, Pleiss," the coach said, without turning round.

Hugo closed the door.

"Sit down," the coach said, still with his back to Hugo, still staring at the photograph of what the coach had once said was the only 100 percent football player he had ever seen.

Hugo sat down.

The coach said. "I'm fining you two hundred and fifty dollars, Pleiss."

"Yes, sir," Hugo said.

The coach finally swung around. He loosened his collar. "Pleiss," he said, "what in the name of Knute Rockne are you up to?"

"I don't know, sir," Hugo said.

"What the hell are you doing staying up until dawn night after night?"

Staying up was not quite an accurate description of what Hugo had been doing, but he didn't challenge the coach's choice of words.

"Don't you know you've been followed, you dummy?" the coach bellowed.

The black car on the empty street. Hugo hung his head. He was disappointed in Sibyl. How could she be so suspicious? And where did she get the money to pay for detectives?

The coach's large hands twitched on the desk, "What are you, a sex maniac?"

"No, sir," Hugo said.

"Shut up!" the coach said.

"Yes, sir," said Hugo.

"And don't think it was me that put a tail on you," the coach said. "It's a lot worse than that. The tail came from the commissioner's office."

Hugo let out his breath, relieved. It wasn't Sibyl. How could he have misjudged her?

"I'll lay my cards on the table, Pleiss," the coach said. "The commissioner's office has been interested in you for a long time now. It's their job to keep this game clean, Pleiss, and I'm with them all the way on that, and make no mistake about it. If there's one thing I won't stand for on my club, it's a crooked ballplayer."

Hugo knew that there were at least 100 things that the coach had from time to time declared he wouldn't stand for on his club, but he didn't think it was the moment to refresh the coach's memory.

"Coach," Hugo began.

"Shut up! When a ballplayer as stupid as you suddenly begin to act as though he has a ouija board under his helmet and is in the middle of one goddamn play after another, naturally they begin to suspect something." The coach opened a drawer in his desk and took out a dark-blue folder from which he extracted several closely typewritten sheets of paper. He put on his glasses to read. "This is the report from the commissioner's office." He ran his eyes over some of the items and shook his head in wonder. "Modesty forbids me from reading to you the account of your sexual exploits, Pleiss," the coach said, "but I must remark that your ability even to trot out onto the field on Sunday after some of the weeks you've spent leaves me openmouthed in awe."

There was nothing Hugo could say to this, so he said nothing.

"So far, you've been lucky," the coach said. "The papers haven't latched onto it yet. But if one word of this comes out, I'll throw you to the wolves so fast you'll pull out of your cleats as you go through the door. Have you heard me?"

"I've heard you, Coach," Hugo said.

The coach fingered the papers on his desk and squinted through his bifocals. "In your sudden career as a lady's man, you also seem to have developed a sense of largess in the bestowal of jewelry. In one shop in this town alone, you have spent well over three thousand dollars in less than two months. At the same time, you buy an eight-room house with a swimming pool, you send your wife on expensive vacations all over the country, you invest fifty thousand dollars in a real-estate deal that is barely legal, you are known to be playing cards for high stakes with the biggest gamblers in the city and you rent a safe-deposit box and are observed stuffing unknown sums of cash into it every week. I know what your salary is, Pleiss. Is it unmannerly of me to inquire whether or not you have fallen upon some large outside source of income recently?"

The coach closed the folder and took off his glasses and sat back. Hugo would have liked to explain, but the words strangled in his throat. All the things that had seemed to him like the smiling gifts of fate now, in that cold blue folder, were arranged against him as the criminal profits of corruption. Hugo liked everyone to like him and he had become used to everyone wishing him well. Now the realization that there were men, the coach among them, who were ready to believe the worst of him and ruin him forever because of it, left him speechless. He waved his hands helplessly.

"Pleiss," the coach said, "I want you to answer one question, and if I ever find out you're lying. . . ." He stopped, significantly. He didn't add the usual coda, "I'll personally nail you by the hands to the locker-room wall." This omission terrified Hugo as he waited numbly for the question.

"Pleiss," the coach said, "are you getting information from gamblers?"

A wave of shame engulfed Hugo. He couldn't remember ever having felt so awful. He began to sob, all 235 pounds of him.

The coach looked at him, appalled. "Use your handkerchief, man," he said.

Hugo used his handkerchief. Damply he said, "Coach, I swear on the head of my mother, I never talked to a gambler in my life."

"I don't want the head of your mother," the coach snarled. But he seemed reassured. He waited for Hugo's sobs to subside. "All right. Get out of here. And be careful. Remember, you're being watched at all times."

Drying his eyes, Hugo dragged himself out of the office. The public-relations man, Brenatskis, was having a beer in the locker room with a small, gray-haired man with cigarette ash on his vest. Hugo recognized the man. It was Vincent Haley, the sports columnist. Hugo tried to get out without being seen. This was no day to be interviewed by a writer. But Brenatskis spotted him and called, "Hey, Hugo, come over here for a minute."

Flight would be damning. Hugo was sure that the whole world knew by now that he was a man under suspicion. So he tried to compose his face as he went over to the two men. He even managed an innocent, deceitful country boy's smile.

"Hello, Mr. Haley," he said.

"Glad to see you, Pleiss," said Haley. "How's your head?"

"Fine, fine," Hugo said hurriedly.

"You're having quite a season, Pleiss," Haley said. His voice was hoarse and whiskeyish and full of contempt for athletes, and his pale eyes were like laser beams. "Yeah, quite a season. I don't think I've ever seen a linebacker improve so much from one game to another."

Hugo began to sweat. "Some years you're lucky," he said. "Things fall into place." He waited, cowering inwardly, for the next doomful inquiry. But Haley merely asked him some routine questions, like who was the toughest man in the league going down the middle and what he thought about the comparative abilities of various passers he had played against. "Thanks, Pleiss," Haley said, "that's about all. Good luck with your head." He held out his hand and Hugo shook it gratefully, glad that in another moment he was going to be out of range of those bone-dissolving eyes. With his hand still in the writer's hand, Hugo heard the whiskeyish voice, but different, as though in some distant echo chamber, saying, in his left ear, "Look at him—two hundred and thirty-five pounds of bone and muscle, twenty-five years old, and he's back here raking in the dough, while my kid, nineteen years old, a hundred and thirty pounds dripping wet, is lying out in the mud and jungle in Vietnam, getting his head shot off. Who did *he* pay off?"

Haley gave Hugo's hand another shake. He even smiled, showing jagged, cynical, tar-stained teeth. "Nice talking to you, Pleiss," he said. "Keep up the good work."

"Thanks, Mr. Haley," Hugo said earnestly. "I'll try."

He went out of the stadium, not watching or caring where he was going, surrounded by enemies.

He kept hearing that rasping, disdainful "Who did *he* pay off?" over and over again as he walked blindly through the streets. At one moment, he stopped, on the verge of going back to the stadium and explaining to the writer about the 63 stitches in his knee and what the Army doctor had said about them. But Haley hadn't said anything aloud and it would be a plunge into the abyss if Hugo had to acknowledge that there were certain moments when he could read minds.

So he continued to walk toward the center of the city, trying to forget the coach and the gamblers, trying to forget Vincent Haley and Haley's 19-year-old son, weight 130 pounds, getting his head shot off in the jungle. Hugo didn't bother much about politics. He had enough to think about trying to keep from being killed every Sunday without worrying about disturbances 10,000 miles away in small Oriental countries. If the United States Army had felt that he wasn't fit for service that was their business.

But he couldn't help thinking about that kid out there, with the mortars bursting around him or stepping on poisoned bamboo stakes or being surrounded by grinning little yellow men with machine guns in their hands.

Hugo groaned in complicated agony. He had walked a long way and he was in the middle of the city, with the bustle of the business section all around him, but he couldn't walk away from that picture of Haley's kid lying torn apart under the burned trees whose names he would never know.

Slowly, he became aware that the activity around him was not just the ordinary traffic of the weekday city. He seemed to be in a parade of some kind and he realized, coming out of his private torment, that people were yelling loudly all around him. They also seemed to be carrying signs. He listened attentively now. "Hell, no, we won't go," they were yelling, and, "U.S. go home," and other short phrases of the same general import. And, reading the signs, he saw, BURN YOUR DRAFT CARDS and DOWN WITH AMERICAN FACISM. Interested, he looked carefully at the hundreds of people who were carrying him along with them. There were quite a few young men with long hair and beards, barefooted in sandals, and rather soiled young girls in blue jeans, carrying large flowers, all intermingled with determined-looking suburban matrons and middle-aged, grim-looking men with glasses, who might have been college professors. My, he thought, this is worse than a football crowd.

Then he was suddenly on the steps of the city hall and there were a lot of police, and one boy burned his draft card and a loud cheer went up from the crowd, and Hugo was sorry he didn't have his draft card on him, because he would have liked to burn it, too, as a sort of blind gesture of friendship to Haley's soldier son. He was too shy to shout anything, but he didn't try to get away from the city-hall steps; and when the police started to use their clubs, naturally, he was one of the first to get hit, because he stood head and shoulders above everybody else and was a target that no self-respecting cop would dream of missing.

Standing in front of the magistrate's bench a good many hours later, with a bloody bandage around his head, Hugo was grateful for Brenatskis' presence beside him, although he didn't know how Brenatskis had heard about the little run-in with the police so soon. But if Brenatskis hadn't come, Hugo would have had to spend the night in jail, where there was no bed large enough to accommodate him.

When his name was called, Hugo looked up at the magistrate. The American flag seemed to be waving vigorously on the wall behind the magistrate's head, although it was tacked to the plaster. Everything had a bad habit of waving after the policeman's club.

The magistrate had a small, scooping kind of face that made him look as though he would be useful in going into small holes to search for vermin. The magistrate looked at him with distaste. In his left ear, Hugo heard the magistrate's voice—"What are you, a fag or a Jew or something?" This seemed to Hugo like a clear invasion of his rights, and he raised his hand as if to say something, but Brenatskis knocked it down, just in time.

"Case dismissed," the magistrate said, sounding like a ferret who could talk. "Next."

A lady who looked like somebody's grandmother stepped up belligerently.

Five minutes later, Hugo was going down the night-court steps with Brenatskis. "Holy man," Brenatskis said, "what came over you? It's a lucky thing they got hold of me or you'd be all over the front page tomorrow. And it cost plenty, I don't mind telling you."

Bribery, too, Hugo recorded in his book of sorrows. Corruption of the press and the judiciary.

"And the coach—" Brenatskis waved his arm hopelessly, as though describing the state of the coach's psyche at this juncture were beyond the powers of literature. "He wants to see you. Right now."

"Can't he wait till morning?" Hugo wanted to go home and lie down. It had been an exhausting day.

"He can't wait until morning. He was very definite. The minute you got out, he said, and he didn't care what time it was."

"Doesn't he ever sleep?" Hugo asked forlornly.

"Not tonight, he's not sleeping," said Brenatskis. "He's waiting in his office."

A stalactite formed in the region of Hugo's liver as he thought of facing the coach, the two of them alone at midnight in naked confrontation in a stadium that could accommodate 60,000 people. "Don't you want to come along with me?" he asked Brenatskis.

"No." said Brenatskis. He got into his car and drove off. Hugo thought of moving immediately to Canada. But he hailed a cab and said "The stadium" to the driver. Perhaps there would be a fatal accident on the way.

There was one 40-watt bulb burning over the players' entrance and the shadows thrown by its feeble glare made it look as though a good part of the stadium had disappeared centuries before, like the ruins of a Roman amphitheater. Hugo wished it *were* the ruins of a Roman amphitheater as he pushed the door open. The night watchman, awakened from his doze on a chair tilted back against the wall, looked up at him. "They don't give a man no rest, none of them," Hugo heard the watchman think as he passed him. "Goddamned prima donnas. I hope they all break their fat necks."

"Evenin', Mr. Pleiss. Nice evenin'," the watchman said.

"Yeah," said Hugo. He walked through the shadows under the stands toward the locker room. The ghosts of hundreds of poor, aching, wounded, lame, contract-haunted football players seemed to accompany him, and the wind sighing through the gangways carried on it the echoes of a billion boos. Hugo wondered how he had ever thought a stadium was a place in which you enjoyed yourself.

His hand on the locker-room door, Hugo hesitated. He had never discussed politics with the coach, but he knew that the coach cried on the field every time the band played *The Star-Spangled Banner* and had refused to vote for Barry Goldwater because he thought Goldwater was a Communist.

Resolutely, Hugo pushed the door open and went into the deserted locker room. He passed his locker. His name was still on it. He didn't know whether it was a good or a bad sign.

The door to the coach's office was closed. After one last look around him at the locker room, Hugo rapped on it.

"Come in," the coach said.

Hugo opened the door and went in. The coach was dressed in a dark suit and his collar was closed and he had a black tie on, as though he were en route to a funeral. His face was ravaged by his vigil, his cheeks sunk, his eyes peered out of purplish caverns. He looked worse than Hugo had ever seen him, even worse than the time they lost 45 to 0 to a first-year expansion club.

"My boy," the coach said in a small, racked voice, "I am glad you came late. It has given me time to think, to take a proper perspective. An hour ago, I was ready to destroy you in righteous anger with my bare hands. But I am happy to say that the light of understanding has been vouchsafed me in the watches of this painful night." The coach was in one of his Biblical periods. "Luckily," he said, "after Brenatskis called me to tell me that he had managed to persuade the judge to dismiss the case against you for a hundred dollars—naturally, your pay will be docked—and that the story would be kept out of the papers for another hundred and fifty—

that will make two hundred and fifty, in all—I had time to consider. After all, the millions of small boys throughout America who look up to you and your fellows as the noblest expression of clean, aggressive American spirit, who model themselves with innocent hero worship after you and your teammates, are now going to be spared the shock and disillusionment of learning that a player of mine so far forgot himself as to be publicly associated with the enemies of his country—Are you following me, Pleiss?"

"Perfectly, Coach," said Hugo. He felt himself inching back toward the door. This new, gentle-voiced, understanding aspect of the coach was infinitely disturbing, like seeing water suddenly start running uphill, or watching the lights of a great city go out all at once.

"As I was saying, as long as no harm has been done to this multitude of undeveloped souls who are, in a manner of speaking, our responsibility, I can search within me for Christian forbearance." The coach came around the desk and put his hand on Hugo's shoulder. "Pleiss, you're not a bad boy—you're a stupid boy, but not a bad boy. It was my fault that you got involved in that sordid exhibition. Yes, my fault. You received a terrible blow on the head on Sunday—I should have spotted the symptoms. Instead of brutally making you do wind sprints and hit the dummy for two hours, I should have said, 'Hugo, my boy, go home and lie down and stay in bed for a week, until your poor head has recovered.' Yes, that's what I should have done. I ask your forgiveness, Hugo, for my shortness of vision."

"Sure, Coach," Hugo said.

"And now," said the coach, "before you go home to your loving wife and a good long rest, I want you to do one thing for me."

"Anything you say, Coach."

"I want you to join me in singing one verse—just one small verse—of *The Star-Spangled Banner.* Will you do that for me?"

"Yes, sir," Hugo said, sure that he was going to forget what came after "the rockets' red glare."

The coach gripped his shoulder hard, then said, "Once, two, three. . . ."

They sang *The Star-Spangled Banner* together. The coach was weeping after the first line.

When they had finished and the echoes had died down under the grandstand, the coach said, "Good. Now go home. I'd drive you home myself, but I'm working on some new plays I want to give the boys tomorrow. Don't you worry. You won't miss them. I'll send them along to you by messenger and you can glance at them when you feel like it. And don't worry about missing practice. When you feel ready, just drop around. God bless you, my boy." The coach patted Hugo a last time on the shoulder and turned to gaze at Jojo Baines, his eyes still wet from the anthem.

Hugo went out softly.

He stayed close to home all the rest of the week, living off canned goods and watching television. Nothing much could happen to him, he figured, in the privacy of his own apartment. But even there, he had his moments of distress.

He was sitting watching a quiz show for housewives at nine o'clock in the morning when he heard the key in the door and the cleaning woman, Mrs. Fitzgerald, came in. Mrs. Fitzgerald was a gray-haired lady who smelled of other people's dust. "I hope you're not feeling poorly, Mr. Pleiss," she said solicitously. "It's a beautiful day. It's a shame to spend it indoors."

"I'm going out later," Hugo lied.

Behind his back, he heard Mrs. Fitzgerald think, "Lazy, hulking slob. Never did an honest day's work in his life. Comes the revolution, they'll take care of the likes of him. He'll find himself with a pick in his hands, on the roads. I hope I live to see the day."

Hugo wondered if he shouldn't report Mrs. Fitzgerald to the FBI, but then decided against it. He certainly didn't want to get involved with *them*.

He listened to a speech by the President and was favorably impressed by the President's command of the situation, both at home and abroad. The President explained that although things at the moment did not seem 100 percent perfect, vigorous steps were being taken, at home and abroad, to eliminate poverty, ill health, misguided criticism by irresponsible demagogs, disturbances in the streets and the unfavorable balance of payments. Hugo was also pleased, as he touched the bump on his head caused by the policeman's club, when he heard the President explain how well the war was going and why we could expect the imminent collapse of the enemy. The President peered out of the television set, masterly, persuasive, confident, including all the citizens of the country in his friendly, fatherly smile. Then, while the President was silent for a moment before going on to other matters, Hugo heard the President's voice, though in quite a different tone, saying, "Ladies and gentlemen, if you really knew what was going on here, you'd *piss.*"

Hugo turned the television set off.

Then, the next day, the television set broke down, and as he watched the repairman fiddle with it, humming mournfully down in his chest somewhere, Hugo heard the television repairman think, "Stupid jerk. All he had to do was take a look and he'd see the only thing wrong is this loose wire. Slap it into the jack and turn a screw and the job's done." But when the television man turned around, he was shaking his head sadly. "I'm afraid you got trouble, mister," the television repairman said. "There's danger of implosion. I'll have to take the set with me. And there's the expense of a new tube."

"What's it going to cost?" Hugo asked.

"Thirty, thirty-five dollars, if we're lucky," said the television repairman.

Hugo let him take the set. Now he knew he was a moral coward, along with everything else.

He was cheered up, though, when his mother and father telephoned, collect, from Maine, to see how he was. They had a nice chat. "And how's my darling Sibyl?" Hugo's mother said. "Can I say hello to her?"

"She's not here," Hugo said. He explained about the trip to Florida with her parents.

"Fine people, fine people," Hugo's mother said. She had met Sibyl's parents once, at the wedding. "I do hope they're all enjoying themselves down South. Well, take care of yourself, Hooey. . . ." Hooey was a family pet name for him. "Don't let them hit you in the face with the ball." His mother's grasp of the game was fairly primitive. "And give my love to Sibyl when she gets home."

Hugo hung up. Then, very clearly, he heard his mother say to his father, 1000 miles away in northern Maine, "With her parents. I bet."

Hugo didn't answer the phone the rest of the week.

Sibyl arrived from Florida late Saturday afternoon. She looked beautiful as she got off the plane and she had a new fur coat that her father had bought her. Hugo had bought a hat to keep Sibyl from noticing the scalp wound inflicted by the policeman's club, at least at the airport, with people around. He had never owned a hat and he hoped Sibyl wouldn't notice this abrupt change in his style of dressing. She didn't notice it. And back in their apartment, she didn't notice the wound, although it was nearly four inches long and could be seen quite clearly through his hair, if you looked at all closely. She chattered gaily on about Florida, the beaches, the color of the water, the flamingos at the race track. Hugo told her how glad he was that she had had such a good time and admired her new coat.

Sibyl said she was tired from the trip and wanted to have a simple dinner at home and get to bed early. Hugo said he thought that was a good idea. He didn't want to see anybody he knew, or anybody he didn't know.

By nine o'clock, Sibyl was yawning and went in to get undressed. Hugo had had three bourbons to keep Sibyl from worrying about his seeming a bit distracted. He started to make up a bed on the living-room couch. From time to time during the week, he had remembered the sound of the low laugh from Sylvia's window and it had made the thought of sex distasteful to him. He had even noticed a certain deadness in his lower regions and he doubted whether he ever could make love to a woman again. "I bet," he thought, "I'm the first man in the history of the world to be castrated by a laugh."

Sibyl came out of the bedroom just as he was fluffing up a pillow. She was wearing a black nightgown that concealed nothing. "Sweetie," Sibyl said reproachfully.

"It's Saturday night," Hugo said, giving a final extra jab at the pillow.

"So?" You'd never guess that she was pregnant as she stood there at the doorway in her nightgown.

"Well, Saturday night, during the season," Hugo said. "I guess I've gotten into the rhythm, you might say, of sleeping alone."

"But there's no game tomorrow, Hugo." There was a tone of impatience in Sibyl's voice.

The logic was unassailable. "That's true," Hugo said. He followed Sibyl into the bedroom. If he was impotent, Sibyl might just as well find it out now as later.

It turned out that his fears were groundless. The three bourbons, perhaps. As they approached the climax of their lovemaking, Hugo was afraid Sibyl was going to have a heart attack, she was breathing so fast. Then, through the turbulence, he heard what she was thinking. "I should have bought that green dress at Bonwit's," Sibyl's thoughtful, calm voice echoed just below his eardrum. "I could do without the belt, though. And then I just might try cutting up that old mink hat of mine and using it for cuffs on that dingy old brown rag I got last Christmas. Maybe my wrists wouldn't look so skinny with fur around them."

Hugo finished his task and Sibyl said "Ah" happily and kissed him and went to sleep, snoring a little. Hugo stayed awake for a long time, occasionally glancing over at his wife's wrists and then staring at the ceiling and thinking about married life.

Sibyl was still asleep when he woke up. He didn't waken her. A church bell was ringing in the distance, inviting, uncomplicated and pure, promising peace to tormented souls. Hugo got out of bed and dressed swiftly but carefully and hurried to the comforts of religion. He sat in the rear, on the aisle, soothed by the organ and the prayers and the upright Sunday-morning atmosphere of belief and remittance from sin.

The sermon was on sex and violence in the modern world and Hugo appreciated it. After what he had gone through, a holy examination of those aspects of today's society was just what he needed.

The minister was a big red-faced man, forthright and vigorous. Violence actually got only a fleeting and rather cursory condemnation. The Supreme Court was admonished to mend its ways and to refrain from turning loose on a Christian society a horde of pornographers, rioters, dope addicts and other sinners because of the present atheistic conception of what the minister scornfully called civil rights, and that was about it.

But when it came to sex, the minister hit his stride. The church resounded to his denunciation of naked and leering girls on magazine stands, of sex education for children, of an unhealthy interest in birth control, of dating and premarital lasciviousness, of Swedish and French moving pictures, of mixed bathing in revealing swimsuits, of petting in parked cars, of all novels that had been written since 1910, of coeducational schools, of the new math, which, the minister explained, was a subtle means of undermining the moral code. Unchaperoned picnics were mentioned, miniskirts got a full two minutes, and even the wearing of wigs, designed to lure the all-too-susceptible American male into lewd and unsocial behavior, came in for its share of condemnation. The way the minister was going on, it would not have surprised some members of the congregation if he finished up with an edict against cross-pollination.

Hugo sat at the rear of the church, feeling chastened. It was a good feeling. That was what he had come to church for, and he almost said "Amen" aloud after one or two of the more spiritedly presented items on the minister's list.

Then, gradually, he became aware of a curious cooing voice in his left ear. "Ah, you, fourth seat to the left in the third row," he heard, "you with that little pink cleft just peeping out, why don't you come around late one weekday afternoon for a little spiritual consolation, ha-ha." Aghast, Hugo realized it was the minister's voice he was hearing.

Aloud, the minister was moving on to a rather unconvincing endorsement of the advantages of celibacy. "And you, the plump one in the fifth row, with the tight brassiere, Mrs. What's-your-name, looking down at your hymnbook as though you were planning to go into a nunnery," Hugo heard, mixed with loud advice on holy thoughts and vigorous, innocent exercise, "I can guess what you're up to when your husband goes out of town. I wouldn't mind if you had *my* private telephone number in your little black book, ha-ha."

Hugo sat rigid in his pew. This was going just a little bit too far.

The minister had swung into chastity. He wanted to end on a note of uplift. His head was tilted back, heavenward, but through slitted eyes, he scanned his Sunday-best parishioners. The minister had a vested interest in chastity and his voice took on a special solemn intonation as he described how particularly pleasing this virtue was in the eyes of God and His angels. "And little Miss Crewes, with your white gloves and white socks," Hugo heard, "ripening away like a tasty little Georgia persimmon, trembling on the luscious brink of womanhood, nobody has to tell me what you do behind the stands on the way home from school. The rectory is only two blocks from school baby, and it's on your way home. Just one timid knock on the door will suffice, ha-ha. There's always tea and little cakes for little girls like you at the rectory, ha-ha."

If Hugo hadn't been afraid of making a scene, he would have got up and run out of the church. Instead, he rapped himself sharply across the left ear. The consequent ringing kept him from hearing anything else. Several people turned around at the sound of the blow and stared disapprovingly at Hugo, but he didn't care. By the time the ringing stopped, the sermon was over and the minister was announcing the number of the hymn.

It was *Rock of Ages.* Hugo wasn't sure of the words, but he hummed, so as not to draw any more attention to himself.

The organ swelled, the sopranos, altos, tenors and bassos joined in, musical and faithful.

"Rock of Ages, cleft for me,
Let me hide myself in Thee.
Let the water and the blood,
From Thy side, a healing flood,
Be of sin the double cure . . ."

Hugo was swept along on the tide of sound. He didn't have much of an ear for music and the only things he played on the phonograph at home were some old 78-rpm Wayne King records that his mother had collected when she was a girl and had given him as a wedding present. But now the diapason of the organ, the pure flutelike tones of the women and young girls addressing God, the deep cello support of the men, combined to give him a feeling of lightness, of floating on spring airs, of being lost in endless fragrant gardens. Virgins caressed his forehead with petaled fingers, waters sang in mountain streams, strong men embraced him in everlasting brotherhood. By the time the congregation reached "Thou must save, and Thou alone," Hugo was out of his pew and writhing in ecstasy on the floor.

It was lucky he was in the last row, and on the aisle.

The hymn was never finished. It started to falter at "While I draw this fleeting breath," as people turned around to see what was happening and came to a final stop on "When I rise to worlds unknown." By that time, everybody in the church was standing up and looking at Hugo, trembling, sprawled on his back, in the middle of the aisle.

The last notes of the organ came to a halt discordantly, at a signal from the minister. Hugo lay still for an instant, conscious of 300 pairs of eyes on him. Then he leaped up and fled.

He rang the bell a long time, but it was only when he roared, "I know you're in there. Open up or I'll break it down," and began to buck at the door with his shoulder that it opened.

"What's going on here?" Miss Cattavi asked, blocking his way. "There are no visiting hours on Sunday."

"There will be this Sunday," Hugo said hoarsely. He pushed roughly past Miss Cattavi. She was all muscle. It was the first time he had ever been rude to a lady.

"He's in Romania," Miss Cattavi said, trying to hold on to him.

"I'll show him Romania," Hugo cried, throwing open doors and dragging Miss Cattavi after him like a junior high school guard.

Dr. Sebastian was behind the fourth door, in a room like a library, practicing dry-fly casting. He was wearing hip-length rubber boots.

"Oh, Mr. Pleiss," Dr. Sebastian said merrily, "you came back."

"I sure did come back," Hugo said. He had difficulty talking.

"You want your other ear done, I wager," said Dr. Sebastian, reeling in delicately.

Hugo grabbed Dr. Sebastian by the lapels and lifted him off the floor so that they were eye to eye. Dr. Sebastian weighted only 140 pounds, although he was quite fat. "I don't want the other ear done," Hugo said loudly.

"Should I call the police?" Miss Cattavi had her hand on the phone.

Hugo dropped Dr. Sebastian, who went down on one knee but made a creditable recovery. Hugo ripped the phone out of the wall. He had always been very careful of other people's property. It was something his father had taught him as a boy.

"Don't tell me," Dr. Sebastian said solicitously, "that the ear has filled up again. It's unusual, but not unheard of. Don't worry about it. The treatment is simple. A little twirl of an instrument and—"

Hugo grabbed the doctor's throat with one hand and kept Miss Cattavi off with the other. "Now, listen to this," Hugo said, "listen to what you did to me."

"Cawlsnhnd on my goddamn windpipe," the doctor said.

Hugo let him go.

"Now, my dear young man," Dr. Sebastian said, "if you'll only tell me what little thing is bothering you. . . ."

"Get her out of the room." Hugo gestured toward Miss Cattavi. The things he had to tell Dr. Sebastian could not be said in front of a woman.

"Miss Cattavi, please . . ." Dr. Sebastian said.

"Animal." Miss Cattavi said, but she went out of the room and closed the door behind her.

Moving out of range, Dr. Sebastian went behind a desk. He remained standing. "I could have sworn that your ear was in superb condition," he said.

"Superb!" Hugo was sorry he had taken his hand off the doctor's throat.

"Well, you can hear your team's signals now, can't you?" Dr. Sebastian said.

"If that's all I could hear," Hugo moaned.

"Ah." Dr. Sebastian brightened. "Your hearing is better then normal. I told you you had an extraordinary aural arrangement. It only took a little cutting, a bold clearing away of certain extraneous matter. . . . You must be having a very good season."

"I am having a season in hell," Hugo said, unconscious that he was now paying tribute to a French poet.

"I'm terribly confused," the doctor said petulantly. "I do better for you than you ever hoped for and what is my reward—you come in here and try to strangle me. I do think you owe me an explanation, Mr. Pleiss."

"I owe you a lot more than that," Hugo said. "Where did you learn your medicine—in the Congo?"

Dr. Sebastian drew himself to his full height. "Cornell Medical School," he said with quiet pride. "Now if you'll only tell me—"

"I'll tell you, all right," Hugo said. He paced up and down the room. It was an old house and the timbers creaked. The sound was like a thousand sea gulls in Hugo's ear.

"First," said Dr. Sebastian, "just what is it that you want me to do for you?"

"I want you to put my ear back the way it was when I came to you," Hugo said.

"You want to be deaf again?" the doctor asked incredulously.

"Exactly."

Dr. Sebastian shook his head. "My dear fellow," he said. "I can't do that. It's against all medical ethics. If it ever got out, I'd be barred forever from practicing medicine anyplace in the United States. A graduate of Cornell—"

"I don't care where you graduated from. You're going to do it."

"You're overwrought, Mr. Pleiss," the doctor said. He sat down at his desk and drew a piece of paper to him and took out a pen. "Now, if you'll only attempt, in a calm and orderly way, to describe the symptoms. . . ."

Hugo paced up and down some more, trying to be calm and orderly. Deep down, he still had a great respect for doctors. "It started," he began, "with hearing the other team's signals."

Dr. Sebastian nodded approvingly and jotted something down.

"In the huddle," Hugo said.

"What's a huddle?"

Hugo explained, as best he could, what a huddle was. "And it's fifteen yards away and they whisper and sixty thousand people are yelling at the top of their lungs all around you."

"I knew it was a successful operation," Dr. Sebastian said, beaming in self-appreciation, "but I had no idea it was *that* successful. It must be very helpful in your profession. Congratulations. It will make a most interesting paper for the next congress of —"

"Shut up," Hugo said. He then went on to describe how he began understanding what the signals meant. Dr. Sebastian's face got a little graver as he asked Hugo to kindly repeat what he had just said and to explain exactly what was the significance of "Brown right! Draw fifty-five . . . on two!" When he finally got it straight and noted that it was a secret code, different for each team, and that the codes were as jealously guarded from opposing teams as the crown jewels, he stopped jotting anything down. And when Hugo went on to the moment when he knew that the opposing quarterback was thinking, "No. . . . It won't work, they're overshifting on us," in just those words, Dr. Sebastian put his pen down altogether and a look of concern came into his eyes.

The description of the poker game only made the doctor shrug. "These days," he said, "we are just beginning to catch a glimmer of the powers of extrasensory perception, my dear fellow. Why, down at Duke University—"

"Keep quiet," Hugo said, and described, with a reminiscent thrill of terror, the radio breakdown in the cockpit of the airplane and hearing the conversation between the pilots.

"I'm sure that could be explained," the doctor said. "A freak electronic phenomenon that—"

Hugo cut in. "I want you to hear what happened to me with a girl," Hugo said. "There was nothing electronic about that."

Dr. Sebastian listened with interest as Hugo relived the experience with Sylvia. Dr. Sebastian licked his lips from time to time but said nothing. He clucked sympathetically, though, when Hugo described the laughter four stories up and Croker's replay in the shower.

Hugo didn't say anything about his conversations with the coach. There were certain things too painful to recall.

In a rush, Hugo let all the rest of it out—Vietnam, the clubbing by the policeman, the interior sneer of the magistrate, Mrs. Fitzgerald's dangerous radical leanings, the President's speech, the television repairman's chicanery, his mother's judgment of his wife.

Dr. Sebastian sat there without saying a word, shaking his head pity-ingly from time to time.

Hugo went on, without mercy for himself, about the green dress and the mink cuffs at a time when you'd bet for sure a woman would be thinking about other things. "Well," he demanded, "what've you got to say about that?"

"Unfortunately," Dr. Sebastian said, "I've never been married. A man my size." He shrugged regretfully. "But there are well-documented cases on record of loving couples who have spent long years together, who are very close together, who have a telepathic sympathy with each other's thoughts. . . ."

"Let me tell you what happened in church this morning," Hugo said desperately. The doctor's scientific ammunition was beginning to take its toll. The fearful thought occurred to him that he wasn't going to shake the doctor and that he was going to walk out of the door no different from the way he had entered.

"It is nice to hear that a big, famous, attractive young man like you still goes to church on Sunday morning," the doctor murmured.

"I've gone to my last church," Hugo said and gave him the gist of what he had heard the minister think while he was delivering his sermon on sex and violence.

The doctor smiled tolerantly. "The men of the cloth are just like us other poor mortals," he said. "It's very probable that it was merely the transference of your own desires and—"

"Then the last thing," Hugo said, knowing he *had* to convince the doc-tor somehow. He told him about writhing on the floor of the church, the spring breezes, the smell of flowers, the unutterable ecstasy during *Rock of Ages.*

The doctor made an amused little *moue.* "A common experience," he said, "for simple and susceptible religious natures. It does no harm."

"Three hundred people watching a two-hundred-and-thirty-five-pound man jerking around on the floor like a hooked tuna!" Hugo shouted. "That does no harm? And you yourself told me that if people could *really* hear, they'd writhe on the floor in ecstasy when they listened to Beethoven."

"Beethoven, yes," the doctor said. "But *Rock of Ages?*" He was a musical snob, Dr. Sebastian. "Tum-tum-tah-dee, tum-tum-dah," he sang contemptuously. Then he became professional. He leaned across the desk and patted Hugo's hand and spoke quietly. "My dear young man, I believe every word you say. You undoubtedly think you have gone through these experiences. The incidents on the playing field can easily be explained. You are highly trained in the intricacies of a certain game, you are coming into your full powers, your understanding of your profession leads you into certain instantaneous practical insights. Be grateful for them. I've already explained the cards, the minister, your wife. The passage with the lady you call Sylvia is a concretization of your sense of guilt, combined with a certain natural young man's sexual appetite. Everything else, I'm afraid, is hallucination. I suggest you see a psychiatrist. I have the name of a good man and I'll give him a call and—"

Hugo growled.

"What did you say?" the doctor asked.

Hugo growled again and went over to the window. The doctor followed him, worried now, and looked out the window. Fifty yards away, on the soft, leaf-covered lawn, a five-year-old boy in sneakers was crossing over toward the garageway of the next house.

The two men stood in silence for a moment.

The doctor sighed. "If you'll come into my operating room," he said.

When he left the doctor's house an hour later, Hugo had a small bandage behind his left ear, but he was happy. The left side of his head felt like a corked-up cider bottle.

Hugo didn't intercept another pass all the rest of the season. He was fooled by the simplest hand-offs and dashed to the left when the play went to the right, and he couldn't hear Johnny Smathers' shouts of warning as the other teams lined up. Johnny Smathers stopped talking to him after two games and moved in with another roommate on road trips. At the end of the season, Hugo's contract was not renewed. The official reason the coach gave to the newspapers was that Hugo's head injury had turned out to be so severe that he would be risking permanent disablement if he ever got hit again.

Dr. Sebastian charged him $500 for the operation and, what with the fine and making up the bribes to the magistrate and the newspapers, that took care of the $1000 raise the coach had promised him. But Hugo was glad to pay for it.

By January tenth, he was contentedly and monogamously selling insurance for his father-in-law, although he had to make sure to sit on the left side of prospects to be able to hear what they were saying.

P. G. Wodehouse is to golf stories what A. Conan Doyle is to mysteries. In this story, Wodehouse deftly displays his patented formula where the "Oldest Member" gives sage advice to a young player on the clubhouse porch. Romance blossoms with a generous dollop of humor in this masterful gem. Besides his dozens of golf stories, Wodehouse wrote plays and ninety-two books, including My Man Jeeves (1919), He Rather Enjoyed It (1924), and The Butler Did It (1957). Born and raised in Britain, Wodehouse spent much of his life in the United States, where he held dual citizenship.

P. G. Wodehouse

THE HEART OF A GOOF (1927)

IT WAS A MORNING WHEN all nature shouted "Fore!" The breeze, as it blew gently up from the valley, seemed to bring a message of hope and cheer, whispering of chip-shots holed and brassies landing squarely on the meat. The fairway, as yet unscarred by the irons of a hundred dubs, smiled greenly up at the azure sky; and the sun, peeping above the trees, looked like a giant golf-ball perfectly lofted by the mashie of some unseen god and about to drop dead by the pin of the eighteenth. It was the day of the opening of the course after the long winter, and a crowd of considerable dimensions had collected at the first tee. Plus fours gleamed in the sunshine, and the air was charged with happy anticipation.

In all that gay throng there was but one sad face. It belonged to the man who was waggling his driver over the new ball perched on its little hill of sand. This man seemed careworn, hopeless. He gazed down the fairway, shifted his feet, waggled, gazed down the fairway again, shifted the dogs once more, and waggled afresh. He waggled as Hamlet might have waggled, moodily, irresolutely. Then, at last, he swung, and, taking from his caddie the niblick which the intelligent lad had been holding in readiness from the moment when he had walked on to the tee, trudged wearily off to play his second.

The Oldest Member, who had been observing the scene with a benevolent eye from his favourite chair on the terrace, sighed.

"Poor Jenkinson," he said, "does not improve."

"No," agreed his companion, a young man with open features and a handicap of six. "And yet I happen to know that he has been taking lessons all the winter at one of those indoor places."

"Futile, quite futile," said the Sage with a shake of his snowy head. "There is no wizard living who could make that man go round in an average of sevens. I keep advising him to give up the game."

"You!" cried the young man, raising a shocked and startled face from the driver with which he was toying. "*You* told him to give up golf! Why I thought—"

"I understand and approve of your horror," said the Oldest Member, gently. "But you must bear in mind that Jenkinson's is not an ordinary case. You know and I know scores of men who have never broken a hundred and twenty in their lives, and yet contrive to be happy, useful members of society. However badly they may play, they are able to forget. But with Jenkinson it is different. He is not one of those who can take it or leave it alone. His only chance of happiness lies in complete abstinence. Jenkinson is a goof."

"A what?"

"A goof," repeated the Sage. "One of those unfortunate beings who have allowed this noblest of sports to get too great a grip upon them, who have permitted it to eat into their souls, like some malignant growth. The goof, you must understand, is not like you and me. He broods. He becomes morbid. His goofery unfits him for the battles of life. Jenkinson, for example, was once a man with a glowing future in the hay, corn, and feed business, but a constant stream of hooks, tops, and slices gradually made him so diffident and mistrustful of himself, that he let opportunity after opportunity slip, with the result that other, sterner, hay, corn, and feed merchants passed him in the race. Every time he had the chance to carry through some big deal in hay, or to execute some flashing *coup* in corn and feed, the fatal diffidence generated by a hundred rotten rounds would undo him. I understand his bankruptcy may be expected at any moment."

"My golly!" said the young man, deeply impressed. "I hope I never become a goof. Do you mean to say there is really no cure except giving up the game?"

The Oldest Member was silent for a while.

"It is curious that you should have asked that question," he said at last, "for only this morning I was thinking of the one case in my experience where a goof was enabled to overcome his deplorable malady. It was owing to a girl, of course. The longer I live, the more I come to see that most things are. But you will, no doubt, wish to hear the story from the beginning."

The young man rose with the startled haste of some wild creature, which, wandering through the undergrowth, perceives the trap in his path.

"I should love to," he mumbled, "only I shall be losing my place at the tee."

"The goof in question," said the Sage, attaching himself with quiet firmness to the youth's coat-button, "was a man of about your age, by name Ferdinand Dibble. I knew him well. In fact, it was to me—"

"Some other time, eh?"

"It was to me," proceeded the Sage, placidly, "that he came for sympathy in the great crisis of his life, and I am not ashamed to say that when he had finished laying bare his soul to me there were tears in my eyes. My heart bled for the boy."

"I bet it did. But—"

The Oldest Member pushed him gently back into his seat.

"Golf," he said, "is the Great Mystery. Like some capricious goddess—"

The young man, who had been exhibiting symptoms of feverishness, appeared to become resigned. He sighed softly.

"Did you ever read 'The Ancient Mariner'?" he said.

"Many years ago," said the Oldest Member. "Why do you ask?"

"Oh, I don't know," said the young man. "It just occurred to me."

Golf (resumed the Oldest Member) is the Great Mystery. Like some capricious goddess, it bestows its favours with what would appear an almost fat-headed lack of method and discrimination. On every side we see big two-fisted he-men floundering round in three figures, stopping every few minutes to let through little shrimps with knock-knees and hollow cheeks, who are tearing off snappy seventy-fours. Giants of finance have to accept a stroke per from their junior clerks. Men capable of governing empires fail to control a small, white ball, which presents no difficulties whatever to others with one ounce more brain than a cuckoo-clock. Mysterious, but there it is. There was no apparent reason why Ferdinand Dibble should not have been a competent golfer. He had strong wrists and a good eye. Nevertheless, the fact remains that he was a dub. And on a certain evening in June I realized that he was also a goof. I found it out quite suddenly as the result of a conversation which we had on this very terrace.

I was sitting here that evening thinking of this and that, when by the corner of the club-house I observed young Dibble in conversation with a girl in white. I could not see who she was, for her back was turned. Presently they parted and Ferdinand came slowly across to where I sat. His air was dejected. He had had the boots licked off him earlier in the afternoon by Jimmy Fothergill, and it was to this that I attributed his gloom. I was to find out in a few moments that I was partly but not entirely correct in this surmise. He took the next chair to mine, and for several minutes sat staring moodily down into the valley.

"I've just been talking to Barbara Medway," he said, suddenly breaking the silence.

"Indeed?" I said. "A delightful girl."

"She's going away for the summer to Marvis Bay."

"She will take the sunshine with her."

"You bet she will!" said Ferdinand Dibble, with extraordinary warmth, and there was another long silence.

Presently Ferdinand uttered a hollow groan. "I love her, dammit!" he muttered brokenly. "Oh golly, how I love her!"

I was not surprised at his making me the recipient of his confidences like this. Most of the young folk in the place brought their troubles to me sooner or later.

"And does she return your love?"

"I don't know. I haven't asked her."

"Why not? I should have thought the point not without its interest for you."

Ferdinand gnawed the handle of his putter distractedly.

"I haven't the nerve," he burst out at length. "I simply can't summon up the cold gall to ask a girl, least of all an angel like her, to marry me. You see, it's like this. Every time I work myself up to the point of having a dash at it, I go out and get trimmed by someone giving me a stroke a hole. Every time I feel I've mustered up enough pep to propose, I take on a bogey three. Every time I'm in good mid-season form for putting my fate to the test, to win or lose it all, something goes all blooey with my swing, and I slice into the rough at every tee. And then my self-confidence leaves me. I become nervous, tongue-tied, diffident. I wish to goodness I knew the man who invented this infernal game. I'd strangle him. But I suppose he's been dead for ages. Still, I could go and jump on his grave."

It was at this point that I understood all, and the heart within me sank like lead. The truth was out. Ferdinand Dibble was a goof.

"Come, come, my boy," I said, though feeling the uselessness of any words. "Master this weakness."

"I can't."

"Try!"

"I have tried."

He gnawed his putter again.

"She was asking me just now if I couldn't manage to come to Marvis Bay, too," he said.

"That surely is encouraging? It suggests that she is not entirely indifferent to your society."

"Yes, but what's the use? Do you know," a gleam coming into his eyes for a moment, "I have a feeling that if I could ever beat some really fairly good player—just once—I could bring the thing off." The gleam faded. "But what chance is there of that?"

It was a question which I did not care to answer. I merely patted his shoulder sympathetically, and after a little while he left me and walked away. I was still sitting there, thinking over his hard case, when Barbara Medway came out of the club-house.

She, too, seemed grave and preoccupied, as if there was something on her mind. She took the chair which Ferdinand had vacated, and sighed wearily.

"Have you ever felt," she asked, "that you would like to bang a man on the head with something hard and heavy? With knobs on?"

I said I had sometimes experienced such a desire, and asked if she had any particular man in mind. She seemed to hesitate for a moment before replying, then, apparently, made up her mind to confide in me. My advanced years carry with them certain pleasant compensations, one of which is that nice girls often confide in me. I frequently find myself enrolled as a father-confessor on the most intimate matters by beautiful creatures from whom many a younger man would give his eye-teeth to get a friendly word. Besides, I had known Barbara since she was a child. Frequently—though not recently—I had given her her evening bath. These things form a bond.

"Why are men such chumps?" she exclaimed.

"You still have not told me who it is that has caused these harsh words. Do I know him?"

"Of course you do. You've just been talking to him."

"Ferdinand Dibble? But why should you wish to bang Ferdinand Dibble on the head with something hard and heavy with knobs on?"

"Because he's such a goop."

"You mean a goof?" I queried, wondering how she could have penetrated the unhappy man's secret.

"No, a goop. A goop is a man who's in love with a girl and won't tell her so. I am certain as I am of anything that Ferdinand is fond of me."

"Your instinct is unerring. He has just been confiding in me on that very point."

"Well, why doesn't he confide in *me,* the poor fish?" cried the high-spirited girl, petulantly flicking a pebble at a passing grasshopper. "I can't be expected to fling myself into his arms unless he gives some sort of a hint that he's ready to catch me."

"Would it help if I were to repeat to him the substance of this conversation of ours?"

"If you breathe a word of it, I'll never speak to you again," she cried. "I'd rather die an awful death than have any man think I wanted him so badly that I had to send relays of messengers begging him to marry me."

I saw her point.

"Then I fear," I said, gravely, "that there is nothing to be done. One can only wait and hope. It may be that in the years to come Ferdinand Dibble will acquire a nice lissom, wristy swing, with the head kept rigid and the right leg firmly braced and—"

"What are you talking about?"

"I was toying with the hope that some sunny day Ferdinand Dibble would cease to be a goof."

"You mean a goop?"

"No, a goof. A goof is a man who—" And I went on to explain the peculiar psychological difficulties which lay in the way of any declaration of affection on Ferdinand's part.

"But I have never heard of anything so ridiculous in my life," she ejaculated. "Do you mean to say that he is waiting till he is good at golf before he asks me to marry him?"

"It is not quite so simple as that," I said sadly. "Many bad golfers marry, feeling that a wife's loving solicitude may improve their game. But they are rugged, thick-skinned men, not sensitive and introspective, like

Ferdinand. Ferdinand has allowed himself to become morbid. It is one of the chief merits of golf that non-success at the game induces a certain amount of decent humility, which keeps a man from pluming himself too much on any petty triumphs he may achieve in other walks of life; but in all things there is a happy mean, and with Ferdinand this humility has gone too far. It has taken all the spirit out of him. He feels crushed and worthless. He is grateful to caddies when they accept a tip instead of drawing themselves up to their full height and flinging the money in his face."

"Then do you mean that things have got to go on like this for-ever?"

I thought for a moment.

"It is a pity," I said, "that you could not have induced Ferdinand to go to Marvis Bay for a month or two."

"Why?"

"Because it seems to me, thinking the thing over, that it is just possible that Marvis Bay might cure him. At the hotel there he would find collected a mob of golfers—I used the term in its broadest sense, to embrace the paralytics and the men who play left-handed—whom even he would be able to beat. When I was last at Marvis Bay, the hotel links were a sort of Sargasso Sea into which had drifted all the pitiful flotsam and jetsam of golf. I have seen things done on that course at which I shuddered and averted my eyes—and I am not a weak man. If Ferdinand can polish up his game so as to go round in a fairly steady hundred and five, I fancy there is hope. But I understand he is not going to Marvis Bay."

"Oh yes he is," said the girl.

"Indeed! He did not tell me that when we were talking just now."

"He didn't know it then. He will when I have had a few words with him."

And she walked with firm steps back into the club-house.

It has been well said that there are many kinds of golf, beginning at the top with the golf of professionals and the best amateurs and working down through the golf of ossified men to that of Scotch University professors. Until recently this last was looked upon as the lowest possible depth; but nowadays, with the growing popularity of summer hotels, we are able to add a brand still lower, the golf you find at places like Marvis Bay.

To Ferdinand Dibble, coming from a club where the standard of play was rather unusually high, Marvis Bay was a revelation, and for some days after his arrival there he went about dazed, like a man who cannot believe it is really true. To go out on the links at this summer resort was like entering a new world. The hotel was full of stout, middle-aged men, who, after a misspent youth devoted to making money, had taken to a game at which real proficiency can only be acquired by those who start playing in their cradles and keep their weight down. Out on the course each morning you could see representatives of every nightmare style that was ever invented. There was the man who seemed to be attempting to deceive his ball and lull it into a false security by looking away from it and then making a lightning slash in the apparent hope of catching it off its guard. There was the man who wielded his mid-iron like one killing snakes. There was the man who addressed his ball as if he were stroking a cat, the man who drove as if he were cracking a whip, the man who brooded over each shot like one whose heart is bowed down by bad news from home, and the man who scooped with his mashie as if he were ladling soup. By the end of the first week Ferdinand Dibble was the acknowledged champion of the place. He had gone through the entire menagerie like a bullet through a cream puff.

First, scarcely daring to consider the possibility of success, he had taken on the man who tried to catch his ball off its guard and had beaten him five up and four to play. Then, with gradually growing confidence, he tackled in turn the Cat-Stroker, the Whip-Cracker, the Heart Bowed Down, and the Soup-Scooper, and walked all over their faces with spiked shoes. And as these were the leading local amateurs, whose prowess the octogenarians and the men who went round in bathchairs vainly strove to emulate, Ferdinand Dibble was faced on the eighth morning of his visit by the startling fact that he had no more worlds to conquer. He was monarch of all he surveyed, and, what is more, had won his first trophy, the prize in the great medal-play handicap tournament, in which he had nosed in ahead of the field by two strokes, edging out his nearest rival, a venerable old gentleman, by means of a brilliant and unexpected four on the last hole. The prize was a handsome pewter mug, about the size of the old oaken bucket, and Ferdinand used to go to his room immediately after dinner to croon over it like a mother over her child.

You are wondering, no doubt, why, in these circumstances, he did not take advantage of the new spirit of exhilarated pride which had replaced his old humility and instantly propose to Barbara Medway. I will tell you. He did not propose to Barbara because Barbara was not there. At the last moment she had been detained at home to nurse a sick parent and had been compelled to postpone her visit for a couple of weeks. He could, no doubt, have proposed in one of the daily letters which he wrote to her, but somehow, once he started writing, he found that he used up so much space describing his best shots on the links that day that it was difficult to squeeze in a declaration of undying passion. After all, you can hardly cram that sort of thing into a postscript.

He decided, therefore, to wait till she arrived, and meanwhile pursued his conquering course. The longer he waited, the better, in one way, for every morning and afternoon that passed was adding new layers to his self-esteem. Day by day in every way he grew chestier and chestier.

Meanwhile, however, dark clouds were gathering. Sullen mutterings were to be heard in corners of the hotel lounge, and the spirit of revolt was abroad. For Ferdinand's chestiness had not escaped the notice of his defeated rivals. There is nobody so chesty as a normally unchesty man who suddenly becomes chesty, and I am sorry to say that the chestiness which had come to Ferdinand was the aggressive type of chestiness which breeds enemies. He had developed a habit of holding the game up in order to give his opponent advice. The Whip-Cracker had not forgiven, and never would forgive, his well-meant but galling criticism of his backswing. The Scooper, who had always scooped since the day when, at the age of sixty-four, he subscribed to the Correspondence Course which was to teach him golf in twelve lessons by mail, resented being told by a snip of a boy that the mashie-stroke should be a smooth, unhurried swing. The Snake-Killer—But I need not weary you with a detailed recital of these men's grievances; it is enough to say that they all had it in for Ferdinand, and one night, after dinner, they met in the lounge to decide what was to be done about it.

A nasty spirit was displayed by all.

"A mere lad telling me how to use my mashie!" growled the Scooper. "Smooth and unhurried my left eyeball! I get it up, don't I? Well, what more do you want?"

"I keep telling him that mine is the old, full St. Andrew's swing," muttered the Whip-Cracker, between set teeth, "but he won't listen to me."

"He ought to be taken down a peg or two," hissed the Snake-Killer. It is not easy to hiss a sentence without a single "s" in it, and the fact that he succeeded in doing so shows to what a pitch of emotion the man had been goaded by Ferdinand's maddening air of superiority.

"Yes, but what can we do?" queried an octogenarian, when this last remark had been passed on to him down his ear-trumpet.

"That's the trouble," sighed the Scooper. "What can we do?" And there was a sorrowful shaking of heads.

"I know!" exclaimed the Cat-Stroker, who had not hitherto spoken. He was a lawyer, and a man of subtle and sinister mind. "I have it! There's a boy in my office—young Parsloe—who could beat this man Dibble hollow. I'll wire him to come down here and we'll spring him on this fellow and knock some of the conceit out of him."

There was a chorus of approval.

"But are you sure he can beat him?" asked the Snake-Killer, anxiously. "It would never do to make a mistake."

"Of course I'm sure," said the Cat-Stroker. "George Parsloe once went round in ninety-four."

"Many changes there have been since ninety-four," said the octogenarian, nodding sagely. "Ah, many, many changes. None of these motorcars then, tearing about and killing—"

Kindly hands led him off to have an egg-and-milk, and the remaining conspirators returned to the point at issue with bent brows.

"Ninety-four?" said the Scooper, incredulously. "Do you mean counting every stroke?"

"Counting every stroke."

"Not conceding himself any putts?"

"Not one."

"Wire him to come at once," said the meeting with one voice.

That night the Cat-Stroker approached Ferdinand, smooth, subtle, lawyer-like.

"Oh, Dibble," he said, "just the man I wanted to see. Dibble, there's a young friend of mine coming down here who goes in for golf a little. George Parsloe is his name. I was wondering if you could spare time to give him a game. He is just a novice, you know."

"I shall be delighted to play a round with him," said Ferdinand kindly.

"He might pick up a pointer or two from watching you." said the Cat-Stroker.

"True, true," said Ferdinand.

"Then I'll introduce you when he shows up."

"Delighted," said Ferdinand.

He was in excellent humour that night, for he had had a letter from Barbara saying that she was arriving on the next day but one.

It was Ferdinand's healthy custom of a morning to get up in good time and take a dip in the sea before breakfast. On the morning of the day of Barbara's arrival, he arose, as usual, donned his flannels, took a good look at the cup, and started out. It was a fine, fresh morning, and he glowed both externally and internally. As he crossed the links, for the nearest route to the water was through the fairway of the seventh, he was whistling happily and rehearsing in his mind the opening sentences of his proposal. For it was his firm resolve that night after dinner to ask Barbara to marry him. He was proceeding over the smooth turf without a care in the world, when there was a sudden cry of "Fore!" and the next moment a golf-ball, missing him by inches, sailed up the fairway and came to a rest fifty yards from where he stood. He looked up and observed a figure coming towards him from the tee.

The distance from the tee was fully a hundred and thirty yards. Add fifty to that, and you have a hundred and eighty yards. No such drive had been made on the Marvis Bay links since their foundation, and such is the generous spirit of the true golfer that Ferdinand's first emotion, after the not inexcusable spasm of panic caused by the hum of the ball past his ear, was one of cordial admiration. By some kindly miracle, he supposed, one of his hotel acquaintances had been permitted for once in his life to time a drive right. It was only when the other man came up that there began to steal over him a sickening apprehension. The faces of all those who hewed divots on the hotel course were familiar to him, and the fact that this fellow was a stranger seemed to point with dreadful certainty to his being the man he had agreed to play.

"Sorry," said the man. He was a tall, strikingly handsome youth, with brown eyes and a dark moustache.

"Oh, that's all right," said Ferdinand. "Er—do you always drive like that?"

"Well, I generally get a bit longer ball, but I'm off my drive this morning. It's lucky I came out and got this practice. I'm playing a match tomorrow with a fellow named Dibble, who's a local champion, or something."

"Me," said Ferdinand, humbly.

"Eh? Oh, you?" Mr. Parsloe eyed him appraisingly. "Well, may the best man win."

As this was precisely what Ferdinand was afraid was going to happen, he nodded in a sickly manner and tottered off to his bathe. The magic had gone out of the morning. The sun still shone, but in a silly, feeble way; and a cold and depressing wind had sprung up. For Ferdinand's inferiority complex, which had seemed cured for ever, was back again, doing business at the old stand.

How sad it is in this life that the moment to which we have looked forward with the most glowing anticipation so often turns out on arrival, flat, cold, and disappointing. For ten days Barbara Medway had been living for that meeting with Ferdinand, when, getting out of the train, she would see him popping about on the horizon with the lovelight sparkling in his eyes and words of devotion trembling on his lips. The poor girl never doubted for an instant that he would unleash his pent-up emotions inside the first five minutes, and her only worry was lest he should give an embarrassing publicity to the sacred scene by falling on his knees on the station platform.

"Well, here I am at last," she cried gaily.

"Hullo!" said Ferdinand, with a twisted smile.

The girl looked at him, chilled. How could she know that his peculiar manner was due entirely to the severe attack of cold feet resultant upon his meeting with George Parsloe that morning? The interpretation which she placed upon it was that he was not glad to see her. If he had behaved like this before, she would, of course, have put it down to ingrowing goofery, but now she had his written statements to prove that for the last ten days his golf had been one long series of triumphs.

"I got your letters," she said, persevering bravely.

"I thought you would," said Ferdinand, absently.

"You seem to have been doing wonders."

"Yes."

There was a silence.

"Have a nice journey?" said Ferdinand.

"Very," said Barbara.

She spoke coldly, for she was madder than a wet hen. She saw it all now. In the ten days since they had parted, his love, she realized, had waned. Some other girl, met in the romantic surroundings of this picturesque resort, had supplanted her in his affections. She knew how quickly Cupid gets off the mark at a summer hotel, and for an instant she blamed herself for ever having been so ivory-skulled as to let him come to this place alone. Then regret was swallowed up in wrath, and she became so glacial that Ferdinand, who had been on the point of telling her the secret of his gloom, retired into his shell and conversation during the drive to the hotel never soared above a certain level. Ferdinand said the sunshine was nice and Barbara said yes, it was nice, and Ferdinand said it looked pretty on the water, and Barbara said yes, it did look pretty on the water, and Ferdinand said he hoped it was not going to rain, and Barbara said yes, it would be a pity if it rained. And then there was another lengthy silence.

"How is my uncle?" said Barbara at last.

I omitted to mention that the individual to whom I have referred as the Cat-Stroker was Barbara's mother's brother, and her host at Marvis Bay.

"Your uncle?"

"His name is Tuttle. Have you met him?"

"Oh yes. I've seen a good deal of him. He has got a friend staying with him," said Ferdinand, his mind returning to the matter nearest his heart. "A fellow named Parsloe."

"Oh, is George Parsloe here? How jolly!"

"Do you know him?" barked Ferdinand, hollowly. He would not have supposed that anything could have added to his existing depression, but he was conscious now of having slipped a few rungs farther down the ladder of gloom. There had been a horribly joyful ring in her voice. Ah, well, he reflected morosely, how like life it all was! We never know what the morrow may bring forth. We strike a good patch and are beginning to think pretty well of ourselves, and along comes a George Parsloe.

"Of course I do," said Barbara. "Why, there he is."

The cab had drawn up at the door of the hotel, and on the porch George Parsloe was airing his graceful person. To Ferdinand's fevered eye he looked like a Greek god, and his inferiority complex began to exhibit symptoms of elephantiasis. How could he compete at love or golf with a fellow who looked as if he had stepped out of the movies and considered himself off his drive when he did a hundred and eighty yards?

"Geor-gee!" cried Barbara blithely. "Hullo, George!"

"Why, hullo, Barbara!"

They fell into pleasant conversation, while Ferdinand hung miserably about in the offing. And presently, feeling that his society was not essential to their happiness, he slunk away.

George Parsloe dined at the Cat-Stroker's table that night, and it was with George Parsloe that Barbara roamed in the moonlight after dinner. Ferdinand, after a profitless hour at the billiard-table, went early to his room. But not even the rays of the moon, glinting on his cup, could soothe the fever in his soul. He practised putting sombrely into his tooth-glass for a while; then, going to bed, fell at last into a troubled sleep.

Barbara slept late the next morning and breakfasted in her room. Coming down towards noon, she found a strange emptiness in the hotel. It was her experience of summer hotels that a really fine day like this one was the cue for half the inhabitants to collect in the lounge, shut all the windows, and talk about conditions in the jute industry. To her surprise, though the sun was streaming down from a cloudless sky, the only occupant of the lounge was the octogenarian with the ear-trumpet. She observed that he was chuckling to himself in a senile manner.

"Good morning," she said, politely, for she had made his acquaintance on the previous evening.

"Hey?" said the octogenarian, suspending his chuckling and getting his trumpet into position.

"I said 'Good morning!' " roared Barbara into the receiver.

"Hey?"

"Good morning!"

"Ah! Yes, it's a very fine morning, a very fine morning. If it wasn't for missing my bun and a glass of milk at twelve sharp," said the octogenarian, "I'd be down on the links. That's where I'd be, down on the links. If it wasn't for missing my bun and glass of milk."

This refreshment arriving at this moment, he dismantled the radio outfit and began to restore his tissues.

"Watching the match," he explained, pausing for a moment in his bun-mangling.

"What match?"

The octogenarian sipped his milk.

"What match?" repeated Barbara.

"Hey?"

"What match?"

The octogenarian began to chuckle again and nearly swallowed a crumb the wrong way.

"Take some of the conceit out of him," he gurgled.

"Out of who?" asked Barbara, knowing perfectly well that she should have said "whom".

"Yes," said the octogenarian.

"Who is conceited?"

"Ah! This young fellow, Dibble. Very conceited. It saw it in his eye from the first, but nobody would listen to me. Mark my words, I said, that boy needs taking down a peg or two. Well, he's going to be this morning. Your uncle wired to young Parsloe to come down, and he's arranged a match between them. Dibble–" Here the octogenarian choked again and had to rinse himself out with milk, "Dibble doesn't know that Parsloe once went round in ninety-four!"

"What?"

Everything seemed to go black to Barbara. Through a murky mist she appeared to be looking at a negro octogenarian, sipping ink. Then her eyes cleared, and she found herself clutching for support at the back of a chair. She understood now. She realized why Ferdinand had been so distrait, and her whole heart went out to him in a spasm of maternal pity. How she had wronged him!

"Take some of the conceit out of him," the octogenarian was mumbling, and Barbara felt a sudden sharp loathing for the old man. For two pins she could have dropped a beetle in his milk. Then the need for action roused her. What action? She did not know. All she knew was that she must act.

"Oh!" she cried.

"Hey?" said the octogenarian bringing his trumpet to the ready.

But Barbara had gone.

It was not far to the links, and Barbara covered the distance on flying feet. She reached the club-house, but the course was empty except for the Scooper, who was preparing to drive off the first tee. In spite of the fact that something seemed to tell her subconsciously that this was one of the sights she ought not to miss, the girl did not wait to watch. Assuming that the match had started soon after breakfast, it must by now have reached one of the holes on the second nine. She ran down the hill, looking to left and right, and was presently aware of a group of spectators clustered about a green in the distance. As she hurried towards them they moved away, and now she could see Ferdinand advancing to the next tee. With a thrill that shook her whole body she realized that he had the honour. So he must have won one hole, at any rate. Then she saw her uncle.

"How are they?" she gasped.

Mr. Tuttle seemed moody. It was apparent that things were not going altogether to his liking.

"All square at the fifteenth," he replied, gloomily.

"All square!"

"Yes. Young Parsloe," said Mr. Tuttle with a sour look in the direction of that lissom athlete, "doesn't seem to be able to do a thing right on the greens. He has been putting like a sheep with the botts."

From the foregoing remark of Mr. Tuttle you will, no doubt, have gleaned at least a clue to the mystery of how Ferdinand Dibble had managed to hold his long-driving adversary up to the fifteenth green, but for all that you will probably consider that some further explanation of this amazing state of affairs is required. Mere bad putting on the part of George Parsloe is not, you feel, sufficient to cover the matter entirely. You are right. There was another very important factor in the situation—to wit, that by some extraordinary chance Ferdinand Dibble had started right off from the first tee, playing the game of a lifetime. Never had he made such drives, never chipped his chips so shrewdly.

About Ferdinand's driving there was as a general thing a fatal stiffness and overcaution which prevented success. And with his chip-shots he rarely achieved accuracy owing to his habit of rearing his head like the lion of the jungle just before the club struck the ball. But today he had been swinging with a careless freedom, and his chips had been true and clean. The thing had puzzled him all the way round. It had not elated him, for, owing to Barbara's aloofness and the way in which she had gambolled about George Parsloe, like a young lamb in the springtime, he was in too deep a state of dejection to be elated by anything. And now, suddenly, in a flash of clear vision, he perceived the reason why he had been playing so well today. It was just because he was not elated. It was simply because he was so profoundly miserable.

That was what Ferdinand told himself as he stepped off the sixteenth, after hitting a screamer down the centre of the fairway, and I am convinced that he was right. Like so many indifferent golfers, Ferdinand Dibble had always made the game hard for himself by thinking too much. He was a deep student of the works of the masters, and whenever he prepared to play a stroke he had a complete mental list of all the mistakes which it was possible to make. He would remember how Taylor had warned against dipping the right shoulder, how Vardon had inveighed against any movement of the head; he would recall how Ray had mentioned the tendency to snatch back the club, how Braid had spoken sadly of those who sin against their better selves by stiffening the muscles and heaving.

The consequence was that when, after waggling in a frozen manner till mere shame urged him to take some definite course of action, he eventually swung, he invariably proceeded to dip his right shoulder, stiffen his muscles, heave, and snatch back the club, at the same time raising his head sharply as in the illustrated plate ("Some Frequent Faults of Beginners—No. 3—Lifting the Bean") facing page thirty-four of James Braid's *Golf Without Tears*. Today, he had been so preoccupied with his broken heart that he had made his shots absently, almost carelessly, with the result that at least one in every three had been a lallapaloosa.

Meanwhile, George Parsloe had driven off and the match was progressing. George was feeling a little flustered by now. He had been given to understand that this bird Dibble was a hundred-at-his-best man, and all the way round the fellow had been reeling off fives in great profusion, and had once actually got a four. True, there had been an occasional six, and even a seven, but that did not alter the main fact that the man was making the dickens of a game of it. With the haughty spirit of one who had once done a ninety-four, George Parsloe had anticipated being at least three up at the turn. Instead of which he had been two down, and had had to fight strenuously to draw level.

Nevertheless, he drove steadily and well, and would certainly have won the hole had it not been for his weak and sinful putting. The same defect caused him to halve the seventeenth, after being on in two, with Ferdinand wandering in the desert and only reaching the green with his fourth. Then, however, Ferdinand holed out from a distance of seven yards, getting a five; which George's three putts just enabled him to equal.

Barbara had watched the proceedings with a beating heart. At first she had looked on from afar; but now, drawn as by a magnet, she approached the tee. Ferdinand was driving off. She held her breath. Ferdinand held his breath. And all around one could see their respective breaths being held by George Parsloe, Mr. Tuttle, and the enthralled crowd of spectators. It was a moment of the acutest tension, and it was broken by the crack of Ferdinand's driver as it met the ball and sent it hopping along the ground for a mere thirty yards. At this supreme crisis in the match Ferdinand Dibble had topped.

George Parsloe teed up his ball. There was a smile of quiet satisfaction on his face. He snuggled the driver in his hands, and gave it a preliminary swish. This, felt George Parsloe, was where the happy ending came. He could drive as he had never driven before. He would so drive that it would take his opponent at least three shots to catch up with him. He drew back his club with infinite caution, poised it at the top of the swing–

"I always wonder–" said a clear, girlish voice, ripping the silence like the explosion of a bomb.

George Parsloe started. His club wobbled. It descended. The ball trickled into the long grass in front of the tee. There was a grim pause.

"You were saying, Miss Medway–" said George Parsloe, in a small, flat voice.

"Oh, I'm so sorry," said Barbara. "I'm afraid put you off."

"A little, perhaps. Possibly the merest trifle. But you were saying you wondered about something. Can I be of any assistance?"

"I was only saying," said Barbara, "that I always wonder why tees are called tees."

George Parsloe swallowed once or twice. He also blinked a little feverishly. His eyes had a dazed, staring expression.

"I am afraid I cannot tell you off-hand," he said, "but I will make a point of consulting some good encyclopaedia at the earliest opportunity."

"Thank you so much."

"Not at all. It will be a pleasure. In case you were thinking of inquiring at the moment when I am putting why greens are called greens, may I venture the suggestion now that it is because they are green?"

And, so saying, George Parsloe stalked to his ball and found it nestling in the heart of some shrub of which, not being a botanist, I cannot give you the name. It was a close-knit, adhesive shrub, and it twined its tentacles so lovingly around George Parsloe's niblick that he missed his first shot altogether. His second made the ball rock, and his third dislodged it. Playing a full swing with his brassie and being by now a mere cauldron of seething emotions he missed his fourth. His fifth came to within a few inches of Ferdinand's drive, and he picked it up and hurled it from him into the rough as if it had been something venomous.

"Your hole and match," said George Parsloe, thinly.

Ferdinand Dibble sat beside the glittering ocean. He had hurried off the course with swift strides the moment George Parsloe had spoken those bitter words. He wanted to be alone with his thoughts.

They were mixed thoughts. For a moment joy at the reflection that he had won a tough match came irresistibly to the surface, only to sink again as he remembered that life, whatever its triumphs, could hold nothing for him now that Barbara Medway loved another.

"Mr. Dibble!"

He looked up. She was standing at his side. He gulped and rose to his feet.

"Yes?"

There was a silence.

"Doesn't the sun look pretty on the water?" said Barbara.

Ferdinand groaned. This was too much.

"Leave me," he said, hollowly. "Go back to your Parsloe, the man with whom you walked in the moonlight beside this same water."

"Well, why shouldn't I walk with Mr. Parsloe in the moonlight beside this same water?" demanded Barbara, with spirit.

"I never said," replied Ferdinand, for he was a fair man at heart, "that you shouldn't walk with Mr. Parsloe beside this same water. I simply said you did walk with Mr. Parsloe beside this same water."

"I've a perfect right to walk with Mr. Parsloe beside this same water," persisted Barbara. "He and I are old friends."

Ferdinand groaned again.

"Exactly! There you are! As I suspected. Old friends. Played together as children, and what not, I shouldn't wonder."

"No, we didn't. I've only known him five years. But he is engaged to be married to my greatest chum, so that draws us together."

Ferdinand uttered a strangled cry.

"Parsloe engaged to be married!"

"Yes. The wedding takes place next month."

"But look here." Ferdinand's forehead was wrinkled. He was thinking tensely. "Look here," said Ferdinand, a close reasoner. "If Parsloe's engaged to your greatest chum, he can't be in love with *you*."

"No."

"And you aren't in love with him?"

"No."

"Then, by gad," said Ferdinand, "how about it?"

"What do you mean?"

"Will you marry me?" bellowed Ferdinand.

"Yes."

"You will?"

"Of course I will."

"Darling!" cried Ferdinand.

"There is only one thing that bothers me a bit," said Ferdinand, thoughtfully, as they strolled together over the scented meadows, while in the trees above them a thousand birds trilled Mendelssohn's Wedding March.

"What is that?"

"Well, I'll tell you," said Ferdinand. "The fact is, I've just discovered the great secret of golf. You can't play a really hot game unless you're so miserable that you don't worry over your shots. Take the case of a chip-shot, for instance. If you're really wretched, you don't care where the ball is going and so you don't raise your head to see. Grief automatically prevents pressing and over-swinging. Look at the top-notchers. Have you ever seen a happy pro?"

"No. I don't think I have."

"Well, then!"

"But pros are all Scotchmen," argued Barbara.

"It doesn't matter. I'm sure I'm right. And the darned thing is that I'm going to be so infernally happy all the rest of my life that I suppose my handicap will go up to thirty or something."

Barbara squeezed his hand lovingly.

"Don't worry, precious," she said, soothingly. "It will be all right. I am a woman, and, once we are married, I shall be able to think of at least a hundred ways of snootering you to such an extent that you'll be fit to win the Amateur Championship."

"You will?" said Ferdinand, anxiously. "You're sure?"

"Quite, quite sure, dearest," said Barbara.

"My angel!" said Ferdinand.

He folded her in his arms, using the interlocking grip.

A man decides to return home the day after a party by swimming the lengths of the swimming pools on his way. Given that he has to traverse a distance of eight miles, this is something of an athletic feat. The story is one of John Cheever's famous tales of American suburbia, originally from the New Yorker *and later included in the bestselling book* The Stories of John Cheever *(1979). "The Swimmer" was made into a movie in 1968 starring Burt Lancaster. Cheever (1912–1982) also wrote distinguished novels such as* The Wapshot Chronicle *(1957),* The Wapshot Scandal *(1964), and* Falconer *(1977).*

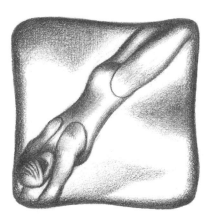

John Cheever

THE SWIMMER (1964)

I T WAS ONE OF THOSE midsummer Sundays when everyone sits around saying, "I *drank* too much last night." You might have heard it whispered by the parishioners leaving church, heard it from the lips of the priest himself, struggling with his cassock in the *vestiarium*, heard it from the golf links and the tennis courts, heard it from the wildlife preserve where the leader of the Audubon group was suffering from a terrible hangover. "I *drank* too much," said Donald Westerhazy. "We all *drank* too much," said Lucinda Merrill. "It must have been the wine," said Helen Westerhazy. "I *drank* too much of that claret."

This was at the edge of the Westerhazys' pool. The pool, fed by an artesian well with a high iron content, was a pale shade of green. It was fine day. In the west there was a massive stand of cumulus cloud so like a city seen from a distance—from the bow of an approaching ship—that it might have had a name. Lisbon. Hackensack. The sun was hot. Neddy Merrill sat by the green water, one hand in it, one around a glass of gin. He was a slender man—he seemed to have the especial slenderness of youth—and while he was far from young he had slid down his banister that morning and given the bronze backside of Aphrodite on the hall table a smack, as he jogged toward the smell of coffee in his dining room. He might have been compared to a summer's day, particularly the last hours of one, and while he lacked a tennis racket or a sail bag the impression was definitely one of youth, sport, and clement weather. He had been swimming and now he was breathing deeply, stertorously as if he could gulp into his lungs the components of that moment, the heat of the sun, the intenseness of his pleasure. It all seemed to flow into his chest. His own house stood in Bullet Park, eight miles to the south, where his four beautiful daughters would have had their lunch and might be playing tennis. Then it occurred to him that by taking a dogleg to the southwest he could reach his home by water.

His life was not confining and the delight he took in this observation could not be explained by its suggestion of escape. He seemed to see, with a cartographer's eye, that string of swimming pools, that quasi-subterranean stream that curved across the county. He had made a discovery, a contribution to modern geography; he would name the stream Lucinda after his wife. He was not a practical joker nor was he a fool but he was determinedly original and had a vague and modest idea of himself as a legendary figure. The day was beautiful and it seemed to him that a long swim might enlarge and celebrate its beauty.

He took off a sweater that was hung over his shoulders and dove in. He had an inexplicable contempt for men who did not hurl themselves into pools. He swam a choppy crawl, breathing either with every stroke or every fourth stroke and counting somewhere well in the back of his mind the one-two one-two of a flutter kick. It was not a serviceable stroke for long distances but the domestication of swimming had saddled the sport with some customs and in his part of the world a crawl was customary. To be embraced and sustained by the light green water was less a pleasure, it seemed, than the resumption of a natural condition, and he would have liked to swim without trunks, but this was not possible considering his project. He hoisted himself up on the far curb—he never used the ladder—and started across the lawn. When Lucinda asked where he was going he said he was going to swim home.

The only maps and charts he had to go by were remembered or imaginary but these were clear enough. First there were the Grahams, the Hammers, the Lears, the Howlands, and the Crosscups. He would cross Ditmar Street to the Bunkers and come, after a short portage, to the Levys, the Welchers, and the public pool in Lancaster. Then there were the Hallorans, the Sachses, the Biswangers, Shirley Adams, the Gilmartins, and the Clydes. The day was lovely, and that he lived in a world so generously supplied with water seemed like a clemency, a beneficence. His heart was high and he ran across the grass. Making his way home by an uncommon route gave him the feeling that he was a pilgrim, an explorer, a man with a destiny, and he knew that he would find friends all along the way; friends would line the banks of the Lucinda River.

He went through a hedge that separated the Westerhazys' land from the Grahams', walked under some flowering apple trees, passed the shed that housed their pump and filter, and came out at the Grahams' pool. "Why, Neddy," Mrs. Graham said, "what a marvelous surprise. I've been trying to get you on the phone all morning. Here, let me get you a drink." He saw then, like any explorer, that the hospitable customs and traditions of the natives would have to be handled with diplomacy if he was ever going to reach his destination. He did not want to mystify or seem rude to the Grahams nor did he have the time to linger there. He swam the length of their pool and joined them in the sun and was rescued, a few minutes later, by the arrival of two carloads of friends from Connecticut. During the uproarious reunions he was able to slip away. He went down by the front of the Grahams' house, stepped over a thorny hedge, and crossed a vacant lot to the Hammers'. Mrs. Hammer, looking up from her roses, saw him swim by although she wasn't quite sure who it was. The Lears heard him splashing past the open windows of their living room. The Howlands and the Crosscups were away. After leaving the Howlands' he crossed Ditmar Street and started for the Bunkers', where he could hear, even at that distance, the noise of a party.

The water refracted the sound of voices and laughter and seemed to suspend it in midair. The Bunkers' pool was on a rise and he climbed some stairs to a terrace where twenty-five or thirty men and women were drinking. The only person in the water was Rusty Towers, who floated there on a rubber raft. Oh, how bonny and lush were the banks of the Lucinda River! Prosperous men and women gathered by the sapphire-colored waters while caterer's men in white coats passed them cold gin. Overhead a red de Haviland trainer was circling around and around and around in the sky with something like the glee of a child in a swing. Ned felt a passing affection for the scene, a tenderness for the gathering, as if it was something he might touch. In the distance he heard thunder. As soon as Enid Bunker saw him she began to scream: "Oh, look who's here! What a marvelous surprise! When Lucinda said that you couldn't come I thought I'd *die.*" She made her way to him through the crowd, and when they had finished kissing she led him to the bar, a progress that was slowed by the fact that he stopped to kiss eight or ten other women and shake the hands of as many men. A smiling bartender he had seen at a hundred parties gave him a gin and tonic and he stood by the bar for a moment, anxious not to get stuck in any conversation that would delay his voyage. When he seemed about to be surrounded he dove in and swam close to the side to avoid colliding with Rusty's raft. At the far end of the pool he bypassed the Tomlinsons with a broad smile and jogged up the garden path. The gravel cut his feet but this was the only unpleasantness. The party was confined to the pool, and as he went toward the house he heard the brilliant, watery sound of voices fade, heard the noise of a radio from the Bunkers' kitchen, where someone was listening to a ball game. Sunday afternoon. He made his way through the parked cars and down the grassy border of their driveway to Alewives Lane. He did not want to be seen on the road in his bathing trunks but there was no traffic and he made the short distance to the Levys' driveway, marked with a PRIVATE PROPERTY sign and a green tube for *The New York Times*. All the doors and windows of the big house were open but there were no signs of life; not even a dog barked. He went around the side of the house to the pool and saw that the Levys had only recently left. Glasses and bottles and dishes of nuts were on a table at the deep end, where there was a bathhouse or gazebo, hung with Japanese lanterns. After swimming the pool he got himself a glass and poured a drink. It was his fourth or fifth drink and he had swum nearly half the length of the Lucinda River. He felt tired, clean, and pleased at that moment to be alone; pleased with everything.

It would storm. The stand of cumulus cloud—that city—had risen and darkened, and while he sat there he heard the percussiveness of thunder again. The de Haviland trainer was still circling overhead and it seemed to Ned that he could almost hear the pilot laugh with pleasure in the afternoon; but when there was another peal of thunder he took off for home. A train whistle blew and he wondered what time it had gotten to be. Four? Five? He thought of the provincial station at that hour, where a waiter, his tuxedo concealed by a raincoat, a dwarf with some flowers wrapped in newspaper, and a woman who had been crying would be waiting for the local. It was suddenly growing dark; it was that moment when the pin-headed birds seem to organize their song into some acute and knowledgeable recognition of the storm's approach. Then there was a fine noise of rushing water from the crown of an oak at his back, as if a spigot there had been turned. Then the noise of fountains came from the crowns of all the tall trees. Why did he love storms, what was the meaning of his excitement when the door sprang open and the rain wind fled rudely up the stairs, why had the simple task of shutting the windows of an old house seemed fitting and urgent, why did the first watery notes of a storm wind have for him the unmistakable sound of good news, cheer, glad tidings? Then there was an explosion, a smell of cordite, and rain lashed the Japanese lanterns that Mrs. Levy had bought in Kyoto the year before last, or was it the year before that?

He stayed in the Levys' gazebo until the storm had passed. The rain had cooled the air and he shivered. The force of the wind had stripped a maple of its red and yellow leaves and scattered them over the grass and the water. Since it was midsummer the tree must be blighted, and yet he felt a peculiar sadness at this sign of autumn. He braced his shoulders, emptied his glass, and started for the Welchers' pool. This meant crossing the Lindleys' riding ring and he was surprised to find it overgrown with grass and all the jumps dismantled. He wondered if the Lindleys had sold their horses or gone away for the summer and put them out to board. He seemed to remember having heard something about the Lindleys and their horses but the memory was unclear. On he went, barefoot through the wet grass, to the Welchers', where he found their pool was dry.

This breach in his chain of water disappointed him absurdly, and he felt like some explorer who seeks a torrential headwater and finds a dead stream. He was disappointed and mystified. It was common enough to go away for the summer but no one ever drained his pool. The Welchers had definitely gone away. The pool furniture was folded, stacked, and covered with a tarpaulin. The bathhouse was locked. All the windows of the house were shut, and when he went around to the driveway in front he saw a FOR SALE sign nailed to a tree. When had he last heard from the Welchers—when, that is, had he and Lucinda last regretted an invitation to dine with them? It seemed only a week or so ago. Was his memory failing or had he so disciplined it in the repression of unpleasant facts that he had damaged his sense of the truth? Then in the distance he heard the sound of a tennis game. This cheered him, cleared away all his apprehensions and let him regard the overcast sky and the cold air with indifference. This was the day that Neddy Merrill swam across the county. That was the day! He started off then for his most difficult portage.

Had you gone for a Sunday afternoon ride that day you might have seen him, close to naked, standing on the shoulders of Route 424, waiting for a chance to cross. You might have wondered if he was the victim of foul play, had his car broken down, or was he merely a fool. Standing barefoot in the deposits of the highway—beer cans, rags, and blowout patches—exposed to all kinds of ridicule, he seemed pitiful. He had known when he started that this was a part of his journey—it had been on his maps—but confronted with the lines of traffic, worming through the summery light, he found himself unprepared. He was laughed at, jeered at, a beer can was thrown at him, and he had no dignity or humor to bring to the situation. He could have gone back, back to the Westerhazys', where Lucinda would still be sitting in the sun. He had signed nothing, vowed nothing, pledged nothing, not even to himself. Why, believing as he did, that all human obduracy was susceptible to common sense, was he unable to turn back? Why was he determined to complete his journey even if it meant putting his life in danger? At what point had this prank, this joke, this piece of horseplay become serious? He could not go back, he could not even re-call with any clearness the green water at the Westerhazys', the sense of in-haling the day's components, the friendly and relaxed voices saying that they had *drunk* too much. In the space of an hour, more or less, he had covered a distance that made his return impossible.

An old man, tooling down the highway at fifteen miles an hour, let him get to the middle of the road, where there was a grass divider. Here he was exposed to the ridicule of the northbound traffic, but after ten or fifteen minutes he was able to cross. From here he had only a short walk to the Recreation Center at the edge of the village of Lancaster, where there were some handball courts and a public pool.

The effect of the water on voices, the illusion of brilliance and suspense, was the same here as it had been at the Bunkers' but the sounds here were louder, harsher, and more shrill, and as soon as he entered the crowded en-closure he was confronted with regimentation. "ALL SWIMMERS MUST TAKE A SHOWER BEFORE USING THE POOL. ALL SWIMMERS MUST USE THE FOOTBATH. ALL SWIMMERS MUST WEAR THEIR IDENTIFICATION DISKS." He took a shower, washed his feet in a cloudy and bitter solution, and made his way to the edge of the water. It stank of chlorine and looked to him like a sink. A pair of lifeguards in a pair of towers blew police whistles at what seemed to be regular intervals and abused the swimmers through a public address system. Neddy remembered the sapphire water at the Bunkers' with longing and thought that he might contaminate himself—damage his own prosperousness and charm—by swimming in this murk, but he reminded himself that he was an explorer, a pilgrim, and that this was merely a stagnant bend in the Lucinda River. He dove, scowling with distaste, into the chlorine and had to swim with his head above water to avoid collisions, but even so he was bumped into, splashed, and jostled. When he got to the shallow end both lifeguards were shouting at him: "Hey, you, you without the identification disk, get outa the water." He did, but they had no way of pursuing him and he went through the reek of sun-tan oil and chlorine out through the hurricane fence and passed the hand-ball courts. By crossing the road he entered the wooded part of the Halloran estate. The woods were not cleared and the footing was treacher-ous and difficult until he reached the lawn and the clipped beech hedge that encircled their pool.

The Hallorans were friends, an elderly couple of enormous wealth who seemed to bask in the suspicion that they might be Communists. They were zealous reformers but they were not Communists, and yet when they were accused, as they sometimes were, of subversion, it seemed to gratify and excite them. Their beech hedge was yellow and he guessed this had been blighted like the Levys' maple. He called hullo, hullo, to warn the Hallorans of his approach, to palliate his invasion of their privacy. The Hallorans, for reasons that had never been explained to him, did not wear bathing suits. No explanations were in order, really. Their nakedness was a detail in their uncompromising zeal for reform and he stepped politely out of his trunks before he went through the opening in the hedge.

Mrs. Halloran, a stout woman with white hair and a serene face, was reading the *Times*. Mr. Halloran was taking beech leaves out of the water with a scoop. They seemed not surprised or displeased to see him. Their pool was perhaps the oldest in the country, a fieldstone rectangle, fed by a brook. It had no filter or pump and its waters were the opaque gold of the stream.

"I'm swimming across the county," Ned said.

"Why, I didn't know one could," exclaimed Mrs. Halloran.

"Well, I've made it from the Westerhazys'," Ned said. "That must be about four miles."

He left his trunks at the deep end, walked to the shallow end, and swam this stretch. As he was pulling himself out of the water he heard

Mrs. Halloran say, "We've been *terribly* sorry to hear about all your misfortunes, Neddy."

"My misfortunes?" Ned asked. "I don't know what you mean."

"Why, we heard that you'd sold the house and that your poor children . . ."

"I don't recall having sold the house," Ned said, "and the girls are at home."

"Yes," Mrs. Halloran sighed. "Yes . . ." Her voice filled the air with an unseasonable melancholy and Ned spoke briskly. "Thank you for the swim."

"Well, have a nice trip," said Mrs. Halloran.

Beyond the hedge he pulled on his trunks and fastened them. They were loose and he wondered if, during the space of an afternoon, he could have lost some weight. He was cold and he was tired and the naked Hallorans and their dark water had depressed him. The swim was too much for his strength but how could he have guessed this, sliding down the banister that morning and sitting in the Westerhazys' sun? His arms were lame. His legs felt rubbery and ached at the joints. The worst of it was the cold in his bones and the feeling that he might never be warm again. Leaves were falling down around him and he smelled wood smoke on the wind. Who would be burning wood at this time of year?

He needed a drink. Whiskey would warm him, pick him up, carry him through the last of his journey, refresh his feeling that it was original and valorous to swim across the county. Channel swimmers took brandy. He needed a stimulant. He crossed the lawn in front of the Hallorans' house and went down a little path to where they had built a house for their only daughter, Helen, and her husband, Eric Sachs. The Sachses' pool was small and he found Helen and her husband there.

"Oh, *Neddy*," Helen said. "Did you lunch at Mother's?"

"Not *really*," Ned said. "I *did* stop to see your parents." This seemed to be explanation enough. "I'm terribly sorry to break in on you like this but I've taken a chill and I wonder if you'd give me a drink."

"Why, I'd *love* to," Helen said, "but there hasn't been anything in this house to drink since Eric's operation. That was three years ago."

Was he losing his memory, had his gift for concealing painful facts let him forget that he had sold his house, that his children were in trouble, and that his friend had been ill? His eyes slipped from Eric's face to his abdomen, where he saw three pale, sutured scars, two of them at least a foot long. Gone was his navel, and what, Neddy thought, would the roving hand, bed-checking one's gifts at 3 A.M., make of a belly with no navel, no link to birth, this breach in the succession?

"I'm sure you can get a drink at the Biswangers'," Helen said. "They're having an enormous do. You can hear it from here. Listen!"

She raised her head and from across the road, the lawns, the gardens, the woods, the fields, he heard again the brilliant noise of voices over water. "Well, I'll get wet," he said, still feeling that he had no freedom of choice about his means of travel. He dove into the Sachses' cold water and, gasping, close to drowning, made his way from one end of the pool to the other. "Lucinda and I want *terribly* to see you," he said over his shoulder, his face set toward the Biswangers'. "We're sorry it's been so long and we'll call you *very* soon."

He crossed some fields to the Biswangers' and the sounds of revelry there. They would be honored to give him a drink, they would be happy to give him a drink. The Biswangers invited him and Lucinda for dinner four times a year, six weeks in advance. They were always rebuffed and yet they continued to send out their invitations, unwilling to comprehend the rigid and undemocratic realities of their society. They were the sort of people who discussed the price of things at cocktails, exchanged market tips during dinner, and after dinner told dirty stories to mixed company. They did not belong to Neddy's set—they were not even on Lucinda's Christmas-card list. He went toward their pool with feelings of indifference, charity, and some unease, since it seemed to be getting dark and these were the longest days of the year. The party when he joined it was noisy and large. Grace Biswanger was the kind of hostess who asked the optometrist, the veterinarian, the real-estate dealer, and the dentist. No one was swimming and the twilight, reflected on the water of the pool, had a wintry gleam. There was a bar and he started for this. When Grace Biswanger saw him she came toward him, not affectionately as he had every right to expect, but bellicosely.

"Why, this party has everything," she said loudly, "including a gate crasher."

She could not deal him a social blow—there was no question about this and he did not flinch. "As a gate crasher," he asked politely, "do I rate a drink?"

"Suit yourself," she said. "You don't seem to pay much attention to invitations."

She turned her back on him and joined some guests, and he went to the bar and ordered a whiskey. The bartender served him but he served him rudely. His was a world in which the caterers' men kept the social score, and to be rebuffed by a part-time barkeep meant that he had suffered some loss of social esteem. Or perhaps the man was new and uninformed. Then he heard Grace at his back say: "They went for broke overnight—nothing but income—and he showed up drunk one Sunday and asked us to loan him five thousand dollars. . . ." She was always talking about money. It was worse than eating your peas off a knife. He dove into the pool, swam its length and went away.

The next pool on his list, the last but two, belonged to his old mistress, Shirley Adams. If he had suffered any injuries at the Biswangers' they would be cured here. Love—sexual roughhouse in fact—was the supreme elixir, the pain killer, the brightly colored pill that would put the spring back into his step, the joy of life in his heart. They had had an affair last week, last month, last year. He couldn't remember. It was he who had broken it off, his was the upper hand, and he stepped through the gate of the wall that surrounded her pool with nothing so considered as self-confidence. It seemed in a way to be his pool, as the lover, particularly the illicit lover, enjoys the possessions of his mistress with an authority unknown to holy matrimony. She was there, her hair the color of brass, but her figure, at the edge of the lighted, cerulean water, excited in him no profound memories. It had been, he thought, a lighthearted affair, although she had wept when he broke it off. She seemed confused to see him and he wondered if she was still wounded. Would she, God forbid, weep again?

"What do you want?" she asked.

"I'm swimming across the county."

"Good Christ. Will you ever grow up?"

"What's the matter?"

"If you've come here for money," she said, "I won't give you another cent."

"You could give me a drink."

"I could but I won't. I'm not alone."

"Well, I'm on my way."

He dove in and swam the pool, but when he tried to haul himself up onto the curb he found that the strength in his arms and shoulders had gone, and he paddled to the ladder and climbed out. Looking over his shoulder he saw, in the lighted bathhouse, a young man. Going out onto the dark lawn he smelled chrysanthemums or marigolds—some stubborn autumnal fragrance—on the night air, strong as gas. Looking overhead he saw that the stars had come out, but why should he seem to see Andromeda, Cepheus, and Cassiopeia? What had become of the constellations of midsummer? He began to cry.

It was probably the first time in his adult life that he had ever cried, certainly the first time in his life that he had ever felt so miserable, cold, tired, and bewildered. He could not understand the rudeness of the caterers' barkeep or the rudeness of a mistress who had come to him on her knees and showered his trousers with tears. He had swum too long, he had been immersed too long, and his nose and his throat were sore from the water. What he needed then was a drink, some company, and some clean, dry clothes, and while he could have cut directly across the road to his home he went on to the Gilmartins' pool. Here, for the first time in his life, he did not dive but went down the steps into the icy water and swam a hobbled sidestroke that he might have learned as a youth. He staggered with fatigue on his way to the Clydes' and paddled the length of their pool, stopping again and again with his hand on the curb to rest. He climbed up the ladder and wondered if he had the strength to get home. He had done what he wanted, he had swum the county, but he was so stupefied with exhaustion that his triumph seemed vague. Stooped, holding on to the gateposts for support, he turned up the driveway of his own house.

The place was dark. Was it so late that they had all gone to bed? Had Lucinda stayed at the Westerhazys' for supper? Had the girls joined her there or gone someplace else? Hadn't they agreed, as they usually did on Sunday, to regret all their invitations and stay at home? He tried the garage doors to see what cars were in but the doors were locked and rust came off the handles onto his hands. Going toward the house, he saw that the force of the thunderstorm had knocked one of the rain gutters loose. It hung down over the front door like an umbrella rib, but it could be fixed in the morning. The house was locked, and he thought that the stupid cook or the stupid maid must have locked the place up until he remembered that it had been sometime since they had employed a maid or a cook. He shouted, pounded on the door, tried to force it with his shoulder, and then, looking in at the windows, saw that the place was empty.

Skulduggery is afoot at the old ballpark as Ellery Queen solves a World Series mystery. This felicitous marriage of baseball and detective story stretches plausibility, but that's part of the fun. Ellery Queen is the pseudonym of cousins Frederic Dannay and Manfred B. Lee. It is also the name of their famous detective, who has appeared in more than thirty novels and seventy short stories. Ellery Queen has won seven Edgar Awards and the coveted Grand Master Award from the Mystery Writers of America. Dannay and Lee also founded and edited Ellery Queen's Mystery Magazine, *which continues to be published.*

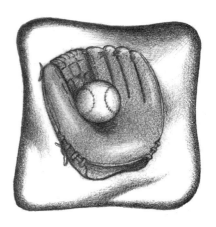

Ellery Queen

MAN BITES DOG (1940)

ANYONE OBSERVING THE tigerish pacings, the gnawings of lip, the contortions of brow, and the fierce melancholy which characterized the conduct of Mr. Ellery Queen, the noted sleuth, during those early October days in Hollywood, would have said reverently that the great man's intellect was once more locked in titanic struggles with the forces of evil.

"Paula," Mr. Queen said to Paula Paris, "I am going mad."

"I hope," said Miss Paris tenderly, "it's love."

Mr. Queen paced, swathed in yards of thought. Queenly Miss Paris observed him with melting eyes. When he had first encountered her,

Miss Paris had been in the grip of a morbid psychology. She had been in deathly terror of crowds. "Crowd phobia," the doctors called it. Mr. Queen had cured her by the curious method of making love to her. And now she was infected by the cure.

"Is it?" asked Miss Paris, her heart in her eyes.

"Eh?" said Mr. Queen. "What? Oh, no. I mean—it's the World Series." He looked savage. "Don't you realize what's happening? The New York Giants and the New York Yankees are waging mortal combat to determine the baseball championship of the world, and I'm three thousand miles away!"

"Oh," said Miss Paris. Then she said cleverly: "You poor darling."

"Never missed a New York series before," wailed Mr. Queen. "Driving me cuckoo. And what a battle! Greatest series ever played. Moore and DiMaggio have done miracles in the outfield. Giants have pulled a triple play. Goofy Gomez struck out fourteen men to win the first game. Hubbell's pitched a one-hit shutout. And today Dickey came up in the ninth inning with the bases loaded, two out, and the Yanks three runs behind, and slammed a homer over the right-field stands!"

"Is that good?" asked Miss Paris.

"Good!" howled Mr. Queen. "It *merely* sent the series into a seventh game."

"Poor darling," said Miss Paris again, and she picked up her telephone. When she set it down she said: "Weather's threatening in the East. Tomorrow the New York Weather Bureau expects heavy rains."

Mr. Queen stared wildly. "You mean—"

"I mean that you're taking tonight's plane for the East. And you'll see your beloved seventh game day after tomorrow."

"Paula, you're a genius!" Then Mr. Queen's face fell. "But the studio, tickets . . . *Bigre!* I'll tell the studio I'm down with elephantiasis, and I'll wire Dad to snare a box. With his pull at City Hall, he ought to—Paula, I don't know what I'd do . . ."

"You might," suggested Miss Paris, "kiss me . . . good-by."

Mr. Queen did so, absently. Then he started. "Not at all! You're coming with me!"

"That's what I had in mind," said Miss Paris contentedly.

And so Wednesday found Miss Paris and Mr. Queen at the Polo Grounds, ensconced in a field box behind the Yankees dugout.

Mr. Queen glowed, he reveled, he was radiant. While Inspector Queen, with the suspiciousness of all fathers, engaged Paula in exploratory conversation, Ellery filled his lap and Paula's with peanut hulls, consumed frankfurters and soda pop immoderately, made hypercritical comments on the appearance of the various athletes, derided the Yankees, extolled the Giants, evolved complicated fifty-cent bets with Detective-Sergeant Velie, of the Inspector's staff, and leaped to his feet screaming with fifty thousand other maniacs as the news came that Carl Hubbell, the beloved Meal Ticket of the Giants, would oppose Señor El Goofy Gomez, the ace of the Yankee staff, on the mound.

"Will the Yanks murder that apple today!" predicted the Sergeant, who was an incurable Yankee worshiper. "And will Goofy mow 'em down!"

"Four bits," said Mr. Queen coldly, "say the Yanks don't score three earned runs off Carl."

"It's a pleasure!"

"I'll take a piece of that, Sergeant," chuckled a handsome man to the front of them, in a rail seat. "Hi, Inspector. Swell day for it, eh?"

"Jimmy Connor!" exclaimed Inspector Queen. "The old Song-and-Dance Man in person. Say, Jimmy, you never met my son Ellery, did you? Excuse me. Miss Paris, this is the famous Jimmy Connor, God's gift to Broadway."

"Glad to meet you, Miss Paris," smiled the Song-and-Dance man, sniffing at his orchidaceous lapel. "Read your *Seeing Stars* column, every day. Meet Judy Starr."

Miss Paris smiled, and the woman beside Jimmy Connor smiled back, and just then three Yankee players strolled over to the box and began to jeer at Connor for having had to take seats behind the hated Yankee dugout.

Judy Starr was sitting oddly still. She was the famous Judy Starr who had been discovered by Florenz Ziegfeld—a second Marilyn Miller, the critics called her; dainty and pretty, with a perky profile and great honey-colored eyes, who had sung and danced her way into the heart of New

York. Her day of fame was almost over now. Perhaps, thought Paula, staring at Judy's profile, that explained the pinch of her little mouth, the fine lines about her tragic eyes, the singing tension of her figure.

Perhaps. But Paula was not sure. There was immediacy, a defense against a palpable and present danger, in Judy Starr's tautness. Paula looked about. And at once her eyes narrowed.

Across the rail of the box, in the box at their left, sat a very tall, leather-skinned, silent and intent man. The man, too, was staring out at the field, in an attitude curiously like that of Judy Starr, whom he could have touched by extending his big, ropy, muscular hand across the rail. And on the man's other side there sat a woman whom Paula recognized instantly. Lotus Verne, the motion-picture actress!

Lotus Verne was a gorgeous, full-blown redhead with deep mercury-colored eyes who had come out of Northern Italy Ludovica Vernicchi, changed her name, and flashed across the Hollywood skies in a picture called *Woman of Bali*, a color-film in which loving care had been lavished on the display possibilities of her dark, full, dangerous body. With fame, she had developed a passion for press-agentry, borzois in pairs, and tall brown men with muscles. She was arrayed in sun-yellow, and she stood out among the women in the field boxes like a butterfly in a mass of grubs. By contrast little Judy Starr, in her flame-colored outfit, looked almost old and dowdy.

Paula nudged Ellery, who was critically watching the Yankees at batting practice. "Ellery," she said softly, "who is that big, brown, attractive man in the next box?"

Lotus Verne said something to the brown man, and suddenly Judy Starr said something to the Song-and-Dance man; and then the two women exchanged the kind of glance women use when there is no knife handy.

Ellery said absently: "Who? Oh! That's Big Bill Tree."

"Tree?" repeated Paula. "Big Bill Tree?"

"Greatest left-handed pitcher major-league baseball ever saw," said Mr. Queen, staring reverently at the brown man. "Six feet three inches of bull-whip and muscle, with a temper as sudden as the hook on his curve ball and a change of pace that fooled the greatest sluggers of baseball for fifteen years. What a man!"

"Yes, isn't he? smiled Miss Paris.

"Now what does that mean?" demanded Mr. Queen.

"It takes greatness to escort a lady like Lotus Verne to a ball game," said Paula, "to find your wife sitting within spitting distance in the next box, and to carry it off as well as your muscular friend Mr. Tree is doing."

"That's right," said Mr. Queen softly. "Judy Starr *is* Mrs. Bill Tree."

He groaned as Joe DiMaggio hit a ball to the clubhouse clock.

"Funny," said Miss Paris, her clever eyes inspecting in turn the four people before her: Lotus Verne, the Hollywood siren; Big Bill Tree, the ex-baseball pitcher; Judy Starr, Tree's wife; and Jimmy Connor, the Song-and-Dance Man, Mrs. Tree's escort. Two couples, two boxes . . . and no sign of recognition. "Funny," murmured Miss Paris. "From the way Tree courted Judy you'd have thought the marriage would outlast eternity. He snatched her from under Jimmy Connor's nose one night at the Winter Garden, drove her up to Greenwich at eighty miles an hour, and married her before she could catch her breath."

"Yes," said Mr. Queen politely. "Come on, you Giants!" he yelled, as the Giants trotted out for batting practice.

"And then something happened," continued Miss Paris reflectively. "Tree went to Hollywood to make a baseball picture, met Lotus Verne, and the wench took the overgrown country boy the way the overgrown country boy had taken Judy Starr. What a fall was there, my baseball-minded friend."

"What a wallop!" cried Mr. Queen enthusiastically, as Mel Ott hit one that bounced off the right-field fence.

"And Big Bill yammered for a divorce, and Judy refused to give it to him because she loved him, I suppose," said Paula softly–"and now this. How interesting."

"Big Bill Tree twisted in his seat a little; and Judy Starr was still and pale, staring out of her tragic, honey-colored eyes at the Yankee bat-boy and giving him unwarranted delusions of grandeur. Jimmy Connor continued to exchange sarcastic greetings with Yankee players, but his eyes kept shifting back to Judy's face. And beautiful Lotus Verne's arm crept about Tree's shoulders.

"I don't like it," murmured Miss Paris a little later.

"You don't like it?" said Mr. Queen. "Why, the game hasn't even started."

"I don't mean your game, silly. I mean the quadrangular situation in front of us."

"Look, darling," said Mr. Queen. "I flew three thousand miles to see a ball game. There's only one angle that interests me—the view from this box of the greatest li'l ol' baseball tussle within the memory of gaffers. I yearn, I strain, I hunger to see it. Play with your quadrangle, but leave me to my baseball."

"I've always been psychic," said Miss Paris, paying no attention. "This is—bad. Something's going to happen."

Mr. Queen grinned. "I know what. The deluge. See what's coming."

Someone in the grandstand had recognized the celebrities, and a sea of people was rushing down on the two boxes. They swamped the aisle behind the boxes, bobbing pencils and papers, and pleading. Big Bill Tree and Lotus Verne ignored their pleas for autographs; but Judy Starr with a curious eagerness signed paper after paper with the yellow pencils thrust at her by people leaning over the rail. Good-naturedly Jimmy Connor scrawled his signature, too.

"Little Judy," sighed Miss Paris, setting her natural straw straight as an autograph-hunter knocked it over her eyes, "is flustered and unhappy. Moistening the tip of your pencil with your tongue is scarcely a mark of poise. Seated next to her Lotus-bound husband, she hardly knows what she's doing, poor thing."

"Neither do I," growled Mr. Queen, fending off an octopus which turned out to be eight pleading arms offering scorecards.

Big Bill sneezed, groped for a handkerchief, and held it to his nose, which was red and swollen. "Hey, Mac," he called irritably to a red-coated usher. "Do somethin' about this mob, huh?" He sneezed again. "Damn this hay-fever!"

"The touch of earth," said Miss Paris. "But definitely attractive."

"Should 'a' seen Big Bill the day he pitched that World Series final against the Tigers," chuckled Sergeant Velie. "He was sure attractive that day. Pitched a no-hit shutout!"

Inspector Queen said: "Ever hear the story behind that final game, Miss Paris? The night before, a gambler named Sure Shot McCoy, who represented a betting syndicate, called on Big Bill and laid down fifty grand in spot cash in return for Bill's promise to throw the next day's game. Bill took the money, told his manager the whole story, donated the bribe to a fund for sick ball players, and the next day shut out the Tigers without a hit."

"Byronic, too," murmured Miss Paris.

"So then Sure Shot, badly bent," grinned the Inspector, "called on Bill for the payoff. Bill knocked him down two flights of stairs."

"Wasn't that dangerous?"

"I guess," smiled the Inspector, "you could say so. That's why you see that plug-ugly with the smashed nose sitting over there right behind Tree's box. He's Mr. Terrible Turk, late of Cicero, and since that night Big Bill's shadow. You don't see Mr. Turk's right hand, because Mr. Turk's right hand is holding on to an automatic under his jacket. You'll notice, too, that Mr. Turk hasn't for a second taken his eyes off that pasty-cheeked customer eight rows up, whose name is Sure Shot McCoy."

Paula stared. "But what a silly thing for Tree to do!"

"Well, yes," drawled Inspector Queen, "seeing that when he popped Mr. McCoy Big Bill snapped two of the carpal bones of his pitching wrist and wrote finis to his baseball career."

Big Bill Tree hauled himself to his feet, whispered something to the Verne woman, who smiled coyly, and left his box. His bodyguard, Turk, jumped up; but the big man shook his head, waved aside a crowd of people, and vaulted up the concrete steps toward the rear of the grandstand.

And then Judy Starr said something bitter and hot and desperate across the rail to the woman her husband had brought to the Polo Grounds. Lotus Verne's mercurial eyes glittered, and she replied in a careless, insulting voice that made Bill Tree's wife sit up stiffly. Jimmy Connor began to tell the one about Walter Winchell and the Seven Dwarfs . . . loudly and fast.

The Verne woman began to paint her rich lips with short, vicious strokes of her orange lipstick; and Judy Starr's flame kid glove tightened on the rail between them.

And after a while Big Bill returned and sat down again. Judy said something to Jimmy Connor, and the Song-and-Dance Man slid over one seat to his right, and Judy slipped into Connor's seat; so that between her and her husband there was now not only the box rail but an empty chair as well.

Lotus Verne put her arm about Tree's shoulders again.

Tree's wife fumbled inside her flame suède bag. She said suddenly: "Jimmy, buy me a frankfurter."

Connor ordered a dozen. Big Bill scowled. He jumped up and ordered some too. Connor tossed the vendor two one-dollar bills and waved him away.

A new sea deluged the two boxes, and Tree turned round, annoyed. "All right, all right, Mac," he growled at the red-coat struggling with the pressing mob. "We don't want a riot here. I'll take six. Just six. Let's have 'em."

There was a rush that almost upset the attendant. The rail behind the boxes was a solid line of fluttering hands, arms, and scorecards.

"Mr. Tree—said—six!" panted the usher; and he grabbed a pencil and card from one of the outstretched hands and gave them to Tree. The overflow of pleaders spread to the next box. Judy Starr smiled her best professional smile and reached for a pencil and card. A group of players on the field, seeing what was happening, ran over to the field rail and handed her scorecards, too, so that she had to set her half-consumed frankfurter down on the empty seat beside her. Big Bill set his frankfurter down on the same empty seat; he licked the pencil long and absently and began to inscribe his name in the stiff, laborious hand of a man unused to writing.

The attendant howled: "That's six, now! Mr. Tree said just six, so that's all!" as if God Himself had said six; and the crowd groaned, and Big Bill waved his immense paw and reached over to the empty seat in the other box to lay hold of his half-eaten frankfurter. But his wife's hand got there first and fumbled round; and it came up with Tree's frankfurter. The big brown man almost spoke to her then; but he did not, and he picked up the remaining frankfurter, stuffed it into his mouth, and chewed away, but not as if he enjoyed its taste.

Mr. Ellery Queen was looking at the four people before him with a puzzled, worried expression. Then he caught Miss Paula Paris's amused glance and blushed angrily.

The groundkeepers had just left the field and the senior umpire was dusting off the plate to the roar of the crowd when Lotus Verne, who thought a double play was something by Eugene O'Neill, flashed a strange look at Big Bill Tree.

"Bill! Don't you feel well?"

The big ex-pitcher, a sickly blue beneath his tanned skin, put his hand to his eyes and shook his head as if to clear it.

"It's the hot dog," snapped Lotus. "No more for you!"

Tree blinked and began to say something, but just then Carl Hubbell completed his warming-up, Crosetti marched to the plate, Harry Danning tossed the ball to his second-baseman, who flipped it to Hubbell and trotted back to his position yipping like a terrier.

The voice of the crowd exploded in one ear-splitting burst. And then silence.

And Crosetti swung at the first ball Hubbell pitched and smashed it far over Joe Moore's head for a triple.

Jimmy Connor gasped as if someone had thrust a knife into his heart. But Detective-Sergeant Velie was bellowing: "What'd I tell you? It's gonna be a massacree!"

"What is everyone shouting for?" asked Paula.

Mr. Queen nibbled his nails as Danning strolled halfway to the pitcher's box. But Hubbell pulled his long pants up, grinning. Red Rolfe was waving a huge bat at the plate. Danning trotted back. Manager Bill Terry had one foot up on the edge of the Giant dugout, his chin on his fist, looking anxious. The infield came in to cut off the run.

Again fifty thousand people made no single little sound.

And Hubbell struck out Rolfe, DiMaggio, and Gehrig.

Mr. Queen shrieked his joy with the thousands as the Giants came whooping in. Jimmy Connor did an Indian war dance in the box. Sergeant Velie looked aggrieved. Señor Gomez took his warm-up pitches, the umpire used his whiskbroom on the plate again, and Jo-Jo Moore, the Thin Man, ambled up with his war club.

He walked. Bartell fanned. But Jeep Ripple singled off Flash Gordon's shins on the first pitch; and there were Moore on third and Ripple on first, one out, and Little Mel Ott at bat.

Big Bill Tree got half out of his seat, looking surprised, and then dropped to the concrete floor of the box as if somebody had slammed him behind the ear with a fast ball.

Lotus screamed. Judy, Bill's wife, turned like a shot, shaking. People in the vicinity jumped up. Three red-coated attendants hurried down, preceded by the hard-looking Mr. Turk. The bench-warmers stuck their heads over the edge of the Yankee dugout to stare.

"Fainted," growled Turk, on his knees beside the prostrate athlete.

"Loosen his collar," moaned Lotus Verne. "he's so p-pale!"

"Have to git him outa here."

'Yes. Oh, yes!"

The attendants and Turk lugged the big man off, long arms dangling in the oddest way. Lotus stumbled along beside him, biting her lips nervously.

"I think . . . " began Judy in a quivering voice, rising.

But Jimmy Connor put his hand on her arm, and she sank back.

And in the next box Mr. Ellery Queen, on his feet from the instant Tree collapsed, kept looking after the forlorn procession, puzzled, mad about something; until somebody in the stands squawked: "SIDDOWN!" and he sat down.

"Oh, I knew something would happen," whispered Paula.

"Nonsense!" said Mr. Queen shortly. "Fainted, that's all."

Inspector Queen said: "There's Sure Shot McCoy not far off. I wonder if—"

"Too many hot dogs," snapped his son. "What's the matter with you people? Can't I see my ball game in peace?" And he howled: "Come o-o-on, Mel!"

Ott lifted his right leg into the sky and swung. The ball whistled into right field, a long long fly, Selkirk racing madly back after it. He caught it by leaping four feet into the air with his back against the barrier. Moore was off for the plate like a streak and beat the throw to Bill Dickey by inches.

"Yip-ee!" Thus Mr. Queen.

The Giants trotted out to their positions at the end of the first inning leading one to nothing.

Up in the press box the working gentlemen of the press tore into their chores, recalling Carl Hubbell's similar feat in the All-Star game when he struck out the five greatest batters of the American League in succession; praising Twinkletoes Selkirk for his circus catch; and incidentally noting that Big Bill Tree, famous ex-hurler of the National League, had fainted in a field box during the first inning. Joe Williams of the *World-Telegram* said it was excitement, Hype Igoe opined that it was a touch of sun—Big Bill never wore a hat—and Frank Graham of the *Sun* guessed it was too many frankfurters.

Paula Paris said quietly: "I should think, with your detective instincts, Mr. Queen, you would seriously question the 'fainting' of Mr. Tree."

Mr. Queen squirmed and finally mumbled: "It's coming to a pretty pass when a man's instincts aren't his own. Velie, go see what really happened to him."

"I wanna watch the game," howled Velie. "Why don't you go yourself, Maestro?"

"And possibly," said Mr. Queen, "you ought to go too, Dad. I have a hunch it may lie in your jurisdiction."

Inspector Queen regarded his son for some time. Then he rose and sighed: "Come along, Thomas."

Sergeant Velie growled something about some people always spoiling other people's fun and why the hell did he ever have to become a cop; but he got up and obediently followed the Inspector.

Mr. Queen nibbled his fingernails and avoided Miss Paris's accusing eyes.

The second inning was uneventful. Neither side scored.

As the Giants took the field again, an usher came running down the concrete steps and whispered into Jim Connor's ear. The Song-and-Dance Man blinked. He rose slowly. "Excuse me, Judy."

Judy grasped the rail. "It's Bill. Jimmy, tell me."

"Now, Judy—"

"Something's happened to Bill!" Her voice shrilled, and then broke. She jumped up. "I'm going with you."

Connor smiled as if he had just lost a bet, and then he took Judy's arm and hurried her away.

Paula Paris stared after them, breathing hard.

Mr. Queen beckoned the redcoat. "What's the trouble?" he demanded.

"Mr. Tree passed out. Some young doc in the crowd tried to pull him out of it up at the office, but he couldn't, and he's startin' to look worried—"

"I knew it!" cried Paula as the man darted away. "Ellery Queen, are you going to sit here and do *nothing?*"

But Mr. Queen defiantly set his jaw. Nobody was going to jockey him out of seeing this battle of giants; no, ma'am!

There were two men out when Frank Crosetti stepped up to the plate for his second time at bat and, with the count two all, plastered a wicked single over Ott's head.

And, of course, Sergeant Velie took just that moment to amble down and say, his eyes on the field: "Better come along, Master Mind. The old man wouldst have a word with thou. Ah, I see Frankie's on first. Smack it, Red!"

Mr. Queen watched Rolfe take a ball. "Well?" he said shortly. Paula's lips were parted.

"Big Bill's just kicked the bucket. What happened in the second inning?"

"He's . . . *dead?*" gasped Paula.

Mr. Queen rose involuntarily. Then he sat down again. "Damn it," he roared, "it isn't fair. I won't go!"

"Suit yourself. Attaboy, Rolfe!" bellowed the Sergeant as Rolfe singled sharply past Bartell and Crosetti pulled up at second base. "Far's I'm concerned, it's open and shut. The little woman did it with her own little hands."

"Judy *Starr?*" said Miss Paris.

"Bill's wife?" said Mr. Queen. "What are you talking about?"

"That's right, little Judy. She poisoned his hot dog." Velie chuckled. "Man bites dog, and–zowie."

"Has she confessed?" snapped Mr. Queen.

"Naw. But you know dames. She gave Bill the business, all right. C'mon, Joe! And I gotta go. What a life."

Mr. Queen did not look at Miss Paris. He bit his lip. "Here, Velie, wait a minute."

DiMaggio hit a long fly that Leiber caught without moving in his tracks, and the Yankees were retired without a score.

"Ah," said Mr. Queen. "Good old Hubbell." And as the Giants trotted in, he took a fat roll of bills from his pocket, climbed onto his seat, and began waving greenbacks at the spectators in the reserved seats behind the box. Sergeant Velie and Miss Paris stared at him in amazement.

"I'll give five bucks," yelled Mr. Queen, waving the money, "for every autograph Bill Tree signed before the game! In this box right here! Five bucks, gentlemen! Come and get it!"

"You nuts?" gasped the Sergeant.

The mob gaped, and then began to laugh, and after a few moments a pair of sheepish-looking men came down, and then two more, and finally a fifth. An attendant ran over to find out what was the matter.

"Are you the usher who handled the crowd around Bill Tree's box before the game, when he was giving autographs?" demanded Mr. Queen.

"Yes, sir. But, look, we can't allow–"

"Take a gander at these five men . . . You, bud? Yes, that's Tree's handwriting. Here's your fin. Next!" and Mr. Queen went down the line, handing out five-dollar bills with abandon in return for five dirty scorecards with Tree's scrawl on them.

"Anybody else?" he called out, waving his roll of bills.

But nobody else appeared, although there was ungentle badinage from the stands. Sergeant Velie stood there shaking his big head. Miss Paris looked intensely curious.

"Who didn't come down?" rapped Mr. Queen.

"Huh?" said the usher, his mouth open.

"There were six autographs. Only five people turned up. Who was the sixth man? Speak up!"

"Oh." The redcoat scratched his ear. "Say, it wasn't a man. It was a kid."

"A *boy?*"

"Yeah, a little squirt in knee-pants."

Mr. Queen looked unhappy. Velie growled: "Sometimes I think society's takin' an awful chance lettin' you run around loose," and the two men left the box. Miss Paris, bright-eyed, followed.

"Have to clear this mess up in a hurry," muttered Mr. Queen. "Maybe we'll still be able to catch the late innings."

Sergeant Velie led the way to an office, before which a policeman was lounging. He opened the door, and inside they found the Inspector pacing. Turk, the thug, was standing with a scowl over a long still thing on a couch covered with newspapers. Jimmy Connor sat between the two women; and none of the three so much as stirred a foot. They were all pale and breathing heavily.

"This is Dr. Fielding," said Inspector Queen, indicating an elderly white-haired man standing quietly by a window. "He was Tree's physician. He happened to be in the park watching the game when the rumor reached his ears that Tree had collapsed. So he hurried up here to see what he could do."

Ellery went to the couch and pulled the newspaper off Bill Tree's still head. Paula crossed swiftly to Judy Starr and said: "I'm horribly sorry, Mrs. Tree," but the woman, her eyes closed, did not move. After a while Ellery dropped the newspaper back into place and said irritably: "Well, well, let's have it."

"A young doctor," said the Inspector, "got here before Dr. Fielding did, and treated Tree for fainting. I guess it was his fault—"

"Not at all," said Dr. Fielding sharply. "The early picture was compatible with fainting, from what he told me. He tried the usual restorative methods—even injected caffeine and picrotoxin. But there was no convulsion, and he didn't happen to catch that odor of bitter almonds."

"Prussic!" said Ellery. "Taken orally?"

"Yes. HCN—hydrocyanic acid, or prussic, as you prefer. I suspected it at once because—well," said Dr. Fielding in a grim voice, "because of something that occurred in my office only the other day."

"What was that?"

"I had a two-ounce bottle of hydrocyanic acid on my desk—I sometimes use it in minute quantities as a cardiac stimulant. Mrs. Tree," the doctor's glance flickered over the silent woman, "happened to be in my office, resting in preparation for a metabolism test. I left her alone. By a coincidence, Bill Tree dropped in the same morning for a physical checkup. I saw another patient in another room, returned, gave Mrs. Tree her test, saw her out, and came back with Tree. It was then I noticed the bottle, which had been plainly marked DANGER—POISON, was missing from my desk. I thought I had mislaid it, but now . . ."

"I didn't take it," said Judy Starr in a lifeless voice, still not opening her eyes. "I never even saw it."

The Song-and-Dance Man took her limp hand and gently stroked it.

"No hypo marks on the body," said Dr. Fielding dryly. "And I am told that fifteen to thirty minutes before Tree collapsed he ate a frankfurter under . . . peculiar conditions."

"I didn't!" screamed Judy. "I didn't do it!" She pressed her face, sobbing, against Connor's orchid.

Lotus Verne quivered. "She made him pick up her frankfurter. I saw it. They both laid their frankfurters down on that empty seat, and she picked up his. So he had to pick up hers. She poisoned her own frankfurter and then saw to it that he ate it by mistake. Poisoner!" She glared hate at Judy.

"Wench," said Miss Paris *sotto voce,* glaring hate at Lotus.

"In other words," put in Ellery impatiently, "Miss Starr is convicted on the usual two counts, motive and opportunity. Motive—her jealousy of Miss Verne and her hatred—an assumption—of Bill Tree, her husband. And opportunity both to lay hands on the poison in your office,

Doctor, and to sprinkle some on her frankfurter, contriving to exchange hers for his while they were both autographing scorecards."

"She hated him," snarled Lotus. "And me for having taken him from her!"

"Be quiet, you," said Mr. Queen. He opened the corridor door and said to the policeman outside: "Look, McGillicuddy, or whatever your name is, go tell the announcer to make a speech over the loudspeaker system. By the way, what's the score now?"

"Still one to skunk," said the officer. "Them boys Hubbell an' Gomez are hot, what I mean."

"The announcer is to ask the little boy who got Bill Tree's autograph just before the game to come to this office. If he does, he'll receive a ball, bat, pitcher's glove, and an autographed picture of Tree in uniform to hang over his itsy-bitsy bed. Scram!"

"Yes, *sir*," said the officer.

"King Carl pitching his heart out," grumbled Mr. Queen, shutting the door, "and me strangulated by this blamed thing. Well, Dad, do you think, too, that Judy Starr dosed that frankfurter?"

"What else can I think?" said the Inspector absently. His ears were cocked for the faint crowd-shouts from the park.

"Judy Starr," replied his son, "didn't poison her husband any more than I did."

Judy looked up slowly, her mouth muscles twitching. Paula said, gladly: "You wonderful man!"

"She didn't?" said the Inspector, looking alert.

"The frankfurter theory," snapped Mr. Queen, "is too screwy for words. For Judy to have poisoned her husband, she had to unscrew the cap of a bottle and douse her hot dog on the spot with the hydrocyanic acid. Yet Jimmy Connor was seated by her side, and in the only period in which she could possibly have poisoned the frankfurter a group of Yankee ball players was *standing before her* across the field rail getting her autograph. Were they all accomplices? And how could she have known Big Bill would lay his hot dog on that empty seat? The whole thing is absurd."

A roar from the stands made him continue hastily: "There was one plausible theory that fitted the facts. When I heard that Tree had died of poisoning, I recalled that at the time he was autographing the six score-cards, *he had thoroughly licked the end of a pencil* which had been handed to him with one of the cards. It was possible, then, that the pencil he licked had been poisoned. So I offered to buy the six autographs."

Paula regarded him tenderly, and Velie said: "I'll be a so-and-so if he didn't."

"I didn't expect the poisoner to come forward, but I knew the inno-cent ones would. Five claimed the money. The sixth, the missing one, the usher informed me, had been a small boy."

"A kid poisoned Bill?" growled Turk, speaking for the first time. "You're crazy from the heat."

"In spades," added the Inspector.

"Then why didn't the boy come forward?" put in Paula quickly. "Go on, darling!"

"He didn't come forward, not because he was guilty but because he wouldn't sell Bill Tree's autograph for anything. No, obviously a hero-worshiping boy wouldn't try to poison the great Bill Tree. Then, just as obviously, he didn't realize what he was doing. Consequently, he must have been an innocent tool. The question was—and still is—of whom?"

"Sure Shot," said the Inspector slowly.

Lotus Verne sprang to her feet, her eyes glittering. "Perhaps Judy Starr didn't poison that frankfurter, but if she didn't then she hired that boy to give Bill—"

Mr. Queen said disdainfully: "Miss Starr didn't leave the box once." Someone knocked on the corridor door and he opened it. For the first time he smiled. When he shut the door they saw that his arm was about the shoulders of a boy with brown hair and quick clever eyes. The boy was clutching a scorecard tightly.

"They say over the announcer," mumbled the boy, "that I'll get a au-tographed pi'ture of Big Bill Tree if . . ." He stopped, abashed at their strangely glinting eyes.

"And you'll certainly get it, too," said Mr. Queen heartily. "What's your name, Sonny?"

"Fenimore Feigenspan," replied the boy, edging toward the door. "Gran' Concourse, Bronx. Here's the scorecard. How about the pi'ture?"

"Let's see that, Fenimore," said Mr. Queen. "When did Bill Tree give you this autograph?"

"Before the game. He said he'd on'y give six—"

"Where's the pencil you handed him, Fenimore?"

The boy looked suspicious, but he dug into a bulging pocket and brought forth one of the ordinary yellow pencils sold at the park with scorecards. Ellery took it from him gingerly, and Dr. Fielding took it from Ellery, and sniffed its tip. He nodded, and for the first time a look of peace came over Judy Starr's still face and she dropped her head tiredly to Connor's shoulder.

Mr. Queen ruffled Fenimore Feigenspan's hair. "That's swell, Fenimore. Somebody gave you that pencil while the Giants were at batting practice, isn't that so?"

"Yeah." The boy stared at him.

"Who was it?" asked Mr. Queen lightly.

"I dunno. A big guy with a coat an' a turned-down hat an' a mustache, an' big black sun-glasses. I couldn't see his face good. Where's my pi'-ture? I wanna see the game!"

"Just where was it that this man gave you the pencil?"

"In the —" Fenimore paused, glancing at the ladies with embarrass-ment. Then he muttered: "Well, I hadda go, an' this guy says—in there—he's ashamed to ask her for her autograph, so would I do it for him—"

"What? What's that?" exclaimed Mr. Queen. "Did you say 'her'?"

"Sure," said Fenimore. "The dame, he says, wearin' the red hat an' red dress an' red gloves in the field box near the Yanks' dugout, he says. He even took me outside an' pointed down to where she was sittin'. Say!" cried Fenimore, goggling. "That's her! That's the dame!" and he leveled a grimy forefinger at Judy Starr.

Judy shivered and felt blindly for the Song-and-Dance Man's hand.

"Let me get this straight, Fenimore," said Mr. Queen softly. "This man with the sun-glasses asked you to get this lady's autograph for him, and gave you the pencil and scorecard to get it with?"

"Yea, an' two bucks too, sayin' he'd meet me after the game to pick up the card, but—"

"But you didn't get the lady's autograph for him, did you? You went down to get it, and hung around waiting for your chance, but then you spied Big Bill Tree, your hero, in the next box and forgot all about the lady, didn't you?"

The boy shrank back. "I didn't mean to, honest, Mister. I'll give the two bucks back!"

"And seeing Big Bill there, your hero, you went right over to get *his* autograph for *yourself,* didn't you?" Fenimore nodded, frightened. "You gave the usher the pencil and scorecard this man with the sun-glasses had handed you, and the usher turned the pencil and scorecard over to Bill Tree in the box—wasn't that the way it happened?"

"Y-yes, sir, an' . . ." Fenimore twisted out of Ellery's grasp, "an' so I–I gotta go." And before anyone could stop him he was indeed gone, racing down the corridor like the wind.

The policeman outside shouted, but Ellery said: "Let him go, officer," and shut the door. Then he opened it again and said: "How's she stand now?"

"Dunno exactly, sir. Somethin' happened out there just now. I think the Yanks scored."

"Damn," groaned Mr. Queen, and he shut the door again.

"So it was Mrs. Tree who was on the spot, not Bill," scowled the Inspector. "I'm sorry, Judy Starr . . . Big man with a coat and hat and mustache and sun-glasses. Some description!"

"Sounds like a phony to me," said Sergeant Velie.

"If it was a disguise, he dumped it somewhere," said the Inspector thoughtfully. "Thomas, have a look in the Men's Room behind the section where we were sitting. And Thomas," he added in a whisper, "find out what the score is." Velie grinned and hurried out. Inspector Queen frowned. "Quite a job finding a killer in a crowd of fifty thousand people."

"Maybe," said his son suddenly, "maybe it's not such a job after all. . . . What was used to kill? Hydrocyanic acid. Who was intended to be killed? Bill Tree's wife. Any connection between anyone in the case and hydrocyanic acid? Yes—Dr. Fielding 'lost' a bottle of it under suspicious circumstances. Which were? That Bill Tree's wife could have taken that bottle . . . *or Bill Tree himself.*"

"Bill Tree!" gasped Paula.

"Bill?" whispered Judy Starr.

"Quite! Dr. Fielding didn't miss the bottle until *after* he had shown you, Miss Starr, out of his office. He then returned to his office with your husband. Bill could have slipped the bottle into his pocket as he stepped into the room."

"Yes, he could have," muttered Dr. Fielding.

"I don't see," said Mr. Queen, "how we can arrive at any other conclusion. We know his wife was intended to be the victim today, so obviously she didn't steal the poison. The only other person who had opportunity to steal it was Bill himself."

The Verne woman sprang up. "I don't believe it! It's a frame-up to protect *her,* now that Bill can't defend himself!"

"Ah, but didn't he have motive to kill Judy?" asked Mr. Queen. "Yes, indeed; she wouldn't give him the divorce he craved so that he could marry *you.* I think, Miss Verne, you would be wiser to keep the peace. . . . Bill had opportunity to steal the bottle of poison in Dr. Fielding's office. He also had opportunity to hire Fenimore today, for he was the *only* one of the whole group who left those two boxes during the period when the poisoner must have searched for someone to offer Judy the poisoned pencil.

"All of which fits for what Bill had to do—get to where he had cached his disguise, probably yesterday; look for a likely tool; find Fenimore, give him his instructions and the pencil; get rid of the disguise again; and return to his box. And didn't Bill know better than anyone his wife's habit of moistening a pencil with her tongue—a habit she probably acquired from *him?*"

"Poor Bill," murmured Judy Starr brokenly.

"Women," remarked Miss Paris, "are *fools.*"

"There were other striking ironies," replied Mr. Queen. "For if Bill hadn't been suffering from a hay-fever attack, he would have smelled the odor of bitter almonds when his own poisoned pencil was handed to him and stopped in time to save his worthless life. For that matter, if he hadn't been Fenimore Feigenspan's hero, Fenimore would not have handed him his own poisoned pencil in the first place.

"No," said Mr. Queen gladly, "putting it all together, I'm satisfied that Mr. Big Bill Tree, in trying to murder his wife, very neatly murdered himself instead."

"That's all very well for *you*," said the Inspector disconsolately. "But *I* need proof."

"I've told you how it happened," said his son airily, making for the door. "Can any man do more? Coming, Paula?"

But Paula was already at a telephone, speaking guardedly to the New York office of the syndicate for which she worked, and paying no more attention to him than if he had been a worm.

"What's the score? What's been going on?" Ellery demanded of the world at large as he regained his box seat. "Three to three! What the devil's got into Hubbell, anyway? How'd the Yanks score? What inning is it?"

"Last of the ninth," shrieked somebody. "The Yanks got three runs in the eighth on a walk, a double, and DiMag's homer! Danning homered in the sixth with Ott on base! Shut up!"

Bartell singled over Gordon's head. Mr. Queen cheered.

Sergeant Velie tumbled into the next seat. "Well, we got it," he puffed. "Found the whole outfit in the Men's Room—coat, hat, fake mustache, glasses and all. What's the score?"

"Three-three. Sacrifice, Jeep!" shouted Mr. Queen.

"There was a rain-check in the coat pocket from the sixth game, with Big Bill's box number on it. So there's the old man's proof. Chalk up another win for you."

"Who cares? . . . *Zowie!*"

Jeep Ripple sacrificed Bartell successfully to second.

"Lucky stiff," howled a Yankee fan near by. "That's the breaks. See the breaks they get? See?"

"And another thing," said the Sergeant, watching Mel Ott stride to the plate. "Seein' as how all Big Bill did was cross himself up, and no harm done except to his own carcass, and seein' as how organized baseball could get along without a murder, and seein' as how thousands of kids like Fenimore Feigenspan worship the ground he walked on—"

"Sew it up, Mel!" bellowed Mr. Queen.

"—and seein' as how none of the newspaper guys know what happened, except that Bill passed out of the picture after a faint, and seein' as everybody's only too glad to shut their traps—"

Mr. Queen awoke suddenly to the serious matters of life. "What's that? What did you say?"

"Strike him out, Goofy!" roared the Sergeant to Señor Gomez, who did not hear. "As I was sayin', it ain't cricket, and the old man would be broke out of the force if the big cheese heard about it . . ."

Someone puffed up behind them, and they turned to see Inspector Queen, red-faced as if after a hard run, scrambling into the box with the assistance of Miss Paula Paris, who looked cool, serene, and starred as ever.

"Dad!" said Mr. Queen, staring. "With a murder on your hands, how can you—"

"Murder?" panted Inspector Queen. "What murder?" And he winked at Miss Paris, who winked back.

"But Paula was telephoning the story—"

"Didn't you hear?" said Paula in a coo, setting her straw straight and slipping into the seat beside Ellery's. "I fixed it all up with your dad. Tonight all the world will know is that Mr. Bill Tree died of heart failure."

They all chuckled then—all but Mr. Queen, whose mouth was open.

"So now," said Paula, "your dad can see the finish of your precious game just as well as *you*, you selfish oaf!"

But Mr. Queen was already fiercely rapt in contemplation of Mel Ott's bat as it swung back and Señor Gomez's ball as it left the Señor's hand to streak toward the plate.

Originally from Esquire, *this story has an ageless theme—a youngster trying to train a horse to race like a champion. Hollywood has done this turn on several occasions in heartwarming movies such as* National Velvet *and* My Friend Flicka. *Occasionally, life imitates art, as a relatively unknown horse like* Seattle Slew *wins triple crown races. Edwin Lanham was a popular novelist and short story writer. Among his books are* One Murder Too Many *(1952),* Death in the Wind *(1955), and* Passage to Danger *(1961).*

Edwin Lanham

THE DENTON MARE (1946)

THE MULE-EARED RABBIT cleared a clump of cactus in a long, stiff jump and shot off at an angle. Clay almost lost his seat as the black filly wheeled to follow. The rabbit dived into the mesquite and Clay pulled the filly in. He laughed and said aloud, "Honey, you could beat the Denton mare."

Tom Drew rode alongside the filly. "Son, how many times have I told you not to run your horse after jackrabbits? You want to break her wind?"

"This little filly just likes to run, Pop." The horse held her small head high, and Clay stroked her foam frothed neck. "Pop, she's part antelope. I bet you she could beat the Denton mare."

Tom Drew shook his head. "No horse ever beat that Sam Bass mare. I seen her run last year."

"I wish I could see her."

"I heard Sam Bass say yesterday that he'd sold her."

"You saw Sam Bass?" Clay asked excitedly. "You mean he's here in town?"

"He was yesterday."

"I'd sure like to see him. Gee, why did he ever sell the Denton mare? Why, she's the fastest horse in North Texas—except Honey!"

Tom chuckled. "Son," he said. "How'd you like to run your little filly in a scrub race?'

"Gee, Pop! You mean it?"

"Kinkead thinks a lot of his long-legged bay, and he wants to make a match. There'll be some races Saturday."

"Give us a chance at him, Pop. Oh, let Honey race him!" The filly caught his excitement and spun on her heels.

"You got to have a stake, Clay."

Clay took quick inventory. All he had to call his own were his star-topped boots and his saddle. He said, "I'll put up my saddle."

"All right. I'll allow you twenty dollars on it. I'll put up the cash for you. But remember, if you lose you're bareback."

When Saturday came Clay had the filly ready under a post-oak tree long before the race. He saw J. P. Kinkead, the storekeeper, holding the big bay near the start of the quarter-mile straightaway.

Clay had to admire the bay, beside which his filly seemed immature and delicate, as Tom Drew led her to the start. Jeff Rogers, the starter, waited, gun in hand. Clay stroked the filly's neck. She was trembling, waiting for his shout. Clay watched Rogers and saw his left eyelid twitch just before he pulled the trigger.

Clay leaned forward and felt the drive of the filly beneath him as he shouted, "Come on, you Honey!" The line of horses beside the track was a blur that quickly came to focus at the finish line ahead. The filly's hoofs drummed over the line and he was out on the prairie, in the open, and the big bay was three lengths behind.

Tom Drew waited for him under the post-oak tree. Clay laughed and cried, "It was easy. Pop, I told you she was fast enough to beat the Denton mare."

Tom smiled and went to get his horse. Clay slid to the ground. He rubbed Honey's broad forehead and put one arm around her neck. He was embarrassed when a low voice said in his ear, "Nice little filly you got there, bub."

A slim young man came into the shade and walked around the filly. He felt her knees, appraised her chest and hocks. "What do you want for her?"

"She ain't for sale," Clay said.

The man's dark eyes had a teasing expression. "Don't blame you. What do they call you, boy?"

Clay sized him up through narrowed lids as he fondled the filly's tapering muzzle. He said, "Clay Drew."

"I'm Sam Bass."

Clay stared. "Sam Bass!" He went around the filly to get near the slim young man. "Say, Mr. Bass, did you see my filly run? How would she make out against the Denton mare?"

"She'd give her a race. You got a quarter horse here, boy."

Clay grinned and called to his father as he came up, leading his dun horse. "Pop, this here is Sam Bass."

"I know Sam," Tom Drew said.

"He says Honey is as good as the Denton mare."

"Get on your filly, Clay, we got to go."

As they rode home Tom said, "He's got a great love of horses, Sam Bass, but he ain't in a class with his mare. They say down Denton way he poisoned a horse trough once to win a race."

Clay chased no more jackrabbits on the filly. He staked out a quarter mile on a level stretch of prairie and began to train her. Several times Sam Bass rode out from town to watch and one day Tom Drew drove past in a wagon while Sam was there.

"I came out to help the boy train," Sam Bass explained. "He's a right smart rider."

Tom looked at Sam. "This is a cattle ranch, not a racing stable. There'll be no more races."

Sam Bass smiled. "That filly is a race horse, and it would be too bad not to run her. Say, I run onto a feller in town this morning wants to make a match. Says his horse can outrun anything in Texas."

"I bet he can't outrun Honey," Clay said.

"That's enough, Clay." Tom Drew frowned. "I'm on my way to town and I won't be back to supper."

Tom Drew did not return until late. Clay sat up in bed and called, "I'm awake, Pop."

Tom opened the door. The lamp in his hand outlined the rueful smile on his face. "Son, I set you a damn bad example," he said.

"What, Pop?"

"There was a feller in town talking mighty big. Feller from San Antone named Joel Collins. Talked about a horse of his and Sam Bass put in about your filly and first thing I knew we'd made a match for a week from Saturday and a mighty big bet. Thousand dollars to be paid at the bank at the end of the race."

"Yippee!" Clay sat up in bed. "Pop, we'll win it. Honey will sure win that race."

"She's got to win it, Son," Tom Drew said.

When the race day came Clay knew that Honey was ready. The tremendous driving leap of her start, so important in a quarter mile race, was drilled to perfection. When he took her to the track he kept her under the trees by the creek and sat on a stump watching the crowd.

Tom Drew came to him a few minutes before the race, his eyes hard. "Clay, that's the horse you're going to race, that sorrel mare."

She was small, quick-moving, and a white hind foot caught Clay's eye. A short man in a dusty black hat held her halter.

"You got a big bite to chew," Tom said. "I've seen that sorrel run. That's the Denton mare."

Clay stared, and his throat tightened. "You sure, Pop?"

"See that nigh hind foot. That's the Denton mare, all right."

"Pop, I'll ask Sam Bass."

"He's on his horse down at the finish line." Tom slumped down on the stump, shaking his head. "Sam Bass tricked me into this match, Clay. It was him took me around to see Joel Collins. Him and Joel are partners."

"Pop, we can beat her," Clay said. "Honey is better than ever, and you ought to see how fast she gets away."

Tom looked up quickly. "Son, you give me an idea. You can ride like an Indian. Rip that saddle off the filly."

"Ride her bareback?"

"Yes. That Denton mare was always slow starting. Over at Denton, Sam had a mound of dirt couple feet high to help her get away, and a colored boy who rode her bareback."

Tom Drew took the saddle from the filly, helped Clay to her bare back and led the horse to the starting line. Joel Collins was a small man but he outweighed Clay by fifty pounds and the mare had a saddle to carry as well.

"Hey," Collins said. "Nothing was said about riding bareback."

"Nothing's going to be said about it now," Tom Drew said in a steely tone. "You can slip off your saddle if you want."

"How about it, Jeff?" Collins said.

The starter shrugged and gave Collins a hostile glance. "The kid can ride naked if he wants."

Collins hesitated then grinned. "Hell, this mare can't be beat. I'll keep my saddle."

Clay knew a trick himself he had said nothing of, even to his father. In the other race he had noticed Jeff closed one eye *before* he pulled the trigger.

Clay's knees pressed the filly's sides. He could feel the gathering of her muscles for the start and he watched Jeff's left eye. He saw the slight twitch of the eyelid.

"Come on, Honey!" he yelled, and his shout was lost in the crash of the gun. But he had a head-start and the sorrel was in the dust at Honey's heels.

Clay's head was down so far that the filly's mane whipped his face. Halfway down the track he heard the sound of the sorrel's hoofs. The mare was creeping up and Clay saw her bleached mane flying at his shoulder. She was all the horse they said she was.

Joel Collins was using his quirt, and the finish line was close ahead. The black and sorrel necks were stretched out together. They were nose to nose. Clay's cheek nearly touched the filly's ear as he shouted, "Honey, beat that mare!" and he felt her drive forward, then they were over the line.

He heard whoops and saw the judges waving as he turned back. He rode slowly up to them. J. B. Kinkead was beating his saddlehorn. Clay was afraid to ask, and his voice trembled, "Who won?"

"Boy, you and her by half a length. I never seen such a drive as that filly put on at the finish."

"Clay!" His father galloped up, waving his hat. "You done it, Son! You beat the Denton mare."

All at once Clay could talk. "It wasn't only the start, Pop. We won the start but we won the race, too. We was all even and Honey pulled ahead and won."

Then Kinkead's voice rose above the clamor. "The Denton mare? Where is she?"

"Why, she ain't stopped running," Tom Drew said. "He don't aim to pay off."

Clay saw the sheen of the sorrel's hide far away. And beside her ran another horse.

"It's Sam Bass with him," Tom Drew said. "I guess they was afraid of the filly all along, and planned to keep going if the mare lost. Well, no use taking after 'em."

"Pop, what do we care?" Clay shouted. "Honey beat the Denton mare!"

As they rode home together, with Honey on a halter beside Clay's cow pony, Tom Drew said, "Clay, you were born knowing about horses, but you got to learn for yourself how some men are made. I reckon you've had your fill of horse racing now."

"I don't know, Pop. I'd like to race that mare again, all even. Honey beat her, but we had to use some tricks ourselves." His eyes shone proudly. "But I know Honey would win again."

"Clay, I reckon you learned something," Tom Drew said, and his eyes held a prouder light than his son's.

Next up is a yarn based on a rowing incident in England that turns into a fascinating mystery. Author Jeffrey Archer was educated at Oxford University, where as a world-class sprinter he represented Great Britain in international competition. He became the youngest member of the House of Commons in 1969, was appointed Deputy Chairman of the Conservative Party in 1985, and was elevated to the House of Lords in 1992. Archer is the author of several international bestsellers, including Not a Penny More, Not a Penny Less *(1974) and* Honor Among Thieves *(1993).*

Jeffrey Archer

DOUGIE MORTIMER'S RIGHT ARM (1994)

ROBERT HENRY KEFFORD III, known to his friends as Bob, was in bed with a girl called Helen when he first heard about Dougie Mortimer's right arm.

Bob was sorry to be leaving Cambridge. He had spent three glorious years at St. John's, and although he hadn't read as many books as he had for his undergraduate degree at the University of Chicago, he had striven every bit as hard to come head of the river.

It wasn't unusual for an American to win a rowing blue in the early

1970s, but to have stroked a victorious Cambridge eight for three years in a row was acknowledged as a first.

Bob's father, Robert Henry Kefford II, known to his friends as Robert, had traveled over to England to watch his son take part in all three races from Putney to Mortlake. After Bob had stroked Cambridge to victory for the third time, his father told him that he must not return to his native Illinois without having presented a memento to the University Boat Club that they would remember him by.

"And don't forget, my boy," declared Robert Henry Kefford II, "the gift must not be ostentatious. Better to show that you have made an effort to present them with an object of historic value than give them something that obviously cost a great deal of money. The British appreciate that sort of thing."

Bob spent many hours pondering his father's words, but completely failed to come up with any worthwhile ideas. After all, the Cambridge University Boat Club had more silver cups and trophies than they could possibly display.

It was on a Sunday morning that Helen first mentioned the name of Dougie Mortimer. She and Bob were lying in each other's arms, when she started prodding his biceps.

"Is this some form of ancient British foreplay that I ought to know about?" Bob asked, placing his free arm around Helen's shoulder.

"Certainly not," Helen replied. "I was simply trying to discover if your biceps are as big as Dougie Mortimer's."

As Bob had never known a girl talk about another man while he was in bed with her, he was unable to think of an immediate response.

"And are they?" he eventually inquired, flexing his muscles.

"Hard to tell," Helen replied. "I've never actually touched Dougie's arm, only seen it at a distance."

"And where did you come across his magnificent specimen of manhood?"

"It hangs over the bar at my dad's local pub, in Hull."

"Doesn't Dougie Mortimer find that a little painful?" asked Bob, laughing.

"Doubt if he cares that much," said Helen. "After all, he's been dead for over sixty years."

"And his arm still hangs above a bar?" asked Bob in disbelief. "Hasn't it begun to smell a bit by now?"

This time it was Helen's turn to laugh. "No, you Yankee fool. It's a bronze cast of his arm. In those days, if you were in the university crew for three years in a row, they made a cast of your arm to hang in the clubhouse. Not to mention a card with your picture on it in every packet of Player's cigarettes. I've never seen *your* picture in a cigarette packet, come to think of it," said Helen as she pulled the sheet over his head.

"Did he row for Oxford or Cambridge?" asked Bob.

"No idea."

"So, what's the name of this pub in Hull?"

"The King William," Helen replied, as Bob took his arm from around her shoulder.

"Is this American foreplay?" she asked after a few moments.

Later that morning, after Helen had left for Newnham, Bob began searching his shelves for a book with a blue cover. He dug out his much-thumbed *History of the Boat Race* and flicked through the index to discover that there were seven Mortimers listed. Five had rowed for Oxford, two for Cambridge. He began to pray as he checked their initials. Mortimer, A.J. (Westminster and Wadham, Oxon), Mortimer, C.K. (Uppingham and Oriel, Oxon), Mortimer, D.J.T. (Harrow and St Catharine's, Cantab), Mortimer, E.L. (Oundle and Magdalen, Oxon). Bob turned his attention to Mortimer, D.J.T., biography page 129, and flicked the pages backward until he reached the entry he sought. Douglas John Townsend Mortimer (St. Catharine's), Cambridge 1907, -08, -09, stroke. He then read the short summary of Mortimer's rowing career.

> Dougie Mortimer stroked the Cambridge boat to victory in 1907, a feat which he repeated in 1908. But in 1909, when the experts considered Cambridge to have one of the finest crews for years, the light blues lost to an Ox-

ford boat that was regarded as the rank outsider. Although many explanations were suggested by the press at the time, the result of the race remains a mystery to this day. Mortimer died in 1914.

Bob closed the book and returned it to the shelf, assuming the great oarsman must have been killed in the First World War. He perched on the end of the bed, considering the information he now possessed. If he could bring Dougie Mortimer's right arm back to Cambridge and present it to the Club at the annual Blues' Dinner, it would surely be a prize that met his father's demanding criterion.

He dressed quickly and went downstairs to the pay phone in the corridor. Once directory inquiries had given him the four numbers he required, he set about trying to remove the next obstacle.

The first calls he made were to the King William—or, to be precise, the King Williams, because the directory had supplied him with the numbers of three pubs in Hull that bore that name. When he was put through to the first, he asked, "Does Dougie Mortimer's right arm hang above your counter?" He couldn't quite make out every word of the broad northern accent that replied, but he was left in no doubt that it didn't.

The second call was answered by a girl who said, "Do you mean that thing that's nailed to the wall above the bar?"

"Yes, I guess that will be it," said Bob.

"Well then, this is the pub you're looking for."

After Bob had taken down the address and checked the pub's opening hours, he made a third call. "Yes, that's possible," he was told. "You can take the 3:17 to Peterborough, where you'll have to change and catch the 4:09 for Doncaster, then change again. You'll arrive in Hull at 6:32."

"What about the last train back?" asked Bob

"8:52, change at Doncaster and Peterborough. You should be back in Cambridge just after midnight."

"Thank you," said Bob. He strolled off to his college for lunch and took a place at the large center table, but proved unusually poor company for those around him.

He boarded the train to Peterborough later that afternoon, still thinking about how he could possibly relieve the pub owners of their prize possession. At Peterborough he jumped out, walked across to a waiting train on platform three and climbed aboard, still deep in thought. When his train pulled into Hull a couple of hours later, he was no nearer to solving the problem. He asked the first taxi on the rank to take him to the King William.

"Market Place, Harold's Corner or Percy Street?" asked the cabbie.

"Percy Street, please," replied Bob.

"They don't open until seven, lad," the cabbie told him once he had dropped Bob outside the front door.

Bob checked the time. Twenty minutes to kill. He walked down a side street at the back of the pub and stopped to watch some young kids playing soccer. They were using the front walls of two houses on either side of the street as goals, and showed amazing accuracy in never hitting any of the windows. Bob wondered if the game would ever catch on in America.

He became so captivated by the youngsters' skill that they stopped to ask him if he wanted to join in. He said, "No thank you," confident that if he did play with them, he would be the one person who ended up breaking a window.

He arrived back outside the King William a few minutes after seven and strolled into the empty pub, hoping that no one would pay much attention to him. But at six feet four inches, and dressed in a double-breasted blue blazer, gray flannels, a blue shirt and college tie, the three people behind the bar might well have wondered if he had dropped in from another planet. He stopped himself from looking above the bar as a young blond barmaid stepped forward and asked him what he would like.

"A half a pint of your best bitter," Bob said, trying to sound like one of his English friends when they ordered a drink from the college watering hole.

The proprietor eyed Bob suspiciously as he took his half-pint glass over to a small round table in the corner and sat down quietly on a stool. He was pleased when two other men entered the pub, so that the proprietor's attention was distracted.

Bob took a sip of the dark liquid and nearly choked. When he had recovered, he allowed his eyes to glance above the bar. He tried to hide his excitement when he saw the bronze cast of a massive arm embedded in a large piece of varnished wood. He thought the object both dreadful and inspiring at the same time. His eyes moved down to the bold lettering printed in gold beneath it:

D. J. T. MORTIMER
1907–08–09
(ST. CATHARINE'S, STROKE)

Bob kept his eye on the proprietor as the pub began to fill up, but he soon became aware that it was his wife—everyone called her Nora—who was not only in charge but who did most of the serving.

When he had finished his drink, he made his way over to her end of the bar.

"What can I do for you, young man?" Nora asked.

"I'll have another, thank you," said Bob.

"An American," she said, as she pulled the pump and began to refill his glass. "We don't get many of you lot up 'ere, at least not since the bases closed." She placed his half-pint on the counter in front of him. "So, what brings you to 'ull?"

"You do," Bob replied, ignoring his drink.

Nora looked suspiciously at the stranger, who was young enough to be her son.

Bob smiled, "Or, to be more accurate, Dougie Mortimer does."

"Now I've figured you out," said Nora. "You phoned this morning, didn't you? My Christie told me. I should 'ave guessed."

Bob nodded. "How did the arm end up in Hull?" he asked.

"Now, that's a long story," said Nora. "It was my grandfather's, wasn't it. Born in Ely 'e was, and 'e used to spend his holidays fishin' the Cam.

Said it was the only catch he managed that year, which I suppose is one better than sayin' it fell off the back of a truck. Still, when 'e died a few years back, my father wanted to throw the bloody thing out with the rest of the rubbish, but I wouldn't 'ear of it, told 'im 'e should 'ang it in the pub, didn't I? I cleaned and polished it, it came up real nice, and then I 'ung it above the bar. Still, it's a long way for you to travel just to 'ave a look at that load of old cobblers."

Bob looked up and admired the arm once again. He held his breath. "I didn't come just to look."

"Then why did you come?" she asked.

"I came to buy."

"Get a move on, Nora," said the proprietor. "Can't you see there are customers waitin' to be served?"

Nora swung round and said, "Just 'old your tongue, Cyril Barnsworth. This young man's come all the way up to 'ull just to see Dougie Mortimer's arm, and what's more, 'e wants to buy it." This caused a ripple of laughter from the regulars standing nearest to the bar, but as Nora didn't join in, they quickly fell silent.

"Then it's been a wasted journey, 'asn't it?" said the proprietor. "Because it's not for sale."

"It's not yours to sell," said Nora, placing her hands on her hips. "Mind you, lad, 'e's right," she said, turning back to face Bob. "I wouldn't part with it for a 'undred quid," said Nora. Several others in the room were beginning to show an interest in the proceedings.

"How about two hundred," said Bob quietly. This time Nora burst out laughing, but Bob didn't even smile.

When Nora had stopped laughing, she stared directly at the strange young man. "My God, 'e means it," she said.

"I certainly do," said Bob. "I would like to see the arm returned to its rightful home in Cambridge, and I'm willing to pay two hundred pounds for the privilege."

The proprietor looked across at his wife, as if he couldn't believe what he was hearing. "We could buy that little second-hand car I've had my eye on," he said.

"Not to mention a summer 'oliday and a new overcoat for next winter," Nora added, staring at Bob as if she still needed to be convinced that he wasn't from another planet. Suddenly she thrust her hand over the counter and said, "You've got yourself a deal, young man."

Bob ended up having to supply several rounds of drinks for those customers who claimed to have been close personal friends of Nora's grandfather, even if some of them looked rather obviously too young. He also had to stay overnight in a local hotel, because Nora wouldn't part with her grandfather's "heirloom," as she now kept referring to it, until her bank manager had phoned Cambridge to check that Robert Henry Kefford III was good for two hundred pounds.

Bob clung onto his treasure all the way back to Cambridge that Monday morning, and then lugged the heavy object from the station to his digs in the Grange Road, where he hid it under the bed. The following day he handed it over to a local furniture restorer, who promised to return the arm to its former glory in time for the night of the Blues' Dinner.

When, three weeks later, Bob was allowed to see the results of the restorer's efforts, he immediately felt confident that he now possessed a prize not only worthy of the C.U.B.C., but that also complied with his father's wishes. He resolved not to share his secret with anyone—not even Helen—until the night of the Blues' Dinner, although he did warn the puzzled president that he was going to make a presentation, and that he required two hooks, eighteen inches apart and eight feet from the floor, to be screwed into the wall beforehand.

The University Blues' Dinner is an annual event held in the Boat House overlooking the Cam. Any former or current rowing blue is eligible to attend, and Bob was delighted to find when he arrived that night that it was a near-record turnout. He placed the carefully wrapped brown paper parcel under his chair, and put his camera on the table in front of him.

Because it was his last Blues' Dinner before returning to America, Bob had been seated at the head table, between the honorary secretary and the current president of boats. Tom Adams, the honorary secretary, had gained his blue some twenty years before, and was recognized as the club's walking encyclopedia because he could name not only everyone in the room, but all the great oarsmen of the past.

Tom pointed out to Bob three Olympic medalists dotted around the room. "The oldest is sitting on the left of the president," he said. "Charles Forester. He rowed at number three for the club in 1908–09, so he must be over eighty."

"Can it be possible?" said Bob, recalling Forester's youthful picture on the clubhouse wall.

"Certainly can," said the secretary. "And what's more, young man," he added, laughing, "you'll look like that one day too."

"What about the man at the far end of the table?" asked Bob. "He looks even older."

"He is," said the secretary. "That's Sidney Fisk. He was boatman from 1912 to 1945, with only a break for the First World War. Took over from his uncle at short notice, if I remember correctly."

"So he would have known Dougie Mortimer," said Bob wistfully.

"Now, there's a great name from the past," said Adams. "Mortimer, D.J.T., 1907-08-09, St. Catharine's, stroke. Oh, yes, Fisk would certainly have known Mortimer, that's for sure. Come to think of it, Charles Forester must have been in the same boat as Mortimer when he was stroke."

During the meal, Bob continued to quiz Adams about Dougie Mortimer, but he was unable to add a great deal to the entry in Bob's *History of the Boat Race,* other than to confirm that Cambridge's defeat in 1909 still remained a mystery, as the light blues demonstrably had the superior crew.

When the last course had been cleared away, the president rose to welcome his guests and to make a short speech. Bob enjoyed the parts he was able to hear above the noise made by the rowdy undergraduates, and even joined in the frenzy whenever Oxford was mentioned. The president ended with the words, "There will be a special presentation to the club this year, by our colonial stroke Bob Kefford, which I'm sure we're all going to appreciate."

When Bob rose from his place, the cheering became even more raucous, but he spoke so softly that the noise quickly died away. He told his fellow members how he had come to discover, and later retrieve, Dougie Mortimer's right arm, leaving out only his exact location when he first learned of its whereabouts.

With a flourish, he unwrapped the parcel that had been secreted under his chair and revealed the newly restored bronze cast. The assembled members rose to their feet and cheered. A smile of satisfaction came over Bob's face as he looked around, only wishing his father could have been present to witness their reaction.

As his eyes swept the room, Bob couldn't help noticing that the oldest blue present, Charles Forester, had remained seated, and was not even joining in the applause. Bob's gaze then settled on Sidney Fisk, the only other person who had not risen to his feet. The old boatman's lips remained fixed in a straight line, and his hands didn't move from his knees.

Bob forgot about the two old men when the president, assisted by Tom Adams, hung the bronze arm on the wall, placing it between a blade that had been pulled by one of the Olympic crew of 1908, and a zephyr worn by the only blue ever to row in a Cambridge boat that had beaten Oxford four years in a row. Bob began to take photographs of the ceremony so that he would have a record to show his father that he had carried out his wishes.

When the hanging was over, many of the members and old blues surrounded Bob to thank and congratulate him, leaving him in no doubt that all the trouble he had taken to track down the arm had been worthwhile.

Bob was among the last to leave that night, because so many members had wanted to wish him good luck for the future. He was strolling along the footpath back to his digs, humming as he went, when he suddenly remembered that he had left his camera on the table. He decided to collect it in the morning, as he was sure that the clubhouse would be locked and deserted by now, but when he turned round to check, he saw a single light coming from the ground floor.

He turned and began walking back towards the clubhouse, still humming. When he was a few paces away, he glanced through the window, and saw that there were two figures standing in the committee room. He strode over to take a closer look, and was surprised to see the elderly blue, Charles Forester, and Sidney Fisk, the retired boatman, trying to shift a heavy table. He would have gone in to assist them if Fisk hadn't suddenly pointed up toward Dougie Mortimer's arm. Bob remained motionless as he watched the two old men drag the table inch by inch nearer to the wall, until it was directly below the plaque.

Fisk picked up a chair and placed it against the wall, and Forester used it as a step to climb onto the table. Forester then bent down and took the arm of the older man, to help him up.

Once they were both safely on the table, they held a short conversation before reaching up to the bronze cast, easing it off its hooks and slowly lowering it until it rested between their feet. Forester, with the help of the chair, stepped back down onto the floor, then turned round to assist his companion again.

Bob still didn't move, as the two old men carried Dougie Mortimer's arm across the room and out of the boathouse. Having placed it on the ground outside the door, Forester returned to switch off the lights. When he stepped back outside into the cold night air, the boatman quickly padlocked the door.

Once again the two old men held a short conversation before lifting Bob's trophy up and stumbling off with it along the towpath. They had to stop, lower the arm to the ground, rest, and start again several times. Bob followed silently in their wake, using the broad-trunked trees to conceal himself, until the elderly pair suddenly turned and made their way down the bank toward the river. They came to a halt at the water's edge and lowered their bounty into a small rowing boat.

The old blue untied the rope, and the two men pushed the boat slowly out into the river, until the water was lapping around the knees of their evening dress trousers. Neither seemed at all concerned about the fact that they were getting soaked. Forester managed to clamber up into the little boat quite quickly, but it took Fisk several minutes to join him. Once they were both aboard, Forester took his place at the oars, while the boatman remained in the bow, clutching on to Dougie Mortimer's arm.

Forester began to row steadily towards the middle of the river. His progress was slow, but his easy rhythm revealed that he had rowed many times before. When the two men calculated that they had reached the center of the Cam, at its deepest point, Forester stopped rowing and joined his companion in the bow. They picked up the bronze arm and, without ceremony, cast it over the side and into the river. Bob heard the splash and saw the boat rock dangerously from side to side. Fisk then took his turn at the oars; his progress back to the riverbank was even slower than Forester's. They eventually reached land, and both men stumbled out and shoved the boat up toward its mooring, the boatman finally securing the rope to a large ring.

Soaked and exhausted, their breath rising visibly in the clear night air, the two old men stood and faced each other. They shook hands like two business tycoons who had closed an important deal before disappearing into the night.

Tom Adams, the club's honorary secretary, rang Bob the following morning to tell him something he already knew. In fact, he had lain awake all night thinking of little else.

Bob listened to Adams's account of the break-in. "What's surprising is that they only took one thing." He paused. "Your arm—or rather, Dougie's arm. It's very strange, especially as someone had left an expensive camera on the head table."

"Is there anything I can do to help?" asked Bob.

"No, I don't think so, old boy," said Adams. "The local police are making inquiries, but my bet is that whoever stole the arm will probably be halfway across the county by now."

"I expect you're right," said Bob. "While you're on the line, Mr. Adams, I wonder if I could ask you a question about the history of the club."

"I'll do my best," said Adams. "But you must remember that it's only a hobby for me, old chap."

"Do you by any chance know who is the oldest living Oxford rowing blue?" There was a long silence on the other end of the line. "Are you still there?" Bob asked eventually.

"Yes. I was just trying to think if old Harold Deering is still alive. I can't remember seeing his obituary in *The Times.*"

"Deering?" said Bob.

"Yes. Radley and Keble, 1909–10–11. He became a bishop, if I remember correctly, but I'm damned if I can recall where."

"Thank you," said Bob, "that's most helpful."

"I could be wrong," Adams pointed out. "After all, I don't read the obituary columns every day. And I'm a bit rusty when it comes to Oxford."

Bob thanked him once again before hanging up.

After a college lunch he didn't eat, Bob returned to his digs and rang the porter's lodge at Keble. He was answered by a curmudgeonly voice.

"Do you have any record of a Harold Deering, a former member of the college?" Bob asked.

"Deering . . . Deering . . ." said the voice. "That's a new one on me. Let me see if he's in the college handbook." Another long pause, during which Bob really did begin to think he'd been cut off, until the voice said, "Good heavens, no wonder. It was just a bit before my time. Deering, Harold, 1909–11, BA 1911, MA 1916 (Theology). Became Bishop of Truro. Is that the one?"

"Yes, that's the man," said Bob. "Do you by any chance have an address for him?'

"I do," said the voice. "The Rt. Revd. Harold Deering, The Stone House, Mill Road, Tewkesbury, Gloucestershire."

"Thank you," said Bob. "You've been very helpful."

Bob spent the rest of the afternoon composing a letter to the former bishop, in the hope that the old blue might agree to see him.

He was surprised to receive a call at his digs three days later from a Mrs. Elliot, who turned out to be Mr. Deering's daughter, with whom he was now living.

"The poor old chap can't see much beyond his nose these days," she explained, "so I had to read your letter out to him. But he'd be delighted to meet you, and wonders if you could call on him this Sunday at 11:30, after Matins—assuming that's not inconvenient for you."

"That's fine," said Bob. "Please tell your father to expect me around 11:30."

"It has to be in the morning," Mrs. Elliot went on to explain, "because, you see, he has a tendency to fall asleep after lunch. I'm sure you understand. By the way, I'll send directions to your college."

On Sunday morning, Bob was up long before the sun rose, and started out on his journey to Tewkesbury in a car he had rented the previous day. He would have gone by train, but British Rail didn't seem willing to rise quite early enough for him to reach his destination on time. As he journeyed across the Cotswolds, he tried to remember to keep the car on the left, and couldn't help wondering how long it would be before the British started to build some highways with more than one lane.

He drove into Tewkesbury a few minutes after eleven, and thanks to Mrs. Elliot's clear directions, quickly found The Stone House. He parked the car outside a little wicket gate.

A woman had opened the door of the house even before Bob was halfway up the scrub-covered path. "It must be Mr. Kefford," she declared. "I'm Susan Elliot." Bob smiled and shook her hand. "I should warn you," Mrs. Elliot explained as she led him toward the front door, "that you'll have to speak up. Father's become rather deaf lately, and I'm afraid his memory isn't what it used to be. He can recall everything that happened to him at your age, but not even the most simple things that I told him yesterday. I've had to remind him what time you would be coming this morning," she said as they walked through the open door. "Three times."

"I'm sorry to have put you to so much trouble, Mrs. Elliot," said Bob.

"No trouble at all," said Mrs. Elliot as she led him down the corridor. "The truth is, my father's been rather excited by the thought of an American blue from Cambridge coming to visit him after all these years. He hasn't stopped talking about it for the past two days. He's also curious about why you wanted to see him in the first place," she added conspiratorially.

She led Bob into the drawing room, where he immediately came face to face with an old man seated in a winged leather chair, wrapped in a warm plaid dressing gown and propped up on several cushions, his legs covered by a tartan blanket. Bob found it hard to believe that this frail figure had once been an Olympic oarsman.

"Is it him?" the old man asked in a loud voice.

"Yes, Father," Mrs. Elliot replied, equally loudly. "It's Mr. Kefford. He's driven over from Cambridge especially to see you."

Bob walked forward and shook the old man's bony outstretched hand.

"Good of you to come all this way, Kefford," said the former bishop, pulling his blanket up a little higher.

"I appreciate your seeing me, sir," said Bob, as Mrs. Elliot directed him to a comfortable chair opposite her father.

"Would you care for a cup of tea, Kefford?"

"No, thank you, sir," said Bob. "I really don't want anything."

"As you wish," said the old man. "Now, I must warn you, Kefford, that my concentration span isn't quite what it used to be, so you'd better tell me straight away why you've come to see me."

Bob attempted to marshal his thoughts. "I'm doing a little research on a Cambridge blue who must have rowed around the same time as you, sir."

"What's his name?" asked Deering. "I can't remember them all, you know."

Bob looked at him, fearing that this going to turn out to be a wasted journey.

"Mortimer. Dougie Mortimer," he said.

"D.J.T. Mortimer," the old man responded without hesitation. "Now, there's someone you couldn't easily forget. One of the finest strokes Cambridge ever produced—as Oxford found out, to their cost." The old man paused. "You're not a journalist, by any chance?"

"No, sir. It's just a personal whim. I wanted to find out one or two things about him before I return to America."

"Then I will certainly try to help if I can," said the old man in a piping voice.

"Thank you," said Bob. "I'd actually like to begin at the end, if I may, by asking if you knew the circumstances of his death."

There was no response for several moments. The old cleric's eyelids closed, and Bob began to wonder if he had fallen asleep.

"Not the sort of thing chaps talked about in my day," he eventually replied. "Especially with its being against the law at the time, don't you know."

"Against the law?" said Bob, puzzled.

"Suicide. A bit silly, when you think about it," the old priest continued, "even if it is a mortal sin. Because you can't put someone in jail who's already dead, now can you? Not that it was ever confirmed, you understand."

"Do you think it might have been connected with Cambridge losing the Boat Race in 1909, when they were such clear favorites?"

"It's possible, I suppose," said Deering, hesitating once again. "I must admit, the thought had crossed my mind. I took part in that race, as you may know." He paused again, breathing heavily. "Cambridge were the clear favorites, and we didn't give ourselves a chance. The result was never properly explained, I must admit. There were a lot of rumors doing the rounds at the time, but no proof—no proof, you understand."

"What wasn't proved?" asked Bob. There was another long silence, during which Bob began to fear that the old man might have thought he'd gone too far.

"My turn to ask you a few questions, Kefford," he said eventually.

"Of course, sir."

"My daughter tells me that you've stroked the winning boat for Cambridge three years in a row."

"That's correct, sir."

"Congratulations, my boy. But tell me: if you had wanted to lose one of those races, could you have done so, without the rest of the crew being aware of it?"

It was Bob's turn to ponder. He realized for the first time since he had entered the room that he shouldn't assume that a frail body necessarily indicates a frail mind.

"Yes, I guess so," he eventually said. "You could always change the stroke rate without warning, or even catch a crab as you took the Surrey bend. Heaven knows, there's always enough flotsam on the river to make it appear unavoidable." Bob looked the old man straight in the eye. "But it would never have crossed my mind that anyone might do so deliberately."

"Nor mine," said the priest, "had their cox not taken holy orders."

"I'm not sure I understand, sir," said Bob.

"No reason you should, young man. I find nowadays that I think in non sequiturs. I'll try to be less obscure. The cox of the 1909 Cambridge boat was a chap called Bertie Partridge. He went on to become a parish priest in some outpost called Chersfield in Rutland. Probably the only place that would have him," he chuckled. "But when I became Bishop of Truro, he wrote and invited me to address his flock. It was such an arduous journey from Cornwall to Rutland in those days, that I could easily have made my excuses, but like you, I wanted the mystery of the 1909 race solved, and I thought this might be my only chance."

Bob made no attempt to interrupt, fearing he might stop the old man's flow.

"Partridge was a bachelor, and bachelors get very lonely, don't you know. If you give them half a chance, they love to gossip. I stayed overnight, which gave him every chance. He told me, over a long dinner accompanied by a bottle of non-vintage wine, that it was well known that Mortimer had run up debts all over Cambridge. Not many undergraduates don't, you might say, but in Mortimer's case they far exceeded even his potential income. I think he rather hoped that his fame and popularity would stop his creditors from pressing their claims. Not unlike Disraeli when he was Prime Minister," he added with another chuckle.

"But in Mortimer's case one particular shopkeeper, who had absolutely no interest in rowing, and even less in undergraduates, threatened to bankrupt him the week before the 1909 boat race. A few days after the race had been lost, Mortimer seemed, without explanation, to have cleared all his obligations, and nothing more was heard of the matter."

Once again the old man paused as if in deep thought. Bob remained silent, still not wishing to distract him.

"The only other thing I can recall is that the bookies made a killing," Deering said without warning. "I know that to my personal cost, because my tutor lost a five-pound wager, and never let me forget that I had told him we didn't have a snowball's chance in hell. Mind you, I was always able to offer that as my excuse for not getting a First." He looked up and smiled at his visitor.

Bob sat on the edge of his seat, mesmerized by the old man's recollections.

"I'm grateful for your candor, sir," he said. "And you can be assured of my discretion."

"Thank you, Kefford," said the old man, now almost whispering. "I'm only too delighted to have been able to assist you. Is there anything else I can help you with?"

"No, thank you, sir," said Bob. "I think you've covered everything I needed to know."

Bob rose from his chair, and as he turned to thank Mrs. Elliot, he noticed for the first time a bronze cast of an arm hanging on the far wall. Below it was printed in gold:

H.R.R. DEERING
1909–10–11
(KEBLE, BOW)

"You must have been a fine oarsman, sir."

"No, not really," said the old blue. "But I was lucky enough to be in the winning boat three years in a row, which wouldn't please a Cambridge man like yourself."

Bob laughed. "Perhaps one last question before I leave, sir."

"Of course, Kefford."

"Did they ever make a bronze of Dougie Mortimer's arm?"

"They most certainly did," replied the priest. "But it mysteriously disappeared from your boathouse in 1912. A few weeks later the boatman was sacked without explanation—caused quite a stir at the time."

"Was it known why he was sacked?" asked Bob.

"Partridge claimed that when the old boatman got drunk one night, he confessed to having dumped Mortimer's arm in the middle of the Cam." The old man paused, smiled, and added, "Best place for it, wouldn't you say, Kefford?"

Bob thought about the question for some time, wondering how his father would have reacted. He then replied simply, "Yes, sir. Best place for it."

John D. MacDonald (1916–1986) is one of the great writers in the mystery/ detective genre. His best-known character is Travis McGee, a Floridian who specializes in getting people out of scrapes. MacDonald's most famous book is The Executioners *(1958), which was twice made into a movie called "Cape Fear." Among his other novels are* No Deadly Drug *(1968),* Condominium *(1977), and* Barrier Island *(1987). MacDonald also wrote about subjects other than crime. The story below concerns a veteran major league baseball player reaching the end of his career.*

John D. MacDonald

A YOUNG MAN'S
GAME (1961)

HE CAME AWAKE IN THE first gray of morning, and saw the palm tops above the mist, coming toward the car and sliding by the window on his side. He rubbed a hand across his face and massaged the back of his neck with big fingers, shifting in the seat and feeling the tingle of circulation along a half-numbed leg. Madge sat small and alert on her cushion, hands tight on the wheel, chin uplifted, as she watched the road ahead where the car lights yellowed the mist.

"Good sleep, honey?" she asked, not taking her eyes from the road ahead.

"I don't know yet. How far we get?"

"Into Florida. We ought to be there in time for lunch."

He stretched in a massive way, hearing the muscles of his right shoulder pop, yawned wide, growled as he yawned. With his left arm still outstretched, he knuckled the back of her fair head lightly.

"Hey!" she said.

"Lots of years, kid. Lots of trips. Lots of blubber to work off every spring."

"Not so much this year, Wally," she said defensively. "Gosh, not like last year."

"About twelve pounds will do it," he agreed.

She gave him a quick glance. "Don't try to do it too fast."

"Want me to drive now?"

"Wait until you're all waked up. I'm not really tired yet."

Usually they managed better, bringing the car down, but this year there had been a hitch in turning the reins of the business over to Thomasson. The accountants wanted to install a new system and Wally Prews wanted to wait and see how it worked out. He hadn't wanted to show up late. Every year, it was just that much harder to get into shape—without complicating matters by losing the first few days. He told Madge he could fly down and then she could bring the car on down, taking her time, but he saw the sharp disappointment in her eyes even as she agreed. So they worked it out, figuring that if they took turns driving, they could make it—just make it. He hoped it would be warm. Heat would make it easier to melt off the winter fat.

Once the sun cut the mist, they began to make better time. He took the wheel and Madge sat beside him, legs pulled up under her. Her head sagged against his shoulder and she slept.

At eleven-thirty, when they were a few miles out of town, he awakened her gently. She patted her hair and fixed her lipstick. He went out of his way to drive by the field. He saw that the stands had been enlarged and repainted. The turf on the field looked new and good. Three men in heavy gray sweat suits were jogging across the outfield grass. The staff would have been in town for a week, getting things lined up, sorting equipment, making up training schedules. The trainer would have the whirlpools set up and the tables and hot lamps. As he drove slowly by it seemed to him that he could detect the familiar locker room smell—socks and sweat and liniments and astringents and oiled leather.

It was a good town, a good place to train. He drove on out to the beach. Old man Giffert was in the rental office. Mrs. Giffert came trotting in moments later.

"By golly," Giffert said. "By golly—Wally Prews. And how you, Miz Prews? It's sure fine to see you folks again. Now the baseball's started for sure. We got you in the same cabaña again. Number seven. Anything you need, just anything at all, you just holler. By golly, Wally, you sure got a-holt of one in that last Cleveland game. By golly, you put it out of the park. Pinch-hit home run. Bet it felt real fine."

"It felt fine, Dan. We'll go get settled in. It's good to be back."

He unloaded the car, and while Madge unpacked, he called Lew at the hotel.

"Lew? This is Wally. Yeah, just got in. What do you mean, shape? I'm a fat old man. Look, we got to get some lunch. Is Alice down yet? Fine. Suppose we stop around later. See you."

He hung up, aware of Madge standing motionless by the dresser, some of his shirts in her hand, watching him.

"All right," he said, too harshly. "He sounded okay. What's he supposed to do? Run over here and kiss me?"

"Please, Wally."

"I'm sorry," he said.

He walked out onto the beach. There had been some erosion. The beach wasn't as large as before. But the sand was clean and white. He snapped his cigarette away. When she came out and said she was ready, they went and ate at the beach restaurant they liked.

"I didn't mean to snap at you," he told her gently.

"I guess he just scares me, honey. He didn't used to. But you know how he is. Oh, he's nice enough, I guess—but people mean absolutely nothing to him."

"It has to be that way. He's an old man. Suppose he gets sentimental. Then he starts fielding teams full of crocks like me and every game is old-timer's day. He'd give me his shirt, his car and his bank account if he thought I needed it. But he sees me dogging it and he yanks me out like he never saw me before. But I'm okay this year. He's got too many kids. He needs balance. I'm okay this year."

"Of course, you are, dear."

And something about the way she said it brought back some of the dull anger. He forced it away and smiled at her. "You going to eat this place clean out of shrimp again this year?"

"Mmmm," she said. "Bushels and tons."

He watched her as she scanned the menu. The booth light touched the gray streak over her ear. Eighteen years in organized ball. Seventeen years married. A long time. So that the words said do not mean much. The real meanings all come clear behind the words.

The front office had sent along the contract in triplicate, in mid-December. The typed figure shocked and angered him. They had given him the maximum cut allowable, the full twenty-five percent. He'd called Lew at his Texas place ten minutes after he ripped open the impressive envelope.

"Well, Wally, you got to look at it this way. That last-year figure, that was figured on a regular. Then you got that slump, and that Whitlock, he come up so good and strong, and that Kimberland was hitting, and so you were—well, reserved for half the season. Then they make out the budget and—"

"Nuts, Lew. This isn't a salary. It's more like a pension. I slumped and I came back. I pinch-hit a three-seventeen for you. I do a clown act on only two flies all year. I won't sign this damn thing."

"Well, it's pretty tough, Wally. You don't sit where I sit. Before television they never got so cautious. Well, you sit tight. Let me see what I can do. But I don't think I can do much."

Two weeks later, another set of contracts was mailed to him. Five percent of the cut had been restored. He had held out for a month, not communicating with them in any way. That month had been hell. Until

Madge had said, "Dear, I'm getting terribly tired of living with a bear. And it's all pride, you know. Not the money. We can get along. You want to play ball. You're afraid they'll let you go on waiver. Just sign, dear. Then you can prove they're wrong."

It made sense. He felt a great weight lift off him when he dropped the signed contracts in the mail. And that was it—now. Prove they were wrong. Get out with the kids. Get the timing working. Get the fat off. Get that jump on the ball every time.

Madge drove him out and left him off the next morning. The town people had put new name signs on the lockers of the regulars. His name had been gaudily, lovingly printed and he had to grin at it.

Pilko, the squat, hairy catcher, patted him smartly across the pale winter softness of his waistline and said, "Old butterball. Old mushmellow."

"Still standing in your hole, Pilk?"

Pilko strained to stand on tiptoe. "Say, Wally, that kid of mine. The boy. Thirteen, he is. And already an inch taller than his old man. A monster, he'll be."

The kids up for their seasonal hack at the big time used the unnamed lockers and made as if they were not the least bit impressed with the large names around them. It was always that way. Always nonchalant, and most of them too smart to grandstand.

Wally Prews bundled himself up. He knew that Christy wouldn't bother him, that Christy would let him pace himself, lean the body down, harden the hands, toughen the legs, build up the wind. And, as always, when he started to jog around the outfield, he felt thick, middle-aged, sweaty and ridiculous. A bulky, overgrown child playing a solitary game with the grimness of all children who pretend.

Pilko ran with him for a time. On the far side of the field, one of the coaches was putting the kids through organized calisthenics. Sweat ran into Wally's eyes, making them sting. At the end of the session, one of Christy's men rubbed him down expertly. He was two pounds lighter. Christy, himself, took care of the threat of a blister on the side of his right heel.

Every night at the cabaña, he tumbled into the deepest of sleeps. At first, he was waking up stiff and sore, taking minutes to work his way out of bed. Then, that began to ease off. At the end of ten days, he was down to one-ninety, where he belonged, and the sun no longer reddened his brown neck.

Yet he knew he was not as relaxed as during other years. There was a tension in him that erupted into anger too easily and too often. He took his turn in the batting cage after batting-tee practice. A new kid was throwing them in. Wally measured his distance from the plate with his bat, planted his feet in his wide, solid stance, bat cocked. He hit two steaming line drives and then a pop-up and then two fouls before he got hold of one in the sweetly remembered way and dumped it out where he wanted it. The kid had been throwing with an easy rhythm. On the next pitch, he made a cute little hesitation. Wally didn't bother to swing. He walked four steps toward the mound and said, "Okay, you pitched a no-hitter. We won thirty to nothing. Now relax and throw."

"I'm sorry, Mr. Prews," the kid said.

The formality of the address shocked Wally. He went back and got hold of several more before Quinn motioned him out. He jogged out through the hole between first and second and took right field, picking up the glove Whitlock had tossed aside as he came in, and feeling an unreasonable annoyance with Whitlock for not holding the glove, tossing it to him as they jogged past one another.

Annoyance kept him full of adrenalin, and when Whitlock hit a sharp line drive into short right, Wally charged it hard, snapped it off the bounce and practiced a peg to the plate. The pitcher cut it off, but not before Wally saw, with satisfaction, that it was straight, true and fast.

When they played the first exhibition game, splitting up into two teams and opening the stands to the public, Wally was pleased by the hand he got. He got two at bat before relinquishing his position to Kimberland. He struck out once and doubled once, driving in a man from first, a new man who ran as if his pants were on fire.

Even then, he couldn't shake off the constant irritation, and he told himself that he was sore because he was being purchased at cut rates this year. It certainly wasn't because he could see that both Kimberland and Whitlock were just as hot as during the last half of the previous season.

The first scheduled exhibition was with the Giants from the other league. Wally started in right. He played three innings but only got one at bat because it was Hearn throwing and he was rough. In his one time at bat, he hit the second ball pitched into a corner for a stand-up double and died there. He knew he had looked good in the field. He threw out Mays when Mays tried to stretch a single into a double. He made a good, long, running catch of a ball that some new kid got a fat piece of, and drew applause on the catch.

But after he came out, he sat sour on the bench, big shoe against the Coke machine, watching without any stir of interest. He knew that Madge was aware of his sourness, and he had seen the little ways in which she had tried to raise his spirits. He tried to respond, and knew his laughter was leaden.

At the end of one day, as he was combing his shower-wet hair over the fifty-cent bald spot, Lew came up behind him and said, "You and Madge, you two going to be home later on?"

"Sure, Lew. Stop on over. Bring Alice."

"Just me. She's got something on."

Wally didn't like the expression on Lew's face. It was too elaborately casual. He made himself smile. "Come on over any time. We'll be there."

Lew came just after dusk. He stood by the screen door and listened to the sound of the Gulf and said, "I stayed on the beach one year. Well, I like to died for not sleeping. Too damn noisy."

"How about a drink, Lew?" Madge asked him.

Lew folded his lean old body into a chair. "Now, if you got a cold brew . . ."

When they were all seated, Lew, looking peculiarly shy, said, "Well, I thought you ought to have a chance to put your two cents in this thing, Madge. Wally's been playing for me a long time."

"Eight seasons, Lew," Madge said quietly. "This will be the ninth."

"Or it won't be the ninth," Wally heard himself say.

"Well, that opens it up," Lew said, a little sharpness in his voice. "I been on the phone a lot. Trading talk. I'll keep the other club out of this. Just say this much. They haven't finished better than fifth in the last four years. They got outfield weakness and power weakness. And they got a kid we want where we're shaky, over there on third. I think maybe we use you for bait and they bite, Wally."

"Then go ahead. Don't come around apologizing in advance."

"You've been one damn miserable man ever since you showed up here, Prews," Lew said.

"I've been playing good ball."

"I know that. I didn't expect that."

Wally stared at him. "That's a hell of a funny thing to say!"

"I don't see how it is. Now, take last year. You were going good. Then you got so hot about whether or not you'd show up good enough to get in another year as a regular that you slumped off. Now, you come down here with a big chip on your shoulder and go around biting on people because already you're wondering about next year. Be honest, Wally Prews. Talk up. Aren't you thinking on next year?"

Wally looked down at his big hands. "Maybe I am, Lew," he said.

"You've got a nice business of your own. You've had a lot of years of ball. You were never a sour guy. What's your trouble now, Wally?"

Wally glanced at Madge and then looked down again. He wanted to put his finger on the trouble. He said the only thing he could think of. 'It—it just doesn't seem to be any fun any more, Lew."

"I figured that. You always played hard. You were always a tough competitor. Now you're fighting yourself and me. You keep it up and you're going to slump worse than last year. Wally, why don't you make this the last year? Only you and me and Madge has to know it. Stop fighting yourself. You do that and I won't trade you. Maybe I'm a little superstitious about you. I've done pretty good in those eight seasons."

Next year, he thought. Watch from the stands. No hard swing and good gutty crack, and the ball sailing high as that great crowd sound came; no running hard for first and then seeing it go and slowing to that jog trot, taking off the cap after you round third. But, also, none of that drawn-down, sick weariness during the hot tag end of the season; none of forcing of muscles which have lost resilience. And Madge would not have to face the brittle, feline politeness of the other baseball wives. It would be down in the record book and all over.

He looked over at Madge. Her eyes were steady. Her expression told him nothing. "It's up to you, Wally," she said quietly.

"But how do you feel?"

"I want what you want. If it isn't any fun any more . . ." She shrugged.

He looked at Lew and then back at Madge. "This will be the last season, Lew," he said. And he saw the gladness in Madge's eyes, quickly masked.

Lew got up and cuffed him on the shoulder. "Okay, Wally. So now I'm fresh out of bait and we don't get that fast feller on third the way I wanted."

They heard him drive away. "Let's take a walk down the beach, honey," Wally said.

They walked on the hard sand where the tide had gone out. The last year. It was funny how thinking about it took weights off him. He held her hand as they walked. The last year in ball. The word had been given. He did not want to change it. And he had a feeling that he would be hot, and stay hot—substituting the ball sense and experience of eighteen years for Whitlock's younger legs, Kimberland's powerful swing. And no slump this year, because it was the last, with everything on the line.

He grunted and it was a sound that was half laugh, half pain.

"Darling?" she said.

"That old carp. That scavenger. All his talk about superstition. Don't you get it? He gets a good year out of me, maybe the best yet if I can keep lucky. Then next year, either Whitlock or Kimberland goes into my slot."

She stopped there, turned to face him. "But, Wally, does that mean you won't . . ."

He took her by the shoulders and turned her a little so that the moonlight was more clearly against her face. There was a feeling of rest, of peace, within him. And love for her.

"This is a fat old man playing his last year, Madge. And it might even be fun again, like they tell you it should be. It's a game, isn't it?"

She smiled in moonlight. "I guess I better be kissed."

So he did, and they walked back to the cabaña through the wave sounds, his big arm around her, their moonlight shadows sharp and clear on the white Florida sand.

Set in Japan after World War I, this story is poignant for its revelations about human character. British writer W. Somerset Maugham (1874–1965) had made a name for himself as a playwright before his masterpiece novel Of Human Bondage *was published in 1915. Other famous novels include* The World Over *(1925),* The Moon and Sixpence *(1941), and* The Razor's Edge *(1945).*

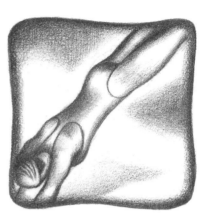

W. Somerset Maugham

A FRIEND IN NEED
(1925)

FOR THIRTY YEARS NOW I have been studying my fellow men. I do not know very much about them. I should certainly hesitate to engage a servant on his face, and yet I suppose it is on the face that for the most part we judge the persons we meet. We draw our conclusions from the shape of the jaw, the look in the eyes, the contour of the mouth. I wonder if we are more often right than wrong. Why novels and plays are so often untrue to life is because their authors, perhaps of necessity, make their characters all of a piece. They cannot afford to make them self-contradictory, for then they become incomprehensible, and yet self-contradictory is what most of us are. We are a haphazard bundle of inconsistent qualities. In books on logic they will tell you that it is absurd to say that yellow is tubular or gratitude heavier than air; but in that mixture of incongruities that makes up the self yellow may very well be a horse and cart and gratitude the middle of next week. I shrug my shoulders when people tell me that their first impressions of a person are always right. I think they must have small insight or great vanity. For my own part I find that the longer I know people the more they puzzle me; my oldest friends are just those of whom I can say that I don't know the first thing about them.

These reflections have occurred to me because I read in this morning's paper that Edward Hyde Burton had died at Kobe. He was a merchant and he had been in business in Japan for many years. I knew him very little, but he interested me because once he gave me a great surprise. Unless I had heard the story from his own lips I should never have believed that he was capable of such an action. It was more startling because both in appearance and manner he suggested a very definite type. Here if ever was a man all of a piece. He was a tiny little fellow, not much more than five feet four in height, and very slender, with white hair, a red face much wrinkled, and blue eyes. I suppose he was about sixty when I knew him. He was always neatly and quietly dressed in accordance with his age and station.

Though his offices were in Kobe Burton often came down to Yokohama. I happened on one occasion to be spending a few days there, waiting for a ship, and I was introduced to him at the British Club. We played bridge together. He played a good game and a generous one. He did not talk very much, either then or later when we were having drinks, but what he said was sensible. He had a quiet, dry humor. He seemed to be popular at the club and afterward, when he had gone, they described him as one of the best. It happened that we were both staying at the Grand Hotel and next day he asked me to dine with him. I met his wife, fat, elderly and smiling, and his two daughters. It was evidently a united and affectionate family. I think the chief thing that struck me about Burton was his kindliness. There was something very pleasing in his mild blue eyes. His voice was gentle; you could not imagine that he could possibly raise it in anger; his smile was benign. Here was a man who attracted you because you felt in him a real love for his fellows. He had charm. But there was nothing mawkish in him; he liked his game of cards and his cocktail, he could tell with point a good and spicy story, and in his youth he had been something of an athlete. He was a rich man and he had made every penny himself. I suppose one thing that made you like him was that he was so small and frail; he aroused your instincts of protection. You felt that he could not bear to hurt a fly.

One afternoon I was sitting in the lounge of the Grand Hotel. This was before the earthquake and they had leather armchairs there. From the windows you had a spacious view of the harbor with its crowded traffic. There were great liners on their way to Vancouver and San Francisco or to Europe by way of Shanghai, Hong Kong and Singapore; there were tramps of all nations, battered and seaworn, junks with their high sterns and great colored sails, and innumerable sampans. It was a busy, exhilarating scene, and yet, I know not why, restful to the spirit. Here was romance and it seemed that you had but to stretch out your hand to touch it.

Burton came into the lounge presently and caught sight of me. He seated himself in the chair next to mine.

"What do you say to a little drink?"

He clapped his hands for a boy and ordered two gin fizzes. As the boy brought them a man passed along the street outside and, seeing me, waved his hand.

"Do you know Turner?" said Burton as I nodded a greeting.

"I've met him at the club. I'm told he's a remittance man."

"Yes, I believe he is. We have a good many here."

"He plays bridge well."

"They generally do. There was a fellow here last year, oddly enough a namesake of mine, who was the best bridge player I ever met. I suppose you never came across him in London. Lenny Burton he called himself. I believe he'd belonged to some very good clubs."

"No, I don't believe I remember the name."

"He was quite a remarkable player. He seemed to have an instinct about the cards. It was uncanny. I used to play with him a lot. He was in Kobe for some time."

Burton sipped his gin fizz.

"It's rather a funny story," he said. "He wasn't a bad chap. I liked him. He was always well dressed and smart-looking. He was handsome, in a way, with curly hair and pink-and-white cheeks. Women thought a lot of him. There was no harm in him, you know, he was only wild. Of course he drank too much. Those sort of fellows always do. A bit of money used to come in for him once a quarter and he made a bit more by cardplaying. He won a good deal of mine, I know that."

Burton gave a kindly chuckle. I knew from my own experiences that he could lose money at bridge with a good grace. He stroked his shaven chin with his thin hand; the veins stood out on it and it was almost transparent.

"I suppose that is why he came to me when he went broke, that and the fact that he was a namesake of mine. He came to see me in my office one day and asked me for a job. I was rather surprised. He told me that there was no more money coming from home and he wanted to work. I asked him how old he was.

"'Thirty-five,' he said.

"'And what have you been doing hitherto?' I asked him.

"'Well, nothing very much,' he said.

"I couldn't help laughing.

"'I'm afraid I can't do anything for you just yet,' I said. 'Come back and see me in another thirty-five years, and I'll see what I can do.'

"He didn't move. He went rather pale. He hesitated for a moment and then he told me that he had had bad luck at cards for some time. He hadn't been willing to stick to bridge, he'd been playing poker, and he'd got trimmed. He hadn't a penny. He'd pawned everything he had. He couldn't pay his hotel bill and they wouldn't give him any more credit. He was down and out. If he couldn't get something to do he'd have to commit suicide.

"I looked at him for a bit. I could see now that he was all to pieces. He'd been drinking more than usual and he looked fifty. The girls wouldn't have thought so much of him if they'd seen him then.

"'Well, isn't there anything you can do except play cards?' I asked him.

"'I can swim,' he said.

"'Swim!'

"I could hardly believe my ears; it seemed such an insane answer to give.

"'I swam for my university.'

"I got some glimmering of what he was driving at. I've known too many men who were little tin gods at their university to be impressed by it.

"'I was a pretty good swimmer myself when I was a young man,' I said.

"Suddenly I had an idea."

Pausing in his story, Burton turned to me.

"Do you know Kobe?" he asked.

"No," I said, "I passed through it once, but I only spent a night there."

"Then you don't know the Shioya Club. When I was a young man I swam from there round the beacon and landed at the creek of Tarumi. It's over three miles and it's rather difficult on account of the currents round the beacon. Well, I told my young namesake about it and I said to him that if he'd do it I'd give him a job.

"I could see he was rather taken aback.

"'You say you're a swimmer,' I said.

"'I'm not in very good condition,' he answered.

"I didn't say anything. I shrugged my shoulders. He looked at me for a moment and then he nodded.

"'All right,' he said. 'When do you want me to do it?'

"I looked at my watch. It was just after ten.

"'The swim shouldn't take you much over an hour and a quarter. I'll drive round to the creek at half past twelve and meet you. I'll take you back to the club to dress and then we'll have lunch together.'

"'Done,' he said.

"We shook hands. I wished him good luck and he left me. I had a lot of work to do that morning and I only just managed to get to the creek at Tarumi at half past twelve. But I needn't have hurried; he never turned up."

"Did he funk it at the last moment?" I asked.

"No, he didn't funk it. He started all right. But of course he'd ruined his constitution by drink and dissipation. The currents round the beacon were more than he could manage. We didn't get the body for about three days."

I didn't say anything for a moment or two. I was a trifle shocked. Then I asked Burton a question.

"When you made him that offer of a job, did you know he'd be drowned?"

He gave a little mild chuckle and he looked at me with those kind and candid blue eyes of his. He rubbed his chin with his hand.

"Well, I hadn't got a vacancy in my office at the moment."

A short story craftsman, André Dubus (1936–1999) wrote his first novel, The Lieutenant, *in 1967. In 1986 he was struck by a car, leaving him wheelchair-bound. Thereafter, he penned some of his finest stories, collected in books such as* Adultery and Other Choices *(1977) and* Dancing After Hours: Stories *(1996). The story here first appeared in the* New Yorker. *It is about a boy, his father, and golf.*

André Dubus

AN AFTERNOON WITH THE OLD MAN (1972)

NOW SUNDAY WAS OVER, and Paul Clement lay in bed in his room and wished for Marshall, his one wish in all the world right now (and he was a boy with many wishes; "If wishes were horses beggars would ride," his mother said when people wished). But Marshall was in Baton Rouge; he had not seen her since the Clements moved from there to Lafayette after the second grade. Maybe he would never see her again. But he would. When he was old enough to drive a car, he would go to Baton Rouge and surprise her. She would squeal and hug him. He saw her, sixteen years old, running down her front steps and sidewalk to meet him; she had breasts and used lipstick and she wore a white dress. Paul knew that now, at ten, he was good-looking—his face was his only pride, it was why Marshall had been his girl—and when he was sixteen he would be even more handsome and bigger and stronger, too, because he had been praying every night and at mass for God to make him an athlete.

He met Marshall in the second grade, a brown-eyed tomboy; she hated dresses, she got dirty when she played, and she brought two cap pistols and a dump truck to the scrap-iron pile at school. ("We sold the Japs our scrap iron, and now they're using it against us," his father said.) Once at recess she drove away with rocks fat Warren, who was kicking dust at Paul. There was a girl named Penny, with long black hair; she sat behind him in class and handed him pictures she drew (he remembered one of her father lying in bed with a broken leg, the leg suspended and weights hanging from it). Penny was prettier than Marshall, but she sometimes irritated him because she always wanted to hold his hand while they waited in line to go into school, and when there was a movie at school she held him captive, pulling him down the auditorium aisle and into a seat beside her, and during the movie her head was warm on his shoulder, her long hair tickling his throat and damp where it pressed his cheek. So he loved Marshall more. His sisters, Amy and Barbara, and his mother knew about Marshall, but his father did not. When Paul told his mother, she said, "Aren't you going to tell Daddy you have a girlfriend?"

"No."

"You should talk more with Daddy. He loves y'all very much, but he doesn't know how to talk to children."

His mother said she would keep his secret. One warm afternoon after school he was to go to a birthday party at a girl's house. His mother asked if Marshall would be there, and he said yes. She smiled and combed his hair with her fingers. "Now don't you kiss her," she said in her tease voice.

At the party, they played hide-and-seek, and he and Marshall sat on a running board in the garage; the boy who was "It" passed by without looking in. The lawn and garage were quiet now; the game had passed them, and Marshall said, "Kiss me."

"No."

"Please." She had olive skin, her brown eyes were large, and a front tooth was missing.

"If you close your eyes," he said. She did, and he kissed her lips and tasted the line of sweat above her mouth.

After hide-and-seek, Marshall and Paul got on the swing hanging from an oak. Marshall wanted him to sit; she stood facing him, her feet squeezed between his hips and the ropes, her skirt moving against this face as she pumped them higher and higher till they swung up level with the branch where the ropes were tied, and she said, "I'd like to go *all* around, over the branch." Paul hoped she wouldn't try.

When he got home his mother asked if he kissed Marshall and he said yes. She smiled and hugged him.

Here in Lafayette he did not have a girl. He did not even know a girl his age, because he didn't go to a public school now; he went to Cathedral, a boys' school taught by Christian Brothers. At the school in Baton Rouge there had been recess, but no one told you what to play and usually he had been with Penny or Marshall, mostly Marshall. But at Cathedral there was physical education for an hour every day, and it was like being in Baton Rouge when his father still played with them, throwing a tennis ball in the backyard. If Barbara or Amy threw to Paul, he sometimes caught it and sometimes did not, but when his father threw it or even if his father was just watching, his muscles stiffened and his belly fluttered and he always missed. At Cathedral it was like that, like being watched by his father.

His father had not played golf in Baton Rouge, or for the first two years in Lafayette; then a priest named Father O'Gorman started coming over and eating supper with them. In summer before supper the men drank beer on the screen porch and listened to the six o'clock news. Father O'Gorman was a bulky man who always smelled like cigars; he liked to tousle Paul's hair. He told Paul's mother not to worry that her husband was an Episcopalian and didn't go to church. "Any man who kneels down and says his prayers every night the way your husband does is a good man." That is what Father O'Gorman told her; she told it to Paul, who had not worried about his father going to hell until the day his mother said the priest said he would not.

Father O'Gorman got Paul's father interested in golf. Soon he had clubs and a bag and shoes, and was taking lessons, playing every Saturday and Sunday, and practicing two or three times a week after work and sometimes on Saturday mornings. One night at supper Paul's mother said to Father O'Gorman, "If I run off with another man it'll be your fault, Father." She was smiling the way she did when she didn't see anything funny. "My husband and I used to be together every weekend, now I'm all by myself."

Paul had not liked those weekends very much. On many Sundays they had gone to New Iberia to visit his mother's family, the Kelleys, who had once had money and lived in a big brick house with Negro women working inside and Negro men working in a yard as big as a school ground, but later all the money was gone and the house, too, and the married aunts and uncles lived like the Clements in small white houses on quiet streets. Those drives to New Iberia were quiet; once there, though, his parents had drinks, and on the way home there was talking.

"I'm home every night," his father said. "She knows that."

"Well, sure you're home, when it's too dark to see the ball, and all your cronies and Betsy Robichaux have gone home, so there's nobody to drink your old beer with." She was smiling at Paul's father, and winking at Father O'Gorman.

Paul's father practiced on a school ground near their house, and he wanted Paul to shag balls for him. The pay was fifty cents, and it was an easy job to stand daydreaming with a canvas bag in his hand and watch his father's small faceless figure, the quick pencil-small flash of swinging golf club, and then spot the ball in the air and stay clear of it till it struck the ground. Easy enough, and he liked earning the money. But he did not like to shag balls, for it wasn't simply a job like raking leaves. He was supposed to like picking up balls that his father hit; afterward, in the car, he was supposed to be interested while his father explained the different irons and woods, and told why sometimes he sliced and sometimes hooked. And he was supposed to want to caddie, to spend all Sunday afternoon following his father around the golf course. "Maybe you'll want to caddie one of these Sundays," his father said as they drove home from the school ground. "I know you can't miss the Saturday picture show, but maybe Sundays—keeps the money in the family that way." Paul sat stiffly, looking through the windshield, smelling the leather golf bag and his father's sweat. "Maybe so," he said.

Now tonight if Marshall were here with him, and if for some reason his parents and Amy and Barbara left the house and went someplace, like visiting in New Iberia, he and Marshall would go to the kitchen and he would make peanut butter and blackberry preserve sandwiches. They would take them with glasses of cold milk to the living room, where the large lazy-sounding oscillating floor fan moved the curtain at one end of its arc, then rustled the Sunday paper on the couch as it swept back. He would sit beside her on the couch, and when they finished the sand-wiches he would rest his head in her lap and look up at her bright eyes and tell her about today, how at Sunday dinner his father had said, "Want to come out today?" and he had chewed a large bite of chocolate cake, trying to think of a reason not to, and then swallowed and said, "Sure."

After dinner, his father got an extra pack of Luckies from the bedroom, and then it was time to go. His mother walked out on the screen porch with them; the wisteria climbing the screen was blooming lavender. "Keep an eye on him in this heat," she said to his father.

"I will."

She kissed them. As they walked to the car, she called, "Look at my two handsome men. Paul, be a good influence on your father, bring him home early."

In the car, they did not talk for six blocks or so. Then his father told him he ought to have a cap to keep the sun off his head, and Paul said he'd be O.K.

"That mama of yours, if I bring you home with a headache she'll say the golf course is the only place the sun shines."

Paul smiled. The rest of the way to the golf course they did not talk. Walking to the clubhouse, Paul trailed a step or two behind his father.

Caddies stood near the sidewalk—tall boys with dirty bare feet or ragged
sneakers and hard brown biceps. Several of them were smoking. ("It
stunts the growth," his mother said.) They were the kind of boys Paul always yielded the sidewalk to when he walked to the cowboy show and
serial in town on Saturdays. Paul looked out at the golf course, shielding
his eyes with one hand, and studied the distant greens and fairways as he
and his father passed the boys and their smell of cigarette smoke and
sweat and sweet hair oil.

"Mr. Clement, you need a caddie?"

"No thanks, Tujack. I got my boy."

From under his shielding hand, Paul stared over the flat fairway at a
tiny red flag, hanging limply over the heat shimmer. As he followed his
father into the clubhouse, he felt their eyes on him; then, turning a corner around the showcase of clubs, he was out of their vision, and he followed his father's broad shoulders and brown hairy arms into the locker
room. His father sat on a bench and put on his golf shoes.

"That Tujack's going to be a hell of a golfer."

"He plays?"

"They all play, these caddies."

Outside, in the hot dust behind the clubhouse, his father strapped the
golf bag onto a cart, and Paul pulled it behind him to the first tee. Tujack
was there, a tall wiry boy of about sixteen, a golf bag slung over his shoulder. Paul shook hands with Mr. Blanchet, Mr. Voorhies, Mr. Peck. Each of
them, as he shook hands, looked Paul up and down, as though to judge
what sort of boy their friend had. Paul gave his father the driver and then
pulled the cart away from the tee, stopping short of the three caddies, who
stood under a sycamore. He was the only one using a cart, and he wished
his father hadn't done that. I can carry it, he wanted to say.

The first hole had a long dogleg going to the left around a field of short
brown weeds. His father shot first, driving two thirds of the way down
the first leg; he came over and gave Paul the driver and stood between
him and the caddies, closing the distance. "You'll be on in two, Mr.
Clement," Tujack said.

"You could, Tujack. Not me."

They were quiet while the others shot, and then Paul walked beside his father, pulling the cart behind him. It seemed badly balanced, and he watched the ground ahead of him for those small rises that might tip the cart over on its side with a shamefaced clanking of clubs. After the first nine, they stopped at the clubhouse for a drink, and his father asked him how he was holding up. "Fine," Paul said. He was. He didn't tire on the second nine, either. It was a hot afternoon, but he liked to sweat, and there was not much need for talking. ("Good shot." "Well, let's see what I can do with the brassie.") Usually, between shots, he walked a little to the rear, and his father talked to one of the men.

When they finished playing, his father gave him a dollar and a quarter and told him he was a good caddie, then asked if he was tired or too hot and what did he want to drink, and took him into the clubhouse and up to the counter. "Give this boy a Grapette and some cheese crackers," his father said, his hand coming down on Paul's shoulder, staying there.

"That your boy?" the man behind the counter said.

"That's him," the hand on Paul's shoulder squeezing now, rocking him back and forth. Paul lowered his eyes and smiled and blushed, just as he did each time his father said, "I'd like you to meet my boy," his father smiling, mussing his hair, Paul shaking the large extended hand, squeezing it ("Always squeeze," his mother told him. "Don't give someone a dead fish"). "He's got a good grip," one man had said, and for a moment Paul had been proud.

Now his father was drinking beer with his friends—what Paul's mother called the nineteenth hole. Paul liked watching him have fun, pouring the good summer-smelling beer in his glass, laughing, talking about the game they just played and other games they had played. They talked about baseball, too; a team called the Dodgers was going to have a colored boy playing this year. Betsy Robichaux and another woman came to their table, and the four men and Paul stood up; Mr. Peck got two chairs from the next table. Paul squeezed the women's hands, too, but not quite as hard.

"He's got his daddy's looks," Betsy Robichaux said.

His father grinned and his blue eyes twinkled. She was not really pretty but she was nice-looking, Paul thought. She sat opposite him with her back to the window that ran the length of the clubhouse, so he watched her, caught himself staring at her now and then, but most of the time he remembered to pretend he was looking past her at the eighteenth green, where long-shadowed men leaned on putters. She was deeply tanned and slender. Her voice was husky, she laughed a lot, she said "hell" and "damn," and she was always smoking a Pall Mall, gesturing with it in her ringless left hand. Paul knew she was not a lady like his mother, but he liked watching women smoke, for a cigarette made them somehow different, like women in movies instead of mothers. She sat there talking golf with the men, and Paul knew his father liked talking golf with her better than with his mother, who only pretended she was interested (Paul could tell by her voice). But thinking about his mother made him feel guilty, as though he were betraying his father, as though he were his mother's spy, recording every time his father said, "Betsy." He decided to count the beers his father drank, so if his mother said something Paul could defend him.

His father drank five beers (Paul had two Grapettes and two packages of cheese crackers with peanut butter), and then it was dusk and they drove home, his father talking all the way in his drinking voice, relaxed, its tone without edges now, rounded by some quality that was almost tenderness, almost affection. He talked golf. Sometimes, when he paused, Paul said yes. As they approached the corner of their street, his father reached over and lightly slapped Paul's leg, then gave it a squeeze.

"Well," he said. "It's not so bad to spend an afternoon with the old man, is it?"

"Nope," Paul said, and knew at once how that sounded, how his father must have heard only their failure in that one little word, because how could his father possibly know, ever forever know, that even that one word had released so much that tears came to his eyes, and it was as if his soul wanted to talk and hug his father but his body could not, and all he could do was in silence love his father as though he were a memory, as the afternoon already was a memory.

His mother met them on the screen porch. "Did my two men have fun together?"

"Sure we did. He's a good caddie."

"Did you have fun?" she asked Paul.

He took a quick deep breath, closed his mouth tightly, pressed a finger under his nose, and pretended to hold back a sneeze as he walked past her.

Now in his bed he grew sleepy to the sound of the fan. He wondered if they would have a new car when he was a big boy. He saw the car as a blue one, and it smelled new inside. Now Marshall came out in her white dress and kissed him in the evening sun right there on her front steps; she had the line of sweat over her lips and smelled of perfume. Holding hands, they walked to the car. Her head came to about his shoulder; just before he opened the car door, she put her hand on his bicep and squeezed it. Her face was lovely and sad for him. "I'm glad you're taking me," she said.

In the car, she slid close to him. Her arms were dark against the lap of her dress. He offered his pack of Luckies, and they lit them from the dashboard lighter. They drove out of town, then on a long road through woods. The road started climbing and they came out above the woods at trimmed bright grass and spreading live oaks, and in their shade old tombstones and crosses. They left the car and very quietly, holding hands, they walked in the oak shade to his father's grave. He made the sign of the cross, bowed his head, and prayed for his father's soul. When Marshall saw the tears in his eyes, she put her arm around his waist and hugged him tightly while he prayed.

Simon Templar, better known as the Saint, is a favorite among devotees of rogue fiction. He has starred in films and a television series that resuscitated the career of Roger Moore. There is also a Saint Mystery Magazine *that publishes detective fiction. As a private investigator in this story, Templar plays a kind of modern-day Robin Hood in a curious game of poker. Author Leslie Charteris (1907–1993) wrote dozens of novels, novelettes, and short stories. Among his books are* The Happy Highwayman *(1939),* The Saint at Large *(1945), and* Vendetta for the Saint *(1965).*

Leslie Charteris

THE MUGS' GAME (1939)

THE STOUT JOVIAL GENTLEMEN in the shapeless suit pulled a card out of his wallet and pushed it across the table. The printing on it said MR. J. J. NASKILL.

The Saint looked at it and offered his cigarette case.

"I'm afraid I don't carry any cards," he said. "But my name is Simon Templar."

Mr. Naskill beamed, held out a large moist hand to be shaken, took a cigarette, mopped his glistening forehead and beamed again.

"Well, it's a pleasure to talk to you, Mr. Templar," he said heartily. "I get bored with my own company on these long journeys and it hurts my eyes to read on a train. Hate travelling, anyway. It's a good thing my business keeps me in one place most of the time. What's your job, by the way?"

Simon took a pull at his cigarette while he gave a moment's consideration to his answer. It was one of the few questions that ever embarrassed him. It wasn't that he had any real objection to telling the truth, but that the truth tended to disturb the tranquil flow of ordinary casual conversation. Without causing a certain amount of commotion, he couldn't say to a perfect stranger, "I'm a sort of benevolent brigand. I raise hell for crooks and racketeers of all kinds, and make life miserable for policemen, and rescue damsels in distress and all that sort of thing." The Saint had often thought of it as a deplorable commentary on the stodgy unadventurousness of the average mortal's mind; but he knew that it was beyond his power to alter.

He said apologetically: "I'm just one of those lazy people. I believe they call it 'independent means.'"

This was true enough for an idle moment. The Saint could have exhibited a bank account that would have dazzled many men who called themselves wealthy, but it was on the subject of how that wealth had been accumulated that several persons who lived by what they had previously called their wits were inclined to wax profane.

Mr. Naskill sighed.

"I don't blame you," he said. "Why work if you don't have to? Wish I was in your shoes myself. Wasn't born lucky, that's all. Still, I've got a good business now, so I shouldn't complain. Expect you recognize the name."

"Naskill?" The Saint frowned slightly. When he repeated it, it did have a faintly familiar ring. "It sounds as if I ought to know it—"

The other nodded.

"Some people call it No-skill," he said. "They're about right, too. That's what it is. Magic for amateurs. Look."

He flicked a card out of his pocket on to the table between them. It was the ace of diamonds. He turned it over and immediately faced it again. It was the nine of clubs. He turned it over again and it was the queen of hearts. He left it lying face down on the cloth and Simon picked it up curiously and examined it. It was the three of spades, but there was nothing else remarkable about it.

"Used to be a conjuror myself," Naskill explained. "Then I got rheumatism in my hands, and I was on the rocks. Didn't know any other job, so I had to make a living teaching other people tricks. Most of 'em haven't the patience to practise sleight of hand, so I made it easy for 'em. Got a fine trade now, and a two-hundred-page catalogue. I can make anybody into just as good a magician as the money they like to spend, and they needn't practise for five minutes. Look."

He took the card that the Saint was still holding, tore it into small pieces, folded his plump fingers on them for a moment and spread out his hands—empty. Then he broke open the cigarette he was smoking and inside it was a three of spades rolled into a tight cylinder, crumpled but intact.

"You can buy that one for a dollar and a half," he said. "The first one I showed you is two dollars. It's daylight robbery, really, but some people like to show off at parties, and they give me a living."

Simon slid back his sleeve from his wrist watch and glanced out of the window at the speeding landscape. There was still about an hour to go before they would be in Miami, and he had nothing else to take up his time. Besides, Mr. Naskill was something novel and interesting in his experience; and it was part of the Saint's creed that a modern brigand could never know too much about the queerer things that went on in the world.

He caught the eye of the waiter at the other end of the dining car and beckoned him over.

"Could you stand a drink?" he suggested.

"Scotch for me," said Mr. Naskill gratefully. He wiped his face again while Simon duplicated the order. "But I'm still talking about myself. If I'm boring you—"

"Not a bit of it." The Saint was perfectly sincere. "I don't often meet anyone with an unusual job like yours. Do you know any more tricks?"

Mrs. Naskill polished a pair of horn-rimmed spectacles, fitted them on his nose and hitched himself forward.

"Look," he said eagerly.

He was like a child with a new collection of toys. He dug into another of his sagging pockets, which Simon was now deciding were probably loaded with enough portable equipment to stage a complete show, and hauled out a pack of cards which he pushed over to the Saint.

"You take 'em. Look 'em over as much as you like. See if you can find anything wrong with 'em. . . . All right. Now shuffle 'em. Shuffle 'em all you want." He waited. "Now spread 'em out on the table. You're doing this trick, not me. Take any card you like. Look at it—don't let me see it. All right. Now, I haven't touched the cards at all, have I, except to give 'em to you? You shuffled 'em and you picked a card without me helping you. I couldn't have forced it on you or anything. Eh? All right. Well, I could put any trimmings I wanted on this trick—any fancy stunts I could think up to make it look more mysterious. They'd all be easy because I know what card you've got all the time. You've got the six of diamonds."

Simon turned the card over. It was the six of diamonds.

"How's that?" Naskill demanded gleefully.

The Saint grinned. He drew a handful of cards towards him, face downwards as they lay, and pored over the backs for two or three minutes before he sat back again with a rueful shrug.

Mr. Naskill chortled.

"There's nothing wrong with your eyes," he said. "You could go over 'em with a microscope and not find anything. All the same, I'll tell you what you've got. The king of spades, the two of spades, the ten of hearts—"

"I'll take your word for it," said the Saint resignedly. "But how on earth do you do it?"

Naskill glowed delightedly.

"Look," he said.

He took off his glasses and passed them over. Under the flat lenses Simon could see the notations clearly printed in the corners of each card—KS, 2S, 10H. They vanished as soon as he moved the glasses and it was impossible to find a trace of them with the naked eye.

"I've heard of that being done with coloured glasses," said the Saint slowly, "but I noticed yours weren't coloured."

Naskill shook his head.

"Coloured glasses are old stuff. Too crude. Used to be used a lot by sharpers but too many people got to hear about 'em. You couldn't get into a card game with coloured glasses these days. No good for conjuring, either. But this is good. Invented it myself. Special ink and special kind of glass. There is a tint in it, of course, but it's too faint to notice." He shoved the cards over the cloth. "Here. Keep the lot for a souvenir. You can have some fun with your friends. But don't go asking 'em in for a game of poker, mind."

Simon gathered the cards together.

"It would be rather a temptation," he admitted. "But don't you get a lot of customers who buy them just for that?"

"Sure. A lot of professionals use my stuff. I know 'em all. Often see 'em in the shop. Good customers—they buy by the dozen. Can't refuse to serve 'em—they'd only get 'em some other way or buy somewhere else. I call it a compliment to the goods I sell. Never bothers my conscience. Anybody who plays cards with strangers is asking for trouble, anyway. It isn't only professionals, either. You'd be surprised at some of the people I've had come in and ask for a deck of readers—that's the trade name for 'em. I remember one fellow . . ."

He launched into a series of anecdotes that filled up the time until they had to separate to their compartments to collect their luggage. Mr. Naskill's pining for company was understandable after only a few minutes' acquaintance; it was clear that he was constitutionally incapable of surviving for long without an audience.

Simon Templar was not bored. He had already had his money's worth. Whether his friends would allow him to get very far with a programme of card tricks if he appeared before them in an unaccustomed set of horn-rimmed windows was highly doubtful; but the trick was worth knowing, just the same.

Almost every kind of craftsman has specialized journals to inform him of the latest inventions and discoveries and technical advances in his trade, but there is as yet no publication called the *Grafter's Gazette and Weekly Skulldugger* to keep a professional freebooter abreast of the newest devices for separating the sucker from his dough, and the Saint was largely dependent on his own researches for the encyclopedic knowledge of the wiles of the ungodly that had brought so much woe to the *chevaliers d'industrie* of two hemispheres. Mr. Naskill's conversation had yielded a scrap of information that would be filed away in the Saint's well-stocked memory against the day when it would be useful. It might lie fallow for a month, a year, five years, before it produced its harvest: the Saint was in no hurry. In the fulness of time he would collect his dividend—it was one of the cardinal articles of his faith that nothing of that kind ever crossed his path without a rendezvous for the future, however distant that future might be. But one of the things that always gave the Saint a particular affection for this story was the promptness with which his expectations were fulfilled.

There were some episodes in Simon Templar's life when all the component parts of a perfectly rounded diagram fell into place one by one with such a sweetly definitive succession of crisp clicks that mere coincidence was too pallid and anemic a theory with which to account for them—when he almost felt as if he were reclining passively in an armchair and watching the oiled wheels of Fate roll smoothly through the convolutions of a supernaturally engineered machine.

Two days later he was relaxing his long lean body on the private beach of the Roney Plaza, revelling in the clean sharp bite of the sun on his brown skin and lazily debating the comparative attractions of iced beer or a tinkling highball as a noon refresher, when two voices reached him sufficiently clearly to force themselves into his drowsy consciousness. They belonged to a man and a girl, and it was obvious that they were quarrelling.

Simon wasn't interested. He was at peace with the world. He concentrated on digging up a small sand castle with his toes and tried to shut them out. And then he heard the girl say: "My God, are you so dumb that you can't see that they must be crooks?"

It was the word "crooks" that did it. When the Saint heard that word, he could no more have concentrated on sand castles than a rabid Egyptologist could have remained aloof while gossip of scarabs and sarcophagi shuttled across his head. A private squabble was one thing, but this was something else that to the Saint made eavesdropping not only pardonable but almost a moral obligation.

He rolled over and looked at the girl. She was only a few feet from him and even at that range it was easier to go on looking than to look away. From her loose raven hair down to her daintily enamelled toenails there wasn't an inch of her that didn't make its own demoralizing demands on the eye, and the clinging silk swimsuit she wore left very few inches any secrets.

"Why must they be crooks?" asked the man stubbornly. He was young and tow-headed but the Saint's keen survey traced hard and haggard lines in his face. "Just because I've been out of luck–"

"Luck!" The girl's voice was scornful and impatient. "You were out of luck when you met them. Two men that you know nothing about, who pick you up in a bar and suddenly discover that you're the bosom pal they've been looking for all their lives–who want to take you out to dinner every night, and take you out fishing every day, and buy you drinks and show you the town–and you talk about luck! D'you think they'd do all that if they didn't know they could get you to play cards with them every night and make you lose enough to pay them back a hundred times over?"

"I won plenty from them to begin with."

"Of course you did! They let you win–just to encourage you to play higher. And now you've lost all that back and a lot more that you can't afford to lose. And you're still going on, making it worse and worse." She caught his arm impulsively and her voice softened. "Oh, Eddie, I hate fighting with you like this, but can't you see what a fool you're being?"

"Well, why don't you leave me alone if you hate fighting? Anyone might think I was a kid straight out of school."

He shrugged himself angrily away from her, and as he turned he looked straight into the Saint's eyes. Simon was so interested that the movement caught him unprepared, still watching them, as if he had been hiding behind a curtain and it had been abruptly torn down.

It was so much too late for Simon to switch his eyes away without looking even guiltier that he had to go on watching, and the young man went on scowling at him and said uncomfortably: "We aren't really going to cut each other's throats, but there are some things that women can't understand."

"If a man told him that elephants laid eggs he'd believe it, just because it was a man who told him," said the girl petulantly, and she also looked at the Saint. "Perhaps if *you* told him—"

"The trouble is, she won't give me credit for having any sense—"

"He's such a baby—"

"If she didn't read so many detective stories—"

"He's so damned pig-headed—"

The Saint held up his hands.

"Wait a minute," he pleaded. "Don't shoot the referee—he doesn't know what it's all about. I couldn't help hearing what you were saying, but it isn't my fight."

The young man rubbed his head shamefacedly, and the girl bit her lip.

Then she said quickly: "Well, please won't you *be* a referee? Perhaps he'd listen to you. He's lost fifteen thousand dollars already, and it isn't all his own money—"

"For God's sake," the man burst out savagely, "are you trying to make me look a complete heel?"

The girl caught her breath, and her lip trembled. And then, with a sort of sob, she picked herself up and walked quickly away without another word.

The young man gazed after her in silence, and his fist clenched on a handful of sand as if he would have liked to hurt it.

"Oh hell," he said expressively.

Simon drew a cigarette out of the packet beside him and tapped it meditatively on his thumbnail while the awkward hiatus made itself at home. His eyes seemed to be intent on following the movements of a small fishing cruiser far out on the emerald waters of the Gulf Stream.

"It's none of my damn business," he remarked at length, "but isn't there just a chance that the girl friend may be right? It's happened before; and a resort like this is rather a happy hunting ground for all kinds of crooks."

"I know it is," said the other sourly. He turned and looked at the Saint again miserably. "But I *am* pig-headed, and I can't bear to admit to her that I could have been such a mug. She's my fiancée–I suppose you guessed that. My name's Mercer."

"Simon Templar is mine."

The name had a significance for Mercer that it apparently had not had for Mr. Naskill. His eyes opened wide.

"Good God, you don't mean–You're not the Saint?"

Simon smiled. He was still immodest enough to enjoy the sensation that his name could sometimes cause.

"That's what they call me."

"Of course I've read about you, but–Well, it sort of . . ." The young man petered out incoherently. "And I'd have argued with you about crooks! . . . But–well, you ought to know. Do *you* think I've been a mug?"

The Saint's brows slanted sympathetically.

"If you took my advice," he answered, "you'd let these birds find someone else to play with. Write it off to experience, and don't do it again."

"But I can't!" Mercer's response was desperate. "She–she was telling the truth. I've lost money that wasn't mine. I've only got a job in an advertising agency that doesn't pay very much, but her people are pretty well off. They've found me a better job here, starting in a couple of months, and they sent us down here to find a home, and they gave us twenty thousand dollars to buy it and furnish it, and that's the money I've been playing with. Don't you see? I've *got* to go on and win it back!"

"Or go on and lose the rest."

"Oh, I know. But I thought the luck must change before that. And yet– But everybody who plays cards isn't a crook, is he? And I don't see how they would have done it. After she started talking about it, I watched them. I've been looking for it. And I couldn't catch them making a single move that wasn't aboveboard. Then I began to think about marked cards—we've always played with their cards. I sneaked away one of the packs we were using last night, and I've been looking at it this morning. I'll swear there isn't a mark on it. Here, I can show you."

He fumbled feverishly in a pocket of his beach robe and pulled out a pack of cards. Simon glanced through them. There was nothing wrong with them that he could see; and it was then that he remembered Mr. J. J. Naskill.

"Does either of these birds wear glasses?" he asked.

"One of them wears pince-nez," replied the mystified young man. "But—"

"I'm afraid," said the Saint thoughtfully, "that it looks as if you are a mug."

Mercer swallowed.

"If I am," he said helplessly, "what on earth am I going to do?"

Simon hitched himself up.

"Personally, I'm going to have a dip in the pool. And you're going to be so busy apologizing to your fiancée and making friends again that you won't have time to think about anything else. I'll keep these cards and make sure about them, if you don't mind. Then suppose we meet in the bar for a cocktail about six o'clock, and maybe I'll be able to tell you something."

When he returned to his own room the Saint put on Mr. Naskill's horn-rimmed glasses and examined the cards again. Every one of them was clearly marked in the diagonally opposite corners with the value of the card and the initial of the suit, exactly like the deck that Naskill had given him; and it was then that the Saint knew that his faith in Destiny was justified again.

Shortly after six o'clock he strolled into the bar and saw that Mercer and the girl were already there. It was clear that they had buried their quarrel.

Mercer introduced her: "Miss Grange—or you can just call her Josephine."

She was wearing something in black-and-white taffeta, with a black-and-white hat and black-and-white gloves and a black-and-white bag, and she looked as if she had just stepped out of a fashion plate. She said: "We're both ashamed of ourselves for having a scene in front of you this afternoon, but I'm glad we did. You've done Eddie a lot of good."

"I hadn't any right to blurt out all my troubles like that," Mercer said sheepishly. "You were damned nice about it."

The Saint grinned.

"I'm a pretty nice guy," he murmured. "And now I've got something to show you. Here are your cards."

He spread the deck out on the table and then he took the horn-rimmed glasses out of his pocket and held them over the cards so that the other two could look through them. He slid the cards under the lenses one by one, face downwards, and turned them over afterwards, and for a little while they stared in breathless silence.

The girl gasped.

"I told you so!"

Mercer's fists clenched.

"By God, if I don't murder those swine—"

She caught his wrist as he almost jumped up from the table.

"Eddie, that won't do you any good."

"It won't do them any good either! When I've finished with them—"

"But that won't get any of the money back."

"I'll beat it out of them."

"But that'll only get you in trouble with the police. That wouldn't help. . . . Wait!" She clung to him frantically. "I've got it. You could borrow Mr. Templar's glasses and play them at their own game. You could break Yoring's glasses—sort of accidentally. They wouldn't dare to stop playing on account of that. They'd just have to trust to luck, like you've been doing, and anyway, they'd feel sure they were going to get it all back again later. And you could win everything back and never see them again." She shook his arm in her excitement. "Go on, Eddie. It'd serve them right. I'll let you play just once more if you'll do that!"

Mercer's eyes turned to the Saint, and Simon pushed the glasses across the table towards him.

The young man picked them up slowly, looked at the cards through them again. His mouth twitched. And then, with a sudden hopeless gesture, he thrust them away and passed a shaky hand over his eyes.

"It's no good," he said wretchedly. "I couldn't do it. They know I don't wear glasses. And I—I've never done anything like that before. I'd only make a mess of it. They'd spot me in five minutes. And then there wouldn't be anything I could say. I—I wouldn't have the nerve. I suppose I'm just a mug after all. . . ."

The Saint leaned back and put a light to a cigarette and sent a smoke ring spinning through the fronds of a potted palm. In all his life he had never missed a cue, and it seemed that this was very much like a cue. He had come to Miami to bask in the sun and be good, but it wasn't his fault if business was thrust upon him.

"Maybe someone with a bit of experience could do it better," he said. "Suppose you let me meet your friends."

Mercer looked at him, first blankly, then incredulously; and the girl's dark eyes slowly lighted up.

Her slim fingers reached impetuously for the Saint's hand.

"You wouldn't really do that—help Eddie to win back what he's lost—"

"What would you expect Robin Hood to do?" asked the Saint quizzically. "I've got a reputation to keep up—and I might even pay my own expenses while I'm doing it." He drew the revealing glasses towards him and tucked them back in his pocket. "Let's go and have some dinner and organize the details."

But actually there were hardly any details left to organize, for Josephine Grange's inspiration had been practically complete in its first outline. The Saint, who never believed in expending any superfluous effort, devoted most of his attention to some excellent lobster thermidor; but he had a pleasant sense of anticipation that lent an edge to his appetite. He knew, even then, that all those interludes of virtue in which he had so often tried to indulge, those brief intervals in which he played at being an ordinary respectable citizen and promised himself to forget that there was such a thing as crime, were only harmless self-deceptions—that for him the only complete life was still the ceaseless hair-trigger battle in which he had found so much delight. And this episode had everything that he asked to make a perfect cameo.

He felt like a star actor waiting for the curtain to rise on the third act of an obviously triumphant first night when they left the girl at the Roney Plaza and walked over to the Riptide—"That's where we usually meet," Mercer explained. And a few minutes later he was being introduced to the other two members of the cast.

Mr. Yoring, who wore the pince-nez, was a small pear-shaped man in a crumpled linen suit, with white hair and bloodhound jowls and a pathetically frustrated expression. He looked like a retired businessman whose wife took him to the opera. Mr. Kilgarry, his partner, was somewhat taller and younger, with a wide mouth and a rich nose and a raffish manner: he looked like the kind of man that men like Mr. Yoring wish they could be. Both of them welcomed Mercer with an exuberant bonhomie that was readily expanded to include the Saint. Mr. Kilgarry ordered a round of drinks.

"Having a good time here, Mr. Templar?"

"Pretty good."

"Ain't we all having a good time?" crowed Mr. Yoring. "I'm gonna buy a drink."

"I've just ordered a drink," said Mr. Kilgarry.

"Well, I'm gonna order another," said Mr. Yoring defiantly. No wife was going to take him to the opera to-night. "Who said there was a Depression? What do you think, Mr. Templar?"

"I haven't found any in my affairs lately," Simon answered truthfully.

"You in business, Mr. Templar?" asked Mr. Kilgarry interestedly.

The Saint smiled.

"My business is letting other people make money for me," he said, continuing strictly in the vein of truth. He patted his pockets significantly. "The market's been doing pretty well these days."

Mr. Kilgarry and Mr. Yoring exchanged glances, while the Saint picked up his drink. It wasn't his fault if they misunderstood him; but it had been rather obvious that the conversation was doomed to launch some tactful feelers into his financial status, and Simon saw no need to add to their coming troubles by making them work hard for their information.

"Well, that's fine," said Mr. Yoring happily. "I'm gonna buy another drink."

"You can't," said Mr. Kilgarry. "It's my turn."

Mr. Yoring looked wistful, like a small boy who has been told that he can't go out and play with his new air gun. Then he wrapped an arm around Mercer's shoulders.

"You gonna play to-night, Eddie?"

"I don't know," Mercer said hesitantly. "I've just been having some dinner with Mr. Templar—"

"Bring him along," boomed Mr. Kilgarry heartily. "What's the difference? Four's better than three, any day. D'you play cards, Mr. Templar?"

"Most games," said the Saint cheerfully.

"That's fine," said Mr. Kilgarry. "Fine," he repeated, as if he wanted to leave no doubt that he thought it was fine.

Mr. Yoring looked dubious.

"I dunno. We play rather high stakes, Mr. Templar."

"They can't be too high for me," said the Saint boastfully.

"Fine," said Mr. Kilgarry again, removing the last vestige of uncertainty about his personal opinion. "Then that's settled. What's holding us back?"

There was really nothing holding them back except the drinks that were lined up on the bar, and that deterrent was eliminated with a discreetly persuasive briskness. Under Mr. Kilgarry's breezy leadership they piled into a taxi and headed for one of the smaller hotels on Ocean Drive, where Mr. Yoring proclaimed that he had a bottle of Scotch that would save them from the agonies of thirst while they were playing. As they rode up in the elevator he hooked his arm affectionately through the Saint's.

"Say, you're awright, ole man," he announced. "I like to meet a young feller like you. You oughta come out fishin' with us. Got our own boat here, hired for the season, an' we just take out fellers we like. You like fishin'?"

"I like catching sharks," said the Saint, with unblinking innocence.

"You ought to come out with us," said Mr. Kilgarry hospitably.

The room was large and uncomfortable, cluttered with that hideous hodgepodge of gilt and lacquer and brocade, assembled without regard to any harmony of style or period, which passes for the height of luxury in American hotel furnishing. In the centre of the room there was a card table already set up, adding one more discordant note to the cacophony of junk, but still looking as if it belonged there. There were bottles and a pail of ice on a pea-green and old-rose butterfly table of incredible awfulness.

Mr. Kilgarry brought up chairs, and Mr. Yoring patted Mercer on the shoulder.

"You fix a drink, Eddie," he said. "Let's all make ourselves at home."

He lowered himself into a place at the table, took off his pince-nez, breathed on them and began to polish them with his handkerchief.

Mercer's tense gaze caught the Saint's for an instant. Simon nodded imperceptibly and settled his own glasses more firmly on the bridge of his nose.

"How's the luck going to be to-night, Eddie?" chaffed Kilgarry, opening two new decks of cards and spilling them on the cloth.

"You'll be surprised," retorted the young man. "I'm going to give you two gasbags a beautiful beating to-night."

"Attaboy," chirped Yoring encouragingly.

Simon had taken one glance at the cards, and that had been enough to assure him that Mr. Naskill would have been proud to claim them as his product. After that, he had been watching Mercer's back as he worked over the drinks. Yoring was still polishing his pince-nez when Mercer turned to the table with a glass in each hand. He put one glass down beside Yoring, and as he reached over to place the other glass in front of the Saint the cuff of his coat sleeve flicked the pince-nez out of Yoring's fingers and sent them spinning. The Saint made a dive to catch them, missed, stumbled and brought his heel down on the exact spot where they were in the act of hitting the carpet. There was a dull scrunching sound, and after that there was a thick and stifling silence.

The Saint spoke first.

"That's torn it," he said weakly.

Yoring blinked at him as he were going to burst into tears.

"I'm terribly sorry," said the Saint.

He bent down and tried to gather up some of the debris. Only the gold bridge of the pince-nez remained in one piece, and that was bent. He put it on the table, started to collect the scraps of glass and then gave up the hopeless task.

"I'll pay for them, of course," he said.

"I'll split it with you," said Mercer. "It was my fault. We'll take it out of my winnings."

Yoring looked from one to another with watery eyes.

"I–I don't think I can play without my glasses," he mumbled.

Mercer flopped into the vacant chair and raked in the cards.

"Come on," he said callously. "It isn't as bad as all that. You can show us your hand and we'll tell you what you've got."

"Can't you manage?" urged the Saint. "I was going to enjoy this game, and it won't be nearly so much fun with only three."

The silence came back, thicker than before. Yoring's eyes shifted despairingly from side to side. And then Kilgarry crushed his cigar butt violently into an ash tray.

"You can't back out now," he said, and there was an audible growl in the fruity tones of his voice.

He broke the other pack across the baize with a vicious jerk of his hand that was as eloquent as a movement could be.

"Straight poker–with the joker wild. Let's go."

To Simon Templar the game had the same dizzy unreality that it would have had if he had been supernaturally endowed with a genuine gift of clairvoyance. He knew the value of every card as it was dealt, knew what was in his own hand before he picked it up. Even though there was nothing mysterious about it, the effect of the glasses he was wearing gave him a sensation of weirdness that was too instinctive to overcome. It was mechanically childish, and yet it was an unforgettable experience. When he was out of the game, watching the others bet against each other, it was like being a cat watching two blind men looking for each other in the dark.

For nearly an hour, curiously enough, the play was fairly even: when he counted his chips he had only a couple of hundred dollars more than when he started. Mercer, throwing in his hand whenever the Saint warned him by a pressure of his foot under the table that the opposition was too strong, had done slightly better; but there was nothing sensational in their advantage. Even Mr. Naskill's magic lenses had no influence over the run of the cards, and the luck of the deals slightly favoured Yoring and Kilgarry. The Saint's clairvoyant knowledge saved him from making any disastrous errors, but now and again he had to bet out a hopeless hand to avoid giving too crude an impression of infallibility.

He played a steadily aggressive game, waiting patiently for the change that he knew must come as soon as the basis of the play had had time to settle down and establish itself. His nerves were cool and serene, and he smiled often with an air of faint amusement; but something inside him was poised and gathered like a panther crouched for a spring.

Presently Kilgarry called Mercer on the third raise and lost a small jackpot to three nines. Mercer scowled as he stacked the handful of chips.

"Hell, what's the matter with this game?" he protested. "This isn't the way we usually play. Let's get some life into it."

"It does seem a bit slow," Simon agreed. "How about raising the ante?"

"Make it a hundred dollars," Mercer said sharply. "I'm getting tired of this. Just because my luck's changed we don't have to start playing for peanuts."

Simon drew his cigarette to a bright glow.

"It suits me."

Yoring plucked at his lower lip with fingers that were still shaky.

"I dunno, ole man—"

"O.K." Kilgarry pushed out two fifty-dollar chips with a kind of fierce restraint. "I'll play for a hundred."

He had been playing all the time with grim concentration, his shoulders hunched as if he had to give some outlet to a seethe of violence in his muscles, his jaw thrust out and tightly clamped; and as the time went by he seemed to have been regaining confidence. "Maybe the game is on the level," was the idea expressed by every line of his body, "but I can still take a couple of mugs like this in any game."

He said, almost with a resumption of his former heartiness:–

"Are you staying long, Mr. Templar?"

"I expect I'll be here for quite a while."

"That's fine! Then after Mr. Yoring's got some new glasses we might have a better game."

"I shouldn't be surprised," said the Saint amiably.

He was holding two pairs. He took a card, and still had two pairs. Kilgarry stood pat on three kings. Mercer drew three cards to a pair, and was no better off afterwards. Yoring took two cards and filled a flush.

"One hundred," said Yoring nervously.

Mercer hesitated, threw in his hand.

"And two hundred," snapped Kilgarry.

"And five," said the Saint.

Yoring looked at him blearily. He took a long time to make up his mind. And then, with a sigh, he pushed his hand into the discard.

"See you," said Kilgarry.

With a wry grin, the Saint faced his hand. Kilgarry grinned also, with a sudden triumph, and faced his.

Yoring made a noise like a faint groan.

"Fix us another drink, Eddie," he said huskily.

He took the next pack and shuffled it clumsily. His fingers were like sausages strung together. Kilgarry's mouth opened on one side and he nudged the Saint as he made the cut.

"Lost his nerve," he said. "See what happens when they get old."

"Who's old?" said Mr. Yoring plaintively. "There ain't more'n three years–"

"But you've got old ideas," Kilgarry jeered. "You could have beaten both of us."

"You never had to wear glasses–"

"Who said you wanted glasses to play poker? It isn't always the cards that win."

Kilgarry was smiling, but his eyes were almost glaring at Yoring as he spoke. Yoring avoided his gaze guiltily and squinted at the hand he had dealt himself. It contained the six, seven, eight and nine of diamonds, and the queen of spades. Simon held two pairs again but the card he drew made it a full house. He watched while Yoring discarded the queen of spades and felt again that sensation of supernatural omniscience as he saw that the top card of the pack, the card Yoring had to take, was the ten of hearts.

Yoring took it, fumbled his hand to the edge of the table, and turned up the corners to peep at them. For a second he sat quite still, with only his mouth working. And then, as if the accumulation of all his misfortunes had at last stung him to a wild and fearful reaction like the turning of a worm, a change seemed to come over him. He let the cards flatten out again with a defiant click and drew himself up. He began to count off hundred-dollar chips. . . .

Mercer, with only a pair of sevens, bluffed recklessly for two rounds before he fell out in response to the Saint's kick under the table.

There were five thousand dollars in the pool before Kilgarry, with a straight, shrugged surrenderingly and dropped his hand in the discard.

The Saint counted two stacks of chips and pushed them in.

"Make it another two grand," he said.

Yoring looked at him waveringly. Then he pushed in two stacks of his own.

"There's your two grand." He counted the chips he had left, swept them with a sudden splash into the pile. "And twenty-nine hundred more," he said.

Simon had twelve hundred left in chips. He pushed them in, opened his wallet and added crisp new bills.

"Making three thousand more than that for you to see me," he said coolly.

Mercer sucked in his breath and whispered: "Oh boy!"

Kilgarry said nothing, hunching tensely over the table.

Yoring blinked at him.

"Len' me some chips, ole man."

"Do you know what you're doing?" Kilgarry asked in a harsh strained voice.

Yoring picked up his glass and half emptied it. His hand wobbled so that some of it ran down his chin.

"I know," he snapped.

He reached out and raked Kilgarry's chips into the pile.

"Eighteen hunnerd," he said. "I gotta buy some more. I'll write you a cheque–"

Simon shook his head.

"I'm sorry," he said quietly. "I'm playing table stakes. We agreed on that when we started."

Yoring peered at him.

"You meanin' something insultin' about my cheque?"

"I don't mean that," Simon replied evenly. "It's just a matter of principle. I believe in sticking to the rules. I'll play you a credit game some other time. To-night we're putting it on the line."

He made a slight gesture towards the cigar box where they had each deposited five thousand-dollar bills when they bought their chips.

"Now look here," Kilgarry began menacingly.

The Saint's clear-blue eyes met his with sapphire smoothness.

"I said cash, brother. Is that clear?"

Yoring groped through his pockets. One by one he untangled crumpled bills from various hiding places until he had built his bet up to thirty-two hundred and fifty dollars. Then he glared at Kilgarry.

"Len' me what you've got."

"But–"

"All of it!"

Reluctantly Kilgarry passed over a roll. Yoring licked his thumb and numbered it through. It produced a total raise of four thousand one hundred and fifty dollars. He gulped down the rest of his drink and dribbled some more down his chin.

"Go on," he said thickly, staring at the Saint. "Raise that."

Simon counted out four thousand-dollar bills. He had one more, and he held it poised. Then he smiled.

"What's the use?" he said. "You couldn't meet it. I'll take the change and see you."

Yoring's hand went to his mouth. He didn't move for a moment, except for the wild swerve of his eyes.

Then he picked up his cards. With trembling slowness he turned them over one by one. The six, seven, eight, nine—and ten of *diamonds.*

Nobody spoke; and for some seconds the Saint sat quite still. He was summarizing the whole scenario for himself, in all its inspired ingenuity and mathematical precision, and it is a plain fact that he found it completely beautiful. He was aware that Mercer was shaking him inarticulately and that Yoring's rheumy eyes were opening wider on him with a flame of triumph.

And suddenly Kilgarry guffawed and thumped the table.

"Go to it," he said. "Pick it up, Yoring. I take it all back. You're not so old, either!"

Yoring opened both his arms to embrace the pool.

"Just a minute," said the Saint.

His voice was softer and gentler than ever, but it stunned the room to another immeasurable silence. Yoring froze as he moved, with his arms almost shaped into a ring. And the Saint smiled very kindly.

Certainly it had been a good trick, and an education, but the Saint didn't want the others to fall too hard. He had those moments of sympathy for the ungodly in their downfall.

He turned over his own cards, one by one. Aces. Four of them. Simon thought they looked pretty. He had collected them with considerable care, which may have prejudiced him. And the joker.

"My pot, I think," he remarked apologetically.

Kilgarry's chair was the first to grate back.

"Here," he snarled, "that's not—"

"The hand he dealt me?" The texture of Simon's mockery was like gossamer. "And he wasn't playing the hand I thought he had, either. I thought he'd have some fun when he got used to being without his glasses," he added cryptically.

He tipped up the cigar box and added its contents to the stack of currency in front of him, and stacked it into a neat sheaf.

"Well, I'm afraid that sort of kills the game for to-night," he murmured, and his hand was in his side pocket before Kilgarry's movement was half started. Otherwise he gave no sign of perturbation, and his languid self-possession was as smooth as velvet. "I suppose we'd better call it a day," he said without any superfluous emphasis.

Mercer recovered his voice first.

"That's right," he said jerkily. "You two have won plenty from me other nights. Now we've got some of it back. Let's get out of here, Templar."

They walked along Ocean Drive, past the variegated modernistic shapes of the hotels, with the rustle of the surf in their ears.

"How much did you win on that last hand?" asked the young man.

"About fourteen thousand dollars," said the Saint contentedly.

Mercer said awkwardly: "That's just about what I'd lost to them before. . . . I don't know how I can ever thank you for getting it back. I'd never have had the nerve to do it alone. . . . And then when Yoring turned up that straight flush—I don't know why—I had an awful moment thinking you'd made a mistake."

The Saint put a cigarette in his mouth and struck his lighter.

"I don't make a lot of mistakes," he said calmly. "That's where a lot of people go wrong. It makes me rather tired, sometimes. I suppose it's just professional pride, but I hate to be taken for a mug. And the funny thing is that with my reputation there are always people trying it. I suppose they think that my reactions are so easy to predict that it makes me quite a setup for any smart business." The Saint sighed, deploring the inexplicable optimism of those who should know better. "Of course I knew that a switch like that was coming—the whole idea was to make me feel so confident of the advantage I had with those glasses that I'd be an easy victim for any ordinary cardsharping. And then, of course, I wasn't supposed to be able to make any complaint because that would have meant admitting that I was cheating, too. It was a grand idea, Eddie—at least you can say that for it."

Mercer had taken several steps before all the implications of what the Saint had said really hit him.

"But wait a minute," he got out. "How do you mean they knew you were wearing trick glasses?"

"Why else do you imagine they planted that guy on the train to pretend he was J. J. Naskill?" asked the Saint patiently. "That isn't very bright of you, Eddie. Now, I'm nearly always bright. I was so bright that I smelt a rat directly you lugged that pack of marked cards out of your beach robe—that was really carrying it a bit too far, to have them all ready to produce after you'd got me to listen in on your little act with Josephine. I must say you all played your parts beautifully, otherwise; but it's little details like that that spoil the effect. I told you at the time that you were a mug," said the Saint reprovingly. "Now why don't you paddle off and try to comfort Yoring and Kilgarry? I'm afraid they're going to be rather hurt when they hear that you didn't manage at least to make the best of a bad job and get me to hand you my winnings."

But Mercer did not paddle off at once. He stared at the Saint for quite a long time, understanding why so many other men who had once thought themselves clever had learned to regard that cool and smiling privateer as something closely allied to the devil himself. And wondering, as they had, why the death penalty for murder had ever been invented.

*The most publicized old-timers' games are those played an[i]
league baseball parks, where grizzled veterans wheeze through [t]
Less known but far more popular are games played in a variety [c]
aging men (and occasionally women) trying to keep in some sem[i]
physical condition. The following story is about old hockey players ree[...][i]ng
the game of their youth with a surprising level of seriousness. It is lovingly written by Peter LaSalle, who is the author of a novel,* Strange Sunlight *(1984),
and two story collections,* The Graves of Famous Writers *(1980) and* Hockey
Sur Glace *(1996). LaSalle's fiction has also appeared in* The Paris Review, The
Best American Short Stories, *and* Prize Stories: The O. Henry Awards.

Peter LaSalle

HOCKEY
(1980)

THE CLUBHOUSE OF THE Winter Club in Lake Forest is American
Tudor with at least a half-dozen gables. The shingled sides are green and
the crisscrossing beams were probably once bright buff. But the buff has
turned to tan under a coating of the thick soot that blows down from the
factories in Waukegan. This particular Saturday morning in 1972, fat
flakes fluttered like moths and every once in a while the sun appeared in
between moving clouds. Chicago lawyer John Fontaine–he had been
starting right defenseman for the Harvard team in 1957 and 1958–
slammed the black lid of the battered white Volvo wagon. He wore his

shin pads underneath the sweatpants. He had bound them tight with hospital tape in the living room while his wife said what she always said:

"I don't know why you put yourself through it. I'm only going to have to listen to you moan about your knees for the rest of the weekend." She kissed him on the top of the head. "You're like a kid."

His stick was a stock Northland "Pro" with a five lie for a right-hander. It was new and one of the four he had bought from the remaining supply in the sports shop on LaSalle Street. The salesman told him that Northland had discontinued the straight blade in its top "Pro" line and the company now turned out only banana curves. They had come into fashion long after John had stopped playing regularly.

The ruddy-faced German attendant, Max, was behind the equipment counter at the club, smiling his usual toothy grin. The dressing room was a long corridor with benches, and framed photographs of old curling teams formed a string like boxcars along each glossily painted wall. Some of the brown-and-white group shots dated back to the twenties and before. The men in heavy coats wore matching tams for the poses and had lined up in front of the same clubhouse. The white script below listed the squad and year of each: "LFWC 1922," "LFWC 1923." Dozens of them.

At the far end of the bench, Ed Ridley laced on his scuffed skates. He seemed to sew the brass tips of the broad, dirty laces through the holes. Half finished, he stretched out one leg and with a grimace he tugged on the two taut strands, as if yanking the reins on a runaway horse. He was only a year or so older than John, but without his hair he looked maybe ten years older. He wore an old Brown University uniform jersey made of wool. The chocolate color had faded and the red stripes at the biceps were sewn-on satin and equally dull. Big moth holes splattered the back. They stretched even bigger as he leaned his overweight body down to continue lacing. John dropped his canvas bag and sat down beside him.

"I keep telling you," John said, "that sweater dates you, Ed. You're as bad as I am with my antique Northlands. I think I've bought out the last of the straight blades in Midwestern captivity. I can't get used to the curves."

Ed didn't seem interested in such talk about equipment.

"He's here," was all he said.

John probed in the bag for his skates. The room smelled of burning and a wood fire glowed like neon behind the door of a cast-iron stove. John knew who Ed meant. In fact, Ed had called him twice that week at his office to pour it all out. John found such confidence embarrassing. He didn't know Ed very well, but, of course, Ed always regarded him as a close friend because they both had played Eastern hockey. At first John feigned ignorance.

"Who's here?"

"That little bastard Lohmayer," Ed said, "that's who. He was just helloing me like I was his long-lost rich uncle."

"Look, Ed, don't jump to any conclusions. I told you that he might have been over there just for a visit. Or to do a chore."

"A chore, that's a laugh. A chore, my ass." Ed tugged again with all his strength. "They were smoking damn marijuana too. I know. Probably going at it the whole afternoon in the bedroom while they were doped. Every time I ask her about it she gives me a different story."

"Well, I hate to parcel out such obvious legal advice, but you know you have only circumstantial evidence."

"My ass. A man can tell. You know that as well as I do. You don't live with a woman for twelve years and not be able to tell. The fruit. I'll fix him today. I'll make my point."

John didn't press the issue and, in truth, he thought that maybe Ed's suspicions were justified. Ed's wife, Delia, must have been a strikingly attractive girl when younger, or, more exactly, before her face started puffing from the alcohol. Nevertheless, her lips were full, her hair a fine natural auburn, and her figure almost slight and certainly slimmer than that of most women her age, probably because she had never borne children. It was at a small dinner get-together that fall that she had gone as far as handling John's knee. She reached under the table cluttered with stylish Swedish dinnerware and smiled. John knew he was singularly naive when it came to such goings-on. He had married his wife, Ruth, while still in college, and that was well before what was eventually to be billed as the Sexual Revolution. Ed was a bond trader for Goldman, Sachs in Chicago. Whenever he was with John at a party, he knitted his eyebrows as if he was thinking very hard and said what John had heard before. "I still can almost picture you from that time we played Harvard in fifty-eight. It was the away game for us, all right, in Cambridge. I remember that. Damn, if it wasn't always the coldest rink I've ever skated in. I never loosened up there until five minutes before the final siren. And you had that Swede. The one who was ECAC scoring leader through the first half of every year, before he always folded."

"Lars. Lars Bjornson," John said.

"That's the one. What a square-headed oaf he was."

Later at the specific get-together the fall before, Delia cornered John in the hallway. John was phoning to tell the baby-sitter that he and Ruth were on their way and that the car she would see coming into the driveway in ten minutes would be theirs. Delia teetered and was very drunk. She pushed herself against his thigh and fingered the hair around his collar.

"You know, John," she said, slurring, "you Harvard man, I just want to go to party after party after party. Always. Is there anything wrong with that?"

"Of course not." What else could John say? "Nothing at all, I suppose."

"That's what I say, nothing at all."

Now John pulled his knit toque down over his ears and, with skates on, awkwardly clomped onto the planks outside. He held his stick like a shepherd's crook. The open rink was in back of the clubhouse and the diesel engine that ran the refrigeration compressor hummed lowly in a steady snore. About a dozen of the players in the makeshift Saturday-morning league were already warming up. In long, smooth strides from the hip, they skated around the oval of ice. Occasionally one would cut in to either blue line and wait for a puck, to take a practice slap. The blades swooshed and swooshed. The hard black disks exploded against the flat of the boards, rattled around the curves behind the nets. The various uniforms ranged from John's own practical sweat suit to a wide assortment of team outfits. Some of the younger high-school kids sported imitation professional jerseys. Of those, at least three had on black Bruins uniform sweaters with the big, yellow-edged "B" in a spoked hub on the chest. Mr. Keane was definitely the oldest skater. He wore a ski parka and a peaked wool lumberman's camp. Lonnie Lohmayer wore his red Lake Forest College game jersey. Lohmayer's father was an important Midwestern banker who had left his vice-presidency of a leading institution in Chicago when the Republicans took over the statehouse. He was now the head of the state's Department of Conservation, while the newspapers speculated that he soon might leave that post to go to Washington as an Assistant Secretary of the Treasury. The family were moneyed Chicagoans of long standing. When Ed had first seen Lonnie play a couple of years before, he had been genuinely excited.

"A natural. A goddamn natural. Maybe even put him on defense like Orr and give him some room to build up speed, and, believe me, with moves like that there's no stopping the kid. We could use him at Brown. A natural. And who says the Canucks still turn out the best." Ed called Providence and arranged for the coach to contact Lonnie in Lake Forest. Lonnie did fly there for an interview and tour of the athletic facilities, and was admitted. But he chose to stay near home and go to Lake Forest College. Ed scolded him when he heard the decision. "Don't be stupid, Lon. Hockey in the East is still the only hockey. And there's always that something about the Ivy League itself. It's tough to explain. But it's something you'll have with you all your life. You don't know how many times I've heard other businessmen talk of me as an Ivy leaguer. Ask John here who went to Harvard. Aren't I right, John? No, Lon, don't pass up a chance for the Ivy League." John remembered him saying just that.

Snow dusted the ice. Everybody agreed to cut short the warm-ups and start play quickly. The weather was obviously worsening and they wouldn't get in the usual two-hour session. The high-powered spotlights on top of the splintery poles around the rink came on and Max yelled from the clubhouse, "Is zat better?"

They simply divided into the two teams they had formed the first Saturday morning they had played, about a month before. The goalies in their rolled leather leg pads pulled down the masks that made them look tribal. They were of markedly different abilities. Coy Stout had played professionally in a West Coast league for a couple of years and had also been on one of those Clarkson College teams in the midsixties that had been so strong. John didn't know the other goalie, a high-schooler. The kid was rubbing one leg pad against the cage's red pipe like a dog trying to get rid of a tick, as he checked it was secure.

"Why don't you give us Coy this week," Ed called to the other team. "I mean, seeing we lost last week."

Nobody complained. The high-schooler lifted his stick as wide as a plank onto his shoulder and started toward the other end. Then there was a mass action of pulling jerseys over heads until one team, John and Ed's, seemed to have mostly dark and the other mostly light. In front of John, curly-haired Lonnie held out the Lake Forest shirt and was shivering a bit. He waited for John to peel off his sweatshirt. It had shrunk from repeated washing and the job wasn't entirely easy. Lonnie's bare arms were more downy than hairy and looked almost womanish. He wore only a T-shirt under the white shoulder pads trimmed with leather to keep the hard plastic from digging in.

"You should wear more than that, Lonnie," John said, "another sweater."

"Not with my speed, Mr. Fontaine." He laughed good-naturedly. He was jokingly cocky and it wasn't offensive. John found it electric, youthful. "I keep going. Don't get time to get cold." Simultaneously they aimed their heads through the necks of the exchanged shirts. "I suppose that's a comedown for you after Harvard, Mr. Fontaine." Lonnie laughed again.

The first time:

Lonnie pumped full speed, holding his stick out in front of him plow style and pushing the puck on the taped flat of it. He wasn't dribbling, because dribbling only slows you down on such breakaways. John watched him from behind the bolted door of the players' compartment. He was surprised that Ed even caught up with the boy—he was so fast. Ed didn't go for the puck. He just threw Lonnie into the direction he was speeding, the way a football linebacker might shove a receiver out of bounds. Actually, it was a clean, legal check. Lonnie hit hard against the boards and the crushing sound brought loud cheers of approval so early in the game.

"All-ri-ight!"

"How you hit, big Ed-dee!"

The flakes were smaller now, but more steady. They were like white gauze in front of the light of the powerful lamps that looked purple in intensity. John himself played a cautious game and he knew he had to be careful of his troublesome knees. In his senior year of college the cartilage had strangely given out. Another operation might leave him with a limp. He usually played on defense with Mr. Keane, who was over fifty. Together, they liked to pass back and forth on the blue line. They would work methodically to confuse completely the organization of the other side, before they fed the puck to the moving forwards, hopefully for a score. The game couldn't last much longer. When John got the puck on his stick, he strained just to keep sight of it. The snow was almost as deep as the blade. Once, he flipped a pass to Mr. Keane and the dragging disk lost momentum at midice. It was left there for galloping Lonnie to pick up. He zigzagged a few strides and then slipped a soft backhand shot to the goal's upper corner, where it hit the netting, a strong hand trying to punch through it. Coy Stout lay sprawled on his stomach. He got up to his knees, pushed the mask back on his sweating face, and laughed, "Nice shot, Lonnie."

John hated watching Ed rough up Lonnie in the congestion that developed in front of the cages. Ed incessantly elbowed the kid's ribs. In the middle of one battering, Lonnie simply forgot about the play and said, "This is ridiculous." He skated to the bench and told somebody else to take his turn on the line.

The second time:

Lonnie must have seen Ed coming. The kid was scrapping with his skate for a loose puck at the boards. Ed charged to flatten him and Lonnie dodged. Without Lonnie's body for a cushion, Ed absorbed the full impact of his own sprint, and his bald head banged hard into the galvanized hexagon-loop wire above the boards. No doubt he was hurt. Most everybody skated onto the ice and Mr. Keane said they should stand back and give him some air. Ed slowly put his gloved hand to the right eye. Red trickled from the bushy brow and he tugged off his glove to feel the cut. Ed loped back to the bench and Mr. Keane told him he best "Call it a day." Ed didn't listen. John sat down beside him. Grinding his yellowed teeth, Ed said, "I'll kill the bastard now. I'll kill him."

John hoped nobody else heard such foolish talk. Coy Stout suggested they abandon the game altogether and one of the high-schoolers, more exuberant, offered the usual, "Next goal wins it." They never kept track of the exact numerical score, but they always seemed to know who won by the feeling that one team had had an easier time of it.

"Damn this," said Ed. "I've always been an easy bleeder. Something about my skin." He scooped some snow off the bench and held it to his head. Its white darkened. "Damn."

"It will be a lot safer," John said, "when they get the new Plexiglas. That wire is damn dangerous. You know, maybe you should get a tetanus shot."

But Ed wasn't listening. He was staring at the game. Across the action of slamming sticks, reddened faces, and pleading shouts for a pass and being in the clear, John could see his wife, Ruth, with their two children. Ruth wore an old camel's-hair coat with the collar upturned. Her hair looked very dark and her skin very clear in the cold. Admittedly, she had become heavier in the last few years. But John, sitting there, thought how handsome she always was in winter. He thought that she had watched him play hockey so often. *Hockey.*

On the ice again, John exchanged passes with Mr. Keane. Ed had missed his turn on defense and now played on wing. John noticed Ed waiting with his stick upraised to signal he was indeed in the clear. John lobbed the puck to him in the air, so it wouldn't drag in the snow on the ice.

"Take it!" somebody yelled.

"All yours, Ed!" somebody else echoed.

John watched and felt a long pang in his stomach. Lonnie, obviously scared, was no more than ten feet in front of Ed, facing him. Lonnie kept his knees close together and his stick blade on the ice, like a goalie, for the block. Ed cocked his own stick up behind him to his shoulder as he readied for the hard slap. He grinned and the blood on his face was running again in a squiggle. It probably lasted only an instant, but to John it seemed forever. He remembered all the injury he had seen in his many years of hockey. A puck to the head *could* kill a man. He remembered noses looking like dough thrown against a breadboard. Teeth hanging from shreds of ragged gum or being spit out like a mess of half-chewed peppermint Lifesavers. He hated to think of the eyes. Above all, he hated to think of a squashed lid immediately starting to swell like a veiny rotten plum. Yes, it seemed forever.

John wanted to save Lonnie with a lunging tackle of Ed. He had to stop Ed or at least shout for Lonnie to protect himself—to duck! But he didn't. Ed grimaced and let go.

Lonnie never flinched. He didn't have to. When Ed's shot finally came, it was a weak, heartless dribbler. John would never know if Ed intended such or simply hit the wrong way, like a nervous golfer. The puck was a wheel as it rolled with a wobble through the snow. Ed appeared blank, lost in the action, and already was leaving. Mr. Keane tipped the puck past Coy Stout and the goalie let him make the score. Play ended for another Saturday. Ed shook his head. He was the first one off the ice and the first one into the clubhouse. The German, Max, held open the door for him and John heard the attendant say, "A bad one, Mr. Ridley. Coming down za lake. Za radio man says all za lakes will be buried by morning."

John walked over the path of boards. His son stood there outside, waiting for him.

"Hey, Dad, where did you get that shirt? It's neat." John's son was ten. "It's almost like a Chicago Black Hawks uniform." The boy ran his mittened hand along the stripes at the waist. "Yeah, red with white stripes just like that. Even the black."

Lonnie came up to them. He had John's sweatshirt in his hand. He looked worried and was pale. He didn't joke.

"Here, Mr. Fontaine." His voice wasn't even strong.

"Oh, you didn't have to worry about me running off with your uniform, Lonnie. I'm on my way to the clubhouse."

"Ah, well, I'm sort of in a hurry. I think I'll just head home."

"Sure," John said.

Lonnie smiled. Ruth and John's daughter, Annie, found them there. The girl was putting a handful of snow and leaves to her mouth.

"Put that down, Annie," Ruth said.

Lonnie had on his own shirt now.

"That's almost like a Black Hawks shirt, mister," Little John said.

Lonnie managed to smile again and tramped off. He didn't go through the clubhouse, though. He headed around the side of the building where there were bare forsythia bushes, white skeletons in the snow.

"Isn't that the Lohmayer boy," Ruth said, "who your friend Ed Ridley wanted to go to Brown? Another one of Ed's famous ideas up in smoke." She never took Ed seriously.

"Yes, that's Lonnie," John said.

"He looks sick. He should have the sense to wear more than that in this cold. It's obvious he's coming down with something."

John was a little weak himself. He was drained, tired, glad it was over. *Hockey.*

It was Saturday afternoon. John felt entirely clean and fit after showering. He followed Ruth and the children through the supermarket, and the slight stiffness in his arms and shoulders from the play was almost pleasant. His knees were fine. Boots dripped and dripped on the market's muddy floor. Low refrigerators with mirrors behind them held the waxy cardboard packages of frozen foods. John watched Ruth reach in for a box of Bird's Eye Oriental Vegetables with a bright picture of fresh pea pods, onions, and mushrooms on a chopping board on the front. He stared at the reflection of the box and her slim fingers holding it in the mirror.

"Did you like these last time we had them?" she asked.

"What?" He was vacant. *Hockey.*

"These vegetables. Did you like them?"

"Yes. Of course."

The shopping cart shivered on wobbly wheels. She described clearly to the butcher exactly how she wanted him to cut the top-round roast that was on sale. The man in his blood-splattered coat appeared pleased to deal with a woman who knew exactly what she wanted. Enamored with the very fullness of his wife's behind, John felt stupid in his affection that sometimes had such adolescent fervor.

Later, John was lying down on the sagging sofa on the sunporch. He was comfortably exhausted from the morning's game by this time. The portable television's gray light was drugging. The program, a wild-animal or adventure show, was narrated by an Englishman with a broad accent, and it was a tour of a game preserve at the very tip of South Africa. The springbok had flowing horns and they grazed right on the beaches. "The beauty of this park," the Englishman said, "is the fantastic juxtaposition of these lovely wild animals and the breathtaking panorama of this beach, these cliffs, and this ocean." Little John came up to the sofa with a sheet of manila drawing paper on which he had sketched a hockey player in brisk strokes. The teachers at his elementary school down the street said he was a natural artist. He got it from his mother. John had bought him a box of artist's chalk for his birthday and the boy treasured the pastels like sticks of gold bullion. He inspected them to make sure they wore evenly and kept them meticulously arranged in the slots of the case provided. The skating figure shed a shadow on the ice. At ten he already knew about light angles and such.

"So, what's this?" asked John. He had one hand behind his head for a pillow.

"A player," his son said. "And he's wearing a red shirt like the one the man let you use today. What does 'LF' stand for?"

"Lake Forest. The college."

"Oh yeah, that's right."

A clanking plow passed outside with the chains on its tires thumping. The sound reminded John of the New Hampshire town where he had grown up. He didn't want to think of Ed Ridley just then. He didn't want to think of Lonnie Lohmayer either. The theme song for the wild-animal show was a classical piece that John seemed to recognize. The white credits rolled up the screen.

"Is your father sleeping?" It was Ruth from the kitchen.

"I don't think so," Little John answered her.

"Well, why don't you turn off that set and let him. Come in and draw in here."

With eyes wide open, John watched the boy fiddle with the switch on the pole lamp, then he got the television set's knob in a single twist. The bright grew smaller to the size of a pinpoint. It was like a distant star and hung on for a long while. Finally, the tube was only a seal-colored bubble of reflection. The outside, where the white birches grew in clusters, was almost dark. The inside, with the light off, was even darker. John liked the winter. He liked hockey. *Hockey.*

He had grown up in the French end of the mill town. The porched, two-story house was like all the others on the street. The lawns were small and divided by driveways of twin cement tracks always sprouting weeds in the summer. Most of the fathers of the other boys worked the humming looms of the textile mills. They were red-brick monstrosities with green-painted windows. John had thought those mills were bona fide castles till he was six. *Hockey.* His father was a schoolteacher and though he never earned very much, he had a regular income. The mill workers were often laid off for months at a time. John hadn't asked his father for the hockey gloves. The man simply returned from monitoring late detention one weekday afternoon and put them on the kitchen table. They smelled of their soft leather and must have cost fifteen dollars even then. On the stiff, gauntletlike cuff, a little armadillo was neatly depicted. The caption below read, ARMOR PLATED. But John wouldn't wear them when he tramped through the woods for the afternoon choose-up games at the pond beside one of the mills. There the ice was hard and black, and they dragged fallen branches onto the surface to mark the goals. In truth, John hid the gloves in the cellar behind the plastered furnace boiler, because he hated to flaunt such opulence in front of the other boys, who were such a scruffy lot. They talked with accents left over from the French they were raised on. They wore gold miraculous medals trimmed with baby-blue ribbons—their mothers pinned them on their jackets in case they fell through. Sometimes John returned home and hit the gloves around the basement. He dribbled them with his stick to scuff that amber leather. If his father saw them, he wanted to make sure the man thought they were being put to hard play.

John always admitted that Harvard took him to play the sport. He had gone to the high school in the town and the year he graduated the team easily won the state championship. Ruth was from Philadelphia and went to Radcliffe. She had gone to a posh boarding school in Germantown. Both her parents were professors and, besides that, they were divorced. Back then it all seemed entirely sophisticated to John. He used to feel like a bumpkin around her. At college she principally wanted to paint and she spent most of her four years frustratedly complaining that Harvard offered no real studio art courses. He knew she noticed him only because he played hockey. She loved to show her friends his glossy photograph in the window of Elsie's Lunch. During the season, pictures of the starters lined the bulletin board there. The camera had caught John coming to a sudden stop. A surf of ice shavings blasted like rhinestones in front of him and he had his stick upraised. He wasn't wearing his bridge and looked menacing indeed without the two side teeth. She once told him that a boarding-school girlfriend had asked her if John was a "ringer."

"A ringer?" Ruth said to her. She thought that the girl was inquiring if John intended marriage—would he give her a ring. "We haven't talked yet about what either of us will do after college."

"Don't be a dummy," the other girl said. "I mean, the name is French. Fontaine. Did they bring him from Canada to play?"

Hockey.

He closed his eyes, opened them, and closed them again.

He fell into a dream in which he heard sirens as he talked on the phone. He might have been in his office or in a downtown restaurant where the white-jacketed waiter had told him during lunch that there was a call for him. On the other end of the line, Ed Ridley said he was at his own house in Lake Forest. He babbled, and at first John didn't want to let himself believe it.

"What?" asked John.

"P-please," stammered Ed Ridley. "Oh, please, John, just tell me what the hell to do now!"

"I knew you were going to do it!"

"I didn't mean to. It just . . . it just happened and . . ."

"Are you *sure?*"

"Oh, God, *am* I sure. I've tried everything. That mouth-to-mouth stuff. It's no good. The rescue is here now, they're outside. I've shot him!"

"I knew you would. You're a fat-headed fool, Ridley! You're. . . ."

John tensed on the sofa as if something electrical had stung him. He felt his whole body jerk. He opened his eyes to see the shadows of the butterfly chairs, the pole lamp, and a contraption that his daughter had been given for Christmas the year before called "Barbie's Penthouse." He rolled to one side and then settled on his back again. He savored the heaviness of just lying there.

The next dream was deeper and maybe he was dozing for a half-hour before it came. It probably had nothing to do with hockey. Or, if it did, he would never know, because he was somewhere else that he would never remember. Here—where he had been, in this world where hockey is played—another clanking plow passed. Its chains thumped and blue sparks blinked along the steel blade nicking the road.

What follows is a highly imaginative tale about the cerebral game of chess. The protagonists are chess masters, competing at the highest level, and the artistry and pressure of intense matches are nicely captured. One of the pleasures of a well-crafted short story is a nifty ending, and the one here is cleverly done. Howard Nemerov won the National Book Award in 1978 and the Pulitzer Prize for Poetry in 1981. He was America's third Poet Laureate, from 1988 to 1990. Among his books are The Collected Poems of Howard Nemerov *(1977) and* Inside the Onion *(1984). W. R. Johnson had a long career working for the U.S. government. Most of his writing is nonfiction and classified by the CIA. He is currently working on two new novels and revising some short stories with Reed Whittemore. The original of this piece appeared in* Story *magazine under the pseudonym of Joseph Cross.*

Howard Nemerov and W. R. Johnson

EXCHANGE OF MEN (1946)

WHEN THE TRAIN PULLED slowly out of Grand Central, Francis Baron took the miniature chessboard from his pocket and began to contemplate it. He did not set out the pieces, but simply studied the sixty-four black and white squares on which, you might say, he played not only chess but his whole life as well. Already as he watched the vacant board, invisible pieces moved and combined in his mind's eye, developing of themselves the studied complexities of his games. It was as he had once said, "When one passes a certain stage, one no longer moves the pieces, but simply watches them move." Francis Baron had passed that stage by the time he was twenty years old. What he was doing now, and expected to be doing until the train reached Boston, might be compared to the five-finger exercises which a great virtuoso performs faithfully every day. A discipline, a regimen, and more: he knew that from these simple diversions might come the inspiration that would save a game, the subtle but definite variation that had never appeared in books. It has happened so before, and the books had modified themselves agreeably: "The following brilliant line of play was employed for the first time in any tournament by the American master, Francis Baron. . . ."

Now, at the age of forty, on his way to the International Tournament, his appearance certainly suggested nothing so artistic and out of the way as a chess master. He was a small man, neatly and not distinctively dressed, and his own peculiarity was a rather oversize round head from which large eyes peered through silver-rimmed glasses. This anonymity of appearance, coupled with his magnificent play, had caused someone to nickname him "the mighty pawn," a title which, with that other more grandiose one of "master" he had retained since his early tournaments.

Conductors and people passing through the car glanced curiously at the little man who nursed in his lap the unoccupied chessboard as though it were a treasure or a secret sorrow; and a personable young man, who sat with a pretty girl across the aisle, leaned over and asked, "Would you care to have a game?"

Baron looked up in some annoyance. "Thank you, no," he said primly, and while he spoke he exchanged queens with his invisible opponent, and came out with the advantage of a pawn. That was one thing about being a master: you could not play with anybody you happened to meet. Even a master dropped games surprisingly often, and such a loss to an unknown opponent in a railroad car would be embarrassing, not to mention the detriment to one's reputation. Also, though Baron was a young man compared to most of the masters he would meet in tournament play, he already had a strong respect, which soon would become fear, for the rising generation. He himself must have looked like a naive innocent when, at twenty-three, he defeated Orimund in the first of many games. Now he could not blame Orimund for behaving so ungraciously afterward.

Fearing he might have been rude, he said now, "I'm terribly busy, you see," and realized that it must have sounded ridiculous.

"Are you going to watch the tournament in Boston?" the young man asked.

Baron hesitated. "Yes," he said finally. "Yes, I expect to be there." Firmly his mind told him, rook takes rook, pawn takes rook, check . . . the ending would be simplicity itself.

"I guess it's really between Orimund, Savard, and Baron," said the young man. "No one else has much chance against those three."

The mate, Baron thought, would be accomplished with a very small force, because the white king was blocked in three directions by his own pawns.

"I admire Orimund very much," the young man continued. "He's the last of the old grand masters. He has the most intense attack I've ever seen. I rather hope he becomes champion again. It would be a victory not only for himself but for his style of play as well."

"You don't much care for the modern way?" asked Baron.

"Too much subtlety, too much caution," said the young man. "Modern chess isn't playing, it's waiting."

"It wins."

"Look," the young man offered. "How about a game? I'll spot you whatever you like—a rook, even."

Baron smiled slowly. "I don't think that will be necessary."

"Well, I feel I should tell you; I'm Richard James, that is—I don't suppose you've heard of me. I won the intercollegiate championship last year."

So this was Richard James. Baron remembered a piece in the papers, not about the intercollegiate tournament, but about another, a small affair in Chicago, in which a young man named Richard James had lost rather badly to Max Tarnes but carried off the brilliancy prize all the same for a rather exciting combination against Jacob Goldman. He could see the familiar old pattern as it began to repeat itself. In a year, or two years, or three, he would be facing the brilliant young master, Richard James, across the tournament board, and everything would be at stake. But nothing need be given away at this moment. He began to set up the pieces.

"I'd still prefer to play even," he said.

"Now are you satisfied?" asked the pretty girl. "You've trapped the innocent bystander into a game. That's what's such fun about being married to Dick," she explained to Baron, "you meet such a lot of interesting people. But by a strange coincidence, they all play chess."

The young man laughed. "I want you to meet my wife, Sally, Mr.—?"

Baron looked at the board. "Springer, John Springer," he said, using the German name for knight. His use of a pseudonym, he told himself, was not in the least disreputable. After all, he had a standing which must be jealously guarded at every moment. Suppose there should be a slip, an accident, the distraction of being aboard a rattling train, the disturbingly informal conditions generally—he did not intend that such an accident should affect the reputation or the tournament play of Francis Baron during the next week.

But in trying, temporarily, at least, to conceal his identity, he must not, he knew, employ his own style of play, which to an expert would at once reveal both his name and his quality. He must accept, then, the disadvantage of meeting Richard James on the latter's own ground, which would probably be the ground of a violent attack, initiated as rapidly as possible. Ordinarily Baron would withdraw before such an attack and use his whole development for defense, for subtle probing and slow exploiting of weaknesses, occupying more and more space in the long wait for his opponent's critical mistake, which must come in time. Then, rapidly, the complexion of the match would change. From the reticence of his beginnings and his control of strategic area, Baron would open out the penetrating, incisive, and fatal counterattack. That was the way, the modern style, which had made Baron a master. But now he must fight by older and riskier methods.

Young James drew the white and opened with the Max Lange attack, quick and straight down the center of the board. It was evident that he was trying for immediate victory, and accepting a disadvantageous position if the attempt failed.

Baron countered along conventional lines, vigorously fighting for the center, for the points from which well-masked and defended powers could extend their grasp on positions within the enemy's lines. Both men were slightly nervous. There was a quality of chess, thought Baron, which made it absurd to say, "It's only a game." On the contrary, as you could judge from the way people played it, it was a warlike and representative struggle for mastery. It was a conspectus of life itself, with the illusion of power over life, which is why, though unthinking people laugh to hear of it, the chess master often dies worn out, overstrained from an incredible depth and complexity of concentration prolonged over a period of years.

As they entered the end game with an exchange of queens, James was a pawn behind, but occupied better immediate attacking position.

"You play extremely well, sir," he said deferentially to Baron, who nodded and smiled. The position, he saw, was critical. If Richard James possessed perfect book knowledge, he had what amounted to a winning game. On the other hand, he was nervous, just about trembling with eagerness for success. If that nervousness could be exploited properly, or improperly, for that matter, but exploited somehow—Francis Baron regretted exceedingly having been drawn into the match. This young man would be present at the tournament, he would recognize his opponent of the railroad car, there would surely be some publicity. He could imagine Savard's wry, crooked grin; and not alone Savard. Baron was not so well liked among the masters; they resented his youth and perhaps his manner as well. There would be a good deal of laughter over this.

Abruptly he said, "I'm afraid I didn't tell you my real name." He smiled in apology, held out his hand. "I'm Francis Baron."

On the surface it was all right. It was even a compliment to the younger man. The master, by revealing his identity, seemed to be acknowledging a worthy opponent. And Richard James tried desperately to take the acknowledgement in that spirit. But there was now too much at stake. He was no longer playing a chess game. He was playing, with a chance to win, against Francis Baron himself. He blushed and stammered, "I hope you didn't think me rude–about Orimund, I mean. I had no idea–"

"Of course not." Francis Baron smiled. "Orimund plays his way, I play mine. It's your move, Mr. James."

Two moves later Richard James moved the pawn that cost him the game. His famous antagonist was gracious in triumph, quiet and assured as he complimented the younger man on playing a very strong game.

"We shall be seeing you in tournament play very soon, I fear," he said cordially when they parted in Back Bay Station.

"You're very kind to say so; we look forward to watching your games."

Both knew what had happened. For Baron the victory was rather empty, achieved by a trick in a class with blowing smoke in your opponent's face throughout a game (this being the favorite stratagem of one Russian master), or whistling, or tapping your fingers on the table. And worst of all, he did not know if he could have won that particular game without such a device.

As for Richard James, he said to his wife, "I don't know why he had to pick that moment to tell me who he was. I was doing all right until then, but Lord! to be up against Francis Baron! I just collapsed right there."

"And that," said Sally, "is just about what he wanted. Your Francis Baron may be a great master, but it strikes me he's just a little bit of a heel at the same time."

"Now, darling, he could have beaten me anyhow."

"Don't 'now darling' me. I don't know much about chess, and he may have been able to beat you hollow; but from what I saw of his face at the time, he didn't think so."

The players in the tournament, thought Baron, had all the solemnity and high seriousness of a conclave of cardinals met to elect a new Pope, and all the jealousy, to be sure, of a boy's ball team electing a captain. It was the first international tournament since before the war, and the meeting was marked by the absence of a few faces formerly well known: Estignan, who was dead; Zinuccio, who had turned Fascist and was in prison; Einrich, who was not allowed to leave his country. But the others he knew well enough: the English master, Cranley, looking in his rich tweeds like an aged schoolboy; Savard, the Frenchman, a dumpy little man who resembled a chef and played the most eccentric games of any master; Jasoff, from Russia, looking more than usually peaked and unhappy; and several other masters from all over the world. Second-rate, thought Baron. And yet, not really second-rate: so little distance, in chess, separated the master from the expert, the merely brilliant player. It was more than probable, he reflected with distaste, that he would lose games to more than one of them. But fortunately, in a chess tournament one was not eliminated for losing a game. Elimination occurred at definite stages, on the basis of point score: one for a win, one-half for a draw. After a complete round, the contestants with the lowest scores went out and the remainder began again.

And there was Orimund, at last. The aged master whose white hair stood out like a wiry halo over his head, who always wore a high white collar and shiny black suit. Orimund, nearing seventy, with his trembling hands, his gentle voice and perfect manners, and that mind whose keenness had probably suffered somewhat during the last years. They said he had spent time in a concentration camp, and looking at him now, Baron found it easy to believe this. He had not remembered the old man as so gentle, so meek. They met in the lobby of the hotel, and Orimund seemed to have forgotten his resentment of Baron. They called each other, conventionally, Master, and were for a moment almost friendly.

"Ech, life passes, Master Baron," the old man said. "You, too, are no longer exactly of the youngsters."

Was that the way of it? Did one creep gently out of life, shedding the old antagonisms, ridding oneself gradually of the vicious desire for success?

"I am glad to have the honor once again, Master," he replied.

"Perhaps for the last time," Orimund said. "You know, years ago, when I was asked 'How can you waste your life playing chess? I was able to reply, 'How can you waste your life writing books, or making money, or painting pictures, or whatever?' And it was a good, an acceptable answer. Now, I confess, I begin to wonder, what have I done? I was given my life, and what have I made of it?"

"You leave an immortal name," replied Baron gravely.

"An immortal name—better to have died ten years ago, much better. Perhaps you will understand that someday, Master." This last, Baron recognized, was said with the familiar cold, deadly anger that he remembered as an element in the former Orimund. But Baron understood what the old man meant: better to have died champion of the world, rather than face the failing of one's powers, the uprising of the young just when one is no longer able to oppose them with success. Better than the last cold years in which, if a master makes a mistake, he believes himself to be losing his mind.

That was the last time they spoke together except over the board. Almost angrily, Baron put down the pity he felt for the old genius. If that's the way it is, that's all, he told himself. When my time comes, I don't expect to weep on the conqueror's shoulder. That's what life is, and if we were the same age I would still be confident of winning. For that matter, if the position were reversed would he show any mercy to me? I doubt it.

The tournament was not easy. Few can go through the nervous strain of game after game against excellent players without feeling a sense of desperation, and Francis Baron was no exception. The competition grew progressively more severe, and in the last matches of the opening round one came up against players who, knowing already that they would be eliminated, played with violence and extravagance in the hope of taking home by way of consolation at least one victory over a possible world's champion. Baron was beaten in this way by Jasoff and Cranley, while Orimund dropped games to Savard and to Baron himself.

Baron, however, was superbly confident. In the first round he had beaten Savard, and his victory over Orimund was achieved, if not easily, at least with certainty and power from the opening move of a solid, invulnerable game. The old man played with a brilliance matching his former great tournament play, but finding his attack met at all points he overextended his defenses slightly and was unable to withstand the vicious counterattack when it finally came.

Richard and Sally were present at all his matches, and though Baron did not in any way acknowledge their interest, he felt intensely and uncomfortably that they had in some sense seen through what had occurred on the train, that it would give them pleasure if he lost, that they were in fact simply waiting for him to make a mistake. He smiled ironically to himself. There would be no mistakes, there must be none—perfection. And forthwith he proceeded roundly to trounce Dr. Anderson, his last opponent in the first round.

Orimund, Savard, Francis Baron and an Irishman named Brian alone escaped elimination. In the second round Brian realized suddenly that he was very close to being world's champion, and simply collapsed, losing to everyone. Savard lost to Baron and Orimund, and these last drew their games and entered the final with a score of two and a half each for the round.

On the night before the last match, Baron was sitting in the hotel lobby, reading, when he was approached by the secretary of the local chess club.

"We have about ten people collected," this functionary said, "and we wondered if you'd care to give some sort of exhibition. We should be honored, greatly honored, Master, and I can say definitely that there will be no publicity. Of course, I realize that you may not feel inclined to make the effort on the eve of the final, but I was instructed to ask you all the same." He hesitated, looked apologetic, and seemed, as though realizing the enormity of his request, to be ready to retire without an answer; but Baron stopped him.

"Under the conditions you specify," he said, "I shouldn't object to the exercise. In fact, I'm grateful for the compliment of your interest. But understand, I'll hold you to strict silence on the subject. In the first place, it would be a reflection on my opponent if it got out that I was so careless of him as to play for fun on the night before our game. I can play tonight only if it is understood that the results don't matter, that it is simply a relaxation from the tournament."

"I quite understand," the secretary said. "This is the arrangement. The members will be told that a master, whose name will not be given, will play blindfolded against all ten of them simultaneously. The master will be in a room apart, and will not meet the other players either before or after the match. In that way the secret of your identity can be kept between the president and myself until after tomorrow night. And besides, the other players will be asked to keep silent about the whole event."

These terms proving to Baron's satisfaction, he was driven to the quarters of the Copley Chess Club, where he was placed in a small antechamber and left alone. Presently the secretary came in.

It has been arranged," he said, "that you are to have white in the even-numbered games and black in the odd. Fair enough?"

"Fair enough," replied Francis Baron.

"Then the first move in all the odd-numbered games is pawn to king four," said the secretary.

"My reply is the same, and my opening move in the even-numbered games is pawn to queen four."

That was the way of it, he thought. In this blindfolded game one allowed the opponents to open up a little, and then when the weak sisters among them disclosed themselves, they must be whipped rapidly, allowing one to concentrate on the difficult games.

The amateurs did show themselves very soon. Games one, two, four, eight, and nine took less than fifteen moves for the establishment of overwhelming superiority on Baron's side. Few of the boards presented any great difficulty. There was the usual zealot who felt that the queenside pawns could do everything necessary, one who thought that to *finchetto* both bishops was to solve all his troubles, another who brought out his queen and proceeded to do damage to the extent of a rook and a pawn before falling into a cleverly prepared trap. Few of the games were in any way rewarding, except as an exercise in concentration for the master.

At last game number seven sorted itself out from the rest; there was something there. A Max Lange attack, with a curious variation in the placement of the queen's knight. Going over the position in his mind, Baron began to recognize the style. His opponent, he was almost certain, could be no one but Richard James. A few minutes later an astonishingly rapid attack confirmed his belief. Baron felt himself being pressed with some severity and marshaled his forces to defend. It would be a close game.

The other games expired in something over the fortieth move. He had won them all, but then, the competition had been very nearly nothing. The seventh game, however, was close and even threatening. James was playing for a brilliant win and as things stood it was well within the possible for him to achieve it. And this time there was no way of breaking the boy's nerve; instead, Baron knew, his own nerve might go. It was so easy to make a mistake; he was holding precariously in his mind the crossing, tangling threads of thirty-two pieces moving altogether more than eighty times over sixty-four squares. The possibilities were infinite. If one forgot a move, or misplaced a move in memory, it was over: defeat. One defeat, of course, in ten blindfold games, is nothing; but to lose to young James! And he was certain that James knew his opponent; he felt an intellectual rapport that enabled him to picture the handsome young face as it bent over the board, and realized that James knew perfectly that he was playing—and winning—against Francis Baron.

And then it came. The secretary entered, said, "Game number seven. pawn to bishop six."

"Is he certain of that?" Baron asked, incredulous.

"That is his move, sir."

"My reply—queen takes rook."

Francis Baron breathed easily. Richard James had made a mistake, a subtle mistake, to be sure, and not immediately apparent, but the master could now foresee the imminent collapse of his opponent's game. After the sacrifice of the queen, knight and two rooks would accomplish the rest. He called after the secretary, "I announce checkmate in six moves."

It went as he planned, now. On the fifth move he forced the white rook to occupy the square adjacent to the white king, thus blocking all escape squares and enabling the knight to mate at bishop seven. He returned to his hotel.

But he was troubled in his mind. A mistake like that, it was unnatural, considering how masterful James's play had been up until then. It was tantamount to deliberate surrender, it was . . . it was deliberate surrender! He saw it now. James had recognized his adversary, had realized that Baron, strained by the tournament, could be upset beyond measure by a defeat of any sort at this moment, and he had deliberately opened up his board so as to be defeated. It was a gesture of the most subtle and keen sportsmanship; it was, in a way, a moral revelation. After all, he reflected, when you consider that he probably dislikes me intensely, and realized that he had it in his power to hurt my game and refrained—that shows the greatest delicacy.

Francis Baron found it difficult to get to sleep. His own face kept appearing to him, saying, "I am Francis Baron, I am Francis Baron," over and over with the utmost pomposity imaginable. What was it for? he asked himself. For a game of chess. Chess is not, after all, life itself. Chess, if you regard it properly, is a game. A great game, true; but is it worth the demands it makes? Fancy a man like Orimund, now, decrepit, feeling bitterly the decline of his powers, yet playing with the most religious courtesy and chivalry.

He could imagine Orimund after the final match, returning alone to Europe. There would still be many admirers, would still be the satisfaction of a good game, not a great game, mind; but deeply, essentially, he would be an old man, nearing death, alone.

Orimund won the final game. Francis Baron would never forget how the reporters gathered around after the game, nor how the old man wept far more over his success than he would have wept over his defeat. And how Orimund called him "Master" and said good-by in the most touching and friendly way, his hand on the younger man's shoulder. "After me," he had said, "in a year, less perhaps, who knows?"

Between dejection and satisfaction, Francis Baron, runner-up for the world's chess championship, packed his bag and prepared to return to New York. The analysis of that final game, he knew, would give many people reason enough to laugh at him.

"Come in," he said in response to a knock.

Richard and Sally James stood at the door. He invited them in, and Richard said, "We just wanted you to know we saw what you did in that game." Sally nodded in agreement. "And we'd like to tell you we thought it was wonderful."

"Did? I didn't do anything—except lose, of course."

"You gave him the game. You did it purposely, and you did it so that no one who didn't know both your styles perfectly would ever realize."

Francis Baron smiled at them. "There's no need to shout it all over the place," he said. "Anyhow, I've got you to thank for my quixotic behavior. You taught me a great deal about games and other things last night."

"Last night?" James looked blank.

"Yes. At the Copley Club, you know, game number seven."

"I don't get it," Richard James said, "I've never been to the Copley Club in my life."

Paul Horgan (1903–1995) was the author of forty-seven books including seventeen novels, four volumes of short stories, five biographies, and several histories. He won the Pulitzer Prize in 1955 for Great River, *a two-volume history of the Rio Grande, and in 1976 for* Lamy of Santa Fe, *a biography. His short stories are particularly effective, and "To the Mountains" is one of his very best. It's about two teenage boys taking responsibility for family survival, with their father away and mother recovering from childbirth. The personal sacrifices on the boys' hunting trip show admirable courage and love.*

Paul Horgan

TO THE MOUNTAINS (1937)

1

JULIO LAY AS QUIETLY as he could. Only his eyes kept moving, turning toward the open door that led into the other room, as if by looking there he could hear better what the women were saying. His brother Luis was asleep beside him. The same blanket of catskins covered them both. Luis could sleep no matter what happened. The firelight on the walls and the ceiling was enough to keep Julio awake, even if his mother were not weeping in the next room. It was a silent night outside; like all the other nights in this place of home.

'When the fire goes out I will go to sleep,' thought Julio; his legs ached from holding them still. Four nights ago his mother had given birth to a baby girl. Josefina Martinez came nine miles from Bernalillo to assist. The father was in Mexico on a wagon train. The trade in the summer and autumn of 1800 was promising, and the weather very fortunate. Rosa's baby came with no one there but her two sons and Josefina the midwife. They made a huge fire in the front room and left the door open so that the heat would wave silently through. The boys stayed outdoors and shuddered like horses under the November moon. From within came the wafting firelight and the nimble sounds of repeated sufferings.

Each boy felt like the deputy of his father. Luis was sixteen and Julio was thirteen. Luis was a stout boy—legs and arms like cottonwood branch, round and wieldy. Julio was slender and something like a half-grown cat in his physical ways. He was wary and respectful of life's dangers. He had grown with caution, because fear slowly told him more as he grew up. Everything Luis did easily, because he was older, Julio had to learn to do because he was younger, and thus everything was harder for him. The boys had no one but each other for companions, mostly; for they lived in the Rio Grande Valley a way out from the village of Bernalillo. They sometimes went there on horseback, when their father could spare the animals from work in the fields. Once, riding to town, Julio's horse had stampeded and run wild, because a hunter in the tall saplings by the field near the river had shot his musket at a rising goose. Julio often dreamed of it, and the triumph of regaining the horse's head.

The brothers slept and the firelight faded down.

In the back room, Rosa presently slept too, and Josefina sat watching her and the new baby.

Josefina was greatly girthed, with two circles of fat at her middle. She was heavy-faced and her eyes were kind, even when her tongue was sharp and filthy. Thus her character: good heart, from instinct; wicked mind, from dealings in the hard world.

The baby lay by its mother's side.

'The face of a *piñón*,' thought Josefina, staring at the tiny brown head and the little open mouth that breathed so roundly.

The house was thick as a fortress, with adobe walls. It stood on a little green flat of land above the fields, beyond which lay the Rio Grande. Over it went two mighty cottonwoods, planted by the grandfather of this house a long time ago, who himself had left the service of the Governor of New Spain to scratch his own land and yield it to his own sons. To the east the fields faded into mesa country, rising face of gravelly sand that held dusty bushes. The mesa rolled away and lifted hills where little pine trees grew. In morning, distant under the early sun, the pine trees seemed to exhale a blue air; and from the blue air rose the mountains, whose mighty trees looked, far away, like scratches upon the face of blue rock.

The mountains were miles away from the house of the family, and sometimes they were altogether hidden by weather: cloud, rain, or wind alive with dust. At other times the mountains were momentously close, as if moved in golden light by the hand of God, and every cañon, every wind course and water hollow in the road stood clear to the eyes of the wondering brothers. Hardly a day of their lives failed to be somehow influenced by the mountains out there to the east.

Josefina came into the front room to kick some more wood on the dying fire; for cold was quick to get through her petulant flesh.

She woke Julio; but he lay with his eyes shut, identifying the noises she made, and the profane rumble of her musing. When she went back, he heard his mother speak sleepily; then the baby squeaked and began to cry, what sounded to him like a mortal utterance and farewell of that alien little life in his mother's bed.

'Yes, if you all four of you get through the winter, that will be one of God's little jokes,' said Josefina, slapping her hands on her cold belly. 'This house never gets warm; and nothing to cover with, those boys out there, freezing on the dirt floor with a dirty old catskin . . .'

'My husband will bring back plenty of money and furs and clothes from Mexico,' said Rosa. But she began to cry again, and mumble little sad doubts against the baby's hot temple.

'So, I will stay as long as I can,' said Josefina. 'But you know that can't be forever.—Be quiet now. You will choke the baby. Here I'll take her, though God knows she may freeze to death. Get back to sleep. I will warm her.'

Josefina took the baby.

Julio leaned and crouched from his bed to see what they did. There was a coldly steady candle burning by the wooden saint in the corner of the bedroom. Josefina held the baby with one arm and with her other hand pulled her tight dress away in front, and her huge bosom lay open and cavernous with shadow. There, at her warmest and most copious being, she laid the baby and folded her breasts to it, and drew her dress together and held her arms like a cradle. Her cheeks quivered at the striving touch of the baby; some pleasure deepened in her being; and for no reason that she could recognize, out of her assortment of past events—midwife, servant, thief, and harlot—she began to blush.

Her eyes watered and she smiled and sighed.

Julio backed into his bed again. His brother Luis flinched and jerked like a dog that is tickled when it dozes. Julio held his breath for fear he would wake Luis. Yet he wanted to talk to him. He wanted to stir his brother into a fury of doing; to save this family; to prove that it was not a world for women—that it was their own little tiny sister who so blindly threatened their mother's life and will, and who opened the disgusting bosom of a fat witch to lie there for warmth!

So his thoughts were confused and furious.

The fire was alive again in little flames like autumn leaves. He could not sleep. He could not forget. He hated his fears. They were with him, vaguely enlivened for Josefina's talk.

It was not long before winter.

In the broken darkness of firelight, Julio lay awake and prayed until he was answered by the same thing that always answered prayers, the earliest voice he had been taught to recognize, which no one else had to hear—the voice of God Himself in his own heart. Father Antonio made him know when he was a very little boy that the stronger a man was, the more he needed the guidance of God. So when he felt afraid and feeble alongside his mild strong brother, he had only to pray, and shut his eyes, and remember Jesus, who would presently come to him and say, 'I see you, Julio Garcia; it is all right. What is it?"

'The mountains, to the mountains,' thought Julio in answer to his own prayer.

'Blessed is the fruit of thy womb: Jesus . . .'

'What is in the mountains?'

'. . . now and at the hour of our death.'

'There is much that my brother and I can do in the mountains, and as soon as he awakens I will tell him; we will take my father's musket and go hunting; we will bring home skins to keep our little sister warm, and show our mother that this is a house of men, who do what is right, no matter how hard it is to do.'

'Amen.'

2

Against the mica panes of the small deep window the early daylight showed like fog, silvery and chill. Luis jumped alive from sleep and went like a pale shadow to the dead fireplace, where he blew ashes off a few remote coals and, shivering in his bare skin, coaxed a fire alive. Then he found his clothes and got into them. He began to laugh at Julio, curled like a cat under the mountain-cat skins, waiting for warmth in the room. Then he thought with pleasure of the work to be done outside, in the marching dawn; cold mist over the river; the horses stirring; animals to feed and release. He went out, already owner of the day.

Julio was awake all that time; and he squinted at the fire, judging nicely just when it would need more wood, lest it go out; and just when the room would be comfortable. He was soon up, listening for sounds in the other room. Presently Josefina came to make breakfast. She felt tragic in the cold morning, and her face drooped with pity for her heart which was abused.

'I am going home,' said she.

'No, you can't do that,' said the boy.

She looked at him with sad delight in his concern.

'Why can't I? What do I get around her for my pains? I was freezing all night.'

'When my father comes home he will pay you plenty. Luis and I can—
we will bring you a glorious piece of fur.'

'Oh, indeed; and where from?'

'We are going to the mountains.'

'A pair of fool children like you? Another thing for your poor mama
to worry about! If she lives through the winter it will be very surprising.'

'What do you mean?'

She had nothing to mean, and so she made it more impressive by quivering her great throat, a ridiculous gesture of melancholy.

Julio ran outside and found his brother. They did not greet each other,
but fell into tasks together.

The sky was coming pale blue over the river, and pale gold edges of light
began to show around the far mountain rims. The house looked like a
lively toy in the defining light, its edges gilded, its shadows dancing.

'Luis.'

'What?'

'I have an idea.'

'Well?'

'Did you feel cold all night?'

'No, but you would not lie still.'

'I am sorry. I heard Josefina talking to Mama.'

'The poor old cow.'

'Do you realize that we are so poor that we haven't got enough things
to keep us warm, especially with the new baby here? And an extra woman
in the house?—She ought to stay with us until Mama is well again.'

'What are you going to do about it?'

'You and I should take the musket and go to hunt cats in the mountains, and bring home enough furs to satisfy everybody.'

'Yes,' said Luis, without any surprise, 'I have thought of that, too.'

'Then I can go?"

'I suppose so—if you behave yourself. It's no child's errand, you know.'

'Of course not. Then will you tell Mama?'

'All right.'

Now the smoke was thick and sweet above the house.

The light spread grandly over the whole valley.

Luis went to his mother's bedside and leaned down. The baby was awake and obscurely busy against her mother's side.

'Mama.'

'My little Luis.'

'Julio and I are going to the mountains for a few days, to get some furs.'

'No, no, you are both too young! That little Julio is just a baby. Now, Luis, don't break my heart with any more troubles!'

'What troubles? We have no troubles!'

'Your father is gone, we have no money, my children shiver all night long, that Josefina is a fat crow, Father Antonio hasn't been near us since the baby was born.'

She wept easily and weakly. Luis was full of guilt, and ideas of flight. He leaned and kissed her cool forehead and laughed like a big man.

'You'll see. My brother and I will come back like merchant princes.'

'Then you are going?'

'Yes, Mummie, we'll go.'

She stared at him in a religious indignation. This was her son! So even sons grew up and went away and did what they wanted to do, in spite of all the things women could think of to keep them back!

Later Julio came to say good-bye, and she shamelessly wooed him to stay, with the name of God, and her love, and his pure dearness, and various coquetries. He felt a lump in his throat, so he shrugged, like his father, and went to the other room, where he paused and said, 'Thank you, Josefina, for staying until my brother and I get back.'

'The devil takes many odd forms,' said Josefina with a pout.

They had two horses and the musket which their father had left at home upon his last departure for Mexico. They had a rawhide pouch containing things to eat, loaves and chilies and dried meat. As soon as they were free of the little fields of home, Julio began to gallop; and Luis overtook him and, saying nothing, reached out for the halter and brought him down to a walk. Julio felt very much rebuked; he sat erect on his horse and squinted his eyes at the mountain rising so far ahead of them, and thought of himself as a relentless hunter.

The boys toiled over the land all morning.

They paused and looked back several times, touched by the change in the look of their farm, which lay now like a box or two on the floor of the valley; and they thought respectively, 'When I have my farm, I shall want to be on higher ground,' and 'What if something dreadful has happened since we left home! If the baby choked to death, or a robber came, I should never forgive myself.'

The mountains looked strangely smaller as they advanced. The foothills raised the riders up, and from various slopes the mountain crowns seemed to lean back and diminish. The blue air in cañons and on the far faces of rock slides and broken mighty shoulders was like a breath of mystery over the familiar facts of memory.

'Let me carry the musket now for a while.'

'No, we might as well decide that now. I am to have it all the time.'

'Why, that isn't right!'

'No, I have had more experience with it. It is our only arm. Now be sensible.'

'Just because I am the younger, you always do this way. I tell you, I am an excellent shot.'

'You may be. But I am nearly four years older, and—I just think it better this way.'

'I wish I'd known before we started.'

'Why don't you go back, then?'

'I will.'

But they rode on together. Easily triumphant, Luis could afford to be indulgent; later on he rode close to Julio and knocked him on the back and winked.

'You think I am not as much of a man as you are,' said Julio bitterly.

'Well, you're not.'

'You'll see! I can show you!'

The brothers' love for each other was equally warm, but derived from different wells of feeling. Sometimes they felt only the love; at other times, only the difference.

Now in afternoon, riding on the windy November plain, and knowing that before nightfall they would be in the very shadow of the nearest mountain reach, they felt their littleness on that world. The air was lighter so high up above the river valley. They looked back: an empire of sand-colored earth, and there, in the far light, the river herself, furred with trees. They looked ahead, but in doing that had to look up.

It was a crazy giant land; a rock that looked like a pebble from here was higher than a tree when they got to it.

'We must find a place to leave the horses.'

'What?'

'You idiot, we can't expect horses to climb straight up cliffs like that over there!'

'Sure, we'll find a place to leave them.'

'It must be nearly too late to go into the mountains tonight.'

'We'll make a fire here.'

'If it is clear enough tonight, they could see our fire from home.'

'They could?'

The thought made Julio shiver. But then it was already getting chill. The sun was going down.

3

They awoke the next morning under the cold mountains, and in their rested souls there was a mood of gods. They caught their horses and rode along the last little flat before the great rise, and before the sun was up over the rocky shoulder they had found a little box cañon where there was a growth of straw-colored grass, and through which there washed a small creek. Leading the horses, they walked far into the narrow shadowy cañon and at last Luis said, 'There!'

'What?'

'Here is the place to leave the animals. We can make a little fence down here, and then be safe when we go off to hunt.'

'What will you build your fence with?'

'Some big rocks and then a lot of branches that will seem high to the horses.'

'Where does that river come from, do you suppose?'

'If you'll stop talking long enough to get to work, we'll go and find out.'

The light of builders came into their eyes, measuring, devising; after a few trials they had a system for their work; they moved harmoniously. Given need, materials, and imagination, nothing wanted. They grew warm, and threw down their coats. The sun quivered in watery brilliance high beyond the rocky crown.

When they were done, they untethered the horses and took up the food, the musket, the powder, balls, their knives, their tinder, and went up the cañon, following the creek. It led them into shadow; they had to wade; the rocks widened—sunlight ahead; then a miniature marsh with moss and creatures' tracks; then a little waterfall, which they heard, a whisper in diamond sunlight, before they saw it; and under it a black pool plumbed by the sun to its still, sandy floor.

The fall came down from a rocky ledge halfway up the face of a gray stone cliff.

The forest shadows beyond it, which they saw looking up, were hazy with sunlight and noon blue.

'We'll swim!'

The boys took off their clothes and fell into the water; for a moment they hated the cold shock, and then they were happily claimed by the animal world. They were away from everything. They were left to their senses. They dived and splashed and bellowed, awakening the silences to echo, which only tempest and beast had awakened before them. This was a bath of a superman; not the idle, slow, muddy, warm current of the Rio Grande, which suggested cows and babies paddling and hot mud drugging boys who swam in summer.

They came out into the warmer air and slapped until they were dry; then they dressed.

'Up there—we've got to get up there someway.'

Luis pointed up to the higher world beyond the fall. There were gigantic pines standing in light-failing ranks; and behind them a great plane of rock shaggy with its own breakage.

So they retreated from the waterfall and went around it, climbing and clawing until they had gained the upper level. They stood to listen. Enormous and pressing, the quiet of the mountains surrounded them. Their eyes, so long limited to a tame river world, hunted ahead. They were explorers, so far as they knew. What no man has ever seen before! There was a mysterious sense of awe in the first eye that owned it.

As they passed in and out of shadow they felt alternately cold and warm.

As they went, they were often forced by the huge silence to stop and let their own sounds die away.

They would laugh at each other at such moments, and then go on.

In midafternoon they thought they must plan to go back, since it took them so long to come. The horses would need company and perhaps protection against beasts.

The sun was yellower and cooler.

The way they had come no longer looked the same; coming, they had watched another face of it; now, retreating, they had to look back often to recognize their course. They lost it, or thought they had, when they came to a bench of gray stone in a spill of light through branches. They then looked aside, and saw the ledge curve and vanish in a stout hillside, and emerge a little farther on and there become the rocky shelf over which rustled their waterfall of the sunny noon.

'It is made by heaven for our purposes!' said Luis.

'Yes, it certainly is—How do you mean?'

'Well, the cats probably come and drink and lie here, and other animals. We could be here on this shelf, you see.'

'And fire down on them?'

'Sure. Come on.'

They started along the ledge and then shagged back and nearly fell down to the cañon floor below when a boom of air and shock arose and smote them from a few feet ahead. It was the thunder of a great bald eagle who beat his way off the rocks and straight up over them, his claws hanging down, his hot red eyes sparkling for one tiny second in the light of the sky. Then he wheeled and raised his claws and extended his head and drifted off in a long slanting line like the descent of the mountain edge over which he vanished.

The boys were breathless.

It scared them.

It also hushed them—the grandeur of that heavy bird leaving earth for air.

'How I should love to get a bird like that!'

'To kill him?'

'Or at least get some of his feathers.'

'Maybe he dropped some.'

Julio moved forward and then crouched and called for his brother.

'Luis, look! Hurry! Here is what he had!'

They were looking at a partially picked mountain-lion cub, off which the eagle had been feeding.

'Julio, you see, now? Here is where the big cats will come. They will roam until they find it, and they will watch. The eagle carried off the baby cat. He'll come back, too!'

Julio acted like a very small boy. He kicked the carcass of the cub off the ledge into the shaly slide below.

'What did you do that for?'

'I don't know.'

'It was wonderful bait! Now it's gone!'

'Well . . .'

'Oh, come on!'

The godlike temper and power of the day were gone for them both—Luis exasperated, Julio tired and guilty.

As they went down to the cañon where the waterfall seemed to stand, not fall, in a mist of blue shadow now that the sun was sinking, they looked up, and saw the eagle so high that he seemed like a spiraling leaf, and Luis shrugged and said, 'Oh, cheer up! I suppose he would have come back anyway and carried his supper off!'

But Luis, though he was again friendly, could not offset the chilling of the whole day; and the rocky clear cold cupping of night in those walled places closed over Julio and confirmed his hunger, his bitterness, his youthful rue at the turn of happiness into misery, like the turn of day into dusk.

All right, if everybody was older than he was, let them parade and give orders. If Luis felt so superior, Julio would show him some day.

They scampered down the cañon as fast as they could, for where they had left the horses was like a station of home to them.

When it was dark enough, they looked for stars, and saw some, but clouds had come, and a damp, warmish wind, and the cañon talked in wind, trees keening, and now and then an almost silent thunder of a wind-blow when it met a distant high rock mountainface.

By the last light of their fire, Luis examined his musket, to see that the day's toil over hard ground hadn't damaged it any.

'Let me see it,' said Julio.

'What for?'

'Oh, can't I just *see* it?'

Luis handed it over.

Julio sighted along the barrel.

'She's a lovely one,' he murmured. Then he gave it back, ready to go to sleep, chuckling with affection for Luis, who would be so surprised.

4

Dawn came with a ghostly diffusion of misty light—the slow march of shapes.

Julio was ready.

He rolled with almost infinite slowness to the ground, free of the blankets, and left Luis slumbering like a mummy who knew the cold of centuries.

He crouched and slowly went around the other side of the bed, and took up the musket and ammunition from the side of his brother.

He sniffed the air, and it was bitter-sweet with cold and some drifting new flavor.

He didn't know, in his excitement and caution, that it was the presage of snow.

He went up the cañon chewing on a hank of jerked meat from his pocket. He was abroad in his own wilderness, with his own gun; in effect, with his own destiny. He remembered yesterday's trail very well, and he toiled while the light grew; yet, there being no sun, everything had a new look, though he had seen it before. He came after a long time to the pool and waterfall. There he stopped and looked back. Now he realized how far it was; how many hours divided him from Luis, who must have been awake and wondering hours ago.

What would Luis do?

Would he kick the hard ground in fury, and halloo for him? Or would he set out in pursuit?

But which way would Luis decide to go?

Or perhaps he was weeping at the conviction that his beautiful young brother Julio had been carried off in the night by beasts of prey.

Then the image of a devouring lion shouldering a musket was too odd, and Julio laughed; then he smartly turned to see where another's laugh came from; then he laughed again, at his echo in the rocky room with the sky roof.

The waterfall was like a wraith made of heavier air than the gray essence that filled the intimate little cañon.

'The cats will come to the ledge,' thought Julio, faithful to his brother's wisdom, even though he outraged it.

He went around the long way, slowly going across the fat roll of the rocky hillside, and found himself then in the tall forest up there. He knew that a hunter must wait; so he settled himself to do so on a tiled shelf of moss, between two big boulders, lacy with fern and dark with shadow.

His stomach was clutched by doubts and partly whetted hunger. Hardest of all was to keep the silence of the mountains, lest he startle his game.

Many times he was ready to get up, relieve the ache of his set legs, go back to Luis and pretend that he had only wandered a few feet from camp.

But he was afraid now. He was afraid of the way the sky looked, dark and soft, and wind very high up which pulled the clouds past the peaks as if tearing gray cloth on the sharp edges.

He was lost, really.

The musket was a heavy sin across his lap. It was loaded. Perhaps he should unload it and scamper back.

But then, if a mountain cat came to the ledge, he would be helpless.

Then he remembered for the first time that he might be in danger from the animals. It sent blood back through him, and he grew angry at such menace.

'If they think they can hurt me, they are crazy, those wildcats!'

So he spent the early day and noon in thoughts of himself and his furies, while the peace of the forest was held, and the sky now came down in darkness and again blew upward in windy jets of silvery light.

And he stayed, watching.

He was so alone and silent that the first touch on his cheek out of the air startled him, and he turned his head quickly to look; but what had touched his cheek was the snow, shortly after noon.

It came down, dandled by the odd currents of airy wind in the irregular mountains, like white dust sifting through the ancient stand of trees up the mountainside.

Julio blinked at the spotty snow falling before his eyes, and he licked the delicious flakes that starred his lips.

The rocks were beginning to look white. The air was white, and the distance was white.

The distance was reduced. When he tried to peer as far as he would, his sight seemed to go so far and then turn black.

All suddenly, a most childish wave of lonesomeness broke over him, and he knew how far away he was, and how solitary; how subject to the mountains.

He got up.

Something else moved, too, in the whitening world.

He saw it, obscurely dark against the white stone shelf below him in line of sight. It was a mountain lion coming down the ledge with beautiful stillness and almost the touch of snow in its own paws.

Its heart-shaped nose was along the ground, smelling the fresh snow and whatever it covered.

Julio lifted the gun, which was as light as he wanted it in this moment, and watched, and licked the snow off his upper lip. Then, with his eyes wide-open and his cheeks blown up, he fired.

He couldn't hear the lion cry, or the echo of the amazing blast through the cañons and the aisles. He was deaf from it. But he sat down behind his rock and watched while he reloaded, and saw the cat spilling its blood on the snow; and then gradually he could hear it moaning as his head cleared. Then it suddenly died. The snow continued on it passively, cooling the blood, and making it pale, and finally thickening over it entirely.

After a long time Julio came down from his rock and touched his game.

He glanced around to see if any more cats happened to be there. There were none. He was exalted and indifferent. He rolled the heavy lion off the ledge down to the sloping hillside below it. There the snow was thinner. There he set to work to skin the cat, as he had watched his father skin animals at home, for leather, for fur, for rawhide.

5

His knife was so wet and cold that it tried to stick to his hands.

He was late in finishing. He felt proud.

Maybe Luis would be annoyed, but not for long. To bring home the first fur? He had a loving warm tender heart for all animals, now that he had conquered one of the greatest. He felt that animals must love men in return, and serve them humbly.

Done, then, he returned to thoughts of others, and then he could have groaned aloud when he really imagined what Luis might feel.

'Do you suppose my brother is in danger because I took away his gun? What if he has been attacked? What if I had not had the gun when the lion came? It would be the same with him, without any protection! Oh, my Jesus and my God, help me to get back in a hurry, and have him safe when I get there!'

Now, with heavying snow and night beginning to fall, the hunter could not scramble fast enough to undo what his day had done.

He shouldered his new skin, which was freezing and heavy, and his gun and his supplies, and went down off the shaly hill. In the bottom of the chasm, where the waterfall entered the stream, it was dark. The black water of the creek alone was clearly visible. He stopped and called out, then turned to listen, but the spiraling flaky darkness was vastly quiet.

He hurried on and sobbed a few times, but he said to himself that it was simply that he was cold, not that he was sorely afraid and sorry.

'Certainly I can see!'

But he paid for this lie when he struck a rock that cut his cheek and threw him down to the ground, where the soft copious snowfall went on secretly to change the mountains, to enrich stony hollows with soft concavities, to stand the bare ridges barer above snowy articulations.

He struggled to make a small fire, scratching twigs and needles and branches from the lee side of rocks, having to feel for his wants. At last he produced a flame, and his heart leaped up, the firelight on the snow was so lovely. In the light he saw where he was, and collected more branches, building craftily to bring up his flames, until the cañon was roaring with light and heat at that spot.

He sat, then lay on his new fur, with the raw side down.

The snowflakes made a tiny, fascinating little hiss of death when they fell into the fire.

'Luis will be all right. I will get to him early in the morning; as soon as it is light I shall start out.'

He dozed and awoke, at last to see his fire gone. Then he knew he must stay awake.

What he knew next was so strange that he felt humble. In spite of trying not to, he had fallen asleep, and was then awakened afterward by wave after wave of sound, through the falling, falling snow which hushed everything but this clamor that had awakened him, the ringing of a bell. The bell clanged and stammered and changed with the wind; like the bell of the church at home, miles up the valley on a still hot summer Sunday morning.

'But this is not—there can be no church in these mountains!' he said in the blackest density of the snowfall that night. And he listened again, but now heard nothing—nothing beyond the faint sense of hushing in the air made by the falling snow.

The bell was gone; it had served to awaken him; somewhere beyond this cold separating fall, it had rung out for him—true, even if it came to him as a dream of security. He did not lie down again; but sat, marveling, and sick for home.

6

The snow continued with daybreak.

He set out again as soon as he could see a few feet in front of him. As the light grew, so did his sense of folly. It was as if he had dreamed of the things that might happen to his brother Luis.

All his greatness of accomplishment disappeared. What good was this smelling and frozen catskin now? He threw it down by an icy rock and found that he could now run, trotting, without the awkward burden of the cat hide, which was stiff and slippery—with its frozen leggings of fur which stuck out, ragged and indignant, the congealed ghost of the cat.

The snow died away as Julio hurried. The wind became capricious and bitter. It scratched in long sweeps down the cañon and bore out over the open plains, which Julio could begin to see as the day grew and he toiled farther down the shadowy chasm.

He kept staring ahead for sight of the spare pines which stood by their camp. He remembered seeing the pines against open sky the first night there—which meant that they were nearly out of the mountain's fold.

He thought he saw the sentinel trees once; broke into a hard run; and then stopped, panting, when he saw that the gray light on a wall of rock had looked for a moment like a misty sky out there over the plain.

The musket was heavy and cold in his grasp. He had it still loaded. Perhaps he ought to shoot it off, a signal for his brother?

But he would call first.

He cried out, and stood to listen, his whole body turned sideways to hear an answer.

There was none.

Now he knew that the bell he had heard last night, waking him up during the snowstorm, was a miracle, sent to keep him from freezing to death in his sleep.

So he began to run again, and his heart nearly burst. He thought perhaps there would be another miracle, to keep Luis safe and bring Julio back to him right away.

The boy crawled over the rocks that seemed cold enough to crack in the weather; he waded where he had to in the glazed creek. Suddenly it was lighter; the sky lay before him as well as above him; and at last he looked down on the miniature meadow of the cañon mouth where the horses were fenced. There! Yes, there were the guardian pine trees.

'Luis, Luis, I am back!' he cried, but he choked and made only a sobbing sound. There was no fire burning at the camp, and Julio was thumped in the breast by fear again, as if Luis had gone back home with the two horses and left him as he deserved to be left, alone in the mountains.

He hurried and then saw the horses, far down the way.

Then he heard a voice, talking to him from a distance; no words; level, careful sounds, it sounded like Luis.

'Luis, where are you?'

Julio came down farther.

He squinted around, and then upward.

'I am glad to see you back. Stop where you are!'

'Luis!'

'Be careful.'

At the same moment, Julio heard how Luis spoke from the tree where he was hanging and he saw the wolf at the base of the tree, which was staring upward, perfectly quiet and ready.

The wolf was huge and looked like a dog, except that he was gray, the color of rock—which was why Julio didn't see him for the first little while.

The wolf must have heard him, for his ears were standing up and the fur on his spine was silvery and alive. Julio stood shocking-still and was perfectly sure that the wolf's eyes were straining toward him as far as they could without the turn of the head; and the animal was ready to turn and attack him if necessary.

So there was a grotesque interval of calm and silence in the cañon.

Luis was hanging to the pine tree, which had a few tough fragments of branch about sixteen feet above the ground.

The sun tried to shine through the bitter and cloudy day.

Luis looked white and sick, half-frozen; his eyes were burning black in new hollow shadows.

'Julio,' said Luis, as lightly as possible, never taking his eyes off the wolf; indeed, as if he were addressing the wolf.

'Yes, Luis,' whispered Julio.

'You have the gun there with you, haven't you?' asked the older brother, in an ingratiating and mollifying tone, to keep the wolf below him still intent upon his first design.

'Yes, Luis.'

'Well, Julio,' said his brother with desperate charm, velvet-voiced and easy, 'see if you can load it without making much disturbance, will you?'

'It is loaded, Luis.'

'Oh, that is fine. Then, Julio, pray Jesus you can manage to shoot the wolf. Julio, be easy and steady now . . . don't–move–fast–or–make–any–noise–Julio–for–the–love–of–God.'

To Julio it was like coming back to the reward of his folly. He held his breath, to be quiet.

He thought Luis was going to fall from the tree–his face was so white and starving, his hands so bony and desperate where they clutched.

'Why, of course I can shoot the terrible wolf,' said Julio to himself; slowly, slowly bringing the musket around to the aim.

Luis, from his tree against the gray pale sky, went on talking in tones of enchantment and courtesy to the wolf, to keep alive the concentration, until Julio fancied the wolf might answer, as animals did in the tales of early childhood.

'We shall see, my dear friend wolf, just sit there–one–more–minute–if you please–until–my–brother gets the thing ready. . . . Are–you–ready–Julio . . .'

The answer was the shot.

The wolf lashed his hindquarters around so that he faced Julio, whence the sound had come.

He roared and spat; but he could not move. His back was broken. He sat and barked and snapped his teeth.

Julio ran a little way forward, then was cautious. He stopped and began to reload.

Luis fell to the ground. He had his knife ready.

But he could not move as quickly as he would. He was cold and stiff and cramped. He hacked his knife into the animal's breast, but the stab was shy and glancing. The wolf made a crying effort and scrabbled its shattered body forward and took Luis by the leg.

'Now, Julio! Your knife!'

Julio dropped the musket and came down to them.

'Where Luis?'

'Under his left forearm!'

'Wolf!' said Julio, and drove his knife.

7

For a moment they all stayed where they were—the brothers panting; the animal dead, and slowly relaxing thus. The brothers sweated and couldn't speak, but hung their heads and spat dry spit and coughed and panted.

'Did he bite you bad?' asked Julio.

'No, he couldn't bite very hard, not even like a dog—he was too hurt.'

'Let me see.'

They peeled the cloth away from the leg just above the knee. The teeth had torn the cloth and the flesh. It did not hurt. It was numb. It bled very little. The skin was blue.

There was nothing to do to the leg except cover it again. They took as long as possible at it, but they had presently to come to the story of the young brother's folly, and as soon as that was done they felt elated—the one penitent and grave, the other pardoning and aware that the terrors of the experience were more useful to his young brother than any words of rebuke.

'. . . And I know right where I left the lion skin; we'll get it later! We can get many more!'

Julio was ballooning with relief, now that it was all over and done with. He felt as he always felt after confession in church—airy and tall.

The physical misery in snow and wind and rocky mountain temper—

this was their outer penalty. But the boys knew an inner joy at the further range of their doing. Simply being where they were, at odds with what menaced them—this was achievement; it was man's doing done.

Late that day the sun did break through and a little while of golden light seemed to relieve the cold. It didn't snow again that night. They kept their fire high. Luis was, oddly, too lame to walk. But he was glad to lie and watch the flames, and smile at Julio's serious bearing, full of thoughtful play in his face which meant plans and intentions.

8

The day after the snowstorm the valley itself came back in a kind of golden resurge of autumn. The house at the little farm was soaked with melting snow; running lines of dark muddy thaw streaked from the round-worn edges of the roof to the walls and the ground.

The temper of the river was warmer than the mountain weather. The willows and cottonwoods lost their snow by noon. The mountains were visible again, after the day of the blind white blowing curtain over the plain.

Not many travelers were abroad; but Father Antonio came down the road shortly after noon, and Josefina saw him, his fat white mare, his robe tucked above his waist, his wool-colored homespun trousers, and his Mexican boots. She went to tell Rosa that the priest was coming at last, and to stop crying, if that was all she was crying for.

The priest dismounted in the yard and let his horse move.

Josefina tidied herself in honor of the visit, and he came in, catching her at wetting her eyebrows. She immediately felt like a fool, from the way he looked at her; and she bowed for his blessing, furious at his kind of power over and against women.

'I didn't get your message about the baby until two days ago, and then I said nothing could keep me from coming as soon as I could. Isn't it fine! Where is he? Or is it a girl? I hope you have a girl. Already those bad boys of yours—where are they?'

Rosa felt as if authority had walked into her house and that she need have no further fear.

Father Antonio was a tall, very spare, bony man nearly fifty, with straw-colored hair, a pale wind-pinked face, and little blue eyes that shone speculatively as he gazed. He was awkward; he couldn't talk without slowly waving his great-knuckled hands in illustration of his mood; and he loved to talk, putting into words the great interest of his days. Everything suggested something else to him; he debated with himself as if he were two Jesuits, they said in Santa Fe, where he was not popular with the clergy because he preferred working in the open land among the scattered families of the river basin.

'Where are the boys?' he asked.

Rosa was at peace. Her cheeks dried and her heart seemed to grow strong. She felt a spell of calm strong breath in her breast. She was proud.

'They have gone hunting. They have been gone several days now. In the mountains.'

Josefina lingered on the outside of a kind of sanctuary which the priest and the mother made, a spiritual confine which she could not enter, a profane and resentful woman. But she could toss her opinions into it.

'They are little fools, a pair of chicken-boned infants, crazy, going to the mountains! It snowed there for two days. They will never come back.'

Rosa watched the priest's face, ready to be frightened or not, by his expression.

He glanced at Josefina, a mild blue fire.

'They are probably all right.'

Josefina mumbled.

'How will a man ever know what goes on,' asked Father Antonio, 'unless he goes out and looks at it?'

'How long can you stay, Father?' asked Rosa.

'Till we christen the baby.'

'But—'

'I'll wait till the brothers come back, so the baby will have a godfather.'

'I—godmother,' simpered Josefina on the outskirts, making a fat and radiant gesture of coquetry.

'Why not?' said the priest mildly, taking the sting out of her scandalous contempt.

It sobered her. She blushed.

'When your husband comes back in the spring with the wagon train,' said Father Antonio, 'you can send some money to my church.'

'Gladly,' said Rosa.

'Those must be big boys by now. I haven't seen them for months. Luis? Julio? That's right. When I was a boy I had all the desires to go and look at what was over the mountains. Then when I was away, there, in Mexico, at the seminary, the world on this side of the mountains was just as inviting and mysterious. Eh? When I came back to go to work, everybody bowed to me, and behaved properly as to a priest. But I always felt a little guilty for that, and went fishing or hunting. The animals had no respect for me, which was a relief, for they knew not of God, whose weight is something to carry, I can tell you!'

This was strange talk to the women.

'Next to catching a sinner and taking away his sin, I like best to fetch a trout, or play a long game of war with a beaver in the river pools. So now I know why your two big brown babies went off to the mountains.'

'Oh,' thought the women. 'That explains it.'

9

Father Antonio stayed over a week. The boys were missing. The priest would go and look at the mountains in all times of day, to see if he could see anything, even in his mind, which might be played with as news for the distracted mother.

But all he saw were the momentous faces of the mountains; light or the absence of light; at dawn, a chalky black atmosphere quivering with quiet air; at noon, silvered by the sun, the great rock wrinkles shining and constant; at evening, the glow of rose, as if there were furnaces within the tumbled stone which heated the surface, until it came to glow for a few moments, then cooling to ashy black from the base upward until it joined the darkening sky like a low heavy cloud.

'I have promised to stay for them, and I will,' said the priest.

He spent the days making Rosa agree to get strong; until she finally arose from her bed and ordered her house again. He did the tasks of the outdoors. There was no need for Josefina to stay now; but stay she did, touched in her vanity by the godmotherhood which had been mentioned once.

She came in one day, still holding her arm over her eyes, as if staring into the distance, the golden chill of the open winter.

'I think I see them coming!' she cried.

They all went outdoors.

'You are crazy,' said the priest.

They looked and looked.

The plain and the slow rise into the mountain-lift were swimming with sunlight. They searched with long looks until they had to blink for vision.

'See! Like a couple of sheep, just barely moving?' insisted Josefina, pointing vaguely at the mountains.

'Where?'

'Yes, I do see! She is right! She must have Indian blood.'

The mother was the last to see and agree.

There was an infinitesimal movement far on the plain, hardly perceptible as a movement; some energy of presence, a fall of light and cast of shadow, just alive enough to be convincing. It was the hunters, coming on their horses on the second day's journey out of the mountains.

Late in the afternoon they arrived.

The marks of their toil were all over them.

To go and come back! This being the common mystery of all journeying, the mother could hardly wait for them to speak; to tell her everything.

She brought the baby and the boys kissed the tiny furred head.

The priest gave them his blessing and they bent their shaggy necks under it.

Josefina stared and then squinted at them, whispering something.

'Luis, you are hurt!'

'Not any more.'

'But you *were!*'

'I will tell you sometime.'

'Now, now!'

'How long have we been away?'

'Ten days!'

The boys talked, confirming each other with looks.

Luis and the wolf; the bite; the fever; the body as the residence of the devil, and the raving nights. Julio and his amazing skill as a marksman; his reckless courage; the two of them together after Luis's recovery; shagging up and down rocky barriers, mountain sprites, and their bag of skins.

'Look at that!'

They got and opened out their two packs of furs, and there were cats, the wolf, a little deer, and a middle-sized brown bear.

'Who got the bear?'

'Luis! It was wonderful! The bear was in a tree, watching us, and what made him nobody knows, but Luis looked up, and *whang!* and *boo!* Down fell the bear, and all it took was one shot!'

'But you should have seen Julio the time he saved my life, when the wolf was waiting for me to fall down, I was so cold and weak! Up in my tree!'

The silence was full of worried love: what had they not done! But safe. Yes, but—what if—!

The brothers looked at each other.

Nothing would ever be said about the other thing. Nobody ever managed to grow up without being foolish at some time or other.

The priest thought, 'The boy Julio looks taller. I suppose it is only natural; last time I was here he was—'

Luis took the baby sister to hold.

There was plenty of fur to keep her warm.

Julio sighed. It was a curiously contented and old man's comment.

Father Antonio felt like laughing; but there was some nobility of bearing in Julio's little mighty shoulders that did not deserve genial patronizing.

The priest glanced at Josefina. He knew his materials like a craftsman. He thought, 'Josefina sees—she even smells as a female—what has taken place in Julio. She stares at him and then squints and whispers to herself. How little is secret! How much makes a life!'

The mother's arms were free of her infant. She went and hugged Julio, because, though she hardly thought it so clearly, she knew that he had gone and conquered the wilderness which was his brother's by birth. She knew that—and what lay behind it—as only a child's mother could know it; with defensive and pitying and pardoning love, so long as it might be needed.

10

'I wish I could write, now,' said Luis.

'Why?'

'Then I would write to my father about it.'

'But he could not read it.'

'No, but he could get somebody to read it to him.'

'Should I write and tell him about it for you?' asked Father Antonio.

'Oh, if you would, Father!'

'I'll be glad to—the minute I get back to my house where I have pens and paper. You have told me the whole adventure.'

But when the priest did return home, and sit down to keep his promise to the delighted brothers, what they had told him seemed to him man's story, and all he finally wrote was:

Dear Garcia:

Your wife has had a dear baby girl, and both are well and happy, with God's grace. Your two sons are proud of their family, and when you return, before hearing from their lips anything of their adventures during your absence, you will see that they are already proper men, for which God be praised in the perfection of His design for our mortal life.

Motor racing is one of the world's most popular sports. With the tragic death in 2001 of NASCAR legend Dale Earnhardt, public attention has probed the motives and emotions of men who risk their lives on the racetrack. Although four decades have passed since this story about Grand Prix racing was written, its fast-paced narrative and intense grip give it a timeless quality. It is doubtful that anyone has written with more knowledge on the subject than Ken W. Purdy. He authored nu-merous fiction and nonfiction books, including Stirling Moss: A Nodding Ac-quaintance with Death *(1962),* All but My Life *(1963), and* Ken Purdy's Book of Automobiles *(1972).*

Ken $W.$ $Purdy$

TELL ME THE REASON, DO (1962)

THE ROUNDED STONES OF THE BEACH warmed in the rising sun. At the water's edge they were dark and wet, laced with green. The spiny odor of salt water and seaweed rose in the hot air. The sea was blue and flat. Half a mile out, a catamaran scudded down the wind under a tea-brown sail, a water bug running. Behind it, pasted to the horizon like a child's paper cutout, a steamer sat under a purple thread of smoke.

Peter Hart knelt on the stony bottom of the sea. There was nothing of consequence so close inshore, no fishes, no shells, no grottoes, no sea-weed jungles, only the marvel of the water, bright and clear, layered in yellows, browns, greens and sapphire blues. He rose slowly until he stood, his head out of water to his chin. He breathed, and sank until the sea lapped at his eyes. He turned slowly, like a searching periscope. On the right, a mile away, St. Martine, white and pink and yellow stucco houses, a stubby church steeple tiled in harsh red-orange. Straight ahead, the hotel, three stories high, sugar-white and shining. Left, the curving horn of the beach, half a mile of it to the jetty and the ruin of the light-house. Behind him, from the wavelets patting the back of his head all the way to the brass-bright shores of Africa, the blue sea. He lay against the water, rolled and began to swim. He swam for ten minutes, or a little more, straight out. Now when he turned to look, the town and the light-house had drawn together, the beach had narrowed. Two figures stood there, black against the sand. One waved. Peter Hart lifted an arm high from the water, dropped it back, stroked, turned. Soft, warm as milk, the sea burbled in his ears, bubbled and foamed behind him. He did not hurry. He believe that he knew what they were going to tell him, and he did not look forward to hearing it.

He waded out of the water. He was tan, and heavily muscled for one who looked, at a little distance, to be lean. He moved indifferently on the hot stones.

"Good morning, Janey," he said. "Tony. Good morning."

"Peter," Janey said. "Ollie Ramirez is dead."

"Yes," he said. "I thought that was what you'd come to tell me." He looked down. The stones were egg-shaped for the most part, white, gray, brown. Lying in a crevice between two white ones he saw a bit of bottle-glass, green, etched and rounded by the scouring sand. He picked it up.

"Was he ever conscious?" he asked. "Ollie?"

"The hospital said no," the girl told him. "Tony phoned."

Tony Markman was tall and thin. His jutting nose seemed to stretch the skin tightly over his face. He wore a black knit shirt and gray slacks that seemed to have nothing to hang to. "He might have been con-scious," he said, "but they didn't think so. At least he never opened his eyes and he never spoke."

"He'd have said something, I think," Peter said.

"That it wasn't your fault, you mean?" Janey said.

"Something like that."

Peter moved off a little way and lifted a robe and a towel from the beach. He pulled the terrycloth robe over his shoulders and looped the towel around his neck. He stood for a moment holding each end of it, feeling the welcome weight of his arms on the back of his neck. He could see three girls walking out on the jetty, single file, one of them carrying a basket. Peter wanted to sit on the beach and watch them, sit with his back to the town. But he turned around.

"We may as well go," he said.

They moved in silence to the walk that pointed, string-straight, to the hotel's main door.

"You know, *I* didn't kill Ollie," Peter said.

"No one says you did, Peter," Janey said.

"Oh, any number of people will say I did," Peter said. "Any number. Point is, though, I didn't. He killed himself. We know that. The question is, why?"

"It isn't quite *that* simple, Peter," Tony said.

"I know it isn't," Peter said. "But it's as close to the truth as we can come just now."

He used the same phrase later in the day when the fellow from the New York paper came to see him. The man's name was Donnell and Hart had read some of his pieces. Donnell had no fixed base, he seemed to move around Europe as he pleased, he was intrigued by exotic sports, pigeon-shooting, chamois-hunting, foldboating and the like.

He had phoned while Peter was dressing after his swim, and had suggested lunch.

"You had better come up here," Peter had said, "if we're to be undisturbed."

Luncheon had been laid on the little balcony table. There was a soufflé and a salad. Donnell drank wine. He was a nervous, red-headed man, committed to his life, to inquiry, to wondering, to finding out. His style was lucid but flat. He was a good reporter, but he had little originality. It saddened him to read the phrasemakers of his trade, men like Red Smith, Murray Kempton, Jimmy Cannon.

He sipped the cold white wine in small mouthfuls and looked out at the sea, brazen now in the vertical rays of the sun. A cream-and-red striped awning shaded the balcony, but Donnell's eyes were light blue, and he squinted.

"When did Ollie die, exactly, do you know?" Peter asked.

"At ten after eight or so," Donnell said. "Dr. Limoutin told us he felt it was all over at four in the morning. You knew it was a depressed frontal fracture?"

"I thought he must be dead when I saw them taking him out of the car," Peter said. "Still, he was strong, you know. He must have had tremendous resistance . . . one time in the Monte, 1956 I think it was, I saw him lift one end of a Citröen onto the road, alone, without help."

"Amazing."

"Still, I suppose that sort of strength's no use when one's badly enough hurt," Peter said. "Ascari was strong, too. So was Behra, if it comes to that."

"Sometimes, watching him drive," Donnell said, "it seemed to me that Ollie Ramirez was too big for the cars, too beefy to be able to move as fast as he had to."

"Bigness hasn't to do with it," Peter said. "Juan Manuel Fangio was big, at least he was thick and stocky, and he was strong as a bull, but he could move very fast when he wanted to."

"Still, Ramirez wasn't really quick, was he?" Donnell said. "Someone told me that if he'd been really quick he'd have got through the corner last night."

"It's sometimes hard to tell," Peter said. "I don't know what happened to Ollie except that he was trying too hard. He went into the bend there at La Pournelle much too fast."

"Yet you were going faster, obviously, since you were about to pass him."

Peter looked at him. The table was a small one and they were close. He has a hunter's face, Donnell thought, I can understand his eyes being slitted here, in this light, but I can't remember ever having seen them any wider open. And his face is all flat, immobile planes, no roundness anywhere. It is the flatness, and the sharp angles where the flatnesses join, that make him seem so cold.

"I always go very fast," Peter said. "I *can* go fast, so I do. I was testing brakes, as well. We'd had some bother, we'd a new kind of pad in the discs, and I was running deeply into the corners and punishing the brakes severely. That was my job, at the moment."

"Were you and Ramirez alone on the circuit?" Donnell asked.

"Not quite. It was just at sundown, and most of the chaps had gone in, but Tommy Reston was still running. He was on the other side of the circuit, over near Douet. He was stroking, just running along, you know. Ollie and I had run past him a couple of minutes before it happened. Ollie was three or four lengths ahead of me when we passed Tommy, and I had cut that to about two lengths when he shut off for La Pournelle . . ."

He looked over the white wrought-iron balcony rail, down at the beach, bright with parasols, and the sea, dotted by the heads of a hundred swimmers. As he stared a red ball loomed and grew in the sea and in his mind's eye and he saw clearly the rounded tail of Olivier Ramirez' car, bordered by rivets half an inch apart. The tail was the gas tank, there was no skin over it. That was all there was to see of Ollie's car: the round, red tail, the wide tires big and black beside it, and Ollie's heavy-shouldered figure hunched in the center of the composition. In that split second it seemed that the car had been cut off at the windshield. But then the nose and a front wheel appeared as Ramirez set it up in a drift for the bend, and reality returned. Down the long straightaway Peter Hart had just touched 8500 engine revolutions a minute in fifth gear, say 180 miles an hour. At this speed he had closed slightly on Ramirez. He intended to pull up to him in the bend and pass him coming out of it. He was perfectly calm. He did not feel competitive. He was practicing. It was an ordinary thing, passing coming out of a bend, he had done it a thousand times. It would take three seconds, or three seconds and a half, and it would be divided into six phases. He didn't think anything of it. He ran a few yards past his normal cutoff point, lifted his foot and hit the brake pedal once, carefully. The pads shrieked on the discs and the car shuddered; the right front wheel brake bit a hair deeper than the others and the car came an inch out of line as the rear tried to pivot around the dragging wheel; Peter felt the movement, or sensed it, caught it with a flick of the steering wheel. He dropped the factor of a potentially grabbing right front brake into the hopper of his mind and stood off and watched, in a way, as the next five phases of the passing maneuver were instantly modified. He hit the brake again, with his toe, anticipating the wheel drag, and dropped his heel to the accelerator as his left foot twice slammed the clutch pedal to the floor and he threw the shift lever across the gate. The engine howled as it was harnessed to the lower gear, and the car slowed, savagely, reluctantly. Once more, and he had it steadied down and level at about 140 miles an hour. He was very close to Ramirez now, ten feet or so, a little too close, perhaps, he thought, watching the man spinning the steering wheel. Ollie was doing something foolish: he had decided not to be passed just there. He had decided to be a little bit competitive. He's gone in over his head, Peter told himself, and he will lose it. They were in the bend now, drifting, all four wheels sliding together, the cars pointing into the bend, the engines screaming under full load in third gear. Intermittent, jerky, soprano screeches were lost in the din as the tires fought the rough concrete. Peter lifted his foot infinitesimally, to lessen the spinning, the slippage of the back wheels on the road by a few times a second, and thus straighten the car a bit, decrease the angle of the drift. Ramirez would go, if he went, toward the outside. Three quarters of the way through the bend he went. The rear of the fat red car broke loose, moved out, accelerated, whipped around, overcame the wheel Ramirez instantly turned against it; the car came broadside, tripped and rolled, three times sideways, twice end-for-end. At the pits they heard the noise come rushing across the field, golden in the dying sun, and the least of them knew what it was, because there is no other sound like it: the maniacal howl of rubber impossibly stretched on concrete, the scream of the engine as the wheels fly into the air, unload it, let it spin 200 times a second and destroy itself, and the crash of a half-ton toy slammed five times to the ground by an idiot giant. Smoke rose into the still air to show the way, and some were there before Peter could stop, turn and come thudding back over the grass of the infield. Three of them lifted Ramirez out, black with oil and rubber dust, red with blood, white with the snowflake foam of the fire extinguishers. His arms hung loose and straight. His head rolled on the yoke of his shoulders. They laid him carefully on the coarse bunched grass, well away from his car, smoking sullenly. The stand-by ambulance came quickly. Peter saw Ollie for the last time through its window as it moved off. He had been wrapped in two thick white blankets; a white towel had been bound around his head like a loose turban; his face was black save where his goggles had been, and there the skin was dead white. The ambulance moved carefully off the turf to the roadway, then very fast downhill along the straight past the pits toward the escape road at Perisot corner, the intersection, and the town.

Peter sighed and turned away from the sea to face Donnell again.

"There was no way in which it could have been avoided, was there?" Donnell said.

"Who can tell?" Peter said. "In these precise circumstances, and with this particular man driving, no, certainly not, or it wouldn't have happened . . . if Ollie had gone into the bend three miles an hour slower . . . but, of course, he didn't."

"You must know that there are people who think it was your fault," Donnell said.

"I'm certain there are," Peter said.

"They say that you were crowding him," Donnell went on.

"One can crowd another car from the side," Peter said, "but not from behind. I've run 160 miles an hour three or four feet behind another car, getting a tow, slip-streaming as you call it, and so has everyone else. The fellow in front simply drives his race and pays no attention."

"I don't think they mean it in that sense," Donnell said. "I think they mean that you were forcing the pace, running up on Ramirez, so that he went into the corner faster than he should have."

Peter Hart shook his head in impatience. "It's not worth talking about," he said. "We weren't racing, we were practicing. No one cared.

There were no prizes, no silver mugs, no money, nothing. Ollie knew I was faster, he knew I'd pass him if I wanted to."

"Wouldn't it have been the ordinary thing for him to have let you go on by?" Donnell asked.

"Yes, that would have been the ordinary thing," Peter said.

"But he didn't do it," Donnell said.

"No, he did the other thing," Peter said. "He decided to compete, he decided to try harder. Whether he was really trying to keep me from going on by, or whether he intended only to make it more interesting for us both, we can't know that."

"Will the accident affect your driving in the race itself tomorrow, do you think?" Donnell said.

There is no point in all this, Peter thought. He could see the starting grid, the cars lined up in threes on the hot white road in front of the green timing tower, the pink staring faces of the crowds, the drivers looking straight ahead, watching the rev-counters, watching the starter's flag, everyone thinking about the red car that was missing, everyone thinking about Ollie Ramirez, heartbroken for him, that dear good jolly man and *do* you remember that girl at Monza who claimed her twins were his, poor fellow, his new fiancée was there and someone had paid the girl to do it, and *do* you remember his drive at Reims in '55, the last 14 laps ten feet from Fangio, ten feet, eight feet, six, the whole way around, 35 miles an hour at Thillois, 185 past the pits, together as if they had been tied with a string, and Ramirez won it by a foot and a half in the last hundred yards? Oh, all that and more . . .

"No, I shan't drive any differently," Peter said. "I shall go faster, that's all, since it's a race, not a practice."

"Still, I suppose you will find yourself thinking about Ramirez every time you go through the bend," Donnell said.

"I doubt it very much," Peter said. "If I think about anything but driving—anything at all, you understand, even for two seconds—I am quite likely to have an accident, and at these speeds, I shall be very badly hurt, in all probability, or killed. If I find myself thinking about Ollie Ramirez tomorrow, I shall pull over, and come in, and let Tommy Reston have the car."

"Do you expect to do that?"

"No, I certainly do not."

Donnell folded his yellow note paper and tucked it away.

"I came here hoping to find out why Olivier Ramirez died," he said. "But I still don't know."

"I would like to know why he died, as well," Peter Hart said. "Some think he died because he did a little thing wrong, that he incorrectly turned a wheel connected through a system of rods to two other wheels; or that he incorrectly arranged a cluster of gears connecting an engine and two wheels; or that he did not understand centrifugal force modified by the slip-angle of natural-rubber tires on rough-finished concrete, something of that sort. I don't think it was anything so simple."

"What, then?"

"I don't know," Peter said. "I don't know why Ollie Ramirez died."

Peter was watching the beach again. A little girl who might have been ten, bright in a daffodil-yellow bathing suit, crouched in water to her waist and leaped up, straight as a stick, arms over her head, then down into the water, up, down, up, down.

"I'll see you at the circuit tomorrow," Donnell said. He nodded, made ritual display of his knowledge of the mystique by not saying anything about good luck, and went away. Peter walked to the door with him.

When the waiter had taken the remains of luncheon, Peter sat on the balcony rail and watched the sea until the sun began to tire him. At the little desk in the blue-white room he wrote three short notes to people in England. The hotel note paper was gauzy and blue, a bright green palm tree engraved over the telephone number. He wrote quickly, in a long round scrawl. ". . . the weather is as always bright. There are vast numbers of tourists about and if possible more yachts than last year. Himself seems to think that he has the brakes set up properly at last and I can find nothing to complain about; I can hold 8000 in top just past the big birch tree before Poivre corner, which should give you a notion.

You will have heard about poor Ollie Ramirez. He lost it completely in the middle of La Pournelle, I was very near him . . ."

He heard a small rattling sound and looked down to see the pen roll off the desk. He did not recall putting it on the blotter pad. He had become just a little bit frightened, and the sensation was strange to him. Since he had come awake at dawn he had had almost no thought that had not to do with Ollie Ramirez. Why? He and Ollie had not been, after all, the best and closest. All right, he was a good sort, a kind man, and all that, but still . . . and he wasn't the only one to die in that way, what of Ascari, Castelotti, Musso, Hawthorn, Portago, Stacey, Bristow, Behra, Sommer, Bouillin-who-called-himself-Levegh-after-his-uncle-who-was-named Veghle, Schell, Marimon, Bonetto, Lewis-Evans, Bueb, Wharton, Scott-Brown, just to name those one could think of immediately, and all contemporaries, all people one had known, all only recently dead, never mind the old boys, the people who'd been killed around Seaman's time. Some he had known better than Ollie Ramirez and liked more and at least three times he had been just as close when it had happened. So why Ollie Ramirez? He knew he hadn't killed Ollie, or perhaps he didn't actually *know* it, because if he hadn't started to move around him, going into La Pournelle, then Ollie would have held his own pace . . . he stopped short as it came to him that he hadn't entertained so juvenile a notion for 15 years and he wholly forbade himself going on. That line was foolishness. If there was anything worth wondering, it was why Ollie had moved out. How could one know why, when Ollie himself might not have known why? The third part of a second was enough to make the decision and put it into being. Peter could recall many such times, times when he had braked without knowing he was going to brake, or bent the floor boards under the accelerator to pass someone, his foot directed by no plan. Everyone did such things, and if one were lucky one lived through and came into years of better judgment. It was unlikely that Ramirez, at 38, still had such moments. Still, he must have done something, there must have been some reason. The man was dead.

The sun had moved away from the balcony. The tide was running out, fewer spots of bright color rode the water. Peter moved in a narrow triangle, from the balcony across the floor to the window that overlooked the courtyard, to the door of the bedroom, to the balcony, slowly over the lemon-yellow carpet. He was happy when the door buzzer sounded with Janey's three little rings. Tony was with her.

"How was Donnell?" Janey said.

"He was all right," Peter said.

"There's to be a commission of inquiry tomorrow night, after the race," Janey said. "Johnny Lurani told Tony."

"Best to them," Peter said. "By that time, even I may have thought of something—but I doubt it." He stood with his back to the balcony. "Did you have lunch, you two?"

"With the Ferrari people," Tony said. "They've found a place on that little narrow street off the market square, four tables in it, they call it The Pub."

"Which it resembles in no way, as you can imagine," Janey said.

He walked his triangle a few times. "Would you like a vermouth or anything?" he said.

"Do run off, Tony," Janey said.

"I?" Tony said.

"Dear boy, you," she said. "I want to take Peter to bed."

Tony wagged his long head back and forth. "*Quel sentiment,*" he said. "I'll occupy myself," he said. "If you like, I'll be at the Ferrari pub, poob, at six." He opened the door a narrow way and went out.

"We could just lie here," Janey said. "I'd be happy with that."

"You're confusing me with somebody else," Peter said.

"You don't have to do anything if you don't want to. I'm competent," she said. "I'm adept, even."

"I know," he said. "I remember. Stop being little earth-mother. Fly now, play later. And talk later."

"Did you think," he said in a little while, "that because Ollie has died, I would take vows of chastity, poverty and abstinence?"

"You said, 'talk later,' " Janey said.

"This is partly later," he said. "This is halfway later, for all you know."

"I didn't think you'd take any vows," she said. "All I know is, you can't stop thinking about it."

"That much is true," Peter said. "The big thing is not that I think about it, but that I apparently *must* think about it. Why, do you suppose? I was closer to Jack Mooney by far, and I never wondered why Jack died, and it was a sadder thing, in some ways: he'd retired, he had everything, his father had been killed in a car and his mother was happy to think that Jack was safe . . . it never occurred to me to wonder why Jack had died. He was doing one hundred in the rain, he turned to wave to someone, he lost it, and a lorry was using some of the road he needed for getting it back. Simple as that."

"I didn't believe you thought much about it," Janey said. "You or any of the others."

"I never have," Peter said. "There's the one thing you learn, and after that you don't think about it, or talk about it, I guess until you start to get old, and one day you realize your eyes are going, or your reflexes are going, and then you're frightened and think about getting killed. But while you have it, all you know is merely that driving is the essence of living, a distillate of it, a concentrate, and since it has more living in it, it must of necessity have more dying in it. I'm putting it badly, but do you know what I mean?"

"Perfectly," Janey said.

"You can see that once you know that, you can be tranquil?" Peter said. "Because then you needn't think any more about dying than a bus conductor does, which is not much. If one's going to have three times as much life, one's going to have to accept three times as much hazard of death, right?"

"Talk later," Janey said. "Peter, talk later!"

They went to the pub place at six. The Ferrari crew had three tables by right of discovery, and Tony had the fourth, and a cassis.

"These types say that Phil Hill got around in 4:5.8 just before they stopped practice," he said when they had squeezed in with him.

"A tiger," Peter said. "A charger, I think they call them in the States."

"Phil Hill is the intellectual's race driver," Janey said. "He is the egghead's *pilote*."

"When he found Moss at Spa," Tony said, "after Stirling's accident, he told a reporter, 'Stirling was lying in a fetal position, hemorrhaging from the mouth, and denouncing, in bad French, two people who were trying to move him.' Nobody else would have put it just that way."

"*Deux Byrrh*," Peter said to the waiter.

They ate *scampi* and said little.

Tony went away before coffee.

"He's having a big thing with a blonde Greek," Janey said. "She's as tall as he is. They have Plattdeutsch for a common language. She wakes him up every morning in the pitch dark and they go outside and wait to make love in the sunrise."

"What a romantic notion," Peter said. "Or, as he said this afternoon, *quel sentiment.*"

"It's not romantic, it's historic," Janey said. "The ancient Greeks, the Greeks of the golden times, much preferred to make love outdoors at dawn. You didn't know that, did you."

"No," Peter said. "Is it true?"

"Yes," Janey said. "Truly. If you think for a little while you will see why it would seem logical to people like that, the most civilized people of all time."

"I'll give it some thought," he said. "Meanwhile, now that your brother's brother has left us, we could go down to the harbor and drink coffee at Mary's."

They threw goodbyes into the din the Ferrari crew was making. The sky was lavender and the air was warm and sweet. He held her wrist as they walked. She hung a quarter-step behind him. She felt leashed and happy. The white houses of the town, spilled like sugar cubes down the slopes, stood rosy in the last of the sun. There was not a trace of movement in the boats crowding the little horseshoe harbor. Their lights were coming on, here and there a yellow glow spilling from a porthole to the black water or a blue-white masthead light glittering like a Christmas-tree star. An accordionist slowly squeezed and played and in another boat farther from the bright shore a girl sang, "Um-de-bol-ay-flum-amour-tooh-le-slu-um-fum-toujour."

"Are you peaceful now?" Janey said.

"You are a dear good girl," Peter said. "You know, there is something about your being such a little thing that makes you very dear. Why is that? Do you weigh eight stone? I doubt it."

"I wish I did weigh eight stone," Janey said. "Answer me: are you peaceful now?"

"Near enough," Peter said. "I wish it were noon tomorrow and I were in the car. I'll be peaceful then." He shrugged. "I ought to go around and say hello to Himself and the people in the garage. Do you want to come?"

"If I may," Janey said. She closed her hand and offered her wrist to him.

It was a Peugeot garage in the ordinary way of things. Now it was a temporary race-car garage, identical with others in the world: bright red Grand Prix cars, or white or blue or bottle-green; tired mechanics, dark-jawed, red-eyed under the unshaded light bulbs hanging from the ceiling; a few people watching, some bored girls, ragged stacks of tires looking bigger and blacker than tires should, silvery tools scattered, electric cables snaked across the floor.

The lowest numbered of the three green cars was 9, Peter's. Two mechanics were working on it.

"What's afoot, Mike?" Peter said.

The stained white jumper-suit stirred and the man came out from under, a slant-jawed, flat-nose specimen.

"Hullo, Peter," he said. "What's afoot? Guv'nor says a hair more camber, here, that's all. Front end's as it was. Everything else done, down to the last split-pin. All it wants now is somebody to steer it and it's home with the lolly for us."

"You think so?" Peter said.

"Why not?" Mike said. "The Eyeties ain't in it, and who else is there?"

"The Eyeties did a 4:5.8 lap," Peter said.

"They ain't in it," Mike said. "They'll blow up. I give 'em an hour." He burrowed under the car again.

Two garages east, a trailer crouched at the curb, a twisted, lumped red car tied down on it.

"Was that it?" Janey whispered.

Peter nodded. He leaned on the trailer and looked in. The wheel was bent on itself, but upward not downward. When the car had flipped, the centrifugal force had tried to tear Ramirez' arms away, but the man's great strength had kept his hands locked to the wheel's rim. There was rust-brown blood on the wheel, on the glasses of the gauges on the dashboard and on the floor.

They left the lights and moved on the dark streets toward the hotel. Strange waxy-leaved trees arched over them. A scent of mimosa followed them, mimosa and jasmine and dew-wet earth. They were disembodied. They had nothing to do with their feet. They moved as if standing in a train in a tunnel. At the end of the tunnel the hotel glowed white under floodlights screwed into the crowns of the palm trees.

They stood on the balcony. Small waves ran in from Egypt. An old man leaned on a cane and stared across the water. He held his hat in his left hand. His hair was so white that it seemed to throw light of its own.

"What do you suppose that old dear is thinking about?" Janey said.

"He sees a yacht anchored out there," Peter said. "It's a steam yacht. The time is July 1909. He's standing at the rail, looking in toward the hotel. A girl is beside him, in a white dress. She has dark red hair loose to her waist. Her eyes are brown, big, gentle and forgiving. His arm is around her. She is hard and strong and beautiful. That old man is thinking about her grave. He knows where it is, a long way from here. In forty-five years he has seen it many times. He is thinking of a terrible thing they taught him in Latin when he was in school, that some Roman said, that the best thing is not to be born at all, and the next best thing is to die young."

"You have made my day," Janey said.

She went in.

"I'm sorry," Peter said.

"Ah, nothing, darling," she said. "Look, you're driving tomorrow, and would you rather I went to my own room?"

"No, I'd rather you stay, if you don't mind," Peter said.

"So would I," she said. "I'll just take a little Nembutal, and a shower, and bid you a soft and passionless good night."

"You can have the bed by the window," he said. "They'll bring tea at eight. I'll call down now."

At five minutes before noon the next day he levered himself into the car. The mechanics had rigged a parasol over the cockpit, but he winced when the heat of the leather seat reached through his driving suit. It was wrinkled and crusty from the fireproofing and he wore nothing under it. He had a helmet upside down in his lap, a pair of cape gloves. He was wearing boxers' shoes with asbestos soles over heavy woolen socks. He was absolutely tranquil, level as the line between sea and sky. He rarely talked about the sensation now growing anew in his belly, the belief that this was life and the rest was something else. Every driver knew it, but few knew it well enough to talk about it, and fewer wished to. Peter had got around to it with Portago one time, the year before he was killed. Portago could talk about it.

"They may get it from the bulls," Portago had said. "I was too old to find out, by the time I wondered. And mountain climbing, maybe. And, I think, a musician a few times in his life. But that's all. Maybe a surgeon. Rarely. But that's all. I really think I know. I've tried most things. Flying? I gave up flying out of boredom. Horses? Jump races? I was amateur champion of Europe. No. Skindiving? No. Hard-hat diving? Nonsense. Skiing? Please. No. In three hours every Sunday, if you're awake and alive, you can live ten years."

He had heard Moss put it another way: "To drive as about ten men in the world can drive is an art, and it is related to ballet."

God bless, Ollie, Peter thought. *Vaya con Dios,* Ollie. Peter did not know any Dios, but never mind.

Engines were started. Peter watched his pit. At 15 seconds Mike waved. Peter pushed the clutch in, nudged the short gear level into first, ran the engine to 4000 and watched for the flag's fall. He was in the second row, cars on all sides. The great flag dropped and they went, 15 cars howling, a noise to make your brain bubble, feeling for the spinning back tires, waiting to get into second and turn it all loose. They hit the first corner bunched like fingers in a fist, everybody in second by then, each trusting in the perfect orthodoxy of the man in front and beside and behind him. They all came through. Past the bend, the two-lane concrete road, snow-bright in the sunshine, ran straight for half a mile across the rolling farmland, two little roller-coaster rises in it. Peter had come out of the corner lying third. The engine screamed, working up to 9000 revolutions a minute, the whole shiny oil-streaming steel complex spinning 150 times a second. He sat well back from the wheel, his arms straight out, his left foot braced hard against the floor, the catapult-thrust pinning him to the seat. The engine raging at his back shook the car; the thin tubing that made its chassis sang and vibrated, and every hill and valley in the road sent a separate shock into the wheels, but none was discernible as an entity; everything, sound, shock, thrust, movement, funneled into one overpowering sensation; the noise was the shout of an organ as high as a hill. He held the wheel lightly. He could look down and see the front road-wheels it guided, tied to the frame by finger-thin steel rods; they were leading him; his life spun with them, he knew delight.

Just ahead and a foot to the right a blood-red Ferrari sat, one might think motionless, since both cars were running at the same rate, working up to 150 miles an hour. The driver wore Hill's white helmet. They ran across the first rise together, flew into the air together, accelerating to land tailfirst. The second rise followed immediately and they flew again. They moved in a blurred green world under a kindly sky. Sensations needled their bodies like rain blown by a gale, they produced the ten decisions a second they must make to stay alive, but they knew the mystic's calm, life narrowed to a knife edge, everything extraneous set aside. At the end of the straight, a point would come to issue: Peter would consider staying off his brakes until a half-second after Hill had hit his in the hope of running around him on the outside. It was a thin hope and they both knew it; Hill was a notable specialist in refinements of braking. Running down to the corner they shifted like twins; Peter moved a little to the left, but Hill, perfectly certain that he would brake last, moved with him, and that was that, they went around as they had gone in, end to end. The cars sat down on their tails as they accelerated out and ran for the esses that led to the straight through the woods.

When they came past the pits for the first time the order was Ferrari Cooper Ferrari Lotus, red green red green, and the first four had opened 20 yards on the rest of the field. They were alone and they all knew it,

Hill, Hart, Gervosa, Dedham. They were having their own race. They were almost in narcosis, sensation-drunk like fliers too high or divers too deep, so that it seemed to them not only normal but desirable and delightful to be doing what they were doing, running three miles a minute ten feet apart, shielded from each other by sheet aluminum so thin it would give under a boy's thumb. They screamed down the straights, towing each other at 170, 175, 180 miles an hour; in orderly sequence they sorted out the gears as corners came; they lurched in the tight-fitting seats when the cars drifted in pairs through the bends, sliding like skiers in a Christy; they schemed for inches of roadway and fractional angles of direction as the cars clawed into the straights again. This went on for 50-odd minutes, until a thrown stone crystallized one side of Gervosa's goggles and put him back into the ruck, but the other three ran like triplets, like a three-car train, and no one could come near. As they burned fuel, lightened the cars, wore the tires down, and more intimately knew the circuit, they went faster, and faster. One of the pits held up a sign REC which they all read to mean that the course record had been broken by Hill, leading; and if by Hill then by the other two as well. They knew without being told. They could run very little faster and stay on the road. All were moving in the same plane: an inch, a hair, a twig from the unmarked notch at which concrete turns to glass-smooth ice, and a car, taking its head, can slide screaming and spinning for a hundred yards.

An hour and a half into the race, the three of them had lapped half the field and were still together. The excitement of the watchers around the circuit, jammed into the tiers of the stands on the finishing straight, three deep on the shorter stretches, standing in sixes and tens on the slow corners, was plain, and it approached hysteria; everyone in the stands was on his feet; in the one hairpin corner they were hanging to each other as if for support, shouting face against face. The drivers saw, and knew it had to do with them, and were untouched. They knew the turmoil was of their making, but they knew as well that it had nothing to do with what was going on in the red automobile and the two green ones.

They were running in their own tracks, running over the black rubber their own tires had laid into the concrete, the same place every time, to an inch or so. They were in echelon most of the time, not in line, and they came into Poivre that way, Hill still leading, Dedham still last. As the white spear of the birch tree left the corner of his eye, Peter laid his weight on the brake, a little harder now than an hour ago; the car dug in, slowed evenly, all of a piece; he dropped his heel on the throttle, hit the clutch, thrust with the gear lever, all as 200 times before, all neat and orderly; he was conscious of an unaccustomed white blank, like a movie projector misbehaving for a second, and then he knew that the rear of the car had moved out; he steered instantly against it, in precise ratio; he gave back some gas pedal but not all of it and he noted that Dedham was now on his right instead of behind him to the left; he felt the off-side of the car rise; and he knew he was moving backward; he looked over his shoulder and was mildly surprised to see a forest falling on him, straight down. He could not hear a sound. He thought of Donnell. He knew Donnell would never find out why, he would never know the reason. Clearly not: there *was* no reason. Naturally not. There was no reason at all. How absurd to think that there had ever been a reason! His world went green. He knew that the forest was receiving him.

That first night, and the next, Janey Sawyer was under such heavy sedation that she slept without a wisp of dream. On the third night she woke laughing from a dream, and it became recurrent, she dreamed it often during the next few months. It was a plain dream: She saw Peter floating on his back in the sea, laughing aloud, speaking, when he could for laughter, to someone out of sight under the water, saying, "Ollie, Ollie, you are a funny man, you are a very funny man, *amigo*, yes, you are."

At first she insisted that this was not a dream, that she could hear Peter Hart's true voice, and when she had waked laughing she would soon weep. But in time the image blurred and the voice faded. In December of that year, in Athens, she met a pleasant Canadian boy. They had passage on the same plane for London, and he arranged for them to sit together. He was attentive and amusing. He made an intangible impression of wealth. He knew nothing about motor racing. They saw much of each other in London. They had a splendid time together. In the spring they went to Montreal.

Although fictional, this story is based on a real-life dog of doubtful pedigree known as Englewood Cold Steel, who was a champion of his breed in Canada. A century old, it is an account of a fighting pit bull who becomes a show dog. Leaving aside the grisly and shocking nature of dog fighting (long since outlawed in North America), the story has the charm of being told by the dog himself, and he's an endearing critter with loads of character. Author Richard Harding Davis (1864–1916) was himself quite a character. The prototype of the adventurous journalist, he was renowned for on-the-spot reporting of big news events, especially during the Spanish-American War. Soon after becoming a newspaperman, he wrote short stories on the side that made him enormously popular and wealthy. "The Bar Sinister," considered his best work, was first published in Scribner's Magazine.

Richard Harding Davis

THE BAR SINISTER (1902)

THE MASTER WAS WALKING most unsteady, his legs tripping each other. After the fifth or sixth round, my legs often go the same way.

But even when the Master's legs bend and twist a bit, you mustn't think he can't reach you. Indeed, that is the time he kicks most frequent. So I kept behind him in the shadow, or ran in the middle of the street. He stopped at many public houses with swinging doors, those doors that are cut so high from the sidewalk that you can look in under them, and see if the Master is inside. At night, when I peep beneath them, the man at the counter will see me first and say, "Here's the Kid, Jerry, come to take you home. Get a move on you"; and the Master will stumble out and follow me. It's lucky for us I'm so white, for no matter how dark the night, he can always see me ahead, just out of reach of his boot. At night the Master certainly does see most amazing. Sometimes he sees two or four of me, and walks in a circle, so that I have to take him by the leg of his trousers and lead him into the right road. One night, when he was very nasty-tempered and I was coaxing him along, two men passed us, and one of them says, "Look at that brute!" and the other asks, "Which?" and they both laugh. The Master he cursed them good and proper.

But this night, whenever we stopped at a public house, the Master's pals left it and went on with us to the next. They spoke quite civil to me, and when the Master tried a flying kick, they gives him a shove. "Do you want us to lose our money?" says the pals.

I had had nothing to eat for a day and a night, and just before we set out the Master gives me a wash under the hydrant. Whenever I am locked up until all the slop pans in our alley are empty, and made to take a bath, and the Master's pals speak civil and feel my ribs, I know something is going to happen. And that night, when every time they see a policeman under a lamppost, they dodged across the street, and when at the last one of them picked me up and hid me under his jacket, I began to tremble; for I knew what it meant. It meant that I was to fight again for the Master.

I don't fight because I like fighting. I fight because if I didn't the other dog would find my throat, and the Master would lose his stakes, and I would be very sorry for him, and ashamed. Dogs can pass me and I can pass dogs, and I'd never pick a fight with none of them. When I see two dogs standing on their hind legs in the streets, clawing each other's ears, and snapping for each other's windpipes, or howling and swearing and rolling in the mud, I feel sorry they should act so, and pretend not to notice. If he'd let me, I'd like to pass the time of day with every dog I meet. But there's something about me that no nice dog can abide. When I trot up to nice dogs, nodding and grinning, to make friends, they always tell me to be off. "Go to the devil!" they bark at me. "Get out!" And when I walk away they shout "Mongrel" and

"Gutter dog!" and sometimes, after my back is turned, they rush me. I could kill most of them with three shakes, breaking the backbone of the little ones and squeezing the throat of the big ones. But what's the good? They *are* nice dogs; that's why I try to make up to them: and, though it's not for them to say it, I *am* a street dog, and if I try to push into the company of my betters, I suppose it's their right to teach me my place.

Of course they don't know I'm the best fighting bull terrier of my weight in Montreal. That's why it wouldn't be fair for me to take notice of what they shout. They don't know that if I once locked my jaws on them I'd carry away whatever I touched. The night I fought Kelley's White Rat, I wouldn't loosen up until the Master made a noose in my leash and strangled me; and, as for that Ottawa dog, if the handlers hadn't thrown red pepper down my nose I *never* would have let go of him. I don't think the handlers treated me quite right that time, but maybe they didn't know the Ottawa dog was dead. I did.

I learned my fighting from my mother when I was very young. We slept in a lumber yard on the river front, and by day hunted for food along the wharves. When we got it, the other tramp dogs would try to take it off us, and then it was wonderful to see mother fly at them and drive them away. All I know of fighting I learned from mother, watching her picking the ash heaps for me when I was too little to fight for myself. No one ever was so good to me as mother. When it snowed and the ice was in the St. Lawrence, she used to hunt alone, and bring me back new bones, and she'd sit and laugh to see me trying to swallow 'em whole. I was just a puppy then; my teeth was falling out. When I was able to fight we kept the whole river range to ourselves. I had the genuine long "punishing" jaw, so mother said, and there wasn't a man or a dog that dared worry us. Those were happy days, those were; and we lived well, share and share alike, and when we wanted a bit of fun, we chased the fat old wharf rats! My, how they would squeal!

Then the trouble came. It was no trouble to me. I was too young to care then. But mother took it so to heart that she grew ailing, and wouldn't go abroad with me by day. It was the same old scandal that they're always bringing up against me. I was so young then that I didn't know. I couldn't see any difference between mother—and other mothers.

But one day a pack of curs we drove off snarled back some new names at her, and mother dropped her head and ran, just as though they had whipped us. After that she wouldn't go out with me except in the dark, and one day she went away and never came back, and, though I hunted for her in every court and alley and back street of Montreal, I never found her.

One night, a month after mother ran away, I asked Guardian, the old blind mastiff, whose Master is the night watchman on our slip, what it all meant. And he told me.

"Every dog in Montreal knows," he says, "except you; and every Master knows. So I think it's time you knew."

Then he tells me that my father, who had treated mother so bad, was a great and noble gentleman from London. "Your father had twenty-two registered ancestors, had you father," old Guardian says, "And in him was the best bull-terrier blood of England, the most ancientest, the most royal; the winning 'blue-ribbon' blood, that breeds champions. He had sleepy pink eyes and thin pink lips, and he was as white all over as his own white teeth, and under his white skin you could see his muscles, hard and smooth, like the links of a steel chain. When your father stood still, and tipped his nose in the air, it was just as though he was saying, 'Oh, yes, you common dogs and men, you may well stare. It must be a rare treat for you colonials to see real English royalty.' He certainly was pleased with hisself, was your father. He looked just as proud and haughty as one of them stone dogs in Victoria Park—them as is cut out of white marble. And you're like him," says the old mastiff—"by that, of course, meaning you're white, same as him. That's the only likeness. But, you see, the trouble is, Kid—well, you see, Kid, the trouble is—your mother—"

"That will do," I said, for then I understood without his telling me, and I got up and walked away, holding my head and tail high in the air.

But I was, oh, so miserable, and I wanted to see mother that very minute, and tell her that I didn't care.

Mother is what I am, a street dog; there's no royal blood in mother's veins, nor is she like that father of mine, nor—and that's the worst—she's not even like me. For while I, when I'm washed for a fight, am as white as clean snow, she—and this is our trouble—she, my mother, is a black-and-tan.

When mother hid herself from me, I was twelve months old and able to take care of myself, and as, after mother left me, the wharves were never the same, I moved uptown and met the Master. Before he came, lots of other menfolks had tried to make up to me, and to whistle me home. But they either tried patting me or coaxing me with a piece of meat; so I didn't take to 'em. But one day the Master pulled me out of a street fight by the hind legs, and kicked me good.

"You want to fight, do you?" says he. "I'll give you all the *fighting* you want!" he says, and he kicks me again. So I knew he was my Master, and I followed him home. Since that day I've pulled off many fights for him, and they've brought dogs from all over the province to have a go at me; but up to that night none, under thirty pounds, had ever downed me.

But that night, so soon as they carried me into the ring, I saw the dog was overweight, and that I was no match for him. It was asking too much of a puppy. The Master should have known I couldn't do it. Not that I mean to blame the Master, for when sober, which he sometimes was—though not, as you might say, his habit—he was most kind to me, and let me out to find food, if I could get it, and only kicked me when I didn't pick him up at night and lead him home.

But kicks will stiffen the muscles, and starving a dog so as to get him ugly-tempered for a fight may make him nasty, but it's weakening to his insides, and it causes the legs to wobble.

The ring was in a hall back of a public house. There was a red-hot whitewashed stove in one corner, and the ring in the other. I lay in the Master's lap, wrapped in my blanket, and, spite of the stove, shivering awful; but I always shiver before a fight: I can't help gettin' excited. While the menfolks were a-flashing their money and taking their last drink at the bar, a little Irish groom in gaiters came up to me and gave me the back of his hand to smell, and scratched me behind the ears.

"You poor little pup," says he; "you haven't no show," he says. "That brute in the taproom he'll eat your heart out."

"That's what *you* think," says the Master, snarling. "I'll lay you a quid the Kid chews him up."

The groom he shook his head, but kept looking at me so sorry-like that I begun to get a bit sad myself. He seemed like he couldn't bear to leave off a-patting of me, and he says, speaking low just like he would to a man-folk, "Well, good luck to you, little pup," which I thought so civil of him that I reached up and licked his hand. I don't do that to many men. And the Master he knew I didn't, and took on dreadful.

"What 'ave you got on the back of your hand?" says he, jumping up.

"Soap!" says the groom, quick as a rat. "That's more than you've got on yours. Do you want to smell of it?" and he sticks his fist under the Master's nose. But the pals pushed in between 'em.

"He tried to poison the Kid!" shouts the Master.

"Oh, one fight at a time," says the referee. "Get into the ring, Jerry. We're waiting." So we went into the ring.

I could never just remember what did happen in that ring. He give me no time to spring. He fell on me like a horse. I couldn't keep my feet against him, and though, as I saw, he could get his hold when he liked, he wanted to chew me over a bit first. I was wondering if they'd be able to pry him off me, when, in the third round, he took his hold; and I begun to drown, just as I did when I fell into the river off the Red C slip. He closed deeper and deeper on my throat, and everything went black and red and bursting; and then, when I were sure I were dead, the handlers pulled him off, and the Master give me a kick that brought me to. But I couldn't move none, or even wink, both eyes being shut with lumps.

"He's a cur," yells the Master, "a sneaking, cowardly cur! He lost the fight for me," says he, "because he's a ——————— cowardly cur." And he kicks me again in the lower ribs, so that I go sliding across the sawdust. "There's gratitude fer yer," yells the Master. "I've fed that dog, and nussed that dog and housed him like a prince; and now he puts his tail between his legs and sells me out, he does. He's a coward! I've done with him, I am. I'd sell him for a pipeful of tobacco." He picked me up by the tail, and swung me for the menfolks to see. "Does any gentleman here want to buy a dog," he says, "to make into sausage meat?" he says. "That's all he's good for."

Then I heard the little Irish groom say, "I'll give you ten bob for the dog."

And another voice says, "Ah, don't you do it; the dog's same as dead—mebbe he is dead."

"Ten shilling!" says the Master, and his voice sobers a bit; "make it two pounds and he's yours."

But the pals rushed in again.

"Don't you be a fool, Jerry," they say. "You'll be sorry for this when you're sober. The Kid's worth a fiver."

One of my eyes was not so swelled up as the other, and as I hung by my tail, I opened it, and saw one of the pals take the groom by the shoulder.

"You ought to give 'im five pounds for that dog, mate," he says; "that's no ordinary dog. That dog's got good blood in him, that dog has. Why, his father—that very dog's father—"

I thought he never would go on. He waited like he wanted to be sure the groom was listening.

"That very dog's father," says the pal, "is Regent Royal, son of Champion Regent Monarch, champion bull terrier of England for four years."

I was sore, and torn, and chewed most awful, but what the pal said sounded so fine that I wanted to wag my tail, only couldn't, owing to my hanging from it.

But the Master calls out: "Yes, his father was Regent Royal; who's saying he wasn't? but the pup's a cowardly cur, that's what his pup is. And why? I'll tell you why: because his mother was a black-and-tan street dog, that's why!"

I don't see how I got the strength, but, some way, I threw myself out of the Master's grip and fell at his feet, and turned over and fastened all my teeth in his ankle, just across the bone.

When I woke, after the pals had kicked me off him, I was in the smoking car of a railroad train, lying in the lap of the little groom, and he was rubbing my open wounds with a greasy yellow stuff, exquisite to the smell and most agreeable to lick off.

II

"Well, what's your name—Nolan? Well, Nolan, these references are satisfactory," said the young gentleman my new Master called "Mr. Wyndham, sir." "I'll take you on as second man. You can begin today."

My new Master shuffled his feet and put his finger to his forehead. "Thank you, sir," says he. Then he choked like he had swallowed a fish bone. "I have a little dawg, sir," says he.

"You can't keep him," says "Mr. Wyndham, sir," very short.

"'E's only a puppy, sir," says my new Master; "'e wouldn't go outside the stables, sir."

"It's not that," says "Mr. Wyndham, sir." "I have a large kennel of very fine dogs; they're the best of their breed in America. I don't allow strange dogs on the premises."

The Master shakes his head, and motions me with his cap, and I crept out from behind the door. "I'm sorry, sir," says the Master. "Then I can't take the place. I can't get along without the dawg, sir."

"Mr. Wyndham, sir," looked at me that fierce that I guessed he was going to whip me, so I turned over on my back and begged with my legs and tail.

"Why, you beat him!" says "Mr. Wyndham, sir," very stern.

"No fear!" the Master says, getting very red. "The party I bought him off taught him that. He never learnt that from me!" He picked me up in his arms, and to show "Mr. Wyndham, sir," how well I loved the Master, I bit his chin and hands.

"Mr. Wyndham, sir," turned over the letters the Master had given him. "Well, these references certainly are very strong," he says. "I guess I'll let the dog stay. Only see you keep him away from the kennels—or you'll both go."

"Thank you, sir," says the Master, grinning like a cat when she's safe behind the area railing.

"He's not a bad bull terrier," says "Mr. Wyndham, sir," feeling my head. "Not that I know much about the smooth-coated breeds. My dogs are St. Bernards." He stopped patting me and held up my nose. "What's the matter with his ears?" he says. "They're chewed to pieces. Is this a fighting dog?" he asks, quick and rough-like.

I could have laughed. If he hadn't been holding my nose, I certainly would have had a good grin at him. Me the best under thirty pounds in the Province of Quebec, and him asking if I was a fighting dog! I ran to the Master and hung down my head modest-like, waiting for him to tell my list of battles; but the Master he coughs in his cap most painful. "Fightin' dawg, sir!" he cries. "Lor' bless you, sir, the Kid don't know the word. 'E's just a puppy, sir, same as you see; a pet dog, so to speak. 'E's a regular old lady's lapdog, the Kid is."

"Well, you keep him away from my St. Bernards," says "Mr. Wyndham, sir," "or they might make a mouthful of him."

"Yes, sir; that they might," says the Master. But when we gets outside he slaps his knee and laughs inside hisself, and winks at me most sociable.

The Master's new home was in the country, in a province they called Long Island. There was a high stone wall about his home with big iron gates to it, same as Godfrey's brewery; and there was a house with five red roofs; and the stables, where I lived, was cleaner than the aërated bakery shop. And then there was the kennels; but they was like nothing else in this world that ever I see. For the first days I couldn't sleep of nights for fear someone would catch me lying in such a cleaned-up place, and would chase me out of it; and when I did fall to sleep I'd dream I was back in the old Master's attic, shivering under the rusty stove, which never had no coals in it, with the Master flat on his back on the cold floor, with his clothes on. And I'd wake up scared and whimpering, and find myself on the new Master's cot with his hand on the quilt beside me; and I'd see the glow of the big stove, and hear the high-quality horses below stairs stamping in their straw-lined boxes, and I'd snoop the sweet smell of hay and harness soap and go to sleep again.

The stables was my jail, so the Master said, but I don't ask no better home than that jail.

"Now, Kid," says he, sitting on top of a bucket upside down, "you've got to understand this. When I whistle it means you're not to go out of this 'ere yard. These stables is your jail. If you leave 'em I'll have to leave 'em too, and over the seas, in the County Mayo, an old mother will 'ave to leave her bit of a cottage. For two pounds I must be sending her every month, or she'll have naught to eat, nor no thatch over 'er head. I can't lose my place, Kid, so see you don't lose it for me. You must keep away from the kennels," says he; "they're not for the likes of you. The kennels are for the quality. I wouldn't take a litter of them woolly dogs for one wag of your tail, Kid, but for all that they are your betters, same as the gentry up in the big house are my betters. I know my place and keep away from the gentry, and you keep away from the champions."

So I never goes out of the stables. All day I just lay in the sun on the stone flags, licking my jaws, and watching the grooms wash down the carriages, and the only care I had was to see they didn't get gay and turn the hose on me. There wasn't even a single rat to plague me. Such stables I never did see.

"Nolan," says the head groom, "some day that dog of yours will give you the slip. You can't keep a street dog tied up all his life. It's against his natur'." The head groom is a nice old gentleman, but he doesn't know everything. Just as though I'd been a street dog because I liked it! As if I'd rather poke for my vittels in ash heaps than have 'em handed me in a washbasin, and would sooner bite and fight than be polite and sociable. If I'd had mother there I couldn't have asked for nothing more. But I'd think of her snooping in the gutters, or freezing of nights under the bridges, or, what's worst of all, running through the hot streets with her tongue down, so wild and crazy for a drink that the people would shout "mad dog" at her and stone her. Water's so good that I don't blame the menfolks for locking it up inside their houses; but when the hot days come, I think they might remember that those are the dog days, and leave a little water outside in a trough, like they do for the horses. Then we wouldn't go mad, and the policemen wouldn't shoot us. I had so much of everything I wanted that it made me think a lot of the days when I hadn't nothing, and if I could have given what I had to mother, as she used to share with me, I'd have been the happiest dog in the land. Not that I wasn't happy then, and most grateful to the Master, too, and if I'd only minded him, the trouble wouldn't have come again.

But one day the coachman says that the little lady they called Miss Dorothy had come back from school, and that same morning she runs over to the stables to pat her ponies, and she sees me.

"Oh, what a nice little, white little dog!" said she. "Whose little dog are you?" says she.

"That's my dog, miss," says the Master. " 'Is name is Kid." And I ran up to her most polite, and licks her fingers, for I never see so pretty and kind a lady.

"You must come with me and call on my new puppies," says she, picking me up in her arms and starting off with me.

"Oh, but please, miss," cries Nolan, "Mr. Wyndham give orders that the Kid's not to go to the kennels."

"That'll be all right," says the little lady; "they're my kennels too. And the puppies will like to play with him."

You wouldn't believe me if I was to tell you of the style of them quality dogs. If I hadn't seen it myself I wouldn't have believed it neither. The Viceroy of Canada don't live no better. There was forty of them, but each one had his own house and a yard—most exclusive—and a cot and a drinking basin all to hisself. They had servants standing round waiting to feed 'em when they was hungry, and valets to wash 'em; and they had their hair combed and brushed like the grooms must when they go out on the box. Even the puppies had overcoats with their names on 'em in blue letters, and the name of each of those they called champions was painted up fine over his front door just like it was a public house or a veterinary's. They were the biggest St. Bernards I ever did see. I could have walked under them if they'd have let me. But they were very proud and haughty dogs, and looked only once at me, and then sniffed in the air. The little lady's own dog was an old gentleman bull dog. He'd come along with us, and when he notices how taken aback I was with all I see, 'e turned quite kind and affable and showed me about.

"Jimmy Jocks," Miss Dorothy called him, but, owing to his weight, he walked most dignified and slow, waddling like a duck, as you might say, and looked much too proud and handsome for such a silly name.

"That's the runway, and that's the trophy house," says he to me, "and that over there is the hospital, where you have to go if you get distemper and the vet gives you beastly medicine."

"And which of these is your 'ouse, sir?" asks I, wishing to be respectful. But he looked that hurt and haughty. "I don't live in the kennels," says he, most contemptuous. "I am a house dog. I sleep in Miss Dorothy's room. And at lunch I'm let in with the family, if the visitors don't mind. They 'most always do, but they're too polite to say so. Besides," says he smiling most condescending, "visitors are always afraid of me. It's because I'm so ugly," says he. "I suppose," says he, screwing up his wrinkles and speaking very slow and impressive, "I suppose I'm the ugliest bull dog in America"; and as he seemed to be so pleased to think hisself so, I said "Yes, sir; you certainly are the ugliest ever I see," at which he nodded his head most approving.

"But I couldn't hurt 'em, as you say," he goes on, though I hadn't said nothing like that, being too polite. "I'm too old," he says; "I haven't any teeth. The last time one of those grizzly bears," said he, glaring at the big St. Bernards, "took a hold of me, he nearly was my death," says he. I thought his eyes would pop out of his head, he seemed so wrought up about it. "He rolled me around in the dirt, he did," says Jimmy Jocks, "an' I couldn't get up. It was low," says Jimmy Jocks, making a face like he had a bad taste in his mouth. "Low, that's what I call it—bad form, you understand, young man, not done in my set—and—and low." He growled way down in his stomach, and puffed hisself out, panting and blowing like he had been on a run.

"I'm not a street fighter," he says, scowling at a St. Bernard marked "Champion." "And when my rheumatism is not troubling me," he says, "I endeavor to be civil to all dogs, so long as they are gentlemen."

"Yes, sir," said I, for even to me he had been most affable.

At this we had come to a little house off by itself, and Jimmy Jocks invites me in. "This is their trophy room," he says, "where they keep their prizes. Mine." he says, rather grand-like, "are on the sideboard." Not knowing what a sideboard might be, I said, "Indeed, sir, that must be very gratifying." But he only wrinkled up his chops as much as to say, "It is my right."

The trophy room was as wonderful as any public house I ever see. On the walls was pictures of nothing but beautiful St. Bernard dogs, and rows and rows of blue and red and yellow ribbons; and when I asked Jimmy Jocks why they was so many more of blue than of the others, he laughs and says, "Because these kennels always win." And there was many shining cups on the shelves, which Jimmy Jocks told me were prizes won by champions.

"Now, sir, might I ask you, sir," says I, "wot is a champion?"

At that he panted and breathed so hard I thought he would bust hisself. "My dear young friend!" says he, "wherever you have been educated? A champion is a—champion," he says. "He must win nine blue ribbons in the 'open' class. You follow me—that is—against all comers. Then he has the title before his name, and they put his photograph in the sporting papers. You know, of course that *I* am a champion," says he. "I am Champion Woodstock Wizard III, and the two other Woodstock Wizards, my father and uncle, were both champions."

"But I thought your name was Jimmy Jocks," I said.

He laughs right out at that.

"That's my kennel name, not my registered name," he says. "Why, certainly you know that every dog has two names. Now, for instance, what's your registered name and number?" says he.

"I've got only one name," I says. "Just Kid."

Woodstock Wizard puffs at that and wrinkles up his forehead and pops out his eyes.

"Who are your people?" says he. "Where is your home?"

"At the stable, sir," I said. "My Master is the second groom."

At that Woodstock Wizard III looks at me for quite a bit without winking, and stares all around the room over my head.

"Oh, well," says he at last, "you're a very civil young dog," says he, "and I blame no one for what he can't help," which I thought most fair and liberal. "And I have known many bull terriers that were champions," says he, "though as a rule they mostly run with fire engines and to fighting. For me, I wouldn't care to run though the streets after a hose cart, nor to fight," says he: "but each to his taste."

I could not help thinking that if Woodstock Wizard III tried to follow a fire engine he would die of apoplexy, and seeing he'd lost his teeth, it was lucky he had no taste for fighting; but, after his being so condescending, I didn't say nothing.

"Anyway," says he, "every smooth-coated dog is better than any hairy old camel like those St. Bernards, and if ever you're hungry down at the stables, young man, come up to the house and I'll give you a bone. I can't eat them myself, but I bury them around the garden from force of habit and in case a friend should drop in. Ah, I see my mistress coming," he says, "and I bid you good day. I regret," he says, "that our different social position prevents our meeting frequent, for you're a worthy young dog with a proper respect for your betters, and in this country there's precious few of them have that." Then he waddles off, leaving me alone and very sad, for he was the first dog in many days that had spoke to me. But since he showed, seeing that I was a stable dog, he didn't want my company, I waited for him to get well away. It was not a cheerful place to wait, the trophy house. The pictures of the champions seemed to scowl at me, and ask what right such as I had even to admire them, and the blue and gold ribbons and the silver cups made me very miserable. I had never won no blue ribbons or silver cups, only stakes for the old Master to spend in the publics; and I hadn't won them for being a beautiful high-quality dog, but just for fighting—which, of course, as Woodstock Wizard III says, is low. So I started for the stables, with my head down and my tail between my legs, feeling sorry I had ever left the Master. But I had more reason to be sorry before I got back to him.

The trophy house was quite a bit from the kennels, and as I left it I see Miss Dorothy and Woodstock Wizard III walking back toward them, and, also, that a big St. Bernard, his name was Champion Red

Elfberg, had broke his chain and was running their way. When he reaches old Jimmy Jocks he lets out a roar like a grain steamer in a fog, and he makes three leaps for him. Old Jimmy Jocks was about a fourth his size; but he plants his feet and curves his back, and his hair goes up around his neck like a collar. But he never had no show at no time, for the grizzly bear, as Jimmy Jocks had called him, lights on old Jimmy's back and tries to break it, and old Jimmy Jocks snaps his gums and claws the grass, panting and groaning awful. But he can't do nothing, and the grizzly bear just rolls him under him, biting and tearing cruel. The odds was all that Woodstock Wizard III was going to be killed; I had fought enough to see that: but not knowing the rules of the game among champions, I didn't like to interfere between two gentlemen who might be settling a private affair, and, as it were, take it as presuming of me. So I stood by, though I was shaking terrible, and holding myself in like I was on a leash. But at that Woodstock Wizard III, who was underneath, sees me through the dust, and calls very faint, "Help, you!" he says. "Take him in the hind leg," he says. "He's murdering me," he says. And then the little Miss Dorothy, who was crying, and calling to the kennel men, catches at the Red Elfberg's hind legs to pull him off, and the brute, keeping his front pats well in Jimmy's stomach, turns his big head and snaps at her. So that was all I asked for, thank you. I went up under him. It was really nothing. He stood so high that I had only to take off about three feet from him and come in from the side, and my long "punishing jaw," as mother was always talking about, locked on his woolly throat, and my back teeth met. I couldn't shake him, but I shook myself and every time I shook myself there was thirty pounds of weight tore at his windpipes. I couldn't see nothing for his long hair, but I heard Jimmy Jocks puffing and blowing on one side, and munching the brute's leg with his old gums. Jimmy was an old sport that day, was Jimmy, or Woodstock Wizard III, as I should say. When the Red Elfberg was out and down I had to run, or those kennel men would have had my life. They chased me right into the stables; and from under the hay I watched the head groom take down a carriage whip and order them to the right about.

Luckily Master and the young grooms were out, or that day there'd have been fighting for everybody.

Well, it nearly did for me and the Master. "Mr. Wyndham, sir," comes raging to the stables. I'd half killed his best prize-winner, he says, and had oughter be shot, and he gives the Master his notice. But Miss Dorothy she follows him, and says it was his Red Elfberg what began the fight, and that I'd saved Jimmy's life, and that old Jimmy Jocks was worth more to her than all the St. Bernards in the Swiss mountains—wherever they may be. And that I was her champion, anyway. Then she cried over me most beautiful, and over Jimmy Jocks, too, who was that tied up in bandages he couldn't even waddle. So when he heard that side of it, "Mr. Wyndham, sir," told us that if Nolan put me on a chain we could stay. So it came out all right for everybody but me. I was glad the Master kept his place, but I'd never worn a chain before, and it disheartened me. But that was the least of it. For the quality dogs couldn't forgive my whipping their champion, and they came to the fence between the kennels and the stables, and laughed through the bars, barking most cruel words at me. I couldn't understand how they found it out, but they knew. After the fight Jimmy Jocks was most condescending to me, and he said the grooms had boasted to the kennel men that I was a son of Regent Royal, and that when the kennel men asked who was my mother they had had to tell them that too. Perhaps that was the way of it, but, however, the scandal got out, and every one of the quality dogs knew that I was a street dog and the son of a black-and-tan.

"These misalliances will occur," said Jimmy Jocks, in his old-fashioned way; "but no well-bred dog," says he, looking most scornful at the St. Bernards, who were howling behind the palings, "would refer to your misfortune before you, certainly not cast it in your face. I myself remember your father's father, when he made his début at the Crystal Palace. He took four blue ribbons and three specials."

But no sooner than Jimmy would leave me the St. Bernards would take to howling again, insulting mother and insulting me. And when I tore at my chain, they, seeing they were safe, would howl the more. It was never the same after that; the laughs and the jeers cut into my heart, and the chain bore heavy on my spirit. I was so sad that sometimes I wished I was back in the gutter again, where no one was better than me, and some nights I wished I was dead. If it hadn't been for the Master being so kind, and that it would have looked like I was blaming mother, I would have twisted my leash and hanged myself.

About a month after my fight, the word was passed through the kennels that the New York Show was coming, and such goings on as followed I never did see. If each of them had been matched to fight for a thousand pounds and the gate, they couldn't have trained more conscientious. But perhaps that's just my envy. The kennel men rubbed 'em and scrubbed 'em, and trims their hair and curls and combs it, and some dogs they fatted and some they starved. No one talked of nothing but the Show, and the chances "our kennels" had against the other kennels, and if this one of our champions would win over that one, and whether them as hoped to be champions had better show in the "open" or the "limit" class, and whether this dog would beat his own dad or whether his little puppy sister couldn't beat the two of 'em. Even the grooms had their money up, and day or night you heard nothing but praises of "our" dogs, until I, being so far out of it, couldn't have felt meaner if I had been running the streets with a can to my tail. I knew shows were not for such as me, and so all day I lay stretched at the end of my chain, pretending I was asleep, and only too glad that they had something so important to think of that they could leave me alone.

But one day, before the Show opened, Miss Dorothy came to the stables with "Mr. Wyndham, sir," and, seeing me chained up and so miserable, she takes me in her arms.

"You poor little tyke!" says she. "It's cruel to tie him up so; he's eating his heart out, Nolan," she says. "I don't know nothing about bull terriers," says she, "but I think Kid's got good points," says she, "and you ought to show him. Jimmy Jocks has three legs on the Rensselaer Cup now, and I'm going to show him this time, so that he can get the fourth; and, if you wish, I'll enter your dog too. How would you like that, Kid? Maybe you'd meet a pal or two," says she. "It would cheer you up, wouldn't it, Kid?" says she. "How would you like to see the most beautiful dogs in the world?" says she. But I was so upset I could only wag my tail most violent. "He says it would!" says she, though, being that excited, I hadn't said nothing.

So "Mr. Wyndham, sir," laughs, and takes out a piece of blue paper and sits down at the head groom's table.

"What's the name of the father of your dog, Nolan?" says he. And Nolan says: "The man I got him off told me he was a son of Champion Regent Royal, sir. But it don't seem likely, does it?" says Nolan.

"It does not!" says "Mr. Wyndham, sir," short like.

"Aren't you sure, Nolan?" says Miss Dorothy.

"No, miss," says the Master.

"Sire unknown," says "Mr. Wyndham, sir," and writes it down.

"Date of birth?" asks "Mr. Wyndham, sir."

"I–I–unknown, sir," says Nolan. And "Mr. Wyndham, sir," writes it down.

"Breeder?" says "Mr. Wyndham, sir."

"Unknown," says Nolan, getting very red around the jaws, and I drops my head and tail. And "Mr. Wyndham, sir," writes that down.

"Mother's name?" says "Mr. Wyndham, sir."

"She was a–unknown," says the Master. And I licks his hand.

"Dam unknown," says "Mr. Wyndham, sir" and writes it down. Then he takes the paper and reads out loud: " 'Sire unknown, dam unknown, breeder unknown, date of birth unknown,' You'd better call him the 'Great Unknown,' " says he. "Who's paying his entrance fee?"

"I am," says Miss Dorothy.

Two weeks after we all got on a train for New York, Jimmy Jocks and me following Nolan in the smoking car, and twenty-two of the St. Bernards in boxes and crates and on chains and leashes. Such a barking and howling I never did hear; and when they sees me going, too, they laughs fit to kill.

"Wot is this–a circus?" says the railroad man.

But I had no heart in it. I hated to go. I knew I was no "show" dog, even though Miss Dorothy and the Master did their best to keep me from shaming them. For before we set out Miss Dorothy brings a man from town who scrubbed and rubbed me, and sandpapered my tail, which hurt most awful, and shaved my ears with the Master's razor, so they could 'most see clear through 'em, and sprinkles me over with pipe clay, till I shines like a Tommy's crossbelts.

"Upon my word!" says Jimmy Jocks when he first sees me. "Wot a swell you are! You're the image of your granddad when he made his début at the Crystal Palace. He took four firsts and and three specials." But I knew he was only trying to throw heart into me. They might scrub, and they might rub, and they might pipe-clay, but they couldn't pipe-clay the insides of me, and they was black-and-tan.

Then we came to a garden, which it was not, but the biggest hall in the world. Inside there was lines of benches a few miles long, and on them sat every dog in America. If all the dog-snatchers in Montreal had worked night and day for a year, they couldn't have caught so many dogs. And they was all shouting and barking and howling so vicious that my heart stopped beating. For at first I thought they was all enraged at my presuming to intrude. But after I got in my place they kept at it just the same, barking at every dog as he come in: daring him to fight, and ordering him out, and asking him what breed of dog he thought he was, anyway. Jimmy Jocks was chained just behind me, and he said he never see so fine a show. "That's a hot class you're in, my lad," he says, looking over into my street, where there were thirty bull terriers. They was all as white as cream, and each so beautiful that if I could have broke my chain I would have run all the way home and hid myself under the horse trough.

All night long they talked and sang, and passed greetings with old pals, and the homesick puppies howled dismal. Them that couldn't sleep wouldn't let no others sleep, and all the electric lights burned in the roof, and in my eyes. I could hear Jimmy Jocks snoring peaceful, but I could only doze by jerks, and when I dozed I dreamed horrible. All the dogs in the hall seemed coming at me for daring to intrude, with their jaws red and open, and their eyes blazing like the lights in the roof. "You're a street dog! Get out, you street dog!" they yells. And as they drives me out, the pipe clay drops off me, and they laugh and shriek; and when I looks down I see that I have turned into a black-and-tan.

They was the most awful dreams, and next morning, when Miss Dorothy come and gives me water in a pan, I begs and begs her to take me home; but she can't understand. "How well Kid is!" she says. And when I jumps into the Master's arms and pulls to break my chain, he says, "If he knew all he had against him, miss, he wouldn't be so gay." And from a book they reads out the name of the beautiful highbred terriers which I have got to meet. And I can't make 'em understand that I only want to run away and hide myself where no one will see me.

Then suddenly men comes hurrying down our street and begins to brush the beautiful bull terriers; and the Master rubs me with a towel so excited that his hands tremble awful, and Miss Dorothy tweaks my ears between her gloves, so that the blood runs to 'em, and they turn pink and stand up straight and sharp.

"Now, then, Nolan," says she, her voice shaking just like his fingers, "keep his head up—and never let the judge lose sight of him." When I hears that my legs breaks under me, for I knows all about judges. Twice the old Master goes up before the judge for fighting me with other dogs, and the judge promises him if he ever does it again he'll chain him up in jail. I knew he'd find me out. A judge can't be fooled by no pipe clay. He can see right through you, and he reads your insides.

The judging ring, which is where the judge holds out, was so like a fighting pit that when I come in it, and finds six other dogs there, I springs into position, so that when they lets us go I can defend myself. But the Master smooths down my hair and whispers, "Hold 'ard, Kid, hold 'ard. This ain't a fight," says he. "Look your prettiest," he whispers. "Please, Kid, look your prettiest"; and he pulls my leash so tight that I can't touch my pats to the sawdust, and my nose goes up in the air. There was millions of people a-watching us from the railings, and three of our kennel men, too, making fun of the Master and me, and Miss Dorothy with her chin just reaching to the rail, and her eyes so big that I thought she was a-going to cry. It was awful to think that when the judge stood up and exposed me, all those people, and Miss Dorothy, would be there to see me driven from the Show.

The judge he was a fierce-looking man with specs on his nose, and a red beard. When I first come in he didn't see me, owing to my being too quick for him and dodging behind the Master. But when the Master drags me round and I pulls at the sawdust to keep back, the judge looks at us careless-like, and then stops and glares through his specs, and I knew it was all up with me.

"Are there any more?" asks the judge to the gentleman at the gate, but never taking his specs from me.

The man at the gate looks in his book. "Seven in the novice class," says he. "They're all here. You can go ahead," and he shuts the gate.

The judge he doesn't hesitate a moment. He just waves his hand toward the corner of the ring. "Take him away," he says to the Master, "over there, and keep him away"; and he turns and looks most solemn at the six beautiful bull terriers. I don't know how I crawled to that corner. I wanted to scratch under the sawdust and dig myself a grave. The kennel men they slapped the rail with their hands and laughed at the Master like they would fall over. They pointed at me in the corner, and their sides just shaked. But little Miss Dorothy she presses her lips tight against the rail, and I see tears rolling from her eyes. The Master he hangs his head like he had been whipped. I felt most sorry for him than all. He was so red, and he was letting on not to see the kennel men, and blinking his eyes. If the judge had ordered me right out it wouldn't have disgraced us so, but it was keeping me there while he was judging the highbred dogs that hurt so hard. With all those people staring, too. And his doing it so quick, without no doubt nor questions. You can't fool the judges. They see inside you.

But he couldn't make up his mind about them highbred dogs. He scowls at 'em, and he glares at 'em, first with his head on the one side and then on the other. And he feels of 'em, and orders 'em to run about. And Nolan leans against the rails, with his head hung down, and pats me. And Miss Dorothy comes over beside him, but don't say nothing, only wipes her eye with her finger. A man on the other side of the rail he says to the Master, "The judge don't like your dog?"

"No," says the Master.

"Have you ever shown him before?" says the man.

"No," says the Master, "and I'll never show him again. He's my dog," says the Master, "and he suits me! And I don't care what no judges think." And when he says them kind words, I licks his hand most grateful.

The judge had two of the six dogs on a little platform in the middle of the ring, and he had chased the four other dogs into the corners, where they was licking their chops, and letting on they didn't care, same as Nolan was.

The two dogs on the platform was so beautiful that the judge hisself couldn't tell which was the best of 'em, even when he stoops down and holds their heads together. But at last he gives a sigh, and brushes the sawdust off his knees, and goes to the table in the ring, where there was a man keeping score, and heaps and heaps of blue and gold and red and yellow ribbons. And the judge picks up a bunch of 'em and walks to the two gentlemen who was holding the beautiful dogs, and he says to each, "What's his number?" and he hands each gentleman a ribbon. And then he turned sharp and comes straight at the Master.

"What's his number?" says the judge. And Master was so scared that he couldn't make no answer.

But Miss Dorothy claps her hands and cries out like she was laughing, "Three twenty-six," and the judge writes it down and shoves Master the blue ribbon.

I bit the Master, and I jumps and bit Miss Dorothy, and I waggled so hard that the Master couldn't hold me. When I get to the gate Miss Dorothy snatches me up and kisses me between the ears, right before millions of people, and they both hold me so tight that I didn't know which of them was carrying of me. But one thing I knew, for I listened hard, as it was the judge hisself as said it.

"Did you see that puppy I gave first to?" says the judge to the gentleman at the gate.

"I did. He was a bit out of his class," says the gate gentleman.

"He certainly was!" says the judge, and they both laughed.

But I didn't care. They couldn't hurt me then, not with Nolan holding the blue ribbon and Miss Dorothy hugging my ears, and the kennel

men sneaking away, each looking like he'd been caught with his nose under the lid of a slop can.

We sat down together, and we all three just talked as fast as we could.
They was so pleased that I couldn't help feeling proud of myself, and I
barked and leaped about so gay that all the bull terriers in our street
stretched on their chains and howled at me.

"Just look at him!" says one of those I had beat. "What's he giving hisself airs about?"

"Because he's got one blue ribbon!" says another of 'em. "Why, when
I was a puppy I used to eat 'em, and if that judge could ever learn to know
a toy from a mastiff, I'd have had this one."

But Jimmy Jocks he leaned over from his bench and says, "Well done,
Kid. Didn't I tell you so?" What he 'ad told me was that I might get a
"commended," but I didn't remind him.

"Didn't I tell you," says Jimmy Jocks, "that I saw your grandfather
make his début at the Crystal—"

"Yes, sir, you did, sir," says I, for I have no love for the men of my
family.

A gentleman with a showing leash around his neck comes up just then
and looks at me very critical. "Nice dog you've got, Miss Wyndham,"
says he; "would you care to sell him?"

"He's not my dog," says Miss Dorothy, holding me tight. "I wish he
were."

"He's not for sale, sir," says the Master, and I was *that* glad.

"Oh, he's yours, is he?" says the gentleman, looking hard at Nolan.
"Well, I'll give you a hundred dollars for him," says he, careless-like.

"Thank you, sir; he's not for sale," says Nolan, but his eyes get very
big. The gentleman he walked away; but I watches him, and he talks to
a man in a golf cap, and by and by the man comes along our street, looking at all the dogs, and stops in front of me.

"This your dog?" says he to Nolan. "Pity he's so leggy," says he. "If he
had a good tail, and a longer stop, and his ears were set higher, he'd be
a good dog. As he is, I'll give you fifty dollars for him."

But, before the Master could speak, Miss Dorothy laughs and says:

"You're Mr. Polk's kennel man, I believe. Well, you tell Mr. Polk from me that the dog's not for sale now any more than he was five minutes ago, and that when he is, he'll have to bid against me for him."

The man looks foolish at that, but he turns to Nolan quick-like. "I'll give you three hundred for him," he says.

"Oh, indeed!" whispers Miss Dorothy, like she was talking to herself. "That's it, is it?" And she turns and looks at me just as though she had never seen me before. Nolan he was a-gaping, too, with his mouth open. But he holds me tight.

"He's not for sale," he growls, like he was frightened; and the man looks black and walks away.

"Why, Nolan!" cried Miss Dorothy, "Mr. Polk knows more about bull terriers than any amateur in America. What can he mean? Why, Kid is no more than a puppy! Three hundred dollars for a puppy!"

"And he ain't no thoroughbred, neither!" cries the Master. "He's 'Unknown,' ain't he? Kid can't help it, of course, but his mother, miss—"

I dropped my head. I couldn't bear he should tell Miss Dorothy. I couldn't bear she should know I had stolen my blue ribbon.

But the Master never told, for at that a gentleman runs up, calling, "Three twenty-six, three twenty-six!" And Miss Dorothy says, "Here he is; what is it?"

"The Winners' class," says the gentleman. "Hurry, please; the judge is waiting for him."

Nolan tries to get me off the chain onto a showing leash, but he shakes so, he only chokes me. "What is it, miss?" he says. "What is it?"

"The Winners' class," says Miss Dorothy. "The judge wants him with the winners of the other classes—to decide which is the best. It's only a form," says she. "He has the champions against him now."

"Yes," says the gentleman, as he hurries us to the ring. "I'm afraid it's only a form for your dog, but the judge wants all the winners, puppy class even."

We had got to the gate, and the gentleman there was writing down my number.

"Who won the open?" asks Miss Dorothy.

"Oh, who would?" laughs the gentleman. "The old champion, of course. He's won for three years now. There he is. Isn't he wonderful?" says he; and he points to a dog that's standing proud and haughty on the platform in the middle of the ring.

I never see so beautiful a dog—so fine and clean and noble, so white like he had rolled hisself in flour, holding his nose up and his eyes shut, same as though no one was worth looking at. Aside of him we other dogs, even though we had a blue ribbon apiece, seemed like lumps of mud. He was a royal gentleman, a king, he was. His master didn't have to hold his head with no leash. He held it hisself, standing as still as an iron dog on a lawn, like he knew all the people was looking at him. And so they was, and no one around the ring pointed at no other dog but him.

"Oh, what a picture!" cried Miss Dorothy. "He's like a marble figure by a great artist—one who loved dogs. Who is he?" says she, looking in her book. "I don't keep up with terriers."

"Oh, you know him," says the gentleman. "He is the champion of champions, Regent Royal."

The Master's face went red.

"And this is Regent Royal's son," cries he, and he pulls me quick into the ring, and plants me on the platform next my father.

I trembled so that I near fell. My legs twisted like a leash. But my father he never looked at me. He only smiled the same sleepy smile, and he still kept his eyes half shut, like as no one, no, not even his own son, was worth his lookin' at.

The judge he didn't let me stay beside my father, but, one by one, he placed the other dogs next to him and measured and felt and pulled at them. And each one he put down, but he never put my father down. And then he comes over and picks me up and sets me back on the platform, shoulder to shoulder with the Champion Regent Royal, and goes down on his knees, and looks into our eyes.

The gentleman with my father he laughs, and says to the judge, "Thinking of keeping us here all day, John?" But the judge he doesn't hear him, and goes behind us and runs his hands down my side, and holds back my ears, and takes my jaws between his fingers. The crowd around the ring is very deep now, and nobody says nothing. The gentleman at the score table, he is leaning forward, with his elbows on his knees and his eyes very wide, and the gentleman at the gate is whispering quick to Miss Dorothy, who has turned white. I stood as stiff as stone. I didn't even breathe. But out of the corner of my eye I could see my father licking his pink chops, and yawning just a little, like he was bored.

The judge he had stopped looking fierce and was looking solemn. Something inside him seemed a-troubling him awful. The more he stares at us now, the more solemn he gets, and when he touches us he does it gentle, like he was patting us. For a long time he kneels in the sawdust, looking at my father and at me, and no one around the ring says nothing to nobody.

Then the judge takes a breath and touches me sudden. "It's his," he says. But he lays his hand just as quick on my father. "I'm sorry," says he.

The gentleman holding my father cries:

"Do you mean to tell me—"

And the judge he answers, "I mean the other is the better dog." He takes my father's head between his hands and looks down at him most sorrowful. "The king is dead," says he. "Long live the king! Good-by, Regent," he says.

The crowd around the railings clapped their hands, and some laughed scornful, and everyone talks fast, and I start for the gate, so dizzy that I can't see my way. But my father pushes in front of me, walking very daintily, and smiling sleepy, same as he had just been waked, with his head high, and his eyes shut, looking at nobody.

So that is how I "came by my inheritance," as Miss Dorothy calls it; and just for that, though I couldn't feel where I was any different, the crowd follows me to my bench, and pats me, and coos at me, like I was a baby in a baby carriage. And the handlers have to hold 'em back so that the gentlemen from the papers can make pictures of me, and Nolan walks me up and down so proud, and the men shake their heads and says, "He certainly is the true type, he is!" And the pretty ladies ask Miss Dorothy, who sits beside me letting me lick her gloves to show the crowd what friends we is, "Aren't you afraid he'll bite you?" And Jimmy Jocks calls to me, "Didn't I tell you so? I always knew you were one of us. Blood will out, Kid; blood will out. I saw your grandfather," says he, "make his début at the Crystal Palace. But he was never the dog you are!"

After that, if I could have asked for it, there was nothing I couldn't get. You might have thought I was a show dog, and they was afeard I'd melt. If I wet my pats, Nolan gave me a hot bath and chained me to the stove; if I couldn't eat my food, being stuffed full by the cook—for I am a house dog now, and let in to lunch, whether there is visitors or not—Nolan would run to bring the vet. It was all tommyrot, as Jimmy says, but meant most kind. I couldn't scratch myself comfortable, without Nolan giving me nasty drinks, and rubbing me outside till it burnt awful; and I wasn't let to eat bones for fear of spoiling my "beautiful" mouth, what mother used to call my "punishing jaw"; and my food was cooked special on a gas stove; and Miss Dorothy gives me an overcoat, cut very stylish like the champions', to wear when we goes out carriage driving.

After the next Show, where I takes three blue ribbons, four silver cups, two medals, and brings home forty-five dollars for Nolan, they gives me a "registered" name, same as Jimmy's. Miss Dorothy wanted to call me "Regent Heir Apparent"; but I was *that* glad when Nolan says, "No; Kid don't owe nothing to his father, only to you and hisself. So, if you please, miss, we'll call him Wyndham Kid." And so they did, and you can see it on my overcoat in blue letters, and painted top of my kennel. It was all too hard to understand. For days I just sat and wondered if I was really me, and how it all come about, and why everybody was so kind. But oh, it was so good they was, for if they hadn't been I'd never have got the thing I most wished after. But, because they was kind, and not liking to deny me nothing, they gave it me, and it was more to me than anything in the world.

It came about one day when we was out driving. We was in the cart they calls the dogcart because it's the one Miss Dorothy keeps to take Jimmy and me for an airing. Nolan was up behind, and me, in my new overcoat, was sitting beside Miss Dorothy. I was admiring the view, and thinking how good it was to have a horse pull you about so that you needn't get yourself splashed and have to be washed, when I hears a dog calling loud for help, and I pricks up my ears and looks over the horse's head. And I sees something that makes me tremble down to my toes. In the road before us three big dogs was chasing a little old lady dog. She had a string to her tail, where some boys had tied a can, and she was dirty with mud and ashes, and torn most awful. She was too far done up to get away, and too old to help herself, but she was making a fight for her life, snapping her old gums savage, and dying game. All this I see in a wink, and then the three dogs pinned her down, and I can't stand it no longer, and clears the wheel and lands in the road on my head. It was my stylish overcoat done that, and I cursed it proper, but I gets my pats again quick, and makes a rush for the fighting. Behind me I hear Miss Dorothy cry: "They'll kill that old dog. Wait, take my whip. Beat them off her! The Kid can take care of himself"; and I hear Nolan fall into the road, and the horse come to a stop. The old lady dog was down, and the three was eating her vicious; but as I come up, scattering the pebbles, she hears, and thinking it's one more of them, she lifts her head, and my heart breaks open like someone had sunk his teeth in it. For, under the ashes and the dirt and the blood, I can see who it is, and I know that my mother has come back to me.

I gives a yell that throws them three dogs off their legs.

"Mother!" I cries. "I'm the Kid," I cries. "I'm coming to you. Mother, I'm coming!"

And I shoots over her at the throat of the big dog, and the other two they sinks their teeth into that stylish overcoat and tears if off me, and that sets me free, and I lets them have it. I never had so fine a fight as that! What with mother being there to see, and not having been let to mix up in no fights since I become a prize-winner, it just naturally did me good, and it wasn't three shakes before I had 'em yelping. Quick as a wink, mother she jumps in to help me, and I just laughed to see her. It was so like old times. And Nolan he made me laugh, too. He was like a hen on a bank, shaking the butt of his whip, but not daring to cut in for fear of hitting me.

"Stop it, Kid," he says, "stop it. Do you want to be all torn up?" says he. "Think of the Boston show," says he. "Think of Chicago. Think of

Danbury. Don't you never want to be a champion?" How was I to think of all them places when I had three dogs to cut up at the same time? But in a minute two of 'em begs for mercy, and mother and me lets 'em run away. The big one he ain't able to run away. Then mother and me we dances and jumps, and barks and laughs, and bites each other and rolls each other in the road. There never was two dogs so happy as we. And Nolan he whistles and calls and begs me to come to him; but I just laugh and play larks with mother.

"Now, you come with me," says I, "to my new home, and never try to run away again." And I shows her our house with the five red roofs, set on the top of the hill. But mother trembles awful, and says: "They'd never let me in such a place. Does the Viceroy live there, Kid?" says she. And I laugh at her. "No; I do," I says. "And if they won't let you live there, too, you and me will go back to the streets together, for we must never be parted no more." So we trots up the hill side by side, with Nolan trying to catch me, and Miss Dorothy laughing at him from the cart.

"The Kid's made friends with the poor old dog," says she. "Maybe he knew her long ago when he ran the streets himself. Put her in here beside me, and see if he doesn't follow."

So when I hears that I tells mother to go with Nolan and sit in the cart; but she says no—that she'd soil the pretty lady's frock; but I tells her to do as I say, and so Nolan lifts her, trembling still, into the cart, and I runs alongside, barking joyful.

When we drives into the stables I takes mother to my kennel, and tells her to go inside it and make herself at home. "Oh, but he won't let me!" says she.

"Who won't let you?" says I, keeping my eye on Nolan, and growling a bit nasty, just to show I was meaning to have my way.

"Why, Wyndham Kid," says she, looking up at the name on my kennel.

"But I'm Wyndham Kid!" says I.

"You!" cries mother. "You! Is my little Kid the great Wyndham Kid the dogs all talk about?" And at that, she being very old, and sick, and nervous, as mothers are, just drops down in the straw and weeps bitter.

Well, there ain't much more than that to tell. Miss Dorothy she settled it.

"If the Kid wants the poor old thing in the stables," says she, "let her stay.

"You see," says she, "she's a black-and-tan, and his mother was a black-and-tan, and maybe that's what makes Kid feel so friendly toward her," says she.

"Indeed, for me," says Nolan, "she can have the best there is. I'd never drive out no dog that asks for a crust nor a shelter," he says. "But what will Mr. Wyndham do?"

"He'll do what I say," says Miss Dorothy, "and if I say she's to stay, she will stay, and I say—she's to stay!"

And so mother and Nolan and me found a home. Mother was scared at first—not being used to kind people; but she was so gentle and loving that the grooms got fonder of her than of me, and tried to make me jealous by patting of her and giving her the pick of the vittles. But that was the wrong way to hurt my feelings. That's all, I think. Mother is so happy here that I tell her we ought to call it the Happy Hunting Grounds, because no one hunts you, and there is nothing to hunt; it just all comes to you. And so we live in peace, mother sleeping all day in the sun, or behind the stove in the head groom's office, being fed twice a day regular by Nolan, and all the day by the other grooms most irregular. And as for me, I go hurrying around the country to the bench shows, winning money and cups for Nolan, and taking the blue ribbons away from father.

Joyce Carol Oates is a prolific writer of fiction, poetry, drama, ⟨
with dozens of novels and hundreds of short stories to her credi
one of today's most honored writers, winning the National Book Award, the
Pushcart Prize, three O. Henry Awards, and numerous awards for lifetime
achievement. Oates lives in New Jersey, where she teaches at Princeton University and helps edit the Ontario Review. Among her books are On Boxing
(1987), First Love: A Gothic Tale (1996), and Will You Always Love Me?
(1996). Oates writes here about a talented racehorse who is injured on the
track. Her story initially appeared in Esquire and was included in The Best
American Short Stories 1985.

Joyce Carol Oates

RAVEN'S WING
(1984)

BILLY WAS AT THE MEADOWLANDS track one Saturday when the
accident happened to Raven's Wing–a three-year-old silky black colt
who was the favorite in the first race, and one of the crowd favorites generally this season. Billy hadn't placed his bet on Raven's Wing. Betting
on the 4:5 favorite held no excitement, and in any case, things were going too well for Raven's Wing, Billy felt, and his owner's luck would be
running out soon. But telling his wife about the accident the next morning Billy was surprised at how important it came to seem, how intense

his voice sounded, as if he was high, or on edge, which he was not, it was just the *telling* that worked him up, and the way Linda looked at him.

"—So there he was in the backstretch, looping around one, two, three, four horses to take the lead—he's a hard driver, Raven's Wing, doesn't let himself off easy—a little skittish at the starting gate, but then he got serious—in fact he was maybe running a little faster than he needed to run, once he got out front—then something happened, it looked like he stumbled, his hindquarters went down just a little—but he was going so fast, maybe forty miles an hour, the momentum kept him going—Jesus, it must have been three hundred feet!—the poor bastard, on three legs. Then the jockey jumped off, the other horses ran by, Raven's Wing was just sort of standing there by the rail, his head bobbing up and down. What had happened was he'd broken his left rear leg—came down too hard on it, maybe, or the hoof sunk in the dirt wrong. Just like that," Billy said. He snapped his fingers. "One minute we're looking at a million-dollar colt, the next minute—nothing."

"Wait. What do you mean, nothing?" Linda said.

"They put them down if they aren't going to race anymore."

"'Put them down'—you mean they kill them?"

"Sure. Most of the time."

"How do they kill them? Do they shoot them?"

"I doubt it, probably some kind of needle, you know, injection, poison in their bloodstream."

Linda was leaning toward him, her forehead creased. "Okay, then what happened?" she said.

"Well—an ambulance came out to the track and picked him up, there was an announcement about him breaking his leg, everybody in the stands was real quiet when they heard. Not because there was a lot of money on him either but because, you know, here's this first-class colt, a real beauty, a million-dollar horse, maybe two million, finished. Just like that."

Linda's eyelids were twitching, her mouth, she might have been going to cry, or maybe, suddenly, laugh, you couldn't predict these days. Near as Billy figured she hadn't washed her hair in more than a week and it looked like hell, she hadn't washed herself in all that time either, wore the same plaid shirt and jeans day after day, not that he'd lower himself to bring the subject up. She was staring at him, squinting. Finally she said, "How much did you lose?—you can tell me," in a breathy little voice.

"How much did *I* lose?" Billy asked. He was surprised as hell. They'd covered all this ground, hadn't they, there were certain private matters in his life, things that were none of her business, he'd explained it—her brother had explained it too—things she didn't need to know. And good reasons for her not to know. "How much did *I* lose—?"

He pushed her aside, lightly, just with the tips of his fingers, and went to the refrigerator to get a beer. It was only ten in the morning but he was thirsty and his head and back teeth ached. "Who says I lost? We were out there for five races. In fact I did pretty well, we all did, what the hell do you know about it," Billy said. He opened the beer, took his time drinking. He knew that the longer he took, the calmer he'd get and it was one of those mornings—Sunday, bells ringing, everybody's schedule off—when he didn't want to get angry. But his hand was trembling when he drew a wad of bills out of his inside coat pocket and let it fall onto the kitchen counter. "Three hundred dollars, go ahead and count it, sweetheart," he said, "you think you're so smart."

Linda stood with her knees slightly apart, her big belly straining at the flannel shirt she wore, her mouth still twitching. Even with her skin grainy and sallow, and pimples across her forehead, she looked good, she was a good-looking girl, hell, thought Billy, it was a shame, a bad deal. She said, so soft he almost couldn't hear her, "I don't think I'm so smart."

"Yeah? What?"

"I don't think I'm anything."

She was looking at the money but for some reason, maybe she was afraid, she didn't touch it. Actually Billy had won almost a thousand dollars but that was his business.

Linda was eight years younger than Billy, just twenty-four though she looked younger, blond, high-strung, skinny except for her belly (she was five, six months pregnant, Billy couldn't remember), with hollowed-out eyes, that sullen mouth. They had been married almost a year and Billy thought privately it was probably a mistake though in fact he loved her, he *liked* her, if only she didn't do so many things to spite him. If she wasn't letting herself go, letting herself get sick, strung-out, weird, just to spite him.

He'd met her through her older brother, a friend of Billy's, more or less, from high school, a guy he'd done business with and could trust. But they had had a misunderstanding the year before and no longer worked together.

Once, in bed, Linda said, "—If the man had to have it, boy, then things would be different. Things would be a lot different."

"What? A baby? How do you mean?" Billy asked. He'd been halfway asleep, he wanted to humor her, he didn't want a fight at two in the morning. "Are we talking about a baby?"

"They *wouldn't* have it, that's all."

"What?"

"The baby. Any baby."

"Jesus—that's crazy."

"Yeah? Who? Would you?" Linda said angrily. "What about your own?"

Billy had two children, both boys, from his first marriage, but as things worked out he never saw them and rarely thought about them—his wife had remarried, moved to Tampa. At one time Billy used to say that he and his ex-wife got along all right, they weren't out to slit each other's throat like some people he knew, but in fact when Billy's salary at GM Radiator had been garnisheed a few years ago he wasn't very happy; he'd gone through a bad time. So he'd quit the job, a good-paying job too, and later, when he tried to get hired back, they were already laying off men, it was rotten luck, his luck had run against him for a long time. One of the things that had driven him wild was the fact that his wife, that is his ex-wife, was said to be pregnant again, and he'd maybe be helping to support another man's kid, when he thought of it he wanted to kill somebody, anybody, but then she got married after all and it worked out and now he didn't have to see her or even think of her very much: that was the advantage of distance. But now he said, "Sure," trying to keep it all light. "What the hell, sure, it beats the Army."

"*You'd* have a baby?" Linda said. Now she was sitting up, leaning over him, her hair in her face, her eyes showing a rim of white above the iris. "Oh don't hand me that. Oh please."

"Sure. If you wanted me to."

"I'm asking about *you*—would *you* want to?"

They had been out drinking much of the evening and Linda was groggy but skittish, on edge, her face very pale and giving off a queer damp heat. The way she was grinning, Billy didn't want to pursue the subject.

"How about *you*, I said," she said, jabbing him with her elbow, "—I'm talking about *you*."

"I don't know what the hell we are talking about."

"You do know."

"What—I don't."

"You do. You do. Don't hand me such crap."

When he and Linda first started going together they'd made love all the time, like crazy, it was such a relief (so Billy told himself) to be out from under that other bitch, but now, married only a year, with Linda dragging around the apartment sick and angry and sometimes talking to herself, pretending she didn't know Billy could hear, now everything had changed, he couldn't predict whether she'd be up or down, high or low, very low, hitting bottom, scaring him with her talk about killing herself (her crazy mother had tried *that* a few times, it probably ran in the family) or getting an abortion (but wasn't it too late, her stomach that size, for an abortion), he never knew when he opened the door what he'd be walking into. She didn't change her clothes, including her underwear, for a week at a time, she didn't wash her hair, she'd had a tight permanent that sprang out around her head but turned flat, matted, blowsy if it wasn't shampooed, he knew she was ruining her looks to spite him but she claimed (shouting, crying, punching her own thighs with her fists) that she just *forgot* about things like that, she had more important things to think about.

One day, a few months before, Billy had caught sight of this great-looking girl out on the street, coat with a fox-fur collar like the one he'd bought for Linda, high-heeled boots like Linda's, blond hair, wild springy curls like a model, frizzed, airy, her head high and her walk fast, almost like strutting—she knew she was being watched, and not just by Billy—and then she turned and it *was* Linda, his own wife, she'd washed her hair and fixed herself up, red lipstick, even eye makeup–he'd just stood there staring, it took him by such surprise. But then the next week she was back to lying around the apartment feeling sorry for herself, sullen and heavy-hearted, sick to her stomach even if she hadn't eaten anything.

The worst of the deal was, he and her brother had had their misunderstanding and didn't do business any longer. When Billy got drunk he had the vague idea that he was getting stuck again with another guy's baby.

The racing news was, Raven's Wing hadn't been killed after all.

It *was* news, people were talking about it, Billy even read about it in the newspaper, an operation on the colt's leg estimated to cost in the six-figure range, a famous veterinary surgeon the owner was flying in from Dallas, and there was a photograph (it somehow frightened Billy, that photograph) of Raven's Wing lying on his side, anesthetized, strapped down, being operated on like a human being. The *size* of a horse–that always impressed Billy.

Other owners had their opinions, was it worth it or not, other trainers, veterinarians, but Raven's Wing's owner wanted to save his life, the colt wasn't just any horse (the owner said) he was the most beautiful horse they'd ever reared on their farm. He was insured for $600,000 and the insurance company had granted permission for the horse to be destroyed but still the owner wanted to save his life. "They wouldn't do that for a human being," Linda said when Billy told her.

"Well," Billy said, irritated at her response, "–this isn't a human being, it's a first-class horse."

"Jesus, a *horse* operated on," Linda said, laughing, "and he isn't even going to run again, you said? How much is all this going to cost?"

"People like that, they don't care about money. They have it, they spend it on what matters," Billy said. "It's a frame of reference you don't know shit about."

"Then what?"

"What?"

"After the operation?"

"After the operation, if it works, then he's turned out to stud," Billy said. "You know what that is, huh?" he said, poking her in the breast.

"Just a minute. The horse is worth that much?"

"A first-class horse is worth a million dollars, I told you, maybe more. Two million. These people take things *seriously*."

"Two million dollars for an animal—?" Linda said slowly. She sounded dazed, disoriented, as if the fact was only now sinking in, but what *was* the fact, what did it mean? "Hey I think that's *sick*."

"I told you, Linda, it's a frame of reference you don't know shit about."

"That's right. I don't."

She was making such a childish ugly face at him, drawing her lips back from her teeth, Billy lost control and shoved her against the edge of the kitchen table, and she slapped him hard, on the side of the nose, and it was all Billy could do to stop right there, just *stop*, not give it back to the bitch like she deserved. He knew, once he got started with this one, it might be the end. She might not be able to pick herself up from the floor when he was done.

Billy asked around, and there was this contact of his named Kellerman, and Kellerman was an old friend of Raven's Wing's trainer, and he fixed it up so that he and Billy could drive out to the owner's farm in Pennsylvania, so that Billy could see the horse, Billy just wanted to *see* the horse, it was always at the back of his mind these days.

The weather was cold, the sky a hard icy blue, the kind of day that made Billy feel shaky, things were so bright, so vivid, you could see something weird and beautiful anywhere you looked. His head ached, he was so edgy, his damn back teeth, he chewed on Bufferin, he and Kellerman drank beer out of cans, tossed the cans away on the road. Kellerman said horse people like these were the real thing, look at this layout, and not even counting Raven's Wing they had a stable worth millions, a Preakness winner, a second-place Kentucky Derby finisher, but was the money even in horses?—hell no it was in some investments or something. That was how rich people worked.

In the stable, at Raven's Wing's stall, Billy hung over the partition and looked at him for a long time, just looked. Kellerman and the trainer were talking but Billy just looked.

The size of the horse, that was one of the things, and the head, the big rounded eyes, ears pricked forward, tail switching, here was Raven's Wing looking at last at him, did he maybe recognize Billy, did he maybe sense who Billy was? Billy extended a hand to him, whispering his name. Hey Raven's Wing. Hey.

The size, and the silky sheen of the coat, the jet-black coat, that skittish air, head bobbing, teeth bared, Billy could feel his warm breath, Billy sucked in the strong *smell*—horse manure, horse piss, sweat, hay, mash, and what was he drinking?—apple juice, the trainer said. *Apple juice,* Christ! Gallons and gallons of it. Did he have his appetite back, Billy asked, but it was obvious the colt did, he was eating steadily, chomping hay, eyeing Billy as if Billy was—was what?—just the man he wanted to see. The man who'd driven a hundred miles to see him.

Both his rear legs were in casts, the veterinarian had taken a bone graft from the good leg, and his weight was down—1,130 pounds to 880—his ribs showing through the silky coat but Jesus did he look good, Jesus this was the real thing wasn't it?—Billy's heart beat fast as if he'd been popping pills, he wished to hell Linda was here, yeah the bitch should see *this,* it'd shut her up for a while.

Raven's Wing was getting his temper back, the trainer said, which was a good thing, it showed he was mending, but he still wasn't 99 percent in the clear, maybe they didn't know how easy it was for horses to get sick—colic, pneumonia, all kinds of viruses, infections. Even the good leg had gone bad for a while, paralyzed, and they'd had to have two operations, a six-hour and a four-hour, the owner had to sign a release, they'd put him down right on the operating table if things looked too bad. But he pulled through, his muscle tone was improving every day, there he was, fiery little bastard, watch out or he'll nip you—a steel plate, steel wire, a dozen screws in his leg, and him not knowing a thing. The way the bone was broken it wasn't *broken,* the trainer told them, it was smashed, like somebody had gone after it with a sledgehammer.

"So he's going to make it," Billy said, not quite listening. "Hey yeah. *You.* You're going to make it, huh."

He and Kellerman were at the stall maybe forty-five minutes and the place was busy, busier than Billy would have thought, it rubbed him the wrong way that so many people were around when he'd had the idea he and Kellerman would be the only ones. But it turned out that Raven's Wing always had visitors. He even got mail. (This Billy snorted to hear— a horse gets *mail?*) People took away souvenirs if they could, good-luck things, hairs from his mane, his tail, that sort of thing, or else they wanted to feed him by hand: there was a lot of that, they had to be watched.

Before they left Billy leaned over as far as he could, just wanting to stroke Raven's Wing's side, and two things happened fast: the horse snorted, stamped, lunged at his hand; and the trainer pulled Billy back.

"Hey I told you," he said. "This is a dangerous animal."

"He likes me," Billy said. "He wasn't going to bite hard."

"Yeah?—sometimes he does. They can bite damn hard."

"He wasn't going to bite actually *hard*," Billy said.

Three dozen blue snakeskin wallets (Venezuelan), almost two dozen up-scale watches (Swiss, German)—chronographs, water-resistant, self-winding, calendar, ultrathin, quartz, and gold tone—and a pair of pierced earrings, gold and pearl, delicate, Billy thought, as a snowflake. He gave the earrings to Linda to surprise her and watched her put them in, it amazed him how quickly she could take out earrings and slip in new ones, position the tiny wires exactly in place, he knew it was a trick he could never do if he was a woman. It made him shiver, it excited him, just to watch.

Linda never said, "Hey where'd you get *these*," the way his first wife used to, giving him that slow wide wet smile she thought turned him on. (Actually it had turned him on, for a while. Two, three years.)

Linda never said much of anything except thank you in her little-girl breathy voice, if she happened to be in the mood for thanking.

One morning a few weeks later Linda, in her bathrobe, came slowly out of the bedroom into the kitchen, squinting at something she held in the air, at eye level. "This looks like somebody's hair, what is it, Indian hair?— it's all black and stiff," she said. Billy was on the telephone so he had an excuse not to give her his fullest attention at the moment. He might be getting ready to be angry, he might be embarrassed, his nerves were always bad this time of day. Linda leaned up against him, swaying a little in her preoccupation, exuding heat, her bare feet planted apart on the linoleum floor. She liked to poke at him with her belly, she had a new habit of standing close.

Billy kept on with his conversation, it was in fact an important conversation, and Linda wound the several black hairs around her forearm, making a little bracelet, so tight the flesh started to turn white, didn't it hurt?—her forehead creased in concentration, her breath warm and damp against his neck.

Here is a story of bullfighting, with its strange mixture of grandeur and cruelty. An American named John Harned becomes mentally unhinged while watching a bullfight in Quito, Ecuador, and leaves his own trail of devastation behind him. Author Jack London (1876–1916) is one of America's best-loved novelists and short story writers. His classic novels are The Call of the Wild *(1903),* The Sea Wolf *(1904), and* White Fang *(1906).*

Jack London

THE MADNESS OF JOHN HARNED (1913)

I TELL THIS FOR A FACT. It happened in the bull-ring at Quito. I sat in the box with John Harned, and with Maria Valenzuela, and with Luis Cervallos. I saw it happen. I saw it all from first to last. I was on the steamer *Ecuadore* from Panama to Guayaquil. Maria Valenzuela is my cousin. I have known her always. She is very beautiful. I am a Spaniard—an Ecuadoriano, true, but I am descended from Pedro Patino, who was one of Pizarro's captains. They were brave men. They were heroes. Did not Pizarro lead three hundred and fifty Spanish cavaliers and four thousand Indians into the far Cordilleras in search of treasure? And

did not all the four thousand Indians and three hundred of the brave cavaliers die on that vain quest? But Pedro Patino did not die. He it was that
lived to found the family of the Patino. I am Ecuadoriano, true, but I am
Spanish. I am Manuel de Jesus Patino. I own many haciendas, and ten
thousand Indians are my slaves, though the law says they are free men
who work by freedom of contract. The law is a funny thing. We Ecuadorianos laugh at it. It is our law. We make it for ourselves. I am Manuel de
Jesus Patino. Remember that name. It will be written some day in history. There are revolutions in Ecuador. We call them elections. It is a
good joke is it not?—what you call a pun?

John Harned was an American. I met him first at the Tivoli hotel in
Panama. He had much money—this I have heard. He was going to Lima,
but he met Maria Valenzuela in the Tivoli hotel. Maria Valenzuela is my
cousin, and she is beautiful. It is true, she is the most beautiful woman
in Ecuador. But also is she most beautiful in every country—in Paris, in
Madrid, in New York, in Vienna. Always do all men look at her, and John
Harned looked long at her at Panama. He loved her, that I know for a
fact. She was Ecuadoriano, true—but she was of all countries; she was of
all the world. She spoke many languages. She sang—ah! like an artiste.
Her smile—wonderful, divine. Her eyes—ah! have I not seen men look in
her eyes? They were what you English call amazing. They were promises
of paradise. Men drowned themselves in her eyes.

Maria Valenzuela was rich—richer than I, who am accounted very rich
in Ecuador. But John Harned did not care for her money. He had a
heart—a funny heart. He was a fool. He did not go to Lima. He left the
steamer at Guayaquil and followed her to Quito. She was coming home
from Europe and other places. I do not see what she found in him, but
she liked him. This I know for a fact, else he would not have followed
her to Quito. She asked him to come. Well do I remember the occasion.
She said:

"Come to Quito and I will show you the bull-fight—brave, clever,
magnificent!"

But he said: "I go to Lima, not Quito. Such is my passage engaged on
the steamer."

"You travel for pleasure—no?" said Maria Valenzuela; and she looked at him as only Maria Valenzuela could look, her eyes warm with the promise.

And he came. No; he did not come for the bull-fight. He came because of what he had seen in her eyes. Women like Maria Valenzuela are born once in a hundred years. They are of no country and no time. They are what you call universal. They are goddesses. Men fall down at their feet. They play with men and run them through their pretty fingers like sand. Cleopatra was such a woman they say; and so was Circe. She turned men into swine. Ha! ha! It is true—no?

It all came about because Maria Valenzuela said:

"You English people are—what shall I say?—savage—no? You prize-fight. Two men hit each other with their fists till their eyes are blinded and their noses are broken. Hideous! And the other men who look on cry out loudly and are made glad. It is barbarous—no?"

"But they are men," said John Harned; "and they prize-fight out of desire. No one makes them prize-fight. They do it because they desire it more than anything else in the world."

Maria Valenzuela—there was scorn in her smile as she said:

"They kill each other often—is it not so? I have read it in the papers."

"But the bull," said John Harned. "The bull is killed many times in the bull-fight, and the bull does not come into the ring out of desire. It is not fair to the bull. He is compelled to fight. But the man in the prize-fight—no; he is not compelled."

"He is the more brute therefore," said Maria Valenzuela. "He is savage. He is primitive. He is animal. He strikes with his paws like a bear from a cave, and he is ferocious. But the bull-fight—ah! You have not seen the bull-fight—no? The toreador is clever. He must have skill. He is modern. He is romantic. He is only a man, soft and tender, and he faces the wild bull in conflict. And he kills with a sword, a slender sword, with one thrust, so, to the heart of the great beast. It is delicious. It makes the heart beat to behold—the small man, the great beast, the wide level sand, the thousands that look on without breath; the great beast rushes to the attack, the small man stands like a statue; he does not move, he is unafraid, and in his hand is the slender sword flashing like silver in the sun; nearer and nearer rushes the great beast with its sharp horns, the man does not move, and then–so–the sword flashes, the thrust is made, to the heart, to the hilt, the bull falls to the sand and is dead, and the man is unhurt. It is brave. It is magnificent! Ah!–I could love the toreador. But the man of the prize-fight–he is the brute, the human beast, the savage primitive, the maniac that receives many blows in his stupid face and rejoices. Come to Quito and I will show you the brave sport, the sport of men, the toreador and the bull."

But John Harned did not go to Quito for the bull-fight. He went because of Maria Valenzuela. He was a large man, more broad of shoulder than we Ecuadorianos, more tall, more heavy of limb and bone. True, he was larger even than most men of his own race. His eyes were blue, though I have seen them gray, and, sometimes, like cold steel. His features were large, too–not delicate like ours, and his jaw was very strong to look at. Also, his face was smooth-shaven like a priest's. Why should a man feel shame for the hair on his face? Did not God put it there? Yes, I believe in God. I am not a pagan like many of you English. God is good. He made me an Ecuadoriano with ten thousand slaves. And when I die I shall go to God. Yes, the priests are right.

But John Harned. He was a quiet man. He talked always in a low voice, and he never moved his hands when he talked. One would have thought his heart was a piece of ice; yet did he have a streak of warm in his blood, for he followed Maria Valenzuela to Quito. Also, and for all that he talked low without moving his hands, he was an animal, as you shall see–the beast primitive, the stupid, ferocious savage of the long ago that dressed in wild skins and lived in the caves along with the bears and wolves.

Luis Cervallos is my friend, the best of Ecuadorianos. He owns three cacao plantations at Naranjito and Chobo. At Milagro is his big sugar plantation. He has large haciendas at Ambato and Latacunga, and down the coast is he interested in oil-wells. Also has he spent much money in planting rubber along the Guayas. He is modern, like the Yankee; and, like the Yankee, full of business. He has much money, but it is in many ventures, and ever he needs more money for new ventures and for the old ones. He has been everywhere and seen everything. When he was a very young man he was in the Yankee military academy what you call West Point. There was trouble. He was made to resign. He does not like Americans. But he did like Maria Valenzuela, who was of his own country. Also, he needed her money for his ventures and for his gold mine in Eastern Ecuador where the painted Indians live. I was his friend. It was my desire that he should marry Maria Valenzuela. Further, much of my money had I invested in his ventures, more so in his gold mine which was very rich but which first required the expense of much money before it would yield forth its riches. If Luis Cervallos married Maria Valenzuela I should have more money very immediately.

But John Harned followed Maria Valenzuela to Quito, and it was quickly clear to us—to Luis Cervallos and me—that she looked upon John Harned with great kindness. It is said that a woman will have her will, but this is a case not in point, for Maria Valenzuela did not have her will—at least not with John Harned. Perhaps it would all have happened as it did, even if Luis Cervallos and I had not sat in the box that day at the bull-ring in Quito. But this I know: we *did* sit in the box that day. And I shall tell you what happened.

The four of us were in the one box, guests of Luis Cervallos. I was next to the Presidente's box. On the other side was the box of General José Eliceo Salazar. With him were Joaquin Endara and Urcisino Castillo, both generals, and Colonel Jacinto Fierro and Captain Baltazar de Echeverria. Only Luis Cervallos had the position and the influence to get that box next to the Presidente. I know for a fact that the Presidente himself expressed the desire to the management that Luis Cervallos should have that box.

The band finished playing the national hymn of Ecuador. The procession of the toreadors was over. The Presidente nodded to begin. The bugles blew, and the bull dashed in—you know the way, excited, bewildered, the darts in its shoulder burning like fire, itself seeking madly whatever enemy to destroy. The toreadors hid behind their shelters and waited. Suddenly they appeared forth, the capadors, five of them, from every side, their colored capes flinging wide. The bull paused at sight of such a generosity of enemies, unable in his own mind to know which to attack. Then advanced one of the capadores alone to meet the bull. The bull was very angry. With its fore-legs it pawed the sand of the arena till the dust rose all about it. Then it charged, with lowered head, straight for the lone capador.

It is always of interest, the first charge of the first bull. After a time it is natural that one should grow tired, a trifle, that the keenness should lose its edge. But that first charge of the first bull! John Harned was seeing it for the first time, and he could not escape the excitement—the sight of the man, armed only with a piece of cloth, and of the bull rushing upon him across the sand with sharp horns, widespreading.

"See!" cried Maria Valenzuela. "Is it not superb?"

John Harned nodded, but did not look at her. His eyes were sparkling, and they were only for the bull-ring. The capador stepped to the side, with a twirl of the cape eluding the bull and spreading the cape on his own shoulders.

"What do you think?" asked Maria Valenzuela. "Is it not a—what-you-call—sporting proposition—no?"

"It is certainly," said John Harned. "It is very clever."

She clapped her hands with delight. They were little hands. The audience applauded. The bull turned and came back. Again the capadore eluded him, throwing the cape on his shoulders, and again the audience applauded. Three times did this happen. The capadore was very excellent. Then he retired, and the other capadore played with the bull. After that they placed the banderillos in the bull, in the shoulders, on each side of the back-bone, two at a time. Then stepped forward Ordonez, the chief matador, with the long sword and the scarlet cape. The bugles blew for the death. He is not so good as Matestini. Still he is good, and with one thrust he drove the sword into the heart, and the bull doubled his legs under him and lay down and died. It was a pretty thrust, clean and sure; and there was much applause, and many of the common people threw their hats into the ring. Maria Valenzuela clapped her hands with the rest, and John Harned, whose cold heart was not touched by the event, looked at her with curiosity.

"You like it?" he asked.

"Always," she said, still clapping her hands.

"From a little girl," said Luis Cervallos. "I remember her first fight. She was four years old. She sat with her mother, and just like now she clapped her hands. She is a proper Spanish woman."

"You have seen it," said Maria Valenzuela to John Harned, as they fastened the mules to the dead bull and dragged it out. "You have seen the bull-fight and you like it—no? What do you think?"

"I think the bull had no chance," he said. "The bull was doomed from the first. The issue was not in doubt. Every one knew, before the bull entered the ring, that it was to die. To be a sporting proposition, the issue must be in doubt. It was one stupid bull who had never fought a man against five wise men who had fought many bulls. It could be possibly a little bit fair if it were one man against one bull."

"Or one man against five bulls," said Maria Valenzuela; and we all laughed, and Luis Cervallos laughed loudest.

"Yes," said John Harned, "against five bulls, and the man, like the bulls, never in the bull-ring before—a man like yourself, Senor Cervallos."

"Yet we Spanish like the bull-fight," said Luis Cervallos; and I hear the devil was whispering then in his ear, telling him to do that which I shall relate.

"Then must it be a cultivated taste," John Harned made answer. "We kill bulls by the thousand every day in Chicago, yet no one cares to pay admittance to see."

"That is butchery," said I; "but this—ah, this is an art. It is delicate. It is fine. It is rare."

"Not always," said Luis Cervallos. "I have seen clumsy matadors, and I tell you it is not nice."

He shuddered, and his face betrayed such what-you-call disgust, that I knew, then, that the devil was whispering and that he was beginning to play a part.

"Senor Harned may be right," said Luis Cervallos. "It may not be fair to the bull. For is it not known to all of us that for twenty-four hours the bull is given no water, and that immediately before the fight he is permitted to drink his fill?"

"And he comes into the ring heavy with water?" said John Harned quickly; and I saw that his eyes were very gray and very sharp and very cold.

"It is necessary for the sport," said Luis Cervallos. "Would you see the bull so strong that he would kill the toreadors?"

"I would that he had a fighting chance," said John Harned, facing the ring to see the second bull come in.

It was not a good bull. It was frightened. It ran around the ring in search of a way to get out. The capadors stepped forth and flared their capes, but he refused to charge upon them.

"It is a stupid bull," said Maria Valenzuela.

"I beg pardon," said John Harned; "but it would seem to me a wise bull. He knows he must not fight man. See! He smells death there in the ring."

True. The bull, pausing where the last one had died, was smelling the wet sand and snorting. And he ran around the ring, with raised head, looking at the faces of the thousands that hissed him, that threw orange-peel at him and called him names. But the smell of blood decided him, and he charged a capador, so without warning that the man just escaped. He dropped his cape and dodged into the shelter. The bull struck the wall of the ring with a crash. And John Harned said, in a quiet voice, as though he talked to himself:

"I will give one thousand sucres to the lazar-house of Quito if a bull kills a man this day."

"You like bulls?" said Maria Valenzuela with a smile.

"I like such men less," said John Harned. "A toreador is not a brave man. He surely cannot be a brave man. See, the bull's tongue is already out. He is tired and he has not yet begun."

"It is the water," said Luis Cervallos.

"Yes, it is the water," said John Harned. "Would it not be safer to ham-string the bull before he comes on?"

Maria Valenzuela was made angry by this sneer in John Harned's words. But Luis Cervallos smiled so that only I could see him, and then it broke upon my mind surely the game he was playing. He and I were to be banderilleros. The big American bull was there in the box with us.

We were to stick the darts in him till he became angry, and then there might be no marriage with Maria Valenzuela. It was a good sport. And the spirit of bull-fighters was in our blood.

The bull was now angry and excited. The capadors had great game with him. He was very quick, and sometimes he turned with such sharpness that his hind legs lost their footing and he plowed the sand with his quarter. But he charged always the flung capes and committed no harm.

"He has no chance," said John Harned. "He is fighting wind."

"He thinks the cape is his enemy," explained Maria Valenzuela. "See how cleverly the capador deceives him."

"It is his nature to be deceived," said John Harned. "Wherefore he is doomed to fight wind. The toreadors know it, the audience knows it, you know it, I know it—we all know from the first that he will fight wind. He only does not know it. It is his stupid beast-nature. He has no chance."

"It is very simple," said Luis Cervallos. "The bull shuts his eyes when he charges. Therefore—"

"The man steps out of the way and the bull rushes by," John Harned interrupted.

"Yes," said Luis Cervallos; "that is it. The bull shuts his eyes, and the man knows it."

"But cows do not shut their eyes," said John Harned. "I know a cow at home that is a Jersey and gives milk, that would whip the whole gang of them."

"But the toreadors do not fight cows," said I.

"They are afraid to fight cows," said John Harned.

"Yes," said Luis Cervallos; "they are afraid to fight cows. There would be no sport in killing toreadors."

"There would be some sport," said John Harned, "if a toreador were killed once in a while. When I become an old man, and mayhap a cripple, and should I need to make a living and be unable to do hard work, then would I become a bull-fighter. It is a light vocation for elderly gentlemen and pensioners."

"But see!" said Maria Valenzuela, as the bull charged bravely and the capador eluded it with a fling of his cape. "It requires skill so to avoid the beast."

"True," said John Harned. "But believe me, it requires a thousand times more skill to avoid the many and quick punches of a prize-fighter who keeps his eyes open and strikes with intelligence. Furthermore, this bull does not want to fight. Behold, he runs away."

It was not a good bull, for again it ran around the ring, seeking to find a way out.

"Yes, these bulls are sometimes the most dangerous," said Luis Cervallos. "It can never be known what they will do next. They are wise. They are half cow. The bull-fighters never like them.—See! He has turned!"

Once again, baffled and made angry by the walls of the ring that would not let him out, the bull was attacking his enemies valiantly.

"His tongue is hanging out," said John Harned. "First, they fill him with water. Then they tire him out, one man and then another, persuading him to exhaust himself by fighting wind. While some tire him, others rest. But the bull they never let rest. Afterward, when he is quite tired and no longer quick, the matador sticks the sword into him."

The time had now come for the banderillos. Three times one of the fighters endeavored to place the darts, and three times did he fail. He but stung the bull and maddened it. The banderillos must go in, you know, two at a time, into the shoulders, on each side the backbone and close to it. If but one be placed, it is a failure. The crowd hissed and called for Ordonez. And then Ordonez did a great thing. Four times he stood forth, and four times, at the first attempt, he stuck in the banderillos, so that eight of them, well placed, stood out of the back of the bull at one time. The crowd went mad, and a rain of hats and money fell upon the sand of the ring.

And just then the bull charged unexpectedly one of the capadors. The man slipped and lost his head. The bull caught him—fortunately, between his wide horns. And while the audience watched, breathless and silent, John Harned stood up and yelled with gladness. Alone, in that hush of all of us, John Harned yelled. And he yelled for the bull. As you see yourself, John Harned wanted the man killed. His was a brutal heart. This bad conduct made those angry that sat in the box of General Salazar, and they cried out against John Harned. And Urcisino Castillo told him to his face that he was a dog of a Gringo and other things. Only it was in Spanish, and John Harned did not understand. He stood and yelled, perhaps for the time of ten seconds, when the bull was enticed into charging the other capadors and the man arose unhurt.

"The bull has no chance," John Harned said with sadness as he sat down. "The man was uninjured. They fooled the bull away from him." Then he turned to Maria Valenzuela and said: "I beg your pardon. I was excited."

She smiled and in reproof tapped his arm with her fan.

"It is your first bull-fight," she said. "After you have seen more you will not cry for the death of the man. You Americans, you see, are more brutal than we. It is because of your prize-fighting. We come only to see the bull killed."

"But I would the bull had some chance," he answered. "Doubtless, in time, I shall cease to be annoyed by the men who take advantage of the bull."

The bugles blew for the death. Ordonez stood forth with the sword and the scarlet cloth. But the bull had changed again, and did not want to fight. Ordonez stamped his foot in the sand, and cried out, and waved the scarlet cloth. Then the bull charged, but without heart. There was no weight to the charge. It was a poor thrust. The sword struck a bone and bent. Ordonez took a fresh sword. The bull, again stung to fight, charged once more. Five times Ordonez essayed the thrust, and each time the sword went part way in or struck the bone. The sixth time, the sword went in to the hilt. But it was a bad thrust. The sword missed the heart and stuck out half a yard through the ribs on the opposite side. The audience hissed the matador. I glanced at John Harned. He sat silent, without movement; but I could see his teeth were set, and his hands were clenched tight on the railing of the box.

All fight was now out of the bull, and, though it was no vital thrust, he trotted lamely what of the sword that stuck through him, in one side and out the other. He ran away from the matador and the capadors, and circled the edge of the ring, looking up at the many faces.

"He is saying: 'For God's sake let me out of this; I don't want to fight,'" said John Harned.

That was all. He said no more, but sat and watched, though sometimes he looked sideways at Maria Valenzuela to see how she took it. She was angry with the matador. He was awkward, and she had desired a clever exhibition.

The bull was now very tired, and weak from loss of blood, though far from dying. He walked slowly around the wall of the ring, seeking a way out. He would not charge. He had had enough. But he must be killed. There is a place, in the neck of a bull behind the horns, where the cord of the spine is unprotected and where a short stab will immediately kill. Ordonez stepped in front of the bull and lowered his scarlet cloth to the ground. The bull would not charge. He stood still and smelled the cloth, lowering his head to do so. Ordonez stabbed between the horns at the spot in the neck. The bull jerked his head up. The stab had missed. Then the bull watched the sword. When Ordonez moved the cloth on the ground, the bull forgot the sword and lowered his head to smell the cloth. Again Ordonez stabbed, and again he failed. He tried many times. It was stupid. And John Harned said nothing. At last a stab went home, and the bull fell to the sand, dead immediately, and the mules were made fast and he was dragged out.

"The Gringos say it is a cruel sport—no?" said Luis Cervallos. "That it is not humane. That it is bad for the bull. No?"

"No," said John Harned. "The bull does not count for much. It is bad for those that look on. It is degrading to those that look on. It teaches them to delight in animal suffering. It is cowardly for five men to fight one stupid bull. Therefore those that look on learn to be cowards. The bull dies, but those that look on live and the lesson is learned. The bravery of men is not nourished by scenes of cowardice."

Maria Valenzuela said nothing. Neither did she look at him. But she heard every word and her cheeks were white with anger. She looked out across the ring and fanned herself, but I saw that her hand trembled. Nor did John Harned look at her. He went on as though she were not there. He, too, was angry, coldly angry.

"It is the cowardly sport of a cowardly people," he said.

"Ah," said Luis Cervallos softly, "you think you understand us."

"I understand now the Spanish Inquisition," said John Harned. "It must have been more delightful than bull-fighting."

Luis Cervallos smiled but said nothing. He glanced at Maria Valenzuela, and knew that the bull-fight in the box was won. Never would she have further to do with the Gringo who spoke such words. But neither Luis Cervallos nor I was prepared for the outcome of the day. I fear we do not understand the Gringos. How were we to know that John Harned, who was so coldly angry, should go suddenly mad? But mad he did go, as you shall see. The bull did not count for much—he said so himself. Then why should the horse count for so much? That I cannot understand. The mind of John Harned lacked logic. That is the only explanation.

"It is not usual to have horses in the bull-ring at Quito," said Luis Cervallos, looking up from the program. "In Spain they always have them. But to-day, by special permission we shall have them. When the next bull comes on there will be horses and picadors—you know, the men who carry lances and ride the horses."

"The bull is doomed from the first," said John Harned. "Are the horses then likewise doomed?"

"They are blindfolded so that they may not see the bull," said Luis Cervallos. "I have seen many horses killed. It is a brave sight."

"I have seen the bull slaughtered," said John Harned. "I will now see the horse slaughtered, so that I may understand more fully the fine points of this noble sport."

"They are old horses," said Luis Cervallos, "that are not good for anything else."

"I see," said John Harned.

The third bull came on, and soon against it were both capadors and picadors. One picador took his stand directly below us. I agree, it was a thin and aged horse he rode, a bag of bones covered with mangy hide.

"It is a marvel that the poor brute can hold up the weight of the rider," said John Harned. "And now that the horse fights the bull, what weapons has it?"

"The horse does not fight the bull," said Luis Cervallos.

"Oh," said John Harned, "then is the horse there to be gored? That must be why it is blindfolded, so that it shall not see the bull coming to gore it."

"Not quite so," said I. "The lance of the picador is to keep the bull from goring the horse."

"Then are horses rarely gored?" asked John Harned.

"No," said Luis Cervallos. "I have seen, at Seville, eighteen horses killed in one day, and the people clamored for more horses."

"Were they blindfolded like this horse?" asked John Harned.

"Yes," said Luis Cervallos.

After that we talked no more, but watched the fight. And John Harned was going mad all the time, and we did not know. The bull refused to charge the horse. And the horse stood still, and because it could not see it did not know that the capadors were trying to make the bull charge upon it. The capadors teased the bull with their capes, and when it charged them they ran toward the horse and into their shelters. At last the bull was well angry, and it saw the horse before it.

"The horse does not know, the horse does not know," John Harned whispered like to himself, unaware that he voiced his thought aloud.

The bull charged, and of course the horse knew nothing till the picador failed and the horse found himself impaled on the bull's horns from beneath. The bull was magnificently strong. The sight of its strength was splendid to see. It lifted the horse clear into the air; and as the horse fell to its side on the ground the picador landed on his feet and escaped, while the capadors lured the bull away. The horse was emptied of its essential organs. Yet did it rise to its feet screaming. It was the scream of the horse that did it, that made John Harned completely mad; for he, too, started to rise to his feet. I heard him curse low and deep. He never took his eyes from the horse, which, still screaming, strove to run, but fell down instead and rolled on its back so that all its four legs were kicking in the air. Then the bull charged it and gored it again and again until it was dead.

John Harned was now on his feet. His eyes were no longer cold like steel. They were blue flames. He looked at Maria Valenzuela, and she looked at him, and in his face was a great loathing. The moment of his madness was upon him. Everybody was looking, now that the horse was dead; and John Harned was a large man and easy to be seen.

"Sit down," said Luis Cervallos, "or you will make a fool out of yourself."

John Harned replied nothing. He struck out his fist. He smote Luis Cervallos in the face so that he fell like a dead man across the chairs and did not rise again. He saw nothing of what followed. But I saw much. Urcisino Castillo, leaning forward from the next box, with his cane struck John Harned full across the face. And John Harned smote him with his fist so that in falling he overthrew General Salazar. John Harned was now in what-you-call Berserker rage—no? The beast primitive in him was loose and roaring—the beast primitive of the holes and caves of the long ago.

"You came for a bull-fight," I heard him say, "and by God I'll show you a man-fight!"

It was a fight. The soldiers guarding the Presidente's box leaped across, but from one of them he took a rifle and beat them on their heads with it. From the other box Colonel Jacinto Fierro was shooting at him with a revolver. The first shot killed a soldier. This I know for a fact. I saw it. But the second shot struck John Harned in the side. Whereupon he swore, and with a lunge drove the bayonet of his rifle into Colonel Jacinto Fierro's body. It was horrible to behold. The Americans and the English are a brutal race. They sneer at our bull-fighting, yet do they delight in the shedding of blood. More men were killed that day because of John Harned than were ever killed in all the history of the bull-ring of Quito, yes, and of Guayaquil and all Ecuador.

It was the scream of the horse that did it. Yet why did not John Harned go mad when the bull was killed? A beast is a beast, be it bull or horse. John Harned was mad. There is no other explanation. He was blood-mad, a beast himself. I leave it to your judgment. Which is worse—the goring of the horse by the bull or the goring of Colonel Jacinto Fierro by the bayonet in the hands of John Harned? And John Harned gored others with that bayonet. He was full of devils. He fought with many bullets in him, and he was hard to kill. And Maria Valenzuela was a brave woman. Unlike the other women, she did not cry out nor faint. She sat still in her box, gazing out across the bull-ring. Her face was white and she fanned herself, but she never looked around.

From all sides came the soldiers and officers and the common people bravely to subdue the mad Gringo. It is true—the cry went up from the crowd to kill all the Gringos. It is an old cry in Latin-American countries, what of the dislike for the Gringos and their uncouth ways. It is true, the cry went up. But the brave Ecuadorianos killed only John Harned, and first he killed seven of them. Besides, there were many hurt. I have seen many bull-fights, but never have I seen anything so abominable as the scene in the boxes when the fight was over. It was like a field of battle. The dead lay around everywhere, while the wounded sobbed and groaned and some of them died. One man, whom John Harned had thrust through the belly with the bayonet, clutched at himself with both his hands and screamed. I tell you for a fact it was more terrible than the screaming of a thousand horses.

No, Maria Valenzuela did not marry Luis Cervallos. I am sorry for that. He was my friend, and much of my money was invested in his ventures. It was five weeks before the surgeons took the bandages from his face. And there is a scar there to this day, on the cheek, under the eye. Yet John Harned struck him but once and struck him only with his naked fist. Maria Valenzuela is in Austria now. It is said she is to marry an Arch-Duke or some high nobleman. I do not know. I think she liked John Harned before he followed her to Quito to see the bull-fight. But why the horse? That is what I desire to know. Why should he watch the bull and say that it did not count, and then go immediately and most horribly mad because a horse screamed? There is no understanding the Gringos. They are barbarians.

Along with Ring Lardner, H. C. Witwer was one of the great early fiction writers on sports. His book The Leather Pushers *was published the year after this story was written for* Collier's. *Witwer's writing style is similar to that of Lardner and Damon Runyon, especially in his use of colorful names like Cockeyed Egan, One-Punch Loughlin, and Dummy Carney. Witwer authored several excellent boxing stories, written in a fractured jargon to provide realism and humor. The narrator of this story is a conniving but lovable boxing promoter.*

H. C. Witwer

THE LEATHER PUSHERS (1920)

ME AND COCKEYED EGAN WAS tourin' "god's own country" (Russian for the West), where the natives would rather be Harold Bell Wright than be president, each with a stable of battlers, pickin' up *beaucoup* sugar by havin' 'em fight each other over the short routes, when Kane Halliday skidded across my path. Besides Beansy Mullen and Bearcat Reed, a coupla heavies, I had a good welter in Battlin' Lewis, and Egan had K. O. Krouse, another tough boy, which made up a set. Them last two babies mixed with each other more times a month than a chorus girl uses a telephone, "without either gaining a decided advantage," as the newspaper innocently remarks. They was steppin' out with each other about four times a week, playin' a different burg each night, and everything was jake till K. O. Krouse shook a mean dice and win $28 from Battlin' Lewis on the ways to Toledo, where we had 'em scheduled to go twelve fast rounds to a draw. Lewis broods and mutters over that for the balance of the railroad ride and knocks Krouse dead in the first frame that night. On account of this cuckoo forgettin' he was a box fighter, and therefore not supposed to get mad, we lose five other bouts we are signed up for with Krouse, which outa petty revenge refused to fight my boy any more. Cockeyed Egan is all for goin' back to New York, because, as he says, if they have took wrestlin' bouts off of the list of felonies there again they certainly oughta stand for the Krouse-Lewis act, where the boys is positively guaranteed to try in the last second of the final round, anyways!

I'm just puttin' a handful of the hotel towels in my suit case on account of you never can tell when they will come in handy, when a bell hop appears at the door and makes me a present of the followin' cable:

Guarantee you thousand Cleveland Bearcat Reed vs. One-Punch Loughlin. Wire if right. DUMMY CARNEY.

Now, this One-Punch Loughlin looked like the next heavyweight champ to the disrobed eye right then. He had clouted his way through the rest of the large boys like Dewey went through Manila Bay, and his knockout record sounded like the first two pages of the phone book. Dummy Carney was his manager, and *him* wirin' me, instead of the club doin' it, was the office that friend Dummy had somethin' cooked up. Sendin' Bearcat Reed into a ring with this rough Loughlin person was like enterin' a armless wonder in a bowlin' tourney. If Loughlin was tryin', my battler wouldn't have a chance if they let him climb through the ropes with a ax in each hand; but for a guarantee of a thousand fish I would let Bearcat Reed box five starvin' lions and a coupla irritated wildcats in the middle of the jungle! I wired Dummy Carney "Sold!" grabbed the Bearcat, and lammed for Cleveland. On the en route the sacrifice wants to know how much they is in this fracas for him. Up to that time the Bearcat had the idea that the only guys in the world which eat regular was Al Vanderbilt and Jack Rockefeller.

"Well," I says, "you oughta grab about three hundred men for your end. That's if you can keep from kissin' the rosin for a coupla rounds. But, of course, they is no use speakin' of the impossible!"

"Three hundred for *me*?" he hollers, leapin' up in the seat. "Say—who am I gonna fight, the Marines?"

"Look here, stupid," I says. "Never mind worryin' about *who* you're gonna battle—you don't see it botherin' *me*, do you? You're the most self-ish guy I ever heard tell of! I gotta be sittin' up night and day gettin' tramps for you to trim, wearin' my fingers to the bone signin' contracts, gettin' a occasional line of hooch about you in the papers, and the etc., and all *you* gotta do is put on a pair of nice white trunks, step through the ropes, take a pastin', and get paid off. Pretty soft for *you*! Suppose I *had* signed you to fight the Marines—as long as you get the sugar, what do *you* care?"

"All right," he grins, pattin' me on the shoulder, "don't get sore. Tell them babies they gotta leave their bay'nets in the dressin' room and *I'll* take a chance!"

Dummy Carney met me at the train in Cleveland and gimme the works. One-Punch Loughlin was gonna let the Bearcat stay the limit if he hadda hold him up, and then we was all goin' to Philly for a return bout a month later, which Dummy would properly work up and at which Loughlin would flatten the Bearcat without no more further formalities. The second mêlée would be level, as Dummy figured the Bearcat was too much of a ham to be worth while savin' for any more. For this last fray I was guaranteed $1,500 for the Bearcat's end, and I never seen a thin dime of it, because the second fight never come off. Bearcat Reed steps through the ropes at Cleveland, squints across the ring, and sees his comin' vis-à-vis just climbin' up and bowin' to the wild applause. Up jumps the Bearcat.

"One-Punch Loughlin, hey?" he yelps. "Nothin' stirrin'! Why, this guy would tear my head off! What d'ye mean by throwin' me in here with that baby? You claimed this would be a spread for me!"

"Shut up, you dumbbell!" I hisses. "We'll fight this guy. He ain't gonna try and—"

"Where d'ye get that *we* stuff?" sneers the Bearcat. "*You* mingle with him—I'll watch it!" and he'd of ducked through the rope if I hadn't grabbed him.

"Listen!" I whispers in his ear. "If you crab this, I'll stick a knife in you the first time you come to your corner! We're gonna fight Loughlin a world series, and this one to-night is only a stall for the *real* sugar, get me? Loughlin's gonna be under wraps all the way, and all *you* gotta do is make a showin'. Tear outa your corner like you're gonna bite his nose off, git mad and make faces—know what I mean? If you make this look good to-night, you drag down five hundred bucks for your next start. How 'bout that?"

"This guy will about croak me!" gasps the Bearcat, as white as the referee's shirt should of been. "But, speakin' of makin' a showin'—I'm gonna *do* that thing for a coupla seconds, anyways!"

Clang! goes the bell.

A wise-lookin' bird, sittin' back of me, jumps up and yells at the Bearcat: "Rush him, kid, *he* ain't got nothin'!"

One-Punch Loughlin comes slowly out, grinnin' at close friends and noddin' politely to acquaintances.

The next minute two thousand innocent bystanders has gone crazy and Dummy Carney has fell into the water bucket in a dead faint!

The second the bell rung Bearcat Reed, lookin' like a guy on his way to the chair and actin' on the principle of kill or get killed, has charged halfway across the ring yellin': "Old men and cripples, get back of the ropes!" A foot from the dumbfounded Loughlin, this bird, which ordinarily could outdive all the seals in the world once he got in a ring, smashes a right to the button of Loughlin's jaw, and Dummy Carney's comin' champ hits the mat so hard I bet he was pickin' rosin outa his face for a month! The referee counted to "six," took another squint at the study in still life at his feet, and waved the dazed Bearcat to his corner. I hadda throw twelve guys outa the ring so's I could get his gloves off. A artist which could of painted the expression on Bearcat Reed's face as he sat there with his eyes and mouth as open as Central Park, gazin' at One-Punch Loughlin asleep at the switch, would of become famous on that one picture. The Bearcat looked like a guy which has struck a match on lower Broadway and seen the Woolworth Buildin' immediately go up in flames!

Of course it was a fluke win. It wouldn't happen again in a million years, but—it happened *then,* which was ample for the Bearcat. That lucky wallop got his name all over the country, and started me toward pilotin' a world's champion. Somebody must of slipped all the four-leaf clovers in the world into the Bearcat's hair, because the next day he puts his cut of the Loughlin fight on a 20 to 1 shot, which win pulled up, and I don't see him again for six months. One-Punch Loughlin fin'ly come back to life, and the first thing he has done was to bust Dummy Carney in the nose, claimin' he had been framed, and then he grabs another manager, which took him over to England, where the set-ups runs wild. And there we will leave them, gentle reader, for the time bein', because this is the story of Kane Halliday, alias "Kid Roberts," and that's as far as the poor old Bearcat and One-Punch Loughlin figures in it right now. Them guys was just the preliminary birds I trotted out to entertain the crowd, and now, boys and girls, the "next ex-e-bition bout of the evenin' is Kid Roberts, Yale '17, vs. Battlin' Fate, nine rounds to a decision. Weights: Roberts, 195; Fate—all the rest. Gents, kindly stop smokin'. I thank you!"

The day after Bearcat Reed flattened One-Punch Loughlin and followed that idiotic act by leavin' me flat, I met Dummy Carney, the other victim, in the lobby of the hotel. One of his eyes is garbed in the conventional black and his nose is a trifle outa true. He let forth a beller of the opposite to joy when he seen me, and I was the best part of a hour convincin' him that I hadn't deliberately double-crossed him, and that me and the Bearcat was more stunned than he was when his battler wilted.

"Well, they is one thing about Loughlin—he proved to the wide, wide world that they is somethin' in a name, anyways!"

"What d'ye mean?" growls Dummy.

"Well," I says, grinnin' demurely, "you called him One-Punch Loughlin, and that's exactly what he was! If you remember the late holocaust, the Bearcat only landed *one* wallop on your ex-mankiller's chin, and he immediately turned in his resignation, didn't he?"

"The big yellah dog!" groans Dummy. "I had him signed for seven fights in the next coupla months that would of win me around twenty thousand berries. From the telegrams I got this mornin' you'd think I had just been elected governor of half a dozen States, and every one of them wires is cancelin' Loughlin. Kin you imagine him runnin' out on me too? If that guy fights for anybody else, I'll have him put in the hoosegow till St. Looey wins a pennant! I can start off by suin' him and—"

"You'll get fat suin' Loughlin!" I shuts him off. "John the Barber sued Dempsey for breach of promise, and all John got was an introduction to all the lawyers in America. Forget about Loughlin—you're well rid of him, anyways. After a exercise boy like Bearcat Reed knockin' him dead with a punch, they wouldn't let Loughlin in a fight club now if he had a ticket! I'm gonna shove off for New York, and you better come along with me. The way they been breakin' for me, I gotta good mind to get outa the fight game altogether and turn square!"

Dummy begins to clear his throat and rub his hands together for a minute, and then suddenly he turns to me and lowers his voice:

"We kin grab a rattler outa here tonight," he says. "Stick around for a coupla minutes, and you'll git a flash at the next heavyweight champion of the world and points west! That's if he shows up," he adds.

"You certainly have become a pig for punishment, Dummy!" I grins. "Who's this guy?"

"Kane Halliday!" he whispers like he was sayin' "The Sheriff of Shantung!" or the like. "How 'bout that?"

"It don't mean nothin' in my young life," I says. "How d'ye play it?"

"You never heard tell of Kane Halliday?" he gasps like his ears is both liars. "The big, now, football star, the weights thrower, the—the—runner, the—ah—what they call a roundabout athalete? *You* know, one of them bimbos which flings a wicked spear and hurls a mean hammer and that there stuff, get me? Why, they claim this baby beat Harvard and the other college all by himself!"

"That ain't my fault," I yawns. "And I can't identify the body yet."

"Was bein' stupid cold, you'd be zero!" snarls Dummy. "Why, the papers was full of this guy!"

"The papers is got nothin' on me," I says, gettin' up. "I'm full of him too! So long!"

But he calls me back, and in about twenty minutes I have got the low down on Monsieur Kane Halliday.

This guy had been committed to college with the idea that when he come out he'd be at the very least a civil engineer, though most of the engineers *I* know learned their trade in a roundhouse and yard and was civil enough as far as that part of it goes. Halliday's people was supposed to have a dollar for every egg in a shad roe, and the boy treated the civil-engineer thing as a practical joke and college as somethin' he had been gave for Christmas to play with. The principal studies he devoted his time and attention to was football, wrestlin', runnin', dancin', boxin', playin' saxophone in the Glee Club and poker in the others. He won more gold and silver cups than the Crown Prince lifted from Belgium, was the most popular guy that ever wore a "Y" on his sweater, and as reward he fin'ly got throwed outa dear old Yale on his ear without even a reference, let alone a diploma, because he had a prejudice against enterin' a classroom. He hit the cruel world about the same time Germany did, and he played with the Allies as a dizzy aviator.

When he come back he was greeted with the delightful information that his old man had gone broke on the war, and it was up to him to make the acquaintance of Manual Labor, provided he wished to continue his daily consumption of proteins and calories, as they wittily refer to food in Battle Creek. Instead of goin' down to the drug store and quaffin' off a beaker of arsenic when he heard of this tough break, Young Halliday borreys enough sugar to send his thoughtless parent down to South America for a rest, brushes back his hair, and starts out to dumfound the universe with stunts that would make a Douglas Fairbanks thriller look reasonable. With the reputation he had grabbed off at college he figured he was in soft, and it was only a question which bank he'd start off bein' president of.

It took the kid about a month to find out that the young men which writes all the movies, novels, and plays in which they is a hero amongst the other characters is slightly addicted to exaggeration. The fact that his father had been granted an absolute divorce from his bank roll had leaked out, and his one-time buddies become the busiest guys in North America when he went to call on 'em.

Now, if Halliday had only known a scenario writer, he would of been tipped off to sneak out immediately for the "great open stretches of the untamed Northwest," where, as a six-day-old infant knows, "a man has his chance to live clean, fight hard and square, and win his way to the top with his pure-hearted, fearless, flashing-eyed, and becomingly, though sensibly, garbed mate at his side." Or he could of gone to punchin' cows, reformin' all the rough yet golden-hearted cowboys by his inability to cuss and his ability to fan a six gun, windin' up by weddin' the rancher's sensationally beautiful daughter, which had been to New York and is through with the cold, merciless, and gilded sham of the city, and craves for the sweet smell of the pines, rodeos, cactus, sagebrush, and steers.

Instead of this, Halliday got as far as Ohio, where, whilst waitin' for somethin' to break, he joined a troupe of professional football players made up of ex-college stars. He played fullback and had been gettin' from fifty to a hundred a game, which was enough to keep him both full and back. Full of food and back in the spotlight. The All-Star Team, however, was bustin' up in Cleveland, and it was at this point that Dummy Carney, which could dive into a haystack and emerge with ten dollars' worth of needles, come across him. Dummy had heard some of the kid's history from Tin-Ear Fagan, a ex-pug, which was with the team as a rubber and some from Halliday himself.

". . . And so," winds up Dummy, pullin' out one of his favorite brand of cigars, which is called "Last One I Got"—"and so I have worked over this baby for a week. He looks like platinum to *me*! You know what the demand is for heavies right now, and if this guy has got anything at all I can take him around the sticks, and then bring him into New York and clean up with him. In about a year or two, if he's still steppin' out, we'll go after the Big Guy. Say—can you imagine *me* pilotin' a world's heavyweight champ?"

"I prob'ly could if you would make me a present of a bite of that opium you musta been chewin'!" I sneers. "A college guy, hey? Well, I'll stake you to him! I'm off them amateur champs."

"Wait till you get a flash at *this* bird!" interrupts Dummy. "Why, he's got a left hand that—ssh!—here he comes. Play dead, now!"

Halliday was class, there's no gettin' away from it. The boy stood well over six foot and was dressed like he had placed all of his football plunder on his back. From my first quick size-up I judged he scaled about 195 ringside when right. He had the light, sure tread of a prowlin' cat, which meant speed, and the clean-cut, smooth-muscled bulk, taperin' gradually from the walkin'-beam shoulders to the unusually slim waist, advertised punchin' power. I knew right away that baby packed a nasty wallop somewheres. Dummy said he was twenty-three. He looked older.

Apart from them shop items, he inventoried about as much like a prize fighter as I'm Mary Pickford's double. I thought what a shock it was gonna be to him the first time somebody flattened his nose. It was! But the thing that struck me odd was his eyes. They didn't seem to fit in with the rest of the layout at all. They should of been baby blue and starin' innocently at the world to go with that golden blond hair. But they wasn't. They was kinda chilled steel gray, and for all the flickin' they did they could of been glass. It was like lookin' into the barrels of a coupla "gats."

He stopped in front of us, nodded kinda nervously to Dummy, and flashed them eyes on me kinda cold.

"S'all right, kid!" says Dummy, catchin' the look. "This guy's my—eh—private secretary. Anything you say in front of him will be used—I mean—well, what *d'ye* say?"

Halliday grinned as we all sat down and pulled his chair closer to Dummy.

"I've decided to accept your proposition, Carney," says Halliday slowly, settlin' back like he was gettin' ready for a long speech. "Now, in the first place, let us—"

But Dummy was on his feet, slappin' him on the shoulder.

"Fine business!" he cackles. "Inside a year your income will sound like the population of China multeyplied by two, and like as not I'll have a couple of pennies myself! Now, they's no use of you gettin' all tired out talkin'; lem*me* take charge of *that* part of it. We start in to-morrow night rakin' in the golden stream. Wait here till I send a wire!"

Oh, Dummy was a fast worker, they's no doubt of that.

Halliday looked after him kinda dazed, and then he wiggles them pliable iron shoulders of his and laughs. We traded a few remarks about this and that, holdin' each other even till Dummy come bustlin' back.

"Now we're all set!" he says to Halliday. "I kinda thought you'd see the light, so I booked you in Sandusky a few days ago at the Crescent A. C. We're gonna box young Du Fresne, heavyweight champion of Canada, twelve rounds to a decision. You'll prob'ly kill that bimbo with a punch, and then we jump to Columbus, and–"

Halliday turns a slow smile on Dummy and holds up his hand.

"Your opinion of my ability is certainly flattering, old man!" he interrupts, "and your system at least seems to have the merit of originality. My first bout is to be with the Canadian champion, eh? What do you propose that I do–start at the top and work my way down?" He chuckled like the kid he was.

"Heh?" snorts Dummy. "Oh–this Du Fresne guy? Say–if he's champion of Canada, then *I'm* next in line for the English throne; get that? He used to fight in the preliminaries around New York under the name of Set-Up Jim Byrnes, and he's wore out more tights reclinin' on the floor of a ring that any fighter which ever pulled on a glove! Lefty Murray's rechristened him and is takin' him around the flatcar circuit till somethin' breaks. D'ye think I'd let you go in there if this guy was any good? All *I* hope is that you don't fracture his skull!"

"But–" begins Halliday.

"This playin' football was a bright idea," goes on Dummy. "It's kept you in steady trainin' all the time, which saves *me* a lotta trouble." He turns to me. "Boy," he says, "that football thing is one tough pastime. Kin you imagine them cuckoos doin' that stuff for *nothin*?" He swings around on Halliday again, which was watchin' him like he was a curiosity. "You ain't mixed up with no dame, are you?" he demands, suspiciously.

The most astonishin' change come over the charmin' features of Monsieur Halliday. His eyebrows becomes one straight line, and them cold eyes gets down to about the size of match heads. I found myself givin' a little shiver, and he wasn't even *lookin'* at *me*. He took a half step forward, and I says to myself: "Fare thee well, Dummy Carney!" and friend Dummy's complexion got a shade lighter, whilst a silly grin appeared on his nervous lips. But they was no bloodshed.

Halliday coughed a coupla times, and then his color come back.

"Eh—we will leave the personal element entirely out of our discussions for the present, Carney," he says, his voice a chill breeze. "As I understand my arrangement with you, it is a purely business affair. We will keep it that way!"

"Sure!" nods Dummy quickly and with the greatest relief. "And there's that! Now, speakin' of business, from now on your name will be Kid Roberts, unless you get trimmed under that name, in which case we will get you a nice fresh new one and start you over again. That Kane Halliday is a swell name for a collar or a hotel, but it don't mean nothin' in the ring—O. K.?"

They was no argument about that end of it—in fact, it seemed to please Halliday, which from now on, gentle reader, we will call Kid Roberts, as they never was no necessity to change it.

"A lulu, hey?" whispers Dummy in my ear when Kid Roberts has gone upstairs to pack up. "He's been workin' out here for a week up at the Arena Club. I've had him under a pull to save his hands, but he's flattened a dozen handlers with a left hook that don't travel over six inches! That's poor, eh?"

"He looks worth a bet," I says, carelessly. "I only hope he don't blow up on you to-morrow night, that's all."

"What d'ye mean blow up?" snarls Dummy. "He oughta be able to take a roomful of guys like Du Fresne—*you* know that!"

"Oughta be able and can do is different," I grins. "A lotta wise birds figured Willard should of let Dempsey come in with a gun to make it a little more even, but look what happened! You wanna figure that this boy will be doin' somethin' to-morrow night he never done before, and that conditions is gonna be a whole lot changed for him. The first shock of that crowd is gonna have *some* effect on your battler, Dummy, and whether it'll be good or bad, I can't guess. I've seen some it made quit cold and some it made fightin' fools; it's accordin' to how a guys' nerves is hooked up. Now–"

"The crowd won't bother this guy," interrupts Dummy. "He's fought before witnesses in college and the like."

"I bet he never heard no ringside prattle like he'll hear to-morrow!" I says. "And they's another thing. Your child wonder may pack a mean wallop, but the thing is–can he *take* it? You know this Du Fresne, bein' led to the slaughter, will be all hopped up to make a terrible flash in the openin' canto. If he shakes Kid Roberts up with a coupla chance swings, and the crowd begins to roar for the Kid's blood, will he stand up under fire or will he wilt? Think of Bearcat Reed knockin' One-Punch Loughlin dead! Can this Roberts baby fight with a closed eye, or a busted nose, or–"

"Aw, shut up!" hollers Dummy. "You should of been a undertaker! Kid Roberts won't *have* to take it–he'll flatten this guy with one clout. I'll lay you a hundred even it don't go two rounds–what d'ye say?"

"Sold!" I says. "Dummy, I ain't figurin' your boy yellah. I'm figurin' on a thing called temperament which I have run up against before. I wouldn't be surprised if the muss went the limit, because I'm afraid if Roberts gets hurt early, bein' green, he'll play safe and be satisfied to stall the rest of it and dog it."

Dummy snorted, but he looked worried. "If he can't take it, I don't wish no part of him," he says. "I'll leave him flat in this Sandusky joint if he don't come through on the bit!"

Well, I went to Sandusky with 'em as Dummy's guest, and also at the sudden request of Kid Roberts to go behind him in his corner for his first fight for money. He seemed to have taken a likin' to me for some reason, and they is no doubt I was for him strong. You couldn't help fall for him; he was just a big, swell-lookin', overgrown boy. For instance, goin' down in the train he made friends with about a dozen kids, and when we pulled into Sandusky he was drawin' pictures for 'em of elephants on the back of his contract with Dummy. Kid Roberts belonged in the ring the same way I belong in the White House!

Dummy was afraid of sendin' him in too cold after the train ride, and, findin' that the club had a gym in connection with it, he sneaks the Kid down there and has him step around a little with a big dinge which was workin' out. They had been at it about a minute when the Kid rocks the tar baby with a right to the body and brings up his left for his man's jaw. But this dark guy knew too much for Roberts, and with a grunt he shifted his bullethead just enough to let the wallop swish by. The force of the punch carried Roberts forward on his toes, and his fist crashed into a steam pipe with everything he had behind it. Dummy let out a wild shriek and waved the dinge away, but the Kid only grinned kinda sheepish, like he was ashamed he had been so clumsy. The hand was red and swollen a bit when we come to tape it before the fight, but it didn't look like nothin' serious, so Dummy soused it with arnica and let it go at that.

The Kid was cool enough, though a trifle pale whilst we was sittin' in the dressin' room waitin' for the semifinal to wind up, and his eyes happened to fall on a newspaper I had brung in. On the front page is a picture of some well-to-do heiress which had just come back to New York from Shantung or some place where she had been wilin' away the winter. Roberts snatches it up and gazes at it with a hungry look. I don't blame him. She looked as pretty as $5,000 a week would to a motorman.

"What a rotten photo!" he mutters, half to himself. "She looks fit, though."

"Friend of yours?" I says, drapin' the bathrobe over his shoulders.

He's still in a trance over the picture.

"Oh—eh—yes—eh—quite so!" he mumbles. "How the devil can I get to New York to-morrow?" he inquires of himself, not even noticin' me.

I filed that one away for future reference. I heard a whole lot about the lady afterward—in fact, I *met* her under exceedin'ly odd conditions. But—

It was about ten o'clock when we swum through the cigarette smoke, pushed down the aisle, and climbed through the ropes, amid the dull rumble of excited voices, as the papers says. The mob, which had never heard tell of Kid Roberts before and, for all they knew, never would again, presented him with a wild cheer. All they knew was that two big guys was gonna mingle, and the chances was excellent that at least one of them would be knocked cold. The Kid bowed very solemnly to the cheer, which act drawed a laugh that didn't help his high-strung nerves a bit.

They was no sign of Young Du Fresne as yet. Roberts shuffled his feet and stared down at 'em, bitin' his lips. A bad sign! The glarin' lights beatin' down on his head, the blood spattered around in his corner from the last brawl, and the noisy crowd was raisin' merry Hades with him.

Some roughneck hollered: "You won't be so pretty, pretty soon, Cutey!"

Another one bawled: "Who brung that chorus man in?"

"Ain't he got lovely skin?" come from somewheres else.

By this time the Kid's feet was doin' a shimmy on the floor. Them sensitive ears of his caught every word, and this rough, sarcastical stuff was like stabbin' him with hot needles, only more so. He was exactly like a two-year-old at the post for the first time. The case-hardened bruiser would of grinned back at the crowd and waved at 'em, and prob'ly got a big hand in return. The sympathies of a fight crowd is as changeable as a woman's mind, but still and all very easy to figure. They're *always* with the winner, no matter if the guy on the floor is their brother.

I gotta hand it to Lefty Murray, Young Du Fresne's pilot. He kept his man outa the ring till the crowd was ready to tear the roof off with impatience, knowin' what the wear and tear would be on the waitin' Roberts. He kicked and argued about every point like the fight was for the world's championship. He found fault with the referee, the paddin' of the ring, the lights, and was startin' a long argument about the way the Kid's hands were taped, when Roberts jumped up and stopped it. His nerves was shot to pieces. Not nerve—*nerves*. Sweet Mamma, but there's a difference!

"Come on!" busts out the Kid. "Let's get it over with!"

Lefty Murray looked him over coolly and grinned. The Kid's drawn face and quiverin' muscles told him aplenty. I knew what he was tellin' his man after they shook hands, just as if I was in Du Fresne's corner: "Get in close and play for his body. Keep on top of him—don't let him set. If you shake him up right off the bat, he's *through*!"

This Du Fresne looked more like a gorilla than a human bein', and prob'ly was. He was a good twenty pounds heavier than the Kid, and what would of been a face on the average guy was simply a puffed, scarred, and pulpy mass. He growled and glared ferociously at the Kid from his corner, and the crowd yelled like a pack of wolves. The Kid grinned back at him faintly and begin wettin' his lips with his tongue.

Dummy had left the handlin' of the Kid entirely up to me, with a coupla boys which had just massacred each other in a preliminary for a purse of $10, as towel wavers. Whilst I was massagin' the Kid's stomach, which felt as tough and ridged as a washboard under my hands, I let fall the remark that Du Fresne couldn't take it and would quit like a dog the minute he got hurt. Then the bell rung.

Du Fresne was off his stool and halfway across the ring before the Kid had hardly straightened up. He smashed a left to the body that shook Roberts from stem to stern, but whilst the mob was still jumpin' up on their chairs and shriekin', the Kid feinted Du Fresne with his own left and then shot a right hook to the head that hurled Du Fresne back a half dozen feet before he crashed down on his face. That wallop landed a bit high, or the quarrel would of been over right then and there. Du Fresne stumbled to his feet at "nine" for the simple reason that he had been told he wouldn't get a nickel if he didn't last at least a coupla rounds. Dummy screamed for the Kid to wade in and finish his man, but the yellin' and excitement upset the boy's judgment, and he allowed Du Fresne to dive into a clinch, where that thankful baby hung on glassy-eyed till the referee pried 'em apart. The Kid dropped him twice more for short counts before the bell, and Du Fresne reeled to his corner, bleedin' from the nose and mouth and practically out on his feet. Roberts didn't even have his hair mussed. The joyful mob was with him to a man. He looked a winner all over, and I figured he'd knock Du Fresne kickin' with the first wallop in the next round. Dummy jumped in and sponged the Kid's face, as happy as a girl with her first engagement ring.

The rest seemed to have done Du Fresne a lotta good, and he come out for the second innin' as fresh as a daisy, but not as good-lookin'. The way some of them tramps can recover from a beatin' that would kill a horse is somethin' I never been able to understand! He missed a wild swing to the jaw, and Roberts jolted him with a wicked right that lifted him a inch from the floor, but he kept his feet and, backin' into a corner like he was ready to call it a day, he covered his head with his arms and waited patiently to get it. Once again the customers jumps up on their chairs; once again they was treated to a disappointment. Instead of steppin' in and polishin' off this guy with a coupla well-placed punches, the Kids stands off and waits for him to recover. I thought Dummy Carney would go crazy. "Bring up that *left*, you boob!" he kept screamin'. The referee walks over to the Kid and slaps him on the shoulders: "Go on, *fight!*" he snarls. "What are you gonna do—*kiss* him?"

Now, the Kid's ace was his left hook, which after one try he put back in the safe. I noticed a queer look on his face, as if he couldn't understand how come he had delivered that man killer and yet Du Fresne was still alive. I caught him glancin' down at the left glove a coupla times like he wanted to be sure the hand was still in it, and then all of a sudden he shakes his head and stop usin' it altogether. He simply give up. As far as his famous left hook was concerned, he could of checked it outside the clubhouse! Du Fresne managed to last out the second round by clinchin' at every chance and holdin' on like rheumatism. Right before the bell he suddenly straightened up and split the Kid's lips with a jab that brought a stream of red when it come away. The mob howled, but Roberts grinned and come back with a smash to the short ribs that dropped Du Fresne gaspin' to his knees.

When the Kid ran to his corner at the end of the second round, the sportsmen which had paid large quantities of lucre to see a knock-out was loudly and bitterly complainin'. They was off Kid Roberts for life and tellin' the world about it. They'd seen him hit Du Fresne with everything but the club's license, yet Du Fresne was still alive, which was all wrong. Evidently this Roberts couldn't hit, and a heavy that can't hit is as popular as foot warmers in Hades.

Dummy begged, cried, and threatened for the Kid to go in and kill Du Fresne, but Kid Roberts had apparently lost all interest in the combat. Du Fresne waddled out to the middle of the ring like he couldn't believe his own eyes that he was still on his feet, but, actin' upon advice from his corner, he got to work again. He put a coupla light lefts to the face without a return from Dummy's hope, and then the Kid started to swing with this guy. The roughhouse stuff was Du Fresne's dish, and in no time at all he had closed the Kid's right eye and had his sore lip puffed up like a balloon. The Kid made a few weak returns with his right, usin' that dynamite left for blockin' and feintin' purposes only, and the dumfounded Du Fresne got more courage every second. Comin' out of a clinch, he swung a vicious right to the Kid's stomach and folleyed that with a clip on the jaw that staggered Roberts and drove whatever judgment he had left outa his head. He missed a dozen right swings, and then fell into one from Du Fresne that opened a gash under his bum eye a inch deep. The crowd was roarin' for a knockout, and Du Fresne's manager was on the verge of the hystericals. At a yell from his corner, Du Fresne shifted his attack to the Kid's mid section and suddenly hooked a left and right to the body that doubled Roberts into a pantin' knot. He was too excited to folley up his advantage, or it would of been curtains for the Kid. He fell wildly into a clinch, but Du Fresne shook him off and stabbed the sore eye with a nasty straight-arm right that sent Roberts staggerin' to his corner, punch drunk and gory.

The fourth and fifth rounds was the same as the third. Du Fresne pasted the Kid from pillar to post, cuttin' him to ribbons with nasty left and right chops, but Roberts still refused to use his left, swingin' wildly with his right and divin' into a clinch whenever he got hurt, which was early and often. He didn't land a half dozen solid punches from the second round on. In Du Fresne's corner they was havin' a party.

In the middle of the sixth round, with Du Fresne chasin' the battered Kid all over the ring and makin' a choppin' block of him, Dummy havin' cussed, cried, and yelled himself hoarse, jumps up and whispers in my ear: "I'm through with this big stiff for life! He's as yellah as a barrel of grapefruit. You was right, they's always somethin' wrong with them gymnasium world beaters. This guy can't take it. Look at him wilt every time he stops one. I'm gonna duck; I don't wanna see no more of it!"

"D'ye wanna get rid of him?" I says innocently.

"Make me an offer!" he snaps.

"Well," I says, watchin' the ring outa the corner of my eye, "you owe me a hundred berries on account of the Kid not winnin' in a round. Gimme his contract and it's even all around!"

That's how I got Kid Roberts. A year and a half later Dummy Carney stood in the lobby of Madison Square Garden and, with tears in his eyes offered me $30,000 for that contract back!

As Dummy snaked his way out through the crowd, I looked up in time to see Du Fresne hang the Kid over the ropes with a volley of lefts and rights, and the referee was lookin' over at *me* for the sponge. A left chop connected solidly and the Kid slid to the floor, resting on his hands and knees. The bell clanged at "eight," and we dragged Roberts to his corner and worked over him with everything but a pulmotor.

It's tough to see your man licked, but they is nothin' tougher in the world than to see him licked when you know he can kill the other guy with one well-placed smash! I begged this boy to try that left once more. I tried everything I could think of except Dummy's stuff of callin' him yellah. That's all wrong with these kinda guys. It don't stir 'em up and make 'em go after the other guy hammer and tongs like the novels claims. They get sore at you and remember it forever after! Fin'ly I got a wild idea. I remembered that dame's picture in the newspaper and what the Kid had said about goin' to New York. I took a chance.

"You're one swell-lookin' baby for Miss Gresham to see!" I says in his ear, sarcastical as possible.

He looked at me in a dazed way, not seemin' to notice me callin' Her by name.

"Why?" he mumbles.

I held the dressin'-room mirror in front of him. You never seen such a change come over nobody in your life. The Kid sees his eye in deep mournin', his lips all purple and puffed outa shape, the bleedin' gash under the glim, and all the rest of his ruined beauty. The one good eye narrows to a pin point and his teeth comes together with a click. He straightens up in his chair and glares across at the leerin' and happy Du Fresne with the benevolent expression of a wounded panther about to charge. The bell rings for the lucky seventh.

The mob took up the bellowin' chant for a knock-out, and Du Fresne come slidin' out with a confident grin, which faded with almost comical speed as he got that glare in the Kid's workin' eye. He faltered in his stride and was short with a right to the face. He commenced to back away and look to his corner for advice, and the Kid stepped in and buried his right to the wrist in his stomach. Du Fresne's grunt could be heard in Paris, and he dropped his guard to protect that tremblin' paunch. The Kid coolly measured him, and, quick as a flash of startled light, brought up his left for the second time in the entire debate. It landed flush on Du Fresne's jaw and crashed him through the ropes into the laps of the newspaper guys, as cold as the middle of Iceland!

"Why didn't you pull that left before?" I demanded, tugging at the Kid's gloves as the perfectly satisfied mob milled out through the doors.

He gimme a odd grin.

I pulled and hauled, but that glove wouldn't move. Fin'ly I took out my penknife and cut it off his wrist. Then I nearly fell over the ropes myself. His left hand was a ugly-lookin' purple and swelled to twice its size.

"I broke a bone or two when I idiotically hit that steam pipe before the fight to-night," he explains cheerfully. "That's why I—eh—rather favored it afterward!"

Imagine goin' into a fight with a broken hand! *Imagine knockin' a two-hundred-and-fifteen-pound guy out with it!*

"But—but," I splutters, "why did you go through with the scrap if you knew that, you darn fool! Why didn't you say somethin'? We could of called it off and—"

"That's exactly what I *thought* you would do," he smiles, "and I couldn't afford to have *that* happen. To be frank with you, I'm broke!"

He looks around curiously. "Where's Carney?" he asks. "He said some things to me I'd like to take up with him!" His voice was hard again.

"Oh, don't mind Dummy," I says. "He got a tough break to-night—lost the best scrapper in his stable!"

"Oh, I'm sorry!" he says. "Influenza?"

"Nope—inexperience!" I tells him. "Well, let's get outa here, hey?"

This little jewel of a story is about three kids fooling around with baseball and poking fun at each other. It first appeared in the New Yorker. *Author Richard Wilbur has taught at Harvard, Wellesley, and Wesleyan. He has published several volumes of poetry, including* Things of the World *(1957) and* Advice to a Prophet *(1961). A recent book is* The Catbird's Song *(1997). Wilbur has won many honors, including the Pulitzer Prize for poetry and the National Book Award for poetry.*

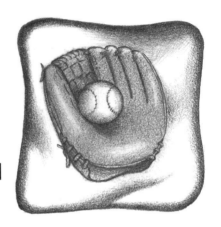

Richard Wilbur

A GAME OF CATCH
(1953)

MONK AND GLENNIE WERE playing a catch on the side lawn of the firehouse when Scho caught sight of them. They were good at it, for seventh-graders, as anyone could see right away. Monk, wearing a catcher's mitt, would lean easily sidewise and back, with one leg lifted and his throwing hand almost down to the grass, and then lob the white ball straight up into the sunlight. Glennie would shield his eyes with his left hand and, just as the ball fell past him, snag it with a little dart of his glove. Then he would burn the ball straight toward Monk, and it would spank into the round mitt and sit, like a still-life apple on a plate, until

Monk flipped it over into his right hand and, with a negligent flick of his hanging arm, gave Glennie a fast grounder.

They were going on and on like that, in a kind of slow, mannered, luxurious dance in the sun, their faces perfectly blank and entranced, when Glennie noticed Scho dawdling along the other side of the street and called hello to him. Scho crossed over and stood at the front edge of the lawn, near an apple tree, watching.

"Got your glove?" asked Glennie after a time. Scho obviously hadn't.

"You could give me some easy grounders," said Scho. "But don't burn 'em."

"All right," Glennie said. He moved off a little, so the three of them formed a triangle, and they passed the ball around for about five minutes, Monk tossing easy grounders to Scho, Scho throwing to Glennie, and Glennie burning them in to Monk. After a while, Monk began to throw them back to Glennie once or twice before he let Scho have his grounder, and finally Monk gave Scho a fast, bumpy grounder that hopped over his shoulder and went in to the brake on the other side of the street.

"Not so hard," called Scho as he ran across to get it.

"You should've had it," Monk shouted.

It took Scho a little while to find the ball among the ferns and dead leaves, and when he saw it, he grabbed it up and threw it toward Glennie. It struck the trunk of the apple tree, bounced back at an angle, and rolled steadily and stupidly onto the cement apron in front of the firehouse, where one of the trucks was parked. Scho ran hard and stopped it just before it rolled under truck, and this time he carried it back to his former position on the lawn and threw it carefully to Glennie.

"I got an idea," said Glennie. "Why don't Monk and I catch for five minutes more, and then you can borrow one of our gloves?"

"That's all right with me," said Monk. He socked his fist into his mitt, and Glennie burned one in.

"All right," Scho said, and went over and sat under the tree. There in the shade he watched them resume their skillful play. They threw lazily fast or lazily slow—high, low, or wide—and always handsomely, their expression serene, changeless, and forgetful. When Monk missed a low backhand catch, he walked indolently after the ball and, hardly even looking, flung it sidearm for an imaginary put-out. After a good while of this, Scho said, "Isn't it five minutes yet?"

"One minute to go," said Monk, with a fraction of a grin.

Scho stood up and watched the ball slap back and forth for several minutes more, and then he turned and pulled himself up into the crotch of the tree.

"Where you going?" Monk asked.

"Just up the tree," Scho said.

"I guess he doesn't want to catch," said Monk.

Scho went up and up through the fat light-gray branches until they grew slender and bright and gave under him. He found a place where several supple branches were knit to make a dangerous chair, and sat there with his head coming out of the leaves into the sunlight. He could see the two other boys down below, the ball going back and forth between them as if they were bowling on the grass, and Glennie's crew-cut head looking like a sea urchin.

"I found a wonderful seat up here," Scho said loudly. "If I don't fall out." Monk and Glennie didn't look up or comment and so he began jouncing gently in his chair of branches and singing "Yo-ho, heave ho" in an exaggerated way.

"Do you know what, Monk?" he announced in a few moments. "I can make you two guys do anything I want. Catch that ball, Monk! Now you catch it, Glennie!"

"I was going to catch it anyway," Monk suddenly said. "You're not making anybody do anything when they're already going to do it anyway."

"I made you say what you just said," Scho replied joyfully.

"No, you didn't," said Monk, still throwing and catching but now less serenely absorbed in the game.

"That's what I wanted you to say," Scho said.

The ball bounded off the rim of Monk's mitt and plowed into a gladiolus bed beside the firehouse, and Monk ran to get it while Scho jounced in his treetop and sang, "I wanted you to miss that. Anything you do is what I wanted you to do."

"Let's quit for a minute," Glennie suggested.

"We might as well, until the peanut gallery shuts up," Monk said.

They went over and sat crosslegged in the shade of the tree. Scho looked down between his legs and saw them on the dim, spotty ground, saying nothing to one another. Glennie soon began abstractedly spinning his glove between his palms; Monk pulled his nose and stared out across the lawn.

"I want you to mess around with your nose, Monk," said Scho, giggling. Monk withdrew his hand from his face.

"Do that with your glove, Glennie," Scho persisted. "Monk, I want you to pull up hunks of grass and chew on it."

Glennie looked up and saw a self-delighted, intense face staring down at him through the leaves. "Stop being a dope and come down and we'll catch for a few minutes," he said.

Scho hesitated, and then said, in a tentatively mocking voice, "That's what I wanted you to say."

"All right, then, nuts to you," said Glennie.

"Why don't you keep quiet and stop bothering people?" Monk asked.

"I made you say that," Scho replied, softly.

"Shut up," Monk said.

"I made you say that, and I want you to be standing there looking sore. And I want you to climb up the tree. I'm making you do it!"

Monk was scrambling up through the branches, awkward in his haste, and getting snagged on twigs. His face was furious and foolish, and he kept telling Scho to shut up, shut up, shut up, while the other's exuberant and panicky voice poured down upon his head.

"Now you shut up or you'll be sorry," Monk said, breathing hard as he reached up and threatened to shake the cradle of slight branches in which Scho was sitting.

"I *want*–" Scho screamed as he fell. Two lower branches broke his rustling, crackling fall, but he landed on his back with a deep thud and lay still, with a strangled look on his face and his eyes clenched. Glennie knelt down and asked breathlessly, "Are you O.K., Scho? Are you O.K.?" while

Monk swung down through the leaves crying that honestly he hadn't even touched him, the crazy guy just let go. Scho doubled up and turned over on his right side, and now both the other boys knelt beside him, pawing at his shoulder and begging to know how he was.

Then Scho rolled away from them and sat partly up, still struggling to get his wind but forcing a species of smile onto his face.

"I'm sorry, Scho," Monk said. "I didn't mean to make you fall."

Scho's voice came out weak and gravelly, in gasps. "I meant—you to do it. You—had to. You can't do—anything—unless I want—you to."

Glennie and Monk looked helplessly at him as he sat there, breathing a bit more easily and smiling fixedly, with tears in his eyes. Then they picked up their gloves and the ball, walked over to the street, and went slowly away down the sidewalk, Monk punching his fist into the mitt, Glennie juggling the ball between glove and hand.

From under the apple tree, Scho, still bent over a little for lack of breath, croaked after them in triumph and misery, "I want you to do whatever you're going to do for the whole rest of your life!"

PERMISSIONS ACKNOWLEDGMENTS

Grateful acknowledgment is extended to the following authors, publications, and agents.

Ring Lardner, "Hurry Kane," from *Round Up*, Charles Scribner's Sons, 1929. Originally published in *Cosmopolitan*, May 1927.

E. Annie Proulx, "On the Antler," originally published in *Harrowsmith* in 1983. Reprinted with the permission of Scribner, a Division of Simon & Schuster, from *Heart Songs and Other Stories*, by E. Annie Proulx. Copyright © 1988 by E. Annie Proulx.

A. Conan Doyle, "The Adventure of Silver Blaze," originally published in *Strand Magazine*, 1892.

Harry Sylvester, "I Won't Do No Dive," originally published in *Esquire*, July 1937. By permission of *Esquire* magazine. © Hearst Communications, Inc. *Esquire* is a trademark of Hearst Property, Inc. All rights reserved.

Frank Dufresne, "The Kelly Rainbow," originally published in *Field and Stream*, July 1933. By permission of Times Mirror Magazines, Inc.

Irwin Shaw, "Whispers in Bedlam," originally published in *Playboy*, February 1969. Reprinted with permission. © Irwin Shaw. All rights reserved.

P. G. Wodehouse, "The Heart of a Goof," from *Divots*, 1927, A. L. Burt, publisher.

John Cheever, "The Swimmer," originally published in the *New Yorker,* July 18, 1964. From *The Stories of John Cheever,* by John Cheever. Used by permission of Alfred A. Knopf, a division of Random House, Inc.

Ellery Queen, "Man Bites Dog." Copyright © 1939 by Ellery Queen. Copyright renewed. Reprinted here with the permission of the Frederic Dannay and Manfred B. Lee Literary Property Trusts and their agent, Jack Time, 3 Erold Court, Allendale, NJ 07401.

Edwin Lanham, "The Denton Mare," originally published in *Esquire,* January 1944. By permission of *Esquire* magazine. © Hearst Communications, Inc. *Esquire* is a trademark of Hearst Property, Inc. All rights reserved.

Jeffrey Archer, "Dougie Mortimer's Right Arm," from *Twelve Red Herrings,* by Jeffrey Archer. Copyright © 1994 by Jeffrey Archer. Reprinted by permission of HarperCollins Publishers, Inc.

John D. MacDonald, "A Young Man's Game," originally published in *Argosy* magazine, May 1961. Copyright © 1961 by Maynard MacDonald. Renewal copyright © 1989 Maynard MacDonald. Used by permission of the estate of John D. MacDonald.

W. Somerset Maugham, "A Friend in Need." From *The World Over,* Doubleday & Co. © 1925 by W. Somerset Maugham.

André Dubus, "An Afternoon with the Old Man," originally published in the *New Yorker,* September 2, 1972. From *Adultery and Other Choices* by André Dubus. Reprinted by permission of David R. Godine, Publisher, Inc. Copyright © 1977 by André Dubus.

Leslie Charteris, "The Mugs' Game," from Leslie Charteris, *The Happy Highwayman,* 1939.

Peter LaSalle, "Hockey," originally published in *The Graves of Famous Writers* in 1980. Reprinted in Peter LaSalle, *Hockey Sur Glace,* 1996. Reprinted here by permission of Breakaway Books, Halcottsville, New York. (800) 548-4348, www.breakawaybooks.com.

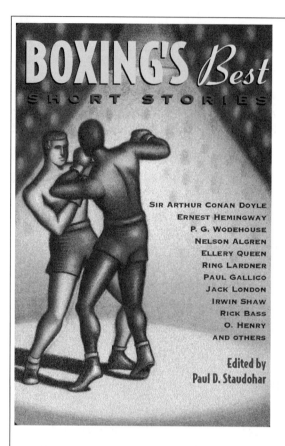

BOXING'S BEST SHORT STORIES
Edited by Paul D. Staudohar

"At once brutish and artistic, primitive and spellbinding, prizefighting provides rich material for talented writers. . . . This collection will delight fight fans, as well as those who just love a good story." —*School Library Journal*

Boxing has always had its share of violence, disreputable characters, and shattered dreams, but as an inspiration for great writing it is unsurpassed. The bone-jarring crack as a glove smashes into a jaw . . . endless seconds as the referee barks "one, two, three" . . . the roar of the crowd as the winner lifts his pulpy face in victory . . . *Boxing's Best Short Stories* brings the action of the ring to life with 22 classic tales.

352 pages, 6 × 9
cloth, $24.00
ISBN 1-55652-364-5

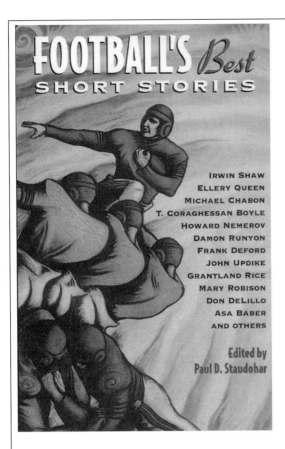

FOOTBALL'S BEST SHORT STORIES

Edited by Paul D. Staudohar

"An exciting collection of some of the best 20th-century writers venturing into some unexpected venues."   —J. C. Martin, *The Arizona Daily Star.*

There are no rookies here—some of America's best writers have penned short stories on football. In this lively anthology of 21 stories and one classic poem about football, fathers and sons tackle their issues, coaches and quarterbacks collide, and ordinary heroes emerge from the blitz. Each decade of the 20th century is tackled, from Ralph D. Paine's 1909 moving story of a down-on-his-luck father who goes to see his son play a big game for Yale, to Ellery Queen's 1940s detective story set in the Rose Bowl, to Frank Deford's spoof on the media hysteria of the Superbowl, written in 1978.

336 pages, 6 × 9
cloth, $22.00, ISBN 1-55652-330-0
paper, $16.95, ISBN 1-55652-365-3

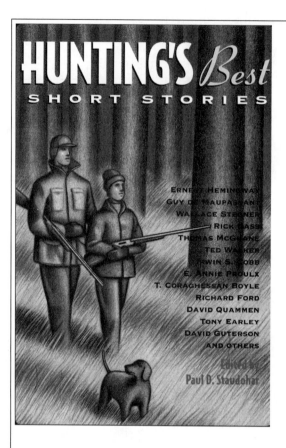

HUNTING'S BEST SHORT STORIES
Edited by Paul D. Staudohar

From duck, goose, and grouse hunting to stiffer contests for deer, elk, moose, bear, and big African game—in one case, even a manhunt—all kinds of hunting and all possible outcomes, from the comic to the heartwarming, disastrous, or bizarre, are explored in *Hunting's Best Short Stories*. Against backdrops of ocean, frozen swamp, forest, or jungle, in this powerful collection of 21 classic and contemporary tales we see the deep bonds between father and son, huntsman and dog, and man and nature being forged or shattered as the line between sport and survival blurs.

336 pages, 6 × 9
cloth, $24.00
ISBN 1-55652-402-1

These books are available from your local bookstore or from Independent Publishers Group by calling (312) 337-0747 or (800) 888-4741.

FISHING'S BEST SHORT STORIES
Edited by Paul D. Staudohar

These twenty-five takes by outstanding authors offer a bounty of fishing adventures: the solitary sportsman casting in a fast trout stream; expensive ocean charters seeking permit and grouper; a couple of kids with bamboo poles and high hopes for the big one. The scenery is as varied as the catch, and passion for the sport goes hand-in-hand with humor, chicanery, surprise endings, friendships between young and old, and romance in unexpected places.

384 pages, 6 × 9
cloth, $24.00
ISBN 1-55652-403-X